Hit and Run

MAIN

Also by Casey Moreton

The Greater Good

Hit and Run

A THRILLER

CASEY MORETON

ATRIA BOOKS

New York   London   Toronto   Sydney

ATRIA BOOKS

1230 Avenue of the Americas
New York, NY 10020

Library of Congress Cataloging-in-Publication Data

Moreton, Casey.
  Hit and run : a thriller / by Casey Moreton.—1st Atria Books trade
  pbk. ed.
      p. cm.
    1. Political fiction. I. Title.

PS3613.O718H58 2006
813'.6—dc22   2005052729

ISBN-13: 978-0-7434-5659-3
ISBN-10:   0-7434-5659-9

First Atria Books trade paperback edition June 2006

10 9 8 7 6 5 4 3 2 1

ATRIA BOOKS is a trademark of Simon & Schuster, Inc.

Designed by Melissa Isriprashad

Manufactured in the United States of America

For information regarding special discounts for bulk purchases, please contact Simon & Schuster Special Sales at 1-800-456-6798 or business@simonandschuster.com.

For Miracle Max
live in peace

PART 1

1

EVERYTHING WAS FINE UNTIL 3:00 A.M., MONDAY. THEY had encountered surprisingly little traffic on the drive from New York, most likely because of the storm that had assaulted much of the East Coast that evening. The rain had mostly tapered off by midnight, leaving in its place occasional patchy fog. Nick Calevetti was at the wheel of Steven Adler's 1967 Ford Mustang, his lead foot hurtling them along at ninety miles an hour. Steven had fallen asleep, his head against the window, exhausted after two days of Nick's whirlwind tour of Manhattan. With the road to themselves, they would be in Boston in less than an hour. They were making good time.

The fog worsened. For long stretches Nick could hardly see the road at all. The headlights weren't much help. But he never let off the gas. If they had his Porsche, he thought with a grin, he'd be doing 110, easy, fog or no fog. Steven's old Mustang could move, but nothing like the Porsche.

The Mustang entered a fog bank and the road disappeared— no white lines, no nothing. Nick pursed his lips and held the wheel steady. He could have been driving off the edge of the earth and not known it. The fog was like a wall. He glanced at the speedometer and then accelerated, fearless. There was just a quick flash of color from out of nowhere, and something slammed into the front of the car, thumping first against the hood, then smashing into the windshield on the passenger side, reducing it to a web of a million sparkling diamonds. The impact was sudden and solid, sending an abrupt shudder through the car. Nick grabbed at the wheel with both hands, jerking it wildly. Tires squealing, the car crossed two lanes of traffic. Again, Nick jerked the wheel and again overcompensated. This reaction was so drastic, given the speed of the car, that the driver-side tires actually lifted off the ground for a moment, and the car nearly flipped.

Steven was thrown against the dash. He hadn't had even a split-second to react, to brace himself with his hands, and his head was forced into the windshield.

Partially out of reflex and partially out of desperation, Nick blindly thrust a foot at the brake pedal, but there was no traction on the wet asphalt. The car went into a full spin. It careened helplessly, skimming across the glasslike asphalt surface. Its momentum carried it nearly seventy feet down the interstate before it began to gradually slow, finally gaining some purchase on some loose gravel on the shoulder. The rear end swung around in a wide arc. When the car finally skidded to a full stop, it rocked on its springs for a few seconds, then settled. It sat at an angle, facing back in the direction from which it had traveled. Its rear driver-side tire was hanging off the shoulder onto wet grass, just two feet shy of a steep embankment.

Lightning flashed in the distance, muted by drifting ribbons of fog.

Steven had been tossed back, falling between the bucket seats, arms flailing, head snapping back as he screamed. Nick's entire upper body had been pressed against the steering wheel, then thrown back into his seat with tremendous force. He still gripped the wheel, an unconscious reflex. His eyes were wide with horror.

When at last all movement had ceased, they remained perfectly still, afraid to move, afraid to breathe.

Steven moaned.

There was blood everywhere. Nick glanced between the seats.

"Steven?"

Another moan.

"Man . . . you okay?" Nick had spatters of blood on his hands. Blood on the steering wheel. On the dash. He glanced all around. There was even a blood pattern on the ceiling of the car.

Nick started trembling. He held his hands out in front of his face. Steven's legs were twisted about. Nick turned in his seat and put a hand on Steven's thigh.

"Steven!" Nick called out. It was dark in the backseat. Nick fumbled with the knobs and switches along the dash, groping for the dome light control. The dim light blinked on. There was more blood than he had imagined. His heart raced.

Nick threw open his door and fumbled to push the seat forward. His fingers were slick and clumsy. The mechanism that controlled the seat was stubborn, and it took him nearly half a minute to finally spring the seat forward so that he could access the backseat and get to Steven. He ducked his head, leaning inside. He braced himself on his knees. Steven had his arms crossed over his face. The pained moans were more frequent now, and longer. Nick's hands were trembling uncontrollably. His throat ached where the steering wheel had caught him under the chin. It was hard to swallow. There was also noticeable pain along the contour of his collarbone. But he had to ignore all of that, at least for the moment.

"Steven!"

Steven managed to unravel his legs. He raised his hands, and Nick got a better look at the damage. Steven's forehead was opened up. His face was covered in blood. "I'm . . . all right," Steven managed to say in barely a whisper. "I'm all right."

"Dude . . . your *head*!" Nick said.

"I know, I feel it. At least it's still attached."

The meat of the forehead was split open, a gash about two inches wide. His nose was bleeding as well.

"Can you move your neck?"

Steven coughed, a thick, throaty cough. "Not sure. Think so."

"Can you get up?"

"Haven't tried. Everything hurts."

Nick piled himself into the backseat, getting an arm around Steven's shoulders. "Careful, man. Let's get you sitting up at least."

Steven got into an upright sitting position without complication. There were numerous aches and pains, and lots of blood, but everything appeared to function normally. With the possible exception of his nose, nothing seemed to be broken. The gash in his forehead felt like a piece of hot metal. He gently probed all around it with a fingertip, hoping it didn't look as bad as it felt.

Nick was trying to catch his breath. He had been fueled by adrenaline for the past few minutes and he couldn't get himself to settle down. It felt like he'd taken a shot to the throat by a work boot. But he could breathe fine. His voice sounded a little hoarse but not too bad. His neck was stiffening, and that would likely worsen in the coming hours.

"What happened?" Steven said finally, leaning up slightly, massaging the back of his head.

"Man . . . I just . . ." Nick shook his head. "Everything's a blur, man."

"Was there another car?"

The fog had dissipated somewhat, and visibility had now increased to maybe a hundred feet. But it was still dark out, the light of the moon shrouded by weather conditions, and all the talking and sudden heavy breathing had fogged the windows even more. Nick raised his head and glanced around. Events had transpired so quickly and dramatically that his mind had become focused solely on survival and thankfulness that both he and Steven were alive. "Another car?"

"Who hit us?"

From where they sat, Nick couldn't see anything beyond the obscured glass. He shook his head. "We hit fog, man. That's what I remember. It was like somebody turned out the lights, and then . . . I don't know."

Steven glanced at his friend. Then he looked over the seats toward the dash and the windshield. "That my blood?"

Nick nodded. "All yours, as far as I can tell."

Steven, still overwhelmed at the sight of the car's upholstery lacquered by his own life-giving blood, noticed the damage to the windshield. "My head tagged the windshield. I wasn't belted in."

"Me neither."

"Serves us right."

"Whatever."

"Look at that. The glass is destroyed." Steven shook his head slowly in awe. "How did I not shatter my skull?"

Nick didn't respond.

"Looks like somebody went at it with a Louisville Slugger!" He glanced back at Nick. "You're telling me my *head* did that, and I'm still sitting here alive, with a scratch above my eyes, talking to you? No way."

The car engine had died. They sat in silence for a long moment.

"Where are we?" Steven asked.

"On I-90. About an hour outside Boston."

"Slide out," Steven said. "I want to get a look at the car."

The early morning air of late spring was cool. Steven shivered.

The passenger-side headlight was smashed so all that remained was a shark's mouth of glass teeth framing the inside of the metal cavity. The glass shards glowed in the light of the remaining headlamp. The quarter-panel had come loose and was nowhere in sight. The grille was busted, half—maybe more—gone, chunks of plastic here and there on the ground and along the edge of the bumper. The hood had taken a shot. The front edge had curled under, and the top had a severe dip, like a three-hundred-pound man had repeatedly parked his rump there. And then there was the windshield, bubbled inward and sagging. Steven leaned forward slightly, extending a hand, gently probing a finger at the glass. Moonlight refracted off the countless individual fragments.

"Something hit us," Steven said. They were standing shoulder to shoulder, their silhouettes set aglow by the lone functioning headlight.

Nick stood still, staring at the damaged Mustang. He didn't blink for a long time.

Steven crouched down in front of the busted headlight, leaning in close for a better look. Then he shook his head, and stood. "Too dark. I've got a flashlight in the trunk." He pulled his key from the ignition and rounded the rear of the car, quickly popping the trunk lid. He returned carrying an inexpensive plastic flashlight, unscrewing one end to make sure it had batteries. He tested it, shining the light in his face.

Nick watched him work, his mind on rewind, desperately thinking back, backpedaling through the past ten minutes, trying to remember what had happened, hoping to get a mental fix on what they had collided with.

Nick had his hands buried in his armpits, standing safely away from the traffic lanes. The sounds of the collision still rang in his ears. He could still see the flash of color, still feel the impact, still feel the unexpected shock of it. He stood with one foot on wet grass, one foot on the edge of the shoulder. "You think it's still drivable?" he said.

Steven's back was to him. He had crouched with the flashlight, inspecting the damage. "Probably," he said. "We can hopefully at least get it home. I'd hate to leave it out here overnight."

"I don't understand what happened," Nick said, mainly to himself.

"This definitely wasn't metal on metal," Steven said, playing the light up the fold in the hood. "I would have lost more paint, for one thing." He drew in close to the busted headlight. Something caught his attention. He held the flashlight under his chin, moving his nose to within inches of the remains of the headlamp. There were spatters of blood on the jagged shards of glass, and a snatch of some kind of cloth. Even in the poor lighting he could tell it was denim. He stared hard. His mind blanked. He opened his mouth to call Nick, but words failed to rise from his throat.

Now it was more obvious. The blood spatters were not just visible on and around the remains of the headlamp but also along the exposed chrome of the bumper. He stood, the cone of white light falling across the hood of the car. More blood. And on the windshield, the most blood of all. A cold chill slithered up his spine, up the back of his neck.

"Nick," he said, his tone thick and dry. He looked over his shoulder, Nick several steps back, as if he were making a subtle effort to withdraw from the scene. "Nick . . . what did you hit?"

Nick shook his head.

Steven rubbed a hand along the stubble of his chin. He stood and looked over the roof of the car into the darkness beyond. He shut the open door, then walked directly out in front of the car, light from the single headlight gradually dimming on the back of his T-shirt. He felt sick to his stomach, with a headache to rival his all-time worst.

Steven began to slowly trace the path of the skid. The embankment to his left was a severe and sudden drop. If the Mustang hadn't stopped at the exact moment it did, they would have tumbled into the darkness below, where they could have been trapped for hours or days. He shined the flashlight down the slope, but the light was too weak to illuminate more than fifteen or twenty feet at a time. He turned and saw Nick following reluctantly at a distance.

Steven flashed back a couple of hours to their departure from Manhattan. Nick had had a few beers earlier that evening at the Yankee game, and a glass or two of wine at his favorite restaurant in midtown before they hit the road. On the way to the car, he had snatched the keys out of Steven's hand and darted for the driver's side. The argument didn't last long. Nick could be aggressive—frighteningly aggressive. He didn't lose many battles. And he hadn't lost that one. Steven had relented and grabbed them each a coffee-to-go on the way out of the city. Nick had seemed fine, in control of all his faculties, at least in Steven's judgment. Now he questioned that judgment. And his view of Nick was suddenly very suspect.

"See anything?" Nick said, catching up now.

Together they watched the beam from the flashlight pass over the wet grass of the embankment. It was too dark and still too foggy to make out anything beyond the range of the flashlight. The silhouettes of trees were vaguely visible on the horizon, and Steven thought he could hear water flowing somewhere nearby, most likely in the form of a stream of unknown size. To his knowledge, the Atlantic was several miles south.

"I've hit deer before," Steven said. "They can tear up a car in a hurry."

Nick nodded.

"But I found this in the headlight." Steven held out the small scrap of denim.

Nick examined it closely, his anxiety level elevating with every breath.

Steven rested the flashlight on his shoulder, panning it back and forth across the gloom. "Nick," he said, still focused on the gloom and the darkness that enveloped the slope of the embankment. "How many deer you know that wear denim?"

The question hung in the air. Then silence fell between them.

Finally, Nick dropped the swath of fabric at his feet. The tumblers were falling into place in his brain, and he had reached a conclusion. It was time to act, time to be decisive. He stepped in front of Steven so that his back was to the slope of the embankment. He stood nose-to-nose with his friend, squaring his shoulders.

"Whatever it is you're thinking, Steven, put it away. Just shut your brain and forget it. We hit a deer, man. Plain and simple. The car knocked it off the road and it ran off to die somewhere in the woods far from here. Okay? Got that? Your car hit Bambi, Steven. End of story. Don't make this complicated. Let's get in the car and get home." Nick offered a mild grin, and he placed a hand on Steven's shoulder.

"What about that denim?"

Nick, glaring deep into his eyes, said slowly and definitively, "I don't know what you're talking about."

"Please get out of my way," Steven said.

"No."

"We have to be sure . . ."

"Of what?"

Another silence filled the moment. It was clear that a lot was going on behind Steven's eyes. An eternity passed before he blinked. A great debate raged in his mind. He let out a long breath, then he nodded. "Fine," he sighed, and lowered the flashlight to his side.

Then they heard the moan.

Nick had already turned back toward the Mustang. He froze. Steven looked at him.

"That was the wind," Nick snapped, unconvincingly.

"Shut up."

The next moan was lower but of longer duration and greater intensity. The haunting sound carried up the grassy slope of the embankment to them.

"Oh my God," Steven said, stunned. He took a step onto the damp grass.

Nick grabbed a fistful of shirt and jerked Steven to him. *"Walk away!"*

Steven couldn't believe what he was hearing. "Are you insane? Someone is down there!"

"Listen to me!" Nick's face was taut with desperation, his eyes wide, threatening. "If we don't leave now, we're in a world of trouble. Don't get involved!"

Steven stiff-armed him, freeing himself with a powerful, defiant shove. "Get out of my *way!*" And down he went, foolhardily hurling himself down the precarious slope of the embankment. And in the same breath, Nick reacted, leaping, arms outstretched, tackling Steven, taking him hard to the ground, both of them rolling and tumbling, limbs flailing, grunting and groaning as they bumped and thrashed and struggled against one another.

Steven got to his feet and put a foot in Nick's chest, knocking

him on his back. Nick grunted, scurried to his feet. The flashlight
had fallen free during the tussle down the embankment. Steven
spotted its diffused glow in a patch of flattened grass. Both men
dived for it.

Steven struck him with an elbow under the chin. Nick fell
back, sliding on his side a few feet down the slope, clutching a
hand at his throat. He coughed and gagged, twisting up onto his
knees.

Steven had the flashlight in hand. For the moment, he disre-
garded Nick. He stood still, listened, arms at his sides.

The moan came from nearby.

The flashlight panned, weak light cutting through the gloom.

Steven took a step forward. "Where . . . where are you?" He
heard slight movement. He redirected the beam of light.

Nick was still on the ground, on his hands and knees, his head
turned in the direction of the sounds of life emanating from the
darkness.

Steven proceeded forward. "Hello?"

"Heeeere . . ."

Steven froze. He stopped breathing, his heart in his throat.
His eyes cut in every direction but saw nothing. "Say again," he
called out.

The only response was an intense, chill-raising moan.

Nick got to his feet, and approached.

Steven took cautious steps, moving deliberately down the
slick terrain. "I can't see you."

"Here . . ."

"Over there," Nick said, pointing to the right of where Steven
stood.

The beam of light shifted slightly, peeling away the veil of
night to uncover a human form. Steven rushed forward. He
stopped suddenly. An adult male lay facedown in the ankle-deep
grass and weeds. Steven swallowed hard. Something inside him
understood that from this moment on things would only get
worse. He approached with caution, as if the body were a viper

preparing to strike. He had no idea what to do, but he had to do something fast.

He turned. "Nick! HE'S ALIVE!"

Nick approached.

"Your cell phone!" Steven said. "Call 911, hurry!"

Nick stared past his friend to the man on the ground.

"Did you hear me?"

Nick just stared, mud and grass on his face and hands. His words came out monotone, "Leave him."

The man on the ground was now making constant guttural sounds, grotesque moans that chilled Steven to the bone.

"How can you say that?" Steven said.

"Leave him, Steven. You don't want to be a part of this."

"He's dying!" Steven yelled, his pulse racing. "Make the call!"

Nick shook his head. Then he began slowly backing away.

Dumbfounded, Steven returned his full attention to the man on the ground. He reached down and tugged at one shoulder, rolling the body faceup. He recoiled at what he saw. The person before him was a male, perhaps forty years of age, with a scraggly partial beard and untrimmed hair. He wore a jeans jacket over a stained white T-shirt and olive green cargo pants. The man's face had taken quite a shot. The nose was pushed to one side, with teeth forced through his lower lip. His face was smeared with blood. One eye was half open, the other swollen shut.

"Hold on, man," Steven said, his voice shaky. "We're gonna get you help. Just hold on." The man mumbled something Steven couldn't understand. "What's your name?" Steven said.

No response.

He worked a hand under the man's backside, feeling for a wallet. The back pocket of the cargo pants was buttoned. His nervous fingers felt fat and clumsy. Finally he managed to twist the button through the buttonhole. The wallet was a cheap nylon tri-fold with a Velcro fastener. Blinking away tears, barely able to focus, he peeled the wallet open, fumbling it to the ground once or twice. He held the light on the man's license. The name was Ronald Calther. The face in the photo was clean-shaven with a half smile.

"Okay, Ronald, everything is going to be fine. Just stay with me. Just stay awake and keep breathing. Can you hear me? Do you understand?"

Calther managed a slight nod. The one eye appeared to find Steven.

"My name's Steven Adler, Ronald. I know you're hurting, but I'll have an ambulance here in no time, and they'll get you patched up. Just focus on me, all right?"

Another, shorter nod.

Calther was badly broken. His legs were twisted, folded in directions they weren't designed to bend, his pants torn and bloody. It didn't take a medical examiner to see that one arm was dislocated, the way it hung loose from the socket, the shoulder severely crushed. Steven didn't want to even speculate at the internal damage. His only goals for the moment were to get his hands on Nick's cell phone, get an ambulance dispatched, and keep Ronald Calther as comfortable as possible until the flashing lights could arrive.

Speaking of Nick, he was nowhere to be seen. Steven pivoted in the muddy slop and glanced up the high embankment, watching, waiting, and fuming inside. *That selfish idiot*, he thought.

He was hesitant to move Calther. The man was in no shape to be jostled around. There were almost certainly spinal injuries. His neck might be broken. Steven hated to keep him down where it was dark and damp, but he was very reluctant to shift his broken body any more than he already had. The best he could hope to do for now was to keep him warm, awake, alert, and distracted from the misery that had befallen him on such a godforsaken night.

He called out to Nick. The Mustang was just beyond view, though he thought he could possibly make out the distant glow of the one headlight. He kept a hand on Calther's chest, his feet shifting on the flattened grass where he was crouched.

No sign of Nick.

"NICK!"

Seconds passed. At last a dark silhouette emerged at the crest of the embankment. Steven waved a hand in the air, signaling for assistance. "COME ON! 911! HURRY!"

For the longest time, Nick did not move a muscle. His silhouette remained steadfast, as if anchored where he stood, midway between the Mustang and Steven. Again, Steven waved a hand. Then, thinking that perhaps his friend had lost sight of him, he hoisted the flashlight over his head, waving it from side to side.

"MAKE THE CALL! THEN GIVE ME A HAND!"

Finally, Nick turned toward the car.

Steven let out a long breath. He bent over Calther's body. "You breathing all right? Need some water? I've got a bottle of water in the car, I think."

Calther managed to move the index finger on one hand. He groaned, his face greasy with mud. Steven put his face in his hands and shook his head, thankful Calther had survived the collision, but praying that the paramedics would make it in time. Nick had already wasted valuable minutes.

A full minute passed. Then another.

"Comeoncomeoncomeon," Steven said under his breath.

He stared down at Calther, the guilt inside him building. Calther was staring back, with that one half-opened eye. The visual exchange lasted for several long seconds, until Calther at last broke eye contact and actually appeared to be looking past Steven's shoulder. Steven followed his gaze, turning to see what might have caught his attention. He was startled to see Nick standing there, nearly right behind him, towering over them, his eyes fully focused on the man on the ground.

With his left hand, Nick held a firm grip on the tire tool from the trunk of the Mustang. It was eighteen inches long, made of solid iron. One end was designed to loosen the lug nuts that held the tires on, with the other end slightly angled and tapered at the very end for use in removing the hubcaps. Nick held it just above the tapered end.

Steven put two and two together a fraction of a second too late.

"No!"

Nick was quick. He clocked Steven in the side of the head with the heel of his shoe. Steven saw stars but not in the sky. The force of the blow spun him away from Calther. The heel had caught him in the jaw. His body twisted and he was down on his knees, and then he went facedown into the muck.

Nick Calevetti lunged forward, raising the tire tool high over his head and bringing it down hard and swift, striking Calther in the skull with deadly precision.

Whack!

The first blow rang out with a grotesque crack. The sound was like the splitting of a ripe coconut. Calther groaned.

Nick swung a second time, with even greater ferocity.

Whack!

Steven brought his head around, his double vision slowly clearing so that he could refocus. He heard the sounds of Nick grunting as he continued the assault. Silhouetted against the gloomy backdrop, the arm came down again and again, blow after blow, the tire tool wielded like a weapon of destruction, each strike wringing ever more life from Ronald Calther.

Whack! Whack!

Nick stood in a stance with his legs spread as he bent at the waist. Blood splattered in the darkness. Calther's body flinched every time the tool made contact with his head, until at last his brain simply died, ending all communication with his nerve endings.

Struggling to his feet, Steven staggered in the general direction of Ronald Calther. Steven dropped to his knees, kneeling beside the body. The moaning and groaning had ceased. He felt for a pulse. There was none. Calther had stopped breathing.

Steven wheeled around, still on his knees.

Nick had taken a half step back.

"He's . . . *dead*," Steven said, short of breath. "You . . . you killed him!"

Nick shook his head. "No, my friend, a car hit him. Accidents happen."

Steven got to his feet, staggered to Nick, clutched his shirt. "*Why?*"

Nick pushed him aside. "You still don't get it. My license has been revoked for six months, and I'm on probation. I have alcohol in my system, and plenty of it. The penal system would crucify me, man! They'd lick their chops, seeing a rich kid like me coming down the pike!"

"You didn't have to do this!"

"What do *you* know?"

"I know you killed a man tonight!"

They locked eyes for an instant; then Nick glanced down at the tire tool still dangling from one hand. Suddenly he took several steps away, reared his arm back, and then with all his might flung the tire tool into the black void of the night. He then turned to Steven and smirked. "No I didn't."

"The police can find that tool. Your fingerprints are on it."

Nick held up a grease rag in his hand. "Guess again."

Steven could only gawk. He felt trapped in a surreal moment. Thunder boomed, shaking the earth. Lightning flashed, and the image of Ronald Calther's battered body was exposed there on the ground before them. The night had morphed into one seemingly endless nightmare.

Nick approached the body, bent at the knees, and clutched Ronald Calther's ankles. He started dragging the body in the direction opposite the interstate.

"What are you doing?"

"Use your brain, Steven. I'm getting rid of the body."

"I'll make sure you don't get away with this."

"Steven, believe me, it's in your best interest to just keep your mouth shut and let this all blow over like it never happened. Clear it from your mind. Let it go. Get over it and move on."

Calther's arms trailed limply behind the rest of his body as Nick labored deeper into the muck and the tall weeds. Nick was breathing hard. Calther was a big man, and his dead body was now two-hundred-plus pounds of dead weight. Nick Calevetti was five-ten and thin. The wet terrain made for poor footing.

Steven found himself overwhelmed with conflicting emotions. To some extent, what Nick was saying made sense, however sick his logic might have sounded. They couldn't bring Calther back to life. Hitting him with the car had been an accident. Tragic, certainly, but an accident nonetheless. Sure, Nick had been driving while under the influence of alcohol, but Steven had let him and had to share the responsibility for the consequences. He had to accept his share of the bla . . .

No . . . no . . . no!

Steven chided himself, ashamed that he'd even considered rationalizing the situation away. Nick had murdered a man! Murdered him in cold blood! *Murder!*

Stepping gingerly through the overgrowth, directing the beam of the flashlight ahead of his path, he began his pursuit. He spotted Nick not too far ahead. There was a stand of trees, ten or twelve of them, bunched together and sticking out of the earth at all angles. Beyond them lay a streambed. The stream was perhaps forty feet across at its widest point. Upon reaching them, Steven realized the trees stood in a marsh. He was soon in it up to his knees. He could hear Nick splashing, battling his load.

"Stop!" Steven called out.

Nick paused, looked in Steven's direction, then continued. Steven quickly caught up. "Wait, we have to talk about this." There was a dirt bluff alongside the stream. An enormous tree had tipped and fallen from atop the bluff, probably decades earlier, exposing its sprawling root system. The unearthed roots created a natural cagelike formation just beneath the surface of the water. Nick floated Calther's body to the fallen tree. Steven grabbed at his elbow but Nick deflected his hand.

"We can find a way out of this."

"I already have," Nick said, working to clear away clumps of mud and thick roots that had rotted after so many years in the water. He commenced stuffing Calther's upper body into the cagelike underwater cavity. Calther was floating faceup, river water and blood gushing from his open mouth. The tire tool had destroyed the bone structure of his face.

Steven backed away, his stomach retching at the sight of Calther and at the thought of how they could have arrived at this moment in their lives. He crawled onto a sandbar and vomited.

Nick made quick work of disposing of the body. He collapsed on the sandbar next to Steven, both of them gasping for breath.

Nick glanced at him, offering a conspiratorial grin. "Me and you, Steven. We're in this thing together."

"No."

"Till death do us part."

"Shut up."

"Don't be stupid. By daylight this will all be behind us. This guy was nobody. There is no one to miss him. Just some drifter. Probably no home or family. Why wreck your life, or mine, over some faceless indigent?"

"Because it isn't right!"

"Oh, grow up!"

Steven hung his head, his fingers clawing into the wet sand. There were too many voices in his head telling him too many different opinions, and he didn't particularly want to hear any of it. It was becoming increasingly impossible to think straight.

"Listen, I did us both a big favor back there," Nick said. "I don't like it any more than you do. But I'm a realist. You've got to take off your rose-colored glasses and see the world for what it is. The world is an ugly, vicious place. To survive, you've got to roll with the punches. I'm on your side here, pal. Back there, what I did, I was just looking out for us."

"Save it." But something shifted inside Steven, something indefinable. Nick was smart, and he had to hand it to him. In finishing off Calther the way he had, he'd taken things to a new level. And he'd had the presence of mind to bring Steven right along with him. It was Steven's car and Steven's tire tool, and, most importantly, it was Nick's word against his. Steven had worked his entire life to get into Harvard University, and now he was twelve months from graduation. Two more semesters and he'd have the world by the tail. Why risk it now? He didn't come from money like Nick, and he worked nights at a warehouse in Boston to afford tuition. Would all the long hours and sweat and perseverance be for nothing?

The truth was, he'd done nothing wrong. All this required was for him to turn a blind eye. Walk away. He had put forth the effort to help Ronald Calther. He couldn't control every action of every other person in the world. He had to let Nick live his own life. Steven's conscience was clear.

They emerged from the trees, both of them wet and shivering.

Still uncertain, unconvinced, Steven said, "What about my car?"

"We drive it back to Cambridge. We stash it for a few days, let things cool off. Or better yet, take it to a body shop. I'll get you the cash for whatever repairs it needs. You won't be out a dime. No reason to get insurance involved."

"I don't like this."

They scrambled to the top of the embankment, exhausted, emotionally spent, drenched from head to toe. They took a moment to catch their breath. Steven could barely remember his life prior to this stretch of I-90. A slight breeze chilled him. The fog had thickened.

"How you feel?" Nick asked.

Steven glared at him. "Don't ask."

"You hear something?" Nick said.

Steven saw them first. He felt the color drain from his face.

A sport-utility vehicle had pulled alongside the Mustang, its doors open, and two individuals had climbed out to investigate the damaged, abandoned vehicle on the side of the road. The taillights glowed bright in the early morning gloom.

"Easy . . . easy . . . easy," Nick said, stepping in front of Steven. "Take it easy, now. Don't panic."

They walked in the direction of the Mustang, Nick a step ahead. A few steps closer and they could identify the make and model of the SUV. It was a Dodge Durango with Pennsylvania tags. A tall man had come around from the driver's side to inspect the Mustang. A heavyset woman cautiously slipped out from the other side, casting quick, furtive glances. She was clearly sheepish about the scenario of an abandoned car in the middle of nowhere. She said something and pointed their way.

Nick whispered, "Remember, we hit a deer. Then we took the time to drag it off the road so that it wouldn't become a safety issue to others."

Steven's throat was suddenly dry. *It's just a matter of time,* he thought, again and again. *It's just a matter of time.*

The man gestured at his female companion to get back in the Durango. She complied and briskly shut the door. He came out as far as the tail end of the Durango, where he stopped and glanced at the damaged front end of the Mustang, then watched them approach.

He made eye contact, first with Nick, then Steven.

"Everything all right?" he asked.

Nick smiled. "Hit a deer."

"That so?"

"Jumped right out of the fog. Never saw it coming." Nick shook his head, shrugging. He hooked a thumb toward the side of the road. "Nailed our front end and went over the top of us.

Landed smack in the middle of the road. By the time that we got turned around and could get back there, she was dead." Nick spoke with such a sense of reality and conviction, Steven almost believed him.

The man turned his chin toward the Mustang. "Did a number on your car, for sure."

"Tell me about it," Nick snorted.

The man sort of grinned, eyed both of them rather skeptically. "Anybody hurt?"

"Just wet and tired."

"Anything I can do to help? Need a ride to town or something? I've got a cell phone if you need to call for a tow truck."

Nick shook his head. "Not necessary, but thanks. We are fine."

Time seemed to stand still while the man assessed the situation. He wasn't fully buying the story, and the three of them knew it. But the tale Nick had spun had sounded just reasonable enough to perhaps do the trick. It appeared that the man had one more question in him, but just then the power window on the Durango rolled down, and the woman stuck her nose out. "Hal?"

He looked over his shoulder. "Yeah, I'm on my way."

She had provided just enough distraction to snap him from his train of thought. He wished them well, and a few heartbeats later the taillights of the Durango had faded into the gloom.

They returned to the Mustang. Steven slid in behind the steering wheel. It suddenly felt incredibly foreign to him. He no longer felt at home in his own skin. The engine started without incident.

"This is the point of no return," Nick said, soberly. "If we play it smart, play it straight, no one will be the wiser. This is our little secret. It's a memory that will fade with time." He glanced at Steven. "Are you with me?"

That was the question, all right. Steven didn't know if he had an answer.

"I'll protect you," Nick added. "I can make your life much more pleasant, Steven. I can make your money problems go away. Or, I can put you through hell. The choice is yours."

Steven put the car in gear, made a U-turn in the middle of I-90, and kept his mouth shut the rest of the way to Boston. He couldn't fathom life getting any worse.

But it would, very quickly.

2

EVERY NIGHT WAS THE SAME. HE AWOKE FOR THE FOURTH or fifth time that night and just lay there in the stillness of his bed, staring at the shadows on the ceiling. According to all the literature he'd read over the past months, the sleeping problem wasn't unusual, given his age and occupation. Even his personal physician could only shrug and write out a prescription. But Kenneth Bourgeous had sworn off sleeping pills. At age eighty-three he took enough medication already. He had no desire to make additions to his daily regimen. No sir, he'd deal with the sleepless nights.

Mrs. Bourgeous was sound asleep in her own bed, directly across the room. They hadn't shared a bed in two decades. On occasion they'd even had separate homes. But at their age it was best not to live alone. No matter whether they got along, it was just comforting to know someone was nearby.

Bourgeous could hear the clock on the wall above his head. He shut his eyes and began counting backward from ten thousand. At nine thousand nine hundred and fifty, his eyes fluttered open again. He gave up. He pushed back the thin blanket, swung his feet to the floor, and shuffled down the hall in his silk robe and ancient slippers. He found a stubby glass and filled it with cranberry juice. A fixture above the sink offered the only light in the kitchen. The display on the microwave oven taunted him with the time: 4:45 a.m.

He shuffled to his recliner in the den, seeking refuge in early morning television. The glass of cranberry juice was within easy reach on the reading table next to his chair. He took a short sip and returned it to its coaster. The pain was short and sudden, like a shot of electrical current ripping through his chest. Bourgeous leaned forward, clutching the front of his robe. Talking heads on the TV screen blurred through his tears. The tightening in his chest intensified, growing unbearable. And then, as suddenly as it had come on, the pain relented. He sank into his chair, sweat across his brow. He hadn't felt one of those in years.

He dabbed his forehead with a folded hanky and reached for his drink. The juice glass was cold against his tongue. He swallowed slowly and couldn't help but smile, knowing he'd dodged a bullet. He had dodged many such bullets. Both physically and professionally. That's what they'd always called him behind his back, Bulletproof Bourgeous.

The TV was muted. He stared at MSNBC. He envied his wife. She could sleep through Hiroshima. But she'd not lived his life. He sat and pondered the past sixty years. Good Lord, no wonder he couldn't sleep. His stomach knotted just casually glancing back at his career. His physician had suggested the cranberry juice for his stomach. He scooted the coaster nearer the edge of the table and reached for his drink.

The glass fell over, crimson liquid spreading out across the small round reading table. Bourgeous had slumped forward, all his fingers digging at his chest, clawing at the robe. The pain was white hot and unrelenting. He slid from the chair to his knees. He tried to call out to his wife, but his voice was reduced to a muted gurgle.

Seconds later he was on his face on the carpet, his arms folded beneath him. His body jerked for a moment or two, then ceased movement. Cranberry juice dripped from the edge of the table, soaking into the deep shag near his feet.

3

FORTY-FIVE MINUTES DOWN THE INTERSTATE, STEVEN HAD both hands on the wheel. He was watching the speedometer like a hawk. The last thing he needed was to be pulled over for speeding. As it stood, it would take a small miracle to not be pulled over for the busted headlight.

The lights of the city sat dazzling on the horizon. His mind jumped from thought to thought. He rolled down the window several inches for some fresh air. Deep breaths . . . deep breaths. Everything he'd worked for, all the sacrifices he'd made, all the sacrifices his parents had made—it was now all in jeopardy.

His wet hair hung in his face but he ignored it. His knuckles were white around the steering wheel. His T-shirt was pasty against his skin.

He was barely ten days past his twenty-first birthday. He'd made it into Harvard University because of his grades and his pure force of will. He had hit the books hard and buckled down during those years when his peers were playing ball, seeing movies, and cruising shopping malls. He had taken it upon himself to reach for the brass ring, to set his sights high, to aim for the stars. By some miracle beyond his comprehension he'd been accepted into Harvard. All he had to do was make it through another year. The next step was Harvard Law. Then he could write his own ticket.

So the gravity of what had occurred back there on that strip of U.S. interstate forty-five minutes ago settled upon him with the weight of the entire cosmos. And as he sped toward the bosom of Boston, he determined within himself that he would not let that one solitary event be the defining moment of his life.

Nick faced out his window. Not a word had passed between them during the entire three-quarters of an hour.

Steven checked his speed, careful to keep the needle a notch or two below the posted limit. That was when he noticed the gas gauge. He didn't like what he saw. They were riding on fumes. That wouldn't do. It was still nearly twenty minutes to Cambridge. They'd have to stop. No big deal, though. He'd pump in a couple bucks, just enough to get home.

At the edge of Boston he wheeled into a 7-Eleven, pulled next to the pumps, and eased out into the glare of the overhead lights. At the pump directly in front of him a thick-chested man in construction boots squeegeed the windshield of his El Camino. He cut a glare toward the Mustang, then went back to his task. Steven felt terribly exposed, as if he were climbing out of the car naked. He grabbed the fuel nozzle from an unleaded pump and squeezed the handle as he surveyed his surroundings. He had the distinct urge to vomit again.

The doors to the 7-Eleven swung open and three punks in leather cut around the corner and disappeared. A police cruiser passed through the intersection. The El Camino pulled away, leaving the Mustang alone at the pumps. It felt like a lifetime since they'd left Manhattan.

He pumped in five dollars' worth and then replaced the nozzle. As he marched toward the entrance, his eyes lingered on the front end of the car. Under the stark lighting, the damage looked much worse. He glanced through the streaked window at Nick. Nick, silent and stoic. All Steven could do was shake his head.

He grabbed a Mountain Dew and put it on the counter. The clerk rang up his total, and he reached for his wallet. His brow creased and he frowned. He patted his back pockets, then patted the front. His blood ran cold. He patted his rear end a second time and held his hands there as he turned his head, looking curiously at the floor all around him. His wallet was gone.

The clerk glared at him with empty eyes.

Steven found a crumpled ten-dollar bill in his front pocket. He dropped it on the counter and turned away without waiting for the change he had coming. He pushed open the door and dashed out to the car, his heart a block of ice in his chest.

"What's up?" Nick said.

"My wallet, have you seen it?" He ran his hands under the seats, then ran his fingers along the creases at the back of the seats. Nothing. He checked the pockets of his jacket. Nothing.

"Look for it!" he barked. Everything of use or value was in the wallet. His driver's license. His student ID. He was hunched over, his knees in the driver's seat, one hand braced against the floorboard, one arm braced against the passenger-side headrest.

He slowly sat upright behind the wheel, facing dead ahead, his face turning to a whitewashed canvas of shock. At that moment there was not a single kernel of doubt about the location of his missing wallet. It had to have fallen out somewhere there along the interstate. He could almost envision it lying in the grass and mud of the embankment. He'd not thought to check. It was out there somewhere. On the ground. In the wide open, for anyone's eyes who cared to look. Under no circumstances could he leave it there.

"It's gone!"

Nick's jaw dropped. "Don't say that."

"Please, God, let this night end."

"Forget about it," Nick said. "Everything is replaceable."

Steven gave him a hard look. "Don't you get it? If it's back there, it's got my ID—that places me at the scene of the crime!"

Nick put his head against the headrest, pushed his fingers through his wet hair. "Unbelievable."

"I've got to go back, right now."

"How could you have been so stupid?"

Steven felt gut shot, like all the air in the universe had been sucked out of him. He could hardly breathe. "*Me?* I'm not the one who got us into this!"

"I can't believe this!"

"Well, believe it."

"We've got to find it. We have no choice."

Steven nodded.

In a heartbeat he was in the car, the engine running, a light mist falling in the glow of the overhead lights. Steven put the Mustang in gear, turned into the street, and headed back toward the one spot on earth he reviled more than any other.

The nightmare seemed to never end.

It had only just begun.

4

SHE HATED SLEEPING ALONE. BUT THAT'S THE WAY KENNETH preferred it. He hated her dog. But she insisted she keep Layla in the house. She could feel Layla's weight at the foot of the bed, and she smiled. For such a tiny dog her body generated an astounding amount of heat. She opened one eye to see what time it was and saw instead a hint of light on the wall, light coming through the door from the hallway. Another sleepless night for Kenneth.

It struck her as a little surprising that Layla hadn't followed him into the room. Even though it was the middle of the night, the dog was always game for some activity. Neither her husband nor her dog was partial to the other, but when the outside world was dark and foreboding, any companionship was better than none at all. But, she figured, Kenneth had probably either perched himself on the toilet and locked the door or fallen asleep in his recliner, boring the dog into returning to bed. She fluffed her pillow and raised her head to make sure Layla had plenty of room to spread out. The dog ignored her. But something caught her attention. There was a stain on the bedspread.

Her arthritis gave her fits as she sat up. She switched on the lamp on the nightstand and put on her glasses. She leaned over and squinted. There were tiny paw-shaped crimson stains on the bedspread. A dozen or more of them. She could see where the dog had leaped onto the bed and ambled around, hunting a comfortable spot to nest.

"Bad, *bad* dog," she scolded in baby talk. "Bad Layla. Bad *girl!*"

What in the world had she gotten into? Mrs. Bourgeous stooped over, pinched up a handful of bedspread, and sniffed a crimson paw print. She frowned.

"What have you been into?"

She climbed out of bed to get the bottle of stain remover from the utility closet. Crossing the kitchen, she saw that the light was coming from the front room. Kenneth watching television.

"Sweetie, you see what a mess Layla made?" She dug out the cleaner from the utility space and crossed to the den. "Sweetie, did you—" The bottle dropped from her hands like a lead sinker and hit with a hollow plastic thump between her bare feet. She wasted precious seconds standing there petrified by shock, staring at his crumpled body, before having the presence of mind to pick up the phone and call 911.

·◆··◆·

They strapped him down on a gurney and loaded him in an ambulance. Mrs. Bourgeous looked on in horror. The colored lights from the ambulance and the police cruisers swirled across the exterior wall of the house and the lawn and the landscaping. They wouldn't let her ride with him. She asked if he was going to make it. The EMTs had few words for her as they rushed to get the old man ready to roll. The good news was he was still showing vital signs. The bad news was those signs were getting weaker by the minute. Mrs. Bourgeous collapsed in tears as she was attended to by uniformed officers.

They escorted her to a cruiser and followed the ambulance

to the hospital emergency room. She demanded to see Kenneth. A pretty nurse with a soothing smile provided her with a paper cup of water and a mild sedative. Mrs. Bourgeous swallowed the pills and sipped the water. She stared up at the nurse with big, frightened eyes. The nurse couldn't have been older than thirty-three or thirty-four. She and Kenneth had been married longer than the girl's parents had been alive. They kept her in a waiting area, seated in a stiff plastic chair with metal legs. From her seat she could hear the doctors scrambling around in a room down the corridor, working desperately to save her husband.

But they couldn't. For twenty minutes they used the best in medical technology to revive the old man's heart. It had stopped beating by the time the ambulance reached the hospital. His time had come. A doctor in a white coat stood in the doorway, searching for the words to tell the widow. The look in his eyes said it all. Before he even opened his mouth, Mrs. Bourgeous put her face in her hands and began shaking her head.

A cop at a pay phone next to an exit put in his change and dialed a number, leaking word of the old man's passing. In the coming hours, the news would spread like a virus: Kenneth Bourgeous, chief justice of the Supreme Court, was dead.

5

IN THE DARK, EVERY MILE OF THE INTERSTATE LOOKED IDENTICAL to the last. Steven could have shut his eyes, driven for ages, then opened them again and not have known the difference. By now they had backtracked several times, going for miles at a time, then cutting back in the opposite direction, looking desperately for something familiar.

Every few minutes they'd pull the car over on the shoulder, get out, and look for any landmarks that might jog their memory. But they could remember little or nothing about the exact place in the road where they had encountered Ronald Calther. In the fog and the gloom, it all appeared interchangeable.

This was all guesswork, a shot in the dark. Their only recollections were of the embankment in the dark of night, the steep slope, the high grass leading down near the water, and the clusters of trees springing up out of the marsh. That was it.

As the morning progressed toward dawn, traffic gradually picked up, and Steven and Nick found it increasingly difficult not to attract attention. The window of opportunity for covering their tracks was quickly slamming shut. Come daylight, their options would be drastically reduced. And daylight was barely an hour away. Already there were streaks of color on the horizon, beginning to break up the night sky.

Nick grew agitated. He cursed, slamming his fist against the dash.

Steven was very near to having a breakdown. His hands were shaking. He was cold and scared. A man had been murdered right before his eyes. And now there seemed every reason to believe that he could go to jail for the rest of his life. He pulled the car to the side of the road. He put his face in his hands and came unglued.

"I can't take it!" Steven burst out. "I can't *take* it! We've got to end this."

Nick looked at him. "What are you saying?"

"Let's just cut our losses. Now my wallet is gone, we're going to be found out anyway, man. If we go to the police, maybe they can—"

"Shut up!" Nick said, getting in his face. "What happened here stays here! You have no idea the fine line you're walking. That wallet could be anywhere. Back at Yankee stadium, back at the restaurant, back at my parents' place. It could be anywhere. There is no reason to assume it's out here. Your paranoia is getting the better of you. You've got to keep your head in the game, bro. And you had better get wise to the fact that my family has the money to save you or break you, buddy boy. A Harvard degree is your meal ticket. You've got a bright future for someone with your background, Steven, so don't screw up or you could end up at the bottom for the rest of your life. How does that sound?"

Tears streaming down his face, Steven could only shake his head. "This isn't right."

"This has nothing to do with right or wrong, man. This is about survival. The weak get eaten. I've got your back—you know that, don't you?"

Steven wiped away tears with his forearm. He blinked several times, then glanced at Nick. They made eye contact. Steven nodded slowly.

Nick said, "And I know that you've got mine. We're blood brothers. Right?"

Again, Steven nodded.

"Blood brothers don't let each other down." Nick extended his hand, and they touched fists, signifying their bond. "All right," Nick said, managing a grin. "So tomorrow, you'll take the car to the shop. I'll give you the cash you'll need before you go. Then we're going to finish out the semester, graduate next spring, and forget that this ever happened."

Steven took a long, deep breath, his hands still shaking. He put the Mustang in gear but kept his foot on the brake pedal. He wanted to say something, to respond, but the inner strength simply wasn't there. He glanced briefly at Nick, who was staring hard at him, then turned to face the road ahead. He heard Nick say one last thing, and those words echoed in his ears for the next several miles.

Nick had said, "Trust me."

6

THE MOST POWERFUL MAN IN THE WORLD WAS ON THE other side of the door. Sometimes it was easy to forget. Especially for a six-term senator. Especially a senator of the same party as the sitting president. Franklin Henbest, Democrat from Idaho, stared at the door to the Oval Office from a comfortable but stiff chair in the waiting area. The bags under his eyes were nothing new, but the catnap he was running on from the night before wasn't helping matters any. He'd been seated twenty minutes, waiting.

By the break of dawn, word had filtered through the capital city of Bourgeous's death. Rumors leaked at the speed of light in D.C. Henbest was already awake when the call came. He refused to believe it at first. It was simply too good to be true. It took the better part of an hour to confirm. Sure enough, the chief justice was dead. A conservative had fallen from the Court. It was a beautiful thing.

Henbest was sixty-three. He was slim, with thinning blond hair turning white. His teeth were blazingly white—*too* white, like the smile on an insurance salesman. As a rule, Franklin Henbest was the tallest in any given room. He was well liked, and personable. Fifty years of cigarettes had reaped for him an artificially baritone voice. During his tenure he had watched two other nominees take the bench. Both by Republican presidents. Both old-school, hard-line conservatives. Bourgeous had been an intimidating beachfront of a man. He'd steered the Court to the right for thirty years. The Democrats had sat patiently, watching and waiting, hoping for a turn at bat. Eventually someone had to retire or expire. Innis Sharp, the fossil of the nine, had more plastic in his chest than a Sony VCR. He'd outlived a half century of presidents. Regardless, though, he was a Democrat to the core. The longer his artificial ticker kept on ticking, the better. He might run on batteries, but he was a vote they could count on. In recent years, seemingly more than any other time in the nation's history, the Court had truly flexed its muscle. And the conservative majority had been the side doing the strong-arming. Suddenly, though, the battlefield had leveled out. A grand opportunity had arisen. With the death of Bourgeous, Henbest and his buddies on the Hill were licking their chops. The droolfest had officially begun.

This morning the West Wing was a hive of activity. Senator Henbest sat and watched with mild detachment. Secretaries and legal aides romped by. Dark suits and knee-length skirts. Wide ties and frowns.

There was no mystery as to why he'd been summoned this morning. He was the Senate minority leader. The figurehead of the left. He'd been summoned to spitball with the president. To bounce names of possible nominees off the wall to see which stuck and which fell hard to the floor. Henbest had made a short list of his own. And he was quite certain that others had come before him with plenty of suggestions. This was their moment to shine. They would swing hard for the fence, go as left as humanly possible. Banging through the Senate Judiciary Committee would be painful and bloody. And waiting on the other side was the Republican majority. What the Democrats needed was a knight in shining armor. Someone deep on the liberal end of the spectrum, as spotless and untouchable as a virgin. Someone beloved. Someone the right couldn't lay a finger on.

A wave of staffers swept by. Henbest fished inside a jacket pocket for a lozenge. He sucked on the mint, his eyes working the room. When the door finally opened, he kept his seat. A half-dozen familiar faces washed through the door. A few of them noticed him and nodded acknowledgment. Others were too busy acting busy. Two of the president's top advisers whispered conspiratorially to one another, creeping along the wall, keeping to themselves. One of them flashed an eye toward the senator but kept moving. Many things, Henbest estimated, had found their way into the president's ear over the past so many hours. There was much to gain and much strategy to consider. He was aware that the president would hear and had heard many opinions about who should be seated on the Court. It was the president's duty to nominate the new chief justice. And nobody had the president's ear like Senator Franklin Henbest. No one's opinion would have greater pull.

After all, that's what family was for.

A secretary told him that the president was ready to see him now. The chief of staff was standing just outside the door, speaking to a staffer. Beyond him, the president stood with one hand in a pocket, smiling. He motioned at Henbest. The senator stepped past the chief of staff and into the office. The president, still grinning, said good morning, patted Henbest on the shoulder, shut the door to the Oval Office so they could be alone, and asked his cousin if he'd like coffee.

•—••—◆—•

The meeting lasted barely ten minutes. Just as Senator Henbest had suspected, the president already had a list in hand. It was the better part of two pages in length. Most of the names Henbest could dispatch from consideration right away. He kept his tongue pinned, though. It wasn't his place to speak out of turn. Soon enough he'd get his chance to whisper in the president's ear and nix whomever he chose. For the time being, though, he'd simply come to float a few names in the spirit of friendly conversation. Sooner or later he'd know exactly whom they needed on the bench. And when that time came, he'd be loaded for bear.

The list was surprisingly interesting. A few of the names on it were a given. They were obvious choices for a liberal nominee. Federal judges, mostly. A few ruled over the lower courts. There was a Hispanic circuit court judge from Miami by the name of Flavia. Henbest had heard of Flavia, in fact thought he might have met him once, a few years back. Probably shook his hand at a Democratic fund-raiser or some such. The Latino was a curious prospect, but his stance on the big issues would either make him or break him. And a Latino, especially, would have to be immaculate in both his personal and professional history if he had half a chance at squeaking by the conservatives in the Senate. There were several women's names listed. A nice thought, for sure. He read on.

The president had seemed fairly enthusiastic about the list. Its contents had come from over a half-dozen sources. Henbest promised to peruse it, roll the names around in his head, and then make additions as he saw fit. One thing was imperative: they needed the first shot over the bow to count. The enemy would smell weakness if it took two or three or four nominees before a confirmation was wrapped up. They needed a power-house of a nominee right out of the gate. They needed the list to boil down to one name, not three. And so the task fell to Franklin Henbest, cousin to the president of the United States, to do the back-alley work, to find their man, to tee up a winning proposition. He didn't take it lightly.

He stepped out into the ever-brightening morning light. He followed the curve of the sidewalk, nodding at an armed guard. His driver was waiting. Henbest ducked inside the back of the Cadillac. They turned into traffic and he stared out the window, the list sealed in a leather portfolio on the seat next to him.

"Back to the office?" his driver asked.

Henbest shook his head. "No. I'm meeting a colleague for a late breakfast. My usual spot."

The driver nodded, then changed lanes and signaled for a left turn at the next light.

Traffic thickened, but the senator was lost in his own little world. Mentally he'd already narrowed the list by close to half. The president wanted the top five names within the next couple of days. For that, he'd need help.

7

THE OFFICE WAS TUCKED IN AN UNIMPRESSIVE STONE BUILD-ing located off a side street in D.C. It wasn't an opulent build-ing, and it wasn't run-down, just remarkably undistinguished. The tenant directory in the foyer didn't have a listing for Chick Mancini's office. He didn't advertise. Nor was he in the phone book. One hundred percent of his business derived from refer-rals.

Chick was standing behind his desk, pulling a manila folder from a filing cabinet against the wall when there came a knock at the door. He checked his watch. He wasn't expecting anyone.

"Door's open," he called out.

The door opened and a familiar face entered the room.

"Have a seat." Chick remained standing behind his desk. Chick had spent much of his adult life working for a number of government bureaucracies, mainly within the intelligence com-munity. He knew everybody who was anybody, and had dirty laundry on them all. His friends and comrades dwelled in low places, and they could find anything. His list of contacts and sources was seemingly infinite. For the better part of a decade he'd made a rather nice living as an information gatherer for those who could afford his services. He didn't look like the shad-owy creature that he was. His expression was always rather chip-per, and his eyes were bright and clear. He was a sleaze with the face of a seminary student. He wore expensive suits that he got from a respected tailor near the Capitol Building on whom Chick kept a nice thick file of unseemly Polaroids. The Lexus out front he got from a lease agent but didn't pay a dime for it. Security in his office was reasonable but it wasn't Fort Knox. He kept anything of any sensitivity in a custom-built vault the size of a grand piano. World War III couldn't open it without the combination.

He put on his used-car-salesman smile and tapped a finger to the manila envelope. "This is going to ruin someone's day," he said with a certain measure of cheer. "Give me just a second to finish up with this."

The man seated across from him nodded. His name was Rowan Lipscomb. Officially, he worked for no one. *Unofficially*, he was on the payroll of Senator Franklin Henbest.

"Easiest money I've made in a month," Chick said with a smile that showed nearly all his teeth. "So, what's the occasion?"

Lipscomb retrieved his attaché case from the floor beside him and removed a thick business envelope. He leaned forward and set the envelope on the front edge of Chick Mancini's desk.

The cheery smiled faded slightly. Chick didn't open his mouth. He snatched up the envelope and fanned through the small brick of cash. Also inside the envelope was a list of names. He gave it a cursory glance.

"I need background checks for everyone listed there, and I need it *yesterday*," Lipscomb said.

"It will take a few hours."

"Fine. Meet me for beers—usual spot, usual time. Be thorough; there can be no surprises."

Chick said, "My reputation speaks for itself. I guarantee no surprises."

"Whatever. Just get it done."

8

THEY COULDN'T FIND JASPER, SO THEY TRACKED DOWN Crystal, which was the next-best thing. If anyone knew where Jasper was—or at least how to find him—she was the one. Crystal Easterling was in the UK, at her parents' estate outside of London when she got the call from the States. Theresa Howell was on the other end of the line, calling from the corporate office in Austin.

"Kenneth Bourgeous is dead," Theresa said. "His wife found him facedown on the floor this morning, at home." She then added that Jasper wasn't answering his cell phone or responding to his pager. In other words, he was being his stubborn, belligerent self again. Everything in the past few weeks had looked so bleak, he'd finally sought exile, from everyone.

"How did he die?"

"Don't know. No word yet about the autopsy. I've been calling you for hours."

Crystal should have been easy enough to find. But she'd left her cell phone at the house and had spent the day out with her mother. They hadn't returned from their day trip until well after dark. Her parents didn't own an answering machine. Theresa had dialed nearly every ten minutes since midmorning. She sounded genuinely taken off guard when Crystal actually answered.

The chief justice was dead. She could hardly believe her ears. There was no time to lose.

Crystal had packed only a carry-on, which made her quick departure possible. Her mother had set a glass of scotch in front of her, but she was already headed for the door, offering each parent a kiss on the cheek. In a flash she was behind the wheel of her rental car and dashing toward Heathrow Airport.

Once in the air, she was on the phone again, dialing Austin, then D.C., then back to Austin. What they were telling her seemed impossible, almost dreamlike. It was the impossible break they'd prayed for. One of the conservative justices was dead. The playing field had been leveled. They were back in the game. All was not lost after all!

Jasper had no idea what had happened.

And nobody could find him.

·◆··◆·

In certain industries, in certain parts of the world, Jasper Cone was a legend. Born and raised in the dust of west Texas, he graduated from high school two years early and dropped out of college less than a full semester into his freshman year. In his world, there was no time or room for academics. Living with a friend's parents, he began writing code for computer software. Cone Intermedia was formed.

Inside of two years, they'd moved their operation to a warehouse, and CI's products were being distributed worldwide. The company's growth was explosive, a fact Jasper wasn't altogether comfortable with. Jasper was a design man, an engineer at heart, a pioneer, a visionary—not a CEO. He was content to hide away and create rather than erect an elaborate business model or develop growth strategies. So a new president was appointed. The guy was an MBA with big plans and little patience for cerebral types. In short order Jasper was edged out. The company he'd founded and nurtured from infancy had been suddenly stripped from him. Crushed and humiliated, he withdrew. Within months, he'd disappeared.

A year or so later he surfaced in Tokyo. Rumors placed him in Europe, then Malaysia, and a few months later in London. By then he had a beard and hadn't cut his hair in ages. Speculation abounded. What was he up to? Had he fallen off the edge? Had his genius finally overwhelmed him? He would surface just long enough to cause a stir. Then just as quickly he'd dip back out of sight.

CI faltered. Without cutting-edge research and development, the company soon floated into the languid waters of mediocrity. The MBA wanted to take the company public, but Wall Street showed little interest in a middling software developer based in the South. Once upon a time, the story went, CI pointed the way toward the future. Now they were just part of the logjam.

The MBA received his walking papers.

Two hired guns were dispatched by the board of directors. Curtis Hubbard and Thomas Bly followed sporadic leads, first to Asia, then on a circuitous route through Europe to Oxford. They found Jasper Cone shacked up with a cute blonde named Crystal Easterling. Jasper refused to talk to them. They offered big money for his return to Austin. He slammed the door in their faces. They returned home empty-handed.

A week later the phone rang in Austin. Jasper Cone was on the line. He wanted the job. But they had to agree to his terms. They didn't hesitate.

In his first six months at the helm, he advanced CI further than they'd managed to move in the five years of his absence. His exile had refreshed him. He worked twenty-hour days, seven days a week.

What many suspected but no one knew for certain was that Crystal was the one who'd urged him to get back into the game. And it was true. They met by chance on a street corner in London. She was thirty-two, five years his junior. In most ways they were opposites, and this was among the chief reasons that their relationship worked and endured. He was the genius, but he relied on her sense of logic. He was the visionary, but without her steadfast common sense he would most certainly have veered off course.

She was a native of Britain and sorely missed the land of her birth during the long months she spent with Jasper in the United States. For a short time they'd traveled the world together. Now, though, Jasper was content to disappear into his work. They had no intention of marrying, though the desire for children burned within her.

Cone Intermedia was once again a player. But Jasper was thinking way ahead. His masterstroke was a product he called "Isis." Isis would revolutionize the personal computer. Isis was what was referred to by the industry as an applications bundle, a handful of software applications packaged together and sold as a single unit for business or home use. The package included all the desired features—word processor, spreadsheet, email, web browser, a multimedia utility, etc. Isis was stunningly user-friendly, uniquely designed, astoundingly stable, and required very minimal training. It was revolutionary. Isis was vastly superior to similar products already on the market. It would be the capstone of CI. But first, they needed the support of computer manufacturers, and it wasn't difficult to convince them to make Isis a standard factory-installed feature on their products. There was no shortage of enthusiasm within the industry. The buzz and excitement was truly phenomenal. But just as CI was gearing up to meet demand, mysteriously the mood changed. Suddenly no one was interested. Manufacturers who'd salivated at the prospect of offering their customers Isis as a factory installation politely rescinded.

Jasper smelled a rat.

It took months to trace the damage back to its source: Amethyst Technologies. A global powerhouse conglomerate based in Seattle, Am-Tech had dominated much of the high-tech marketplace for two decades, growing at an unprecedented rate year after year. Am-Tech, headed by founder and resident genius Costas Goodchapel, was a bulldozer, a ravenous beast, conquering new territory almost at will. The techno-giant manufactured mainly processor chips. The best in the world. The chips were blazingly fast. Nothing compared. And they were cheap. All of which made them very much in demand. Upward of 87 percent of all desktop computers and 70 percent of all laptop computers manufactured in the United States alone carried Amethyst processor chips. Which, of course, made Amethyst, and Goodchapel, very, very rich. And very, very powerful.

Jasper and his legal team did extensive research on IMM Development, the company that produced the software applications being carried standard on the great majority of computers at the time, and in the process, uncovered a dirty little secret: IMM Development was owned by Amethyst Technologies.

The cry "MONOPOLY" could be heard across the globe. Cone Intermedia went into full litigation mode. They sued on the basis of anticompetitive practices. Potentially, billions of dollars were at stake. The battle began.

No one, least of all Jasper or Crystal, could have imagined that the ensuing conflict would eventually lead them to the steps of the Supreme Court. Until twelve hours ago, the Court had been split five-four in favor of the conservatives, in favor of free trade and Am-Tech. The Amethyst team had strutted its stuff. Chief Justice Bourgeous had been the swing vote. But with Bourgeous on a slab in the morgue, the Court was at a dead heat, four against four. It was up for grabs. This was the president's opportunity to shift the power of the Court. The president was a classic liberal, and he held all the cards. Yesterday, Cone Intermedia had been sinking further into a deep dark hole. But now, with the right nominee seated on the bench, they could turn near-bankruptcy into a multibillion-dollar jackpot.

◆━◆━◆

Crystal wasn't worried for Jasper. It was his way to retreat from the world when everything seemed to be closing in on him. But if what she was hearing was true, Jasper needed to know about

it. The Court was now even. And whoever the president nominated could drastically alter how the Court might eventually
rule in *Cone Intermedia v. Amethyst Technologies*. That one rul-
ing, she understood all too well, would likely mean the difference between hundreds of millions in revenue or bankruptcy
for CI.

She had to find Jasper. There were decisions to be made,
strategies to discuss. Fate had winked at them. What would
come of it was anybody's guess. But for the moment, Bourgeous's death would keep them afloat.

9

THE BAR WAS QUIET FOR A MONDAY NIGHT. LIPSCOMB WAS
in and out in under three minutes. He ordered a beer, and by the
time it arrived he was out the door. Chick Mancini hadn't said a
word. He placed the package on the bar in front of Lipscomb,
and then took a long swig of his Amstel Light.

The dossier was four inches thick, with narrow margins and
small print. Lipscomb turned through the intersection and
headed back toward Georgetown. The senator had given specific
instructions. He wanted the dossier *tonight*. Lipscomb phoned
ahead.

Senator Henbest was waiting at the preordained spot. He
read through the night, confident that the next chief justice was
somewhere in those pages.

10

DINNER WAS LONG OVER, BUT LANNA ADLER WAS JUST NOW getting to the dishes. She stood at the kitchen sink in jeans and a tank top, up to her forearms in sudsy dishwater. The TV was on in the next room, the volume up loud enough to hear in the surrounding counties, but she ignored it. The dinner table had been cleared with help from the kids. The kitchen counter beside her was a landslide of dinner plates, knives, forks, spoons, and glasses.

It was getting late. She yawned as she worked. Her eyes were watery. If she ever got to bed, she'd be lucky to catch five hours. The younger kids were already asleep. The teenagers were either studying or finishing up chores. She could hear Parker struggling with the food cans out back. They kept the dog food in oil drums, scooping it out using an old Cool Whip dish. The lid of the drum clanged down, and she could hear her son mumbling under his breath. The screen door clapped against its frame, and Parker shuffled through the kitchen, the shoelaces of one sneaker trailing behind.

Lanna had tucked Claire, the four-year-old, and Cody, the seven-year-old, into bed before trudging downstairs to wipe off the table and start on the dishes. They'd gotten into the habit of staying up an hour or two past their bedtimes, a habit Lanna was determined to put an end to. They were ornery as dirt, though. They shared a room and would spend a half hour whispering back and forth in the dark before finally fading off to sleep. Cody, without fail, requested a glass of water every night just before bed. The request was uniformly denied on a nightly basis. That glass of water would keep him up for at least another hour, zipping up and down the hall to the bathroom, which of course was his plan.

The oldest child still living at home was Dermott. He was

outside helping his father and Mitchell Lundberg work on Mitchell's 1963 Corvette, the three of them struggling desperately to get a few more thousand miles out of the vintage sports car. Lanna pulled a gravy boat into the soapy water and ran her sponge over it. That blasted TV was too loud.

She called, "Parker."

No response.

"Parker!"

A head poked around the corner from the hallway. "Huh?"

"Turn down the television. It's a wonder anybody can even hear themselves think. The little ones are trying to sleep."

The boy shrugged, and headed for the living room, dutifully obeying his mother.

"Thank you!" she called out over the splash of the running water, but got no response. Parker was fourteen and had little or no use for any form of contact with a parental unit. The dogs were fed—the last of his daily chores—so he quickly withdrew to his bedroom and locked the door. She could only guess what went on behind that closed door of his. If she hadn't already been through this behavior with Steven and Dermott, she'd have probably been concerned. They'd survived unscathed, and so would he. Like it or not, teenage boys just needed their space.

One of the cats brushed against her leg, probably hoping for dinner scraps. She looked at the clock and groaned. She had to get to bed. Her shift at the hospital would start just after sunup. There was no telling what time Allan and Dermott would make it to bed. She wouldn't wait up, though.

Sometimes it overwhelmed her that she still had a four-year-old left to raise. Steven was completing his third year of college. Claire would finish college in eighteen years! Just doing the math made her feel old. Maybe they should have stopped after Parker. Having her last kid out of the house in eight years didn't sound nearly as daunting. In all likelihood, she'd be a grandmother before either Claire or Cody reached elementary school. It wouldn't shock her if Steven showed up at the door at any time with a fiancée in tow. It was bound to happen eventually. That meant that her youngest child would be just a few years older than her first grandchild . . .

When she got to the bathroom and flipped on the light, she stood at the mirror and wiped at her makeup, avoiding the sight of possible gray hairs. I'm barely forty-two, she reminded herself.

She collapsed into bed. The remote was on Allan's pillow. Ted Koppel was still rambling when she finally closed her eyes.

.•◦••◦•.

Allan Adler rolled out from beneath the front end of the Corvette and snatched a metric socket from the bumper inches above his face. It snapped easily onto the ratchet wrench, and back underneath he went, metal caster wheels scraping against the cement slab. Looking up past the engine block, he could see Mitchell's face squinting down at him from above. Mitchell had a grease rag in his hands, working hard to look busy.

This routine had gone on for years. Mitchell had bought the car the summer before their senior year of high school. It had been wrecked, and he got a good deal on it. It was to be a summer project. They spent many long nights that summer pounding out dents, buffing out scratches, and applying an insane amount of primer to the body of the old girl. By the end of that August, they were barely beyond where they'd started, but it was at least roadworthy. The money ran out and Mitchell eventually put the Vet up on blocks awaiting an infusion of cash that never seemed to materialize. It was years before the work would resume.

Life interceded.

Allan served his time in the military and got married. Mitchell battled his way through college and two divorces.

Mitchell now lived in Dallas and had made and lost several fortunes playing the markets. He was currently on a downward slide and was determined to turn things around, one way or another. He was a man well versed in making, moving, and blowing money. He lived alone and worked ridiculous hours, routinely making the three-hour drive up to Allan's place in Oklahoma City on a moment's notice just to decompress. He usually drove the Vet—if he could get it started—and they still spent endless hours under the hood, talking, laughing, and reminiscing. The Vet was a happy connection to the past, a reminder of simpler times that they weren't quite prepared to part with.

"Lundberg." Allan Adler sighed. "I hate to tell you this—"

"Then don't."

"Your alternator won't hold a charge. It's living on borrowed time."

"Fix it. I need every penny I can get my hands on."

In the dark beneath the truck, Allan shook his head. Back in Dallas, Mitchell drove around in a leased Mercedes that he probably couldn't afford. He wasn't broke, but the demise of the dot-com bubble had certainly sucked the wind out of his sails. So lately he made the drive north much more frequently than he had a decade earlier. There was no way to accurately tabulate exactly how many evenings and weekends had been frittered away tinkering on the old Vet.

Allan wiped sweat from his eyes. "Talk to your banker about your money problems. I'm just the mechanic here."

Dermott was leaning against the front fender, holding the work light. He was eighteen, with barely a month left until high school graduation. He was the tallest of the family, standing even above Steven and their father. He possessed neither the grades nor the ambition to do what Steven had achieved. His future was pretty much still up in the air. His grades wouldn't get him a scholarship. He might spend a year saving money, then take a stab at a community college. Though none of that interested him. He'd thought about following in his father's footsteps and joining the army, though Allan certainly hadn't encouraged any of his kids to invest time in the military as he had. Though the truth be told, Allan had signed up way-back-when for the same reasons Dermott was now facing.

Dermott yawned. Tomorrow was a school day. The praise and attention Steven received for being the "Harvard Man" bothered him only a little. He didn't begrudge his brother what he'd earned. He'd spent many a night in bed staring restlessly at the ceiling wondering why he'd been the one who'd fallen short. But now, to some extent, he'd come to terms with it all. He'd have to be his own man, seek his own fortune down his own path. He yawned again, rubbing his eyes with his free hand. No telling how late they'd be up working on Mitchell's car. No matter, though. He'd just sleep in the morning during class.

A tool clanged against something beneath the engine. Allan muttered something the other two didn't catch. Mitchell glanced at Dermott and grinned. Dermott chuckled knowingly.

The workshop sat out back of the house. It was the size of a two-car garage. Half of it stored the Adlers' boat, an inboard vessel that Allan spent about as much time working on as he did Mitchell's car. The boat hadn't been within fifty feet of water in three years. Every summer he swore they'd spend every other Saturday at the lake. The other half of the workshop was just that, a work area. A long workbench stood against the back wall. Tools hung from pegboard. Sawhorses stood in the open on the cement slab, just waiting for the next important project to come along. The cement slab extended eighteen or twenty feet beyond the workshop edifice itself. When the two halves of the shop were tied up, for whatever reasons, as they were now, they'd use the extended surface of the slab as a work area. A netless basketball rim hung above one of the big doors. Thousands of games of hoops had been played on that section of cement.

The floodlight shining down from the gable in the roof helped Allan little to not at all. He pushed himself out on the rolling board and sat up with a groan. He put a hand to his lower back and grimaced.

"I might not charge for the work on the Vet, Mitchell, but I'm sending my chiropractor bill straight to you."

"Yeah, you do that. I'll get right on it." He winked at Dermott.

"Pick up an alternator at a salvage. Won't cost too much. That's your best bet. The alternator's not your only problem, but the rest will keep for now. It's late, and I have to be at the lumberyard early in the morning. Got a meeting with a big contractor. He's planning a couple of subdivisions. Just take it easy on the old girl, will ya?" He rolled over onto his knees, then slowly stood. Mitchell tossed him a grease rag, and he went to work on his fingers with it.

"You're a lifesaver, Adler. You know that?"

Allan gestured to his son. "Unplug that light, roll up the extension cord, and set it on the corner of the bench in there. Grab a shower before you climb into bed. I'll see you in the morning. All right?"

Dermott nodded and dropped the light to his side, dangling it by its cord. Mitchell patted him on the butt as he slouched by.

Allan said, "Hey, Derm. Thanks for your help. You're a good hand."

Dermott disappeared inside the workshop.

Mitchell turned the key, and the Vet's old engine started up hesitantly. He called out through the open window, "Ah, yeah, boy! Purrs like a kitten! Like the day she rolled off the line!"

Allan dragged his rolling board into the shop and hit the light switch on his way out. He shook hands with his old friend. "You know, Lundberg, this car is in no better shape than it was twenty-five years ago."

"You gripe like my ex-wife."

"Which one?"

"All of them."

"Go home, old man."

The vintage car took out across the lawn, through the open

gate, and slipped on into the night. It would be a long drive back to Texas.

Allan stood for a moment in the newfound quiet, content to be alone, listening to the locusts and other peaceful night sounds. The light to Dermott's room winked out, leaving the only light on in the house that of the kitchen.

Allan stripped and left his dirty clothes in a heap in the utility room. He poured himself a glass of milk and drank it on his way to the bedroom, walking in his underwear. The house was now totally dark. Setting the empty glass on the windowsill, he stared out the window, exhausted, his back aching from the hours lying on that board. Moonlight cast shadows all across the backyard. He smiled for no reason at all. As tired as he was, he had no complaints. Life, he figured, could be worse.

11

IT WAS BARELY LATE SPRING, BUT ALREADY THE SOUTHERN half of Texas had begun its climb near the hundred-degree mark. By midmorning, Tuesday, when her plane touched down in Austin, Crystal Easterling was already sick of the Lone Star State. For the millionth time she asked herself why she'd followed Jasper there. It was a place where the sun always beat down and the humidity was thick enough to spread on toast. She'd spent her youth chomping at the bit to get out from under the dreary skies of Britain, and now she couldn't wait to return.

There was a car waiting for her at the airport. A familiar face greeted her. Sarah Brighton looked flustered. She was Thomas Bly's personal assistant. Thomas Bly had been among those who got Cone Intermedia off the ground back when it was nothing more than a crazy pipe dream. Sarah was fueled by stress and could barely function in its absence. Her face was stretched tight, and she was all teeth and eyes.

"We can't find him," Sarah said.

Crystal said nothing. She wasn't the chatty type. And she'd never been too keen on Sarah.

As they sat in traffic, a cell phone rang and Sarah yapped into it as she pressed the accelerator to the floor.

"I know that," Sarah was saying, "but try Ryan in distribution. Yes, I understand that, but this is what Thomas wants. I don't care. It's specific in the memo he emailed everyone in your area. Just take care of it!" She snapped the phone shut and honked at someone who'd cut her off.

The front end of the car dipped slightly as they turned into the entrance to the grounds of CI. Sarah manhandled the car like a test pilot. The car skidded to a stop in a narrow parking space. The latest incarnation of the CI headquarters stood two floors aboveground and two beneath. It was obscenely modern in its architectural design. It had been conceptualized, financed, and built at a time when the future of the company seemed destined for glory and infinite riches. The company had shouldered massive debt to see it built. Nine months after the ribbon was cut, the very earth beneath them seemed to crumble away. Now everything hinged on the lawsuit against Amethyst. As long as Amethyst continued to squeeze the competition from the marketplace, CI would never be able to meet its obligations. The debt had become an albatross. It was on everyone's mind all the time. And the debt changed things. Before, if the company had dried up and blown away, it would have been simply a failure. No longer. They had borrowed nearly ninety million dollars. There were expectations. The time for walking away had passed. If they'd waited ten months, things would be different now. But the days to second-guess themselves were four years behind them. What was done was done. All they could do now was find a fissure in Amethyst's defense.

Crystal pushed open the front door to the atrium and went straight to the elevator. She marched out and headed for Jasper Cone's office on the second floor. His assistant was sitting at her desk. She lowered her phone to her shoulder and looked up at Crystal as she swooshed by and pushed open the glass door into Jasper's office.

"Ms. Easterling," Anna called after her. "Ms. East . . ."

The office was empty. It was the largest office space in the complex. It was all clean lines and smooth surfaces, titanium and redwood. A sleek laptop sat closed on the surface of the desk. The only other object on the desk was a multiple-line phone. From the phone on the desk Crystal dialed Jasper's cell phone. No answer. She'd already dialed him from the plane with her cell. Jasper wasn't responding. She logged onto his laptop and sent an email to his pager. She knew exactly what was going on. Jasper had gone off to pout. Things had gotten bleak, and he'd run off to suck his thumb and stick out his lip. Jasper was a genius. That wasn't up for debate. But heavy-duty business issues freaked him out.

She'd noticed outside that his parking slot was vacant. He was a multimillionaire yet drove a 1975 Toyota Land Cruiser. His brain processed like a computer, and he'd made his fortune in the computer field, but he liked to drive vehicles built without computer chips. Her Porsche convertible was in the slot next to Jasper's. The air-cooled engine catapulted her onto the freeway, and she was soon headed toward the outskirts of the city. She drove with the top down and the wind in her hair, doing ninety-five for the better part of an hour.

If you weren't looking for the turnoff you'd miss it. It was a narrow asphalt strip cut through a gap in the trees. It wound through pine needles for several hundred yards, heavily shaded on either side of the path by dense, overhanging vegetation. The Porsche passed over a short bridge that spanned a bone-dry creek bed. The lakeside getaway was just beyond the bridge. She was pissed at Jasper. He was a brilliant man, and a phenomenal lover, but he had an immature side. It was his tendency to run from conflict, like a child who doesn't get his way. She was beginning to boil inside as she parked the car.

She was startled to see a helicopter on the cement landing paddock in the grassy strip to the north of the house. It meant that she wasn't Jasper's only visitor. Her pace slowed, and she somewhat hesitantly tried the front door. It was locked. She had one hand in her purse looking for her key when she heard voices. She eased around the corner of the house and down a path of aggregate stone to the steps that led up to the deck at the rear of the house. Before she'd taken a step she recognized at least two of the voices, and it gave her pause. Something was going on.

They were seated in a circle of wood deck chairs. None of them seemed surprised to see Crystal as she mounted the top step and crossed the deck to them.

Jasper got up from his chair and came over to her with an awkward grin. "What took you so long?"

She wanted to backhand him. "I must've misplaced my invitation."

No one else stood. They barely acknowledged her. These were men drunk with ego. Newton Highfill. Sandy Strunyin. Anwar Claussen. Highfill was on the board of directors, a shady character with dark, sunken eyes. Strunyin, along with Thomas Bly, had been with Jasper from the very beginning, and from the beginning he'd been the master strategist, lifting Jasper's creative brilliance from the drawing-room table to the highways and byways of the marketplace. He focused on his drink, not even raising his eyes to her. And finally, Anwar Claussen, CI's lead legal counsel in the suit brought against Amethyst.

Something was going on.

And she'd been left out.

Jasper fetched her a deck chair and she sat down.

"Hope I haven't missed out on anything important," she said.

"We knew you were in Europe," said Strunyin. "There was no

time to waste. Bourgeous is dead, and decisions had to be made in a hurry. I guess we could have sat and played cards while we waited for you."

Heat was rising in Crystal's cheeks.

She decided to listen for a while, observing the conversation rather than participating. One thing was clear: she'd caught them in the middle of something. Exactly what didn't stand out at first. She simply waited and listened. Her presence there wasn't welcome, and she could feel the coolness coming from the surrounding eyes. But each of them was there on behalf of Cone Intermedia, a fact that required her good faith.

There were glasses of iced tea that didn't appear to have been touched. Each man held a printout several pages thick. The printouts were the central focus.

Attention shifted to Anwar Claussen, indicating that he was the one interrupted by Crystal's unannounced arrival. He turned a page of the printout and cleared his throat. Claussen was thick chested and dark skinned, and of Iranian lineage. He had big, meaty hands, a wide nose, and a great surplus of body hair, which peeked out from the cuffs and collar of his shirt. His voice was so deep it seemed to arise from the bottom of a well. He started to speak, but was cut off by Newton Highfill.

Highfill sat at the edge of his seat, his hands on his knees. "Come on, she is on the board of directors. Right? She's here, and we've got to narrow this down, and she's sharper than the lot of us put together. Am I wrong?"

"I agree," Jasper said. He didn't like keeping anything from Crystal, but it was a big relief not having to be the one to broach the subject. He didn't want to be seen as forcing his terms on everyone all the time.

Sandy Strunyin cut an eye toward Claussen. "It's all the same to me. We've just got to move on this thing," Strunyin said.

Claussen shifted his big, black eyes from face to face. A lot was going on behind those eyes. Calculations. He was thinking ten steps ahead. That's why he charged eight hundred dollars an hour. That's why they'd put him up in a four-hundred-dollar-a-night hotel in D.C. for the past six months. That's why his judgment was rarely if ever questioned. Because it was his job to find a way to win the case. He was an assassin in the courtroom. Without a word, Claussen reached a hand down to his briefcase and lifted out another copy of the printout.

It passed from hand to hand around the gathering of chairs until it reached Crystal.

Claussen wasn't at all pleased by this turn of events. They could easily have reached Crystal in London. But it had been his decision to move in quickly, keeping matters between just the men. Perhaps it had to do with his heritage, where women were valued below cattle, though he would have vehemently denied such a notion. What they were doing here was highly unethical but necessary, given their precarious position, and so he understood the importance of keeping the matter well contained.

"A pot of gold has fallen in our lap," Highfill began, shrugging off Claussen's glare. "For the moment it seems that we've been spared. The conservative side of the Court has taken a major hit. Though only days ago our fate seemed sealed, a new hope has sprung up. And so, we've gathered here to do our best to not let this opportunity slip through our fingers. Within the next few days the president will name his nominee to replace the chief justice." Highfill paused, searching the faces surrounding him as if seeking approval to continue on this course. He gathered his thoughts for a moment, and lowering the tone of his voice just slightly, he added, "And it is our intention to take whatever steps necessary to ensure that he nominate an individual we can count on to cast his or her vote in our favor. The new chief justice will be the swing vote. If we can influence the president's choice, we'll own that vote. One vote can change everything."

"We're going to buy the vote?" Crystal said.

"Whoa, whoa, whoa!" Highfill reared back in his deck chair, the tapered slats of wood beneath him and behind him groaning with a shift of weight. "Slow down. Nobody here is using words like that, Crystal. I'd suggest you be careful what comes out of your mouth. What I said—*specifically*—is that we should be prepared to do *whatever necessary*. Please do not be putting words in my mouth."

Anwar Claussen's gaze was steadfastly focused on Crystal Easterling, trying to detect whether there was anything there that she hadn't yet betrayed with her tongue, any sort of hesitancy.

"I apologize," Crystal said, very businesslike and very British, and very much understanding she'd interpreted correctly. This was a sticky position for them as a group, and as a publicly held company, to find themselves in. One solitary vote separated riches from ruin. To do nothing at all sounded pathetic and illogical. But to even consider taking action to alter the Court by felonious means was risky at best and held imponderable repercussions at worst. Surely there had to be a better alternative. "The president is a staunch, lifelong Democrat," she said very evenly, tucking long strands of blond hair behind her ear. "He's every bit as liberal as we could ever hope for. Why would he even consider nominating a conservative for chief justice? Just the prospect seems inconceivable."

Highfill opened his mouth to speak but Strunyin beat him to the punch.

"This isn't rocket science, Crystal. He's facing a Republican majority in the Senate. He's got to appease them at the same time he's attempting to squeeze through a nominee of like mind. The Senate Judiciary Committee will be ready to blast the first left-winger the president offers up. And a moderate would be of no use to us at all. Because a moderate is a wild card—that vote could go one way or the other. What we have to do—if we choose to do *anything at all*—is whisper a name in the president's ear, a name we can put complete faith in. And we have to have an iron-clad guarantee that the president will listen. And that is likely to get expensive."

Jasper Cone listened pensively. This sort of garbage was the

reason he'd been hesitant to return to the company he'd
founded in his youth. This was business. He was not a business-
man. He was a visionary. His gift was to imagine the impossible,
then form something great where before there had been nothing. This conversation had nothing to do with him other than
the fact that he was ultimately responsible for the outcome. This
was war. These were generals drawing up battle plans. Jasper
Cone was no soldier.

As he listened, his stomach twisted into knots. How had it
come to this? Cone Intermedia was an innovator. Isis was an entire generation ahead of anything Amethyst or any other com-
petitor had to offer. On paper it looked so simple. But on paper
CI was rushing headlong into the abyss. And Amethyst was the
responsible party. As much as Jasper despised involving himself
in these machinations, he simply couldn't deny the obvious.

A further intrusion was having these three jackals out to his
private retreat. This was his oasis. Only he and Crystal spent
time there. It was strictly off-limits. The few who knew of its existence dared not trespass. At this moment he felt grossly vio-
lated. But the instant that word of Bourgeous's death reached
Claussen, then Highfill, then Jasper, it was clear there could be
no delay. And they needed to meet in seclusion.

Jasper Cone was tall. This always shocked people on first encounter. He was six foot ten and slim. Unlike many in his chosen
profession, he'd always adhered to a strict vegan diet. He
avoided carbonated drinks and fried foods of any kind. He rarely
consumed anything made of refined sugars, and avoided complex carbohydrates and red meat at all costs. More fresh water
passed through him in a given day than through a brook trout.
One of his great passions was organic gardening. To the east of
the house he'd built an impressive, state-of-the-art, climate-
controlled greenhouse. It was an obsession. The roof of the
greenhouse was easily visible from the deck railing. His radically
healthy lifestyle deeply irritated many of those closest to him.
Including, at times, Crystal.

His hair was grown out longer now than he'd ever worn it. And his beard was getting out of hand. It was fine for a lowly programmer or some such basement-dwelling gnome permanently stuck in the dark in front of a monitor, but not for a chief executive officer of a major software company. He was thirty-seven and hadn't yet caved in to adulthood, though he did actually have on full-length pants today, Crystal noted. She mused silently that Jasper must have truly considered this little shindig to be a deadly serious matter. He lived in baggy shorts and T-shirts. But even the wrinkled T-shirt had been replaced today with a navy Polo shirt. His footwear, however, remained the same. Beneath the Polo and the chinos were his familiar leather sandals. He'd come so close, she thought, to looking like a mature adult.

Jasper and Strunyin were an unlikely pairing, and it was rather evident that had they not bonded as they had in college, their paths might never have crossed later in life. A decade earlier when the board forced Jasper's hand and showed him the door, Sandy Strunyin failed his old friend. At a moment when friendship should have trumped all else, Strunyin sided with the opposition, insisting he had only the company's best interest in mind, a company they both loved. It was a wound that hadn't fully healed and likely never would. And it was an act of treason that Crystal refused to let Jasper forget. Every friendship had to face the shifting sands of adulthood, and few made it safely to the other side, unscarred and intact. And seldom were there hundreds of millions of dollars at stake.

The board of directors had clawed and scratched at one another before the decision was made to go groveling back to Jasper to please fix what they'd screwed up. He was impossible to control. Dealing with him was like blindly grabbing at a wet bar of soap on the shower floor. Given his size and his obvious intelligence, Jasper could be quite intimidating, especially if confronted or contradicted. He didn't mince words and was not one to leash his tongue or tone down his temper. Bringing him back into the fold caused no small amount of anxiety. It had not been a personal decision but business. They needed him. He could build a better mousetrap. His price? A 25 percent stake in the company.

"So where are we then? Where do we stand?" Crystal said, one leg crossed over the other in a very feminine posture. "And what is this about?" She waved the stapled pages over her knee.

It was Claussen who answered.

"That's the list," he said.

"List?"

"Straight from the Oval Office. The president's nominee will be chosen from the names in those pages."

"Astounding," she said. She briefly scanned through the pages.

Claussen continued. "What we've discussed up to now is the fact that we have no time to waste. Zero. A nominee will be named within days, with or without us. It should go without saying that we will not be following official channels in pursuing this course of action. The list you have in your hands was leaked to us by a source on Capitol Hill who shall remain nameless. What is important is that we now have a window of opportunity, however small that window may be. It is my understanding that these names have already undergone a preliminary inquest regarding each individual's personal background and professional history. Our selection must be made with the utmost care. There is no going back to the drawing board if we choose poorly. This is a one-shot deal."

Full attention had shifted to the list in their hands. Crystal's eyes moved across the page. Strunyin's lips moved as he read silently.

So that was it, was it? A course of action had been put forth and agreed upon in her absence. That stung. If Sarah hadn't tracked her down in England, she'd have been left out of the loop altogether. She wondered why Jasper had allowed this to happen.

It was clear that Anwar Claussen wanted her input kept to a minimum, and Strunyin and Highfill were apparently following his lead without objection. As intimidating as Jasper could be, in certain circumstances he could be very easily manipulated. And she'd understood early on that Claussen was the master manipulator.

Their options were few. And heading into the past weekend it had looked as though all hope was lost. She was still far from optimistic. What Claussen was suggesting was beyond scandalous. But the ultimate truth was she wanted to emerge from the lawsuit victorious as badly as anyone. This was perhaps the one shot they had. So much was riding on it. Everything, it seemed.

She simply hated being sucked into a decision made without her input.

"How long do we have?" she asked.

"Less than twenty-four hours," Claussen injected without hesitation. "By this time tomorrow the process must be in full motion."

Silence followed.

Then Claussen added, "And of course there is the issue of what you are willing to . . . invest."

Another long silence; this time it felt as though the air around them had changed. After an extended moment, Newton Highfill broke the hush by tearing a strip of paper from the bottom edge of the last page of his copy of the list. He clicked his pen. His eyes drifted, wandering toward the bright, cloudless sky. He took a long, deep breath. When his eyes returned to his lap, he exhaled, then scribbled a dollar amount on the small strip of paper. The pen stopped. He took a second to ponder his work, then passed the strip of paper to Strunyin for his consideration.

Strunyin glanced at it, and immediately his eyebrows arched. Finally, though, he nodded his approval. He passed it to Jasper Cone.

Jasper paid it no mind, passing it on to Crystal.

Her eyes went wide, and she cut them toward Highfill with an understated yet unmistakable expression that conveyed what they all were thinking: *this is insane.* But she followed suit and simply shrugged her consent. She looked to meet Jasper's eyes, but he averted them, suddenly interested in a fire ant moving across the deck near his feet. Finally, she passed the strip to Claussen.

Claussen's expression never changed. He studied the figure for a few seconds, then lifted his briefcase to his lap. He neatly folded the strip of paper and slid it inside. Then he stood, briefcase at his side.

"I'll see what I can do," he said.

12

FIFTY YEARS EARLIER, ON A NARROW DIRT ROAD IN BRAZIL, a group of small, brown-skinned boys dribbled homemade soccer balls and laughed in the afternoon sun. Each day was pretty much the same as the day before. They were as poor as humans could be. They lived in mud huts with thatched roofs and ate a single meal per day if all went well. Their future was bleak. But that was life. They were prisoners of their environment. The joy of soccer was all they had.

One of the boys was named Costas Daya. His father was an alcoholic with a raging temper who rarely worked. His was a childhood of fear and hunger. His father spent most of his days sleeping and most of his nights out with other men of the village, drinking. One night his father never returned. It made his mother neither happy nor sad. Her husband's absence changed her life very little. She earned their bread money harvesting in the fields. Her face was hardened to leather and cracked by the Brazilian sun. Hers was a bitterly hard life. Costas learned early on that he would do anything necessary not to duplicate his parents' path.

On his eighth birthday, his mother was kicked in the head by a mule as she trailed behind it in the muddy track that divided the field. The blow shattered her skull and she died before she hit the ground. It was the most fortuitous day of young Costas's life.

The orphan would have starved if not for the Baptist missionaries who regularly passed through the village. They washed and fed him, clothed him, and taught him to read. It turned out that the dark-skinned boy was a fast learner. While in their company he experienced his first ride in an automobile. He enjoyed three meals a day, plus plenty of snacks, was given a store-bought soccer ball, and spent his mornings in the Baptist school in the company of pretty girls. It was indeed a blissful evolution from the life he'd been born into.

He traveled with the missionaries to São Paulo, then on to Rio de Janeiro. His young mind was transfixed by the sights and sounds and bright lights of the big city. He vowed never to return to the dirty little village or to the life it held for him. The missionaries told him of a family in another country who very much wanted to make him a part of their home. He wasn't altogether sure what a country was, but he trusted the missionaries, and if they thought it was a good idea, then so did he. The greatest thrill of his life was the flight on the jet plane, which took him to a place called the United States of America.

The Goodchapels took him into their home and legally adopted him, and he became Costas Goodchapel. They lived in a beautiful home in a beautiful place called Seattle. His new family provided even more and better food than the Baptist missionaries. Costas gained weight and his bones grew strong. His thin body filled out, and he soon grew into a strapping, healthy young boy. Every night he thanked God for the alcohol that lured away his father and for the mule that struck his mother.

His adoptive father worked at a place called a bank. It looked like a castle, like in the picture books he'd read in the small school in Brazil. Nothing in his short life had prepared him for such a place. It was grand and beautiful and filled him with awe. The bank, he learned, had to do with money. And you needed money to buy food and clothing and a fine home—with enough money you could have anything your heart desired. Costas did not understand money, but he did understand the desires of the heart. From that moment on, whenever he dreamed, he dreamed of money.

He excelled in school, rising to the top of his class. His undergraduate years were spent at the most prestigious business school in the nation. Unlike most of the students he encountered in his classes, Costas knew what it meant to hunger so badly as to not be able to sleep at night because of the stomach pains. This was his great advantage. This was his great secret. It gave him the edge. His great fear was going back to where he'd begun. He would simply never let that happen.

Whatever faith in God he'd ever had was soon eclipsed by love of the dollar. God equaled love, but money equaled happiness.

And money translated into power.

His adult life was a procession of conquests. He was feared and admired. Over the course of twenty-five years he built an empire in the technologies industry and enjoyed wealth beyond his wildest childhood imagination. But no matter how great the heights he reached or how immense a fortune he'd amassed, he was forever haunted by the nightmare of being cast back into unspeakable poverty.

All those years ago, as an eight-year-old child, on his last day in the village of his birth, as the Baptist missionaries were preparing to scoop him away to a better life, Costas had knelt down in a muddy stream and taken a handful of rocks from the streambed. He formed a sieve with his fingers, the sand and smaller pebbles falling through the gaps. Among the collection of smooth river stones that remained, one stood out. It was a purple quartz, a gemstone. It was beautiful. It astounded him that such a gorgeous gemstone could have come from such a lowly stream. He palmed the purple stone and decided to keep it forever to remind him of this day. As they were loading into the automobile, he approached one of the nice missionary women and held out his hand, unfurling his fingers from around his treasure.

"What kind of stone is it?" he asked.

She studied it for only a moment, then answered him in his native Portuguese. "Amethyst," she said with a nod and a slight smile. "That is an amethyst."

Costas closed his fingers around the quartz and clung to it with all his might. For the next half century he would never be without it.

13

THE FIRST CALL CAME AT WORK WHILE ALLAN WAS BUSY and was taken by one of the clerks at the front desk before they'd closed for the day. It was Lanna, phoning to say she was having to work several hours late because one of the second-shift nurses had called in sick and there was no one else to cover. The second call was long-distance and came to the house, where the answering machine picked up, and which no one would hear until hours later. The clerk who took the first call scratched the message on a sticky note and stuck it in the center of the computer screen in Allan's office, up the short flight of carpeted stairs around the corner from the contractors' sales desk.

Allan couldn't take the call himself because he was outside in the yard, helping unload a huge order of windows that had arrived seven hours late. It was probably not in his job description to be out there in the dust and heat with a back belt on, killing himself, pitching in with the hourly laborers, unloading the thirty-foot trailer. The problem was he didn't actually have a job description, at least not in writing. And if he didn't offer his own muscle to get the task done, it simply would not get done. It was already 6:00 p.m. He'd grabbed something packaged in plastic from one of the poorly stocked vending machines for lunch. That was six hours ago, and he was by now quite simply running out of juice.

Allan was standing on the back of the big truck, wearing leather work gloves. The driver would hand him a window, and he'd hand it down to the men waiting on the ground, ready to distribute the new inventory to the wood racks along the outside wall of the building. He leaned out of the truck. To the west the sky was looking mean. Ominous-looking clouds had bunched together and appeared to be blowing in his direction. They'd have a storm tonight. A big, nasty one, too, he thought, standing with his hands on his hips, sweat dripping from his nose as he waited for the driver to loosen the straps from around the next batch of Anderson windows. If they hurried they might be able to get the load off the truck and stocked before it started getting wet.

Allan bailed off the rear of the truck, coming down with a slap of his boots against the broken pavement that ran between the truck and the store. He patted one of his men in the chest with his gloved hand. "Yo, Mark," he said with a depleted expression. "Take over for me for a minute?"

"Not a problem," Mark said, hooking his fingers on the trailer and swinging his legs up. He was half Allan's age and shirtless. His upper body was bronzed from the long days loading and unloading lumber in the yard. He was lean and muscular and friendly, and Allan had no doubt the kid would never strive for anything more in life than ten or twelve bucks an hour and cold beer at the end of the day.

Still out of breath, Allan plucked off his work gloves and hobbled over to one of the wooden racks that shelved the windows. His can of Diet Mountain Dew was on the ground beneath a two-by-ten that ran horizontal. His knees popped and crackled as he squatted to pick up his soda and then stood. Bad knees ran in the family. He'd put off surgery most of his adult life. One day he'd probably regret it. He'd deal with that when the time came.

He dug the bill of lading from his back pocket and unfolded it. He patted his shirt pocket for a pen. An enormous picture window was being hoisted out of the back of the truck. Allan held his breath. The amount of faith he put in those guys was amazing. They laughed and talked as they spun the thing and then tucked it into its spot along the wall.

A copy of the invoice was kept at the contractors' sales desk. Allan went in through a side door and past the plumbing department. Most of the lights were off. He pulled on a file cabinet drawer, and it rattled down its track, jarring to a halt. He pulled out the vendor file and spotted the invoice. The carpeted stairs to his immediate right led to his office. He grabbed a ballpoint from the pencil tray in his desk drawer and tucked it behind his ear. Then he spotted the note on his computer screen. He groaned, knowing he'd now be responsible for his own dinner, wadded the message, and pitched it in the general vicinity of the wastebasket. A long day had just got longer.

He could assume Lanna had instructed Dermott to pick up Parker from soccer practice. And he could only hope the kids wouldn't destroy the house before he got home. When Lanna worked late, the microwave oven got a workout. He pondered stopping for Chinese carryout, but the checkbook was getting low, and neither of them would be getting paid for another week.

Again he felt an old, familiar stab of pain in his ribs. He'd never dreamed that he would find himself in his midforties living paycheck to paycheck, unable to afford to even treat his kids to carryout for dinner. Once upon a time he'd believed he might really become something. Now he glanced at his reflection in the computer screen. Sweaty and dirty, bad knees and a bad back, barely clearing thirty-five grand a year after taxes. His one opportunity had been the short time immediately following his service in the military. He'd had a couple of promising job offers out east. But he couldn't stand city life. He'd wanted a rural existence. Just the peace and quiet of a modest home on a few hundred acres. Raise a family, raise some livestock. Be an honest American man.

That all sounded good on paper. But that was about it.

By the time he came around to his senses, he had a mortgage he could barely handle, a couple of car payments, and a mess of screaming kids. If Lanna hadn't become a registered nurse, they would have never made it. As it stood, they had just enough in savings to repair her car if and when the transmission fell out. Part of what made him feel like such a failure was his wife's having to work, let alone work such long hours. She should be at home with the kids, not . . .

Stop it.

He shut it out. From the pencil tray in his desk he grabbed a roll of Rolaids and popped three or four in his mouth, crunching them, then washing them down with the Diet Mountain Dew.

Back outside he rounded the corner and nearly smashed head-on into his crew.

"Truck's unloaded, chief," Mark said, his well-defined upper body glistening with sweat. "The driver's over there waiting for your signature."

"Great. Good job, guys. Thanks for your help today. Get on out of here and I'll see you in the morning."

Allan signed off on the paperwork and shook hands with the driver.

"See you in a couple weeks, probably," the driver said, slamming his door. The pipe above the cab of the truck pumped a cloud of black exhaust into the air as the big rig roared through the gate and turned onto the street.

Allan filed the paperwork, shut off the lights, and locked the door. As he turned the ignition in his Dodge, the clock in the dash rolled over to 7:00 p.m. He groaned. He couldn't readily identify a single muscle that didn't ache. His head throbbed. The small bottle of Excedrin in the ashtray was empty. He turned the vents so that the air conditioner was blowing in his face. He said a silent prayer of thanks that Steven was getting the best education money could buy. Steven had his head on straight. Steven had a bright future ahead of him. He was the one kid they wouldn't have to worry about. Allan had never been so sure of anything in his life.

14

THE SUN WAS DIRECTLY IN ALLAN ADLER'S FACE AS HE SAT waiting for traffic to pass so he could turn into his driveway. That was one of the things he hated most about not coming home right at closing time. By now the sun was hanging just above the horizon, making it all but impossible to see if anything was approaching in the oncoming lane. The visor was down and his hand was up, cutting the glare as best he could. A half-dozen motorists had queued behind him, waiting impatiently to be on their way.

The house was literally about a stone's throw from the highway, but the meandering gravel driveway took you on a quarter-mile jaunt up and down and around, over deep ruts and a pair of cattle guards. As he ever so slowly crossed the first cattle guard,

Allan cast an eye at the tiny pond to his left. An inch-thick layer of scum covered the surface, unbroken except where a flight of ducks had blazed a rift across the center. He watched them paddle contentedly, bathing and dipping their heads into the murky water looking for an evening meal. He accelerated up a steep incline that leveled off about a hundred yards from the front porch. The gate was secured by a simple hand latch. He swung the gate wide, pulled through, then hopped out and drew the gate shut.

Dermott's Chevy had a flat. It was parked out front in its usual spot. Flat tires were a common occurrence on the Adler farm. The driveway was abusive. Allan figured his boy had no idea. He'd be out after dark with a hand jack and lug wrench, fumbling with a flashlight. Another common occurrence.

The kids were inside. Not surprisingly, the TV was on. He could hear it before he opened the front door. Cody was sprawled on the floor with his head propped up on his hands, his elbows in the carpet. Claire was in the recliner, legs folded beneath her, a doll in her lap. Their eyes were glued to the set.

"Turn that thing down."

Cody waddled forward on his elbows and punched down the volume. The remote had been missing for the better part of two weeks. A major inconvenience.

Parker had been standing at the edge of the kitchen, bouncing a Nerf football off the wall. But he suddenly caught it and stealthily stashed it on the counter beside the microwave.

"Considering that the TV's on and everybody looks so relaxed, I'm assuming everybody's room is clean and the chores are done. Cody, you watered your mother's plants?"

"I will in a minute," Cody said. "Soon as this is over."

After the day he'd had, Allan was near the end of his rope. "You do it now, mister."

The boy pouted under his breath as he stomped to the kitchen for the water can they kept under the sink.

"What about you?" he said, palming Parker's head of sandy blond hair. "I guess the dogs are fed and watered."

"Did it soon as I got home."

"All right. You made dinner yet?"

"No."

Allan collected his thoughts for a moment. He walked over and opened the pantry, taking quick inventory of menu possibilities. "Here's some Ragù. Put a pan of water on the stove and wait for it to boil. Then throw in some spaghetti noodles, here . . ." He turned and handed his son a package of fettuccine. "That's a brand-new package. When the water's hot enough, snap those in half and pitch them in. Get some ground beef from the fridge and brown it. Drain the grease and then stir in this sauce. Got that?"

Parker nodded, not at all pleased with his new assignment.

Four-year-old Claire had flattened herself as best she could, molding her body against the seat of the recliner, hoping to camouflage herself and escape her father's notice. It didn't work.

"Claire, get in here and help your brother. Set the table."

She put her chin on the arm of the chair. "I can't reach."

"Then pick up your toys. It's a mess in here. Where's Dermott?"

Nobody answered.

"Parker, where's your older brother?"

"Don't know," Parker said, setting a pan of water on a burner. "Out back, maybe."

There was a package of Chips Ahoy! on the kitchen table, and it had been left sitting wide open. He told Claire to close the bag and seal it with a rubber band. It was frustrating. "You all know better than to snack before dinner."

About that time a mighty rumble radiated up from the middle of his belly. Claire looked up at him and giggled.

"Hold on a second," he said. He snatched the bag from her and grabbed out three or four of the chocolate chip cookies for himself. He winked at his daughter. "Do as I say, not as I do."

She giggled again. "Silly Daddy!"

Allan went through the kitchen door to the backyard. He

stood on the back stoop, looking for Dermott. There was no sign of him. He wanted the boy to get to that tire before sundown.

"Dermott!" he yelled as he stood holding the screen door open with one hand. No answer. He called out his son's name once more. No answer. He shook his head. "That boy," he said under his breath.

In his bedroom Allan shut the door and stripped for the shower. Steam billowed out, fogging the mirror. He could have stayed in there forever. He couldn't hear the phone, couldn't hear the kids, couldn't hear customer complaints. It was his ten-minute vacation.

He and Lanna had secretly ferreted away a few thousand dollars in a sock drawer in hopes of sneaking away somewhere special that summer. She dreamed of the Caribbean. That was fine, though he preferred someplace cool and quiet. She wanted white sand beaches. Didn't matter, really. The money wasn't there to spend. And they realistically couldn't afford the time off. Maybe someday.

He found some freshly laundered jeans folded on a shelf in the closet. The aroma of simmering spaghetti sauce filtered in from beneath the bedroom door. He was starving. His heart went out to Lanna. She'd risen before him that morning. And after a long day with patients, she had to be there for more of the same until well into the evening.

To his surprise, Parker had been extra industrious and had baked some garlic bread in the oven. He'd even set the table. Even though the kid had no notable culinary skills, Allan wasn't worried. After all, how could you screw up Ragù?

Claire was back in front of the television.

"Claire, come on, baby, wash up. Dinnertime."

Cody had hijacked Parker's Nerf ball and was trying to stuff it into an empty Folger's can.

"Put that away and wash your hands."

Parker lifted the pan of boiling water from the red-hot burner and drained it in a colander in one side of the sink.

"Parker, any sign of Dermott?"

Concentrating on his work, the chef simply shook his head.

"Cody, run up and check Dermott's bedroom. See if he's hiding out. Tell him dinner's on."

Cody shot down the hall like a rocket.

Allan navigated around Claire, who was swaying from side to side in bored fashion between the kitchen counter and the wall. He sank into his chair at the head of the dining room table. He sighed deeply and closed his eyes.

The phone rang, and Claire sprang across the kitchen, snatching up the receiver and saying hello in her chipper voice.

"Hi, Mommy."

Allan opened his eyes.

"Yeah, Parker's burning the sketti."

"Am not!"

"Yes, ma'am, I been helping."

"Have not!"

"Yeah, he's at the table." Claire held out the phone. "Daddy, Mommy wants to talk to you."

Allan nodded, motioning her over.

Claire set the phone in his lap and quickly departed.

"Hey, babe."

"I'm sorry I couldn't be there to fix dinner," Lanna said on the other end of the line. "It's been a nuthouse here all day. I'm hoping to be relieved in the next ninety minutes or so. It's that bug that's been going around. The nursing staff has been dropping like flies." She sounded exhausted.

"Yeah, it's been all over town. Don't worry about dinner, we'll survive. Just be careful on the drive home. If you're really good, you might even be able to talk me into a foot rub. Sound good?"

"Un*believably* good, actually."

"You may have to wake me when you get home, though. It's been one of those days."

"We get any mail?"

"Actually, I didn't even check." Allan put the phone to his chest. "Parker, did you check the mail?"

Parker freed himself from his food duties long enough to acknowledge a haphazard pile of envelopes at the end of the counter.

"Ah. Would you bring it over here, please."

Allan held the phone to his ear with one hand and sorted through the mail with the other. "Junk, junk . . . credit card offer. Yeah, that's what we need more of. Junk, junk. Gas bill . . . great. Junk. Sales fliers. Got a statement from the bank. That's big fun. And . . . that looks like the end of it."

"One bill, huh? Slow day," Lanna said. "Any messages?"

"Haven't checked the machine."

"Don't worry about it, sweetie."

There was a lengthy silence, during which they both sighed.

"You okay?" he asked.

"Mmmhmm." She yawned into the receiver.

"Hang in there, babe," he said.

"Anyway, I better go. Be there shortly, or soon thereafter. Love you."

"Love you." Allan set the phone on the table.

"Mommy coming home?" Claire was seated at the far end of the table, her chin resting on her forearms.

"She'll be here in a bit. Let's eat."

"Want me to hang up the phone?" she asked.

Allan smiled warmly at his little girl, then shook his head. "Nah, keep your seat. I got it." He rose from his chair and lumbered across the tiled floor to a corner of the kitchen where the linoleum counter butted into the pantry. The telephone charger/answering machine was plugged into the wall. He snapped the phone into the charger. The answering machine showed one message. He pressed Play and stared at the cabinetry as he listened. He wasn't prepared for what he was about to hear.

"*Mom . . . Dad . . . please . . . somebody pick up . . .*"

The voice was barely more than a whisper, but at the same

time it was frantic, full of desperation. And the voice was un-mistakable. When he first recognized Steven's voice, a small smile started forming, tugging at the corners of Allan's mouth. His eyes dropped to the machine. But as the message progressed, the smile rapidly evaporated.

> *Oh, please, somebody be there . . . somebody please pick up! Uh . . . I've just got a minute . . . I'm in serious trou-ble. There's been an accident and I . . . I'm in jail. There's too much to explain right now. I'm sorry.*

There were noises in the background and other voices. Steven was beginning to stutter. He'd clearly been crying, or was still.

"Daddy, is that—"

"Shhh!" Allan put a hand out to shush all talking.

> *They've assigned an attorney to me . . . here's his cell phone number. Please . . . please write it down and call him back as soon as possible. I'm in real trouble, Dad. I need help. But whatever they tell you, it didn't happen the way it sounds. Please believe that. I've gotta go, they're coming. Please call that number. His name is Swanson.*

The line went dead.

The room stood in silence.

Allan jerked open a catchall drawer and grabbed something to write with. He hastily scribbled the public defender's cell number on the surface of the counter. He then spun around. All of his kids were standing at the edge of the kitchen, staring at him, open-mouthed. Dermott included. He'd come into the house and Allan hadn't noticed. Their eyes met.

"I didn't even think to check that when I got home," Dermott said, clearly stunned. "I'm sorry, Dad."

Allan nodded.

For a long moment he stood still, paralyzed.

Finally, he looked at the younger kids. "Cody, Claire, Parker. You all take your dinner into the living room. You can eat in front of the TV. Try not to make a mess. But stay out of here and stay out of the way. Go on now."

He wasn't sure what, if anything, he needed Dermott's help with. It just seemed like a sound idea to have him close by until he got his bearings.

He couldn't decide whom to call first, Lanna or this Swanson character. When the kitchen was clear of the youngsters, he made his decision, picked up the handset, and dialed the number.

15

THEY KNEW THERE HAD TO BE A LIST. IF IT HAD BEEN leaked, nobody on their side of the fence had seen it. But it was out there. They were sure of it.

Les Faulkenberry, Republican senator from South Carolina, had spent the day in more meetings than he could count. The phone was ringing off the hook. Everybody wanted answers from him he didn't have. Everybody wanted a look at the list. He couldn't help them, he insisted. Sure, he had his spies out. But the Democrats were clearly doing a splendid job of keeping the president's list under tight wraps. Who could blame them?

The week had only just begun and already what a week it had been. Faulkenberry was fully aware of the fact that Washington would likely hear of the president's nominee for chief justice very shortly. Within weeks if not days. And that was eating the Republicans alive. The not knowing. The uncertainty. Not that it would do them any good. But the mystery would be causing more than a few upset stomachs in the coming days.

Faulkenberry sat in his office alone, the only light coming from a brass lamp on his desk. It was nearly midnight. His phone was quiet for the first time all day. He lit a cigarette and kicked his feet up onto the corner of his desk. He was late for a meeting. But they could wait.

Outside his window the lights of Capitol Hill sparkled. The events of Monday morning had turned the power stratum in the Capitol on its head. Of all the justices that could have keeled over, he mused, why'd it have to be Bourgeous? What a headache that caused. After decades of suffering through a Court controlled by the left, the Republicans had finally managed to enjoy a five-to-four majority for a few years. Bourgeous was a rock. He was batter-dipped in the dogma of the right. He'd never swayed. His was a vote they could count on. When the other conservatives teetered with indecision, the old school Republican had stood his ground. Now the president would almost certainly take advantage of this opportunity to wipe clean all the progress that had been made. What a headache.

The phone rang and startled him.

"Yeah. I'm on my way." He hung up the phone. He was late for the meeting. And they were anxious to get their hands around his neck. Why *he'd* been picked was anybody's guess. But the members of his party had made him their mouthpiece, shoved out front to mollify any concerns regarding the week's turn of events. Thus the meeting tonight.

He dropped his feet to the carpet and squashed out his cigarette in a crystal ashtray on the desk. He stood and put on his suit coat. His driver drove without saying a word. He knew when the senator was in no mood for conversation.

At the hotel, he was met outside by a tall young man dressed impeccably in a tailored suit who escorted him inside to an elevator and up to the eighteenth floor. These occasions invariably made him uncomfortable. These people simply didn't understand politics. They understood only money. And they were usually willing to spend whatever amount necessary to get things done.

"Senator," another very tall man in his late twenties said as Faulkenberry was shown to a luxurious suite of rooms. "You're very gracious for accommodating us like this on such short notice."

He counted four faces in the suite, excluding the gentleman who'd escorted him from the elevator. But he did not yet see the one face that mattered most. He knew that Costas Goodchapel had concerns, but Goodchapel didn't make a habit of making personal appearances. He'd sent his representatives instead. There was clearly a lot at stake here.

Faulkenberry knew that Goodchapel was a major contributor to the Republican Party and had been for years. That kind of financial support assured that his voice be heard. Goodchapel had a reputation, and the senator was aware of that reputation, which did nothing to put him at ease as he shook hands with the representatives from Amethyst Technologies.

Relatively speaking, Faulkenberry was fresh meat in Washington. He was in his second term, having practiced law for over a decade in his home state. But he'd made the right connections and had been appointed to the right committees. He wasn't afraid to stick his nose where it didn't belong. That was where the money and the power were found in D.C., after all. He was forty, with a full head of hair and a winning smile.

He recognized Ben Clement right away. Costas Goodchapel's top lawyer and right-hand man. Clement was standing behind a wet bar pouring a drink.

"Senator, good evening," Clement said, holding the bottle uncorked. "Sherry?" he offered.

"Please."

"It helps with the jet lag, you know." Clement handed him a glass and they shook hands. "Please, have a seat."

It was late, and no one had any real desire to be there. No

time was wasted. They arrived at the meat of the conversation in a hurry.

"We're concerned about the Court, Senator. About the direction it could take in the very near future." Clement had almost aqua blue eyes. They were startling, nearly hypnotic in their intensity. He hadn't touched his drink. He had one leg crossed over the other, holding the cut-crystal glass atop his knee. The man was clearly not here to entertain. He'd come to deliver a message.

"Our concern lies in maintaining the Court as an *effective* instrument of justice. As I'm sure you are aware, Amethyst, as a corporate entity—and Mr. Goodchapel, specifically—has been deeply involved in the American political system. And we would certainly be distressed to see the cumulative value of our investment simply tossed aside."

Faulkenberry nodded his head ever so slightly, putting forth a look of deep interest and understanding, as if he himself wielded the decision-making power to move mountains. The truth was that he was so far out of his depth that at this moment he was absolutely terrified. He sipped from his drink. He was way out of his league dealing personally with Amethyst. The man across from him was essentially a Mafia goon dispatched to turn the screws.

"I don't think I need to spell out the effects that a Democrat-controlled Court would have on free enterprise in this country," Clement continued.

"Indeed," Faulkenberry managed. Sweat droplets were running down from his armpits.

"Prior to the untimely and unfortunate demise of Chief Justice Bourgeous, the wheels of justice seemed to be right on track to produce an acceptable verdict in this unmerited lawsuit that has been brought against the most groundbreaking company in the technologies sector since the days of Thomas Edison himself. Because of frivolous suits such as this, Amethyst is forced to waste valuable resources that could be better invested in our ongoing research and development. The Republican Party has always seen fit to support and promote the interests of free enterprise, and we can only hope that such steadfast support will continue, unthreatened and unfettered."

The words hung in the air. Clement ended the statement with a shadow of a thin smile, intended to soften the edge. His liquor remained untouched. The booze was intended to sooth the senator's nerves and loosen his tongue. They wanted to know what he knew. But Faulkenberry was smart enough to be on guard. If he'd heard anything, any buzz coming from the White House, he wouldn't have wasted it on these guys. Sure, the Republican Party needed to keep the funds flowing, and nobody had more to throw around than Amethyst Technologies, but you couldn't just hand them whatever they wanted at the drop of a hat.

Senator Faulkenberry was well informed of the *Amethyst v. Cone Intermedia* face-off. Sure, he knew that Amethyst was just a bunch of thugs, that they'd muscled away the competition. It was just business, and nothing in the business world was fair.

They were gathered in an open sitting area, two armchairs flanked by matching sofas. A stunning Tibetan rug served as the centerpiece of the room. Senator Faulkenberry sat in one of the comfy chairs, now ignoring his glass of sherry. Clement stared at him across the rug. His Ivy League associates inhabited the sofas. They all had that same look about them. Polished and snobby, educated beyond all reason. Faulkenberry had done all right in the practice of law. He'd wandered the halls of a moderate-size private firm in Charlottesville. But he'd hated it. So he'd gone to the next logical step and taken a crack at politics. Now he hated politics. It wasn't the corruption that sickened his stomach—that was the only thing that made either vocation interesting. He couldn't even put into words what he so despised. But he could tell, sitting there across from this parasite wearing five-hundred-dollar shoes, that corporate law and corporate politics were every bit as corrosive to the soul.

Sitting there, Faulkenberry had nothing of value to offer but felt the white-hot spotlight on his face. He put on his plastic campaign-trail look that conveyed deep understanding and empathy.

"Right. Right," he nodded, furrowing his brow. "Your concern is understandable. After all, free enterprise is the cornerstone of the American economy. And I can say without the slightest hesitation that the Republican Party is *the* party of free enterprise. My peers and I have dedicated ourselves to assuring that government allow industry to thrive and grow. And we would vehemently oppose anyone or any institution that would seek to impede that constitutionally protected freedom."

Clement said, "The Supreme Court is on the verge of being threatened, Senator. We have a sitting president who happens to not share the views which you've just finished expressing to me. You know as well as I do that he will nominate a liberal, and that that would all but destroy an opportunity for our company to get a fair and just decision from the Court. At the moment, from where I sit, you and yours seem terribly impotent."

The bottom dropped out of Faulkenberry's gut. The real message of the night was now ready to be served up.

"Senator," Clement continued. "Next year is an election year. You'll be awfully busy, out and about, working tirelessly to raise campaign funds. What a shame it would be for you and your party to lose the large-scale contributions of corporate America. How many millions of dollars would that take from your coffers? And believe me, Senator, we can make that happen. We can also see to it that your time in Washington comes to an untimely end. Or, your cup could runneth over. It's all up to you. There's no room on the Court for a liberal."

Clement abruptly stood. "Get the job done, Senator. Otherwise we have no further use for you."

Clement left the room.

Those seated on the sofas stood and faced Faulkenberry, signaling that the meeting had adjourned. The pleasantries had officially ended. He was shown to the elevator.

The message had been delivered.

Deliver us a nominee, or the money tree dies.

Faulkenberry emerged into the night. He waited at the curb for his driver to pull around. He felt humiliated. He was a United States senator, for crying out loud. They should have come to him on their knees, pleading for his help. Not demanding results. He was so incensed he could barely breathe.

He'd been given a message. And he'd take that message back with him. Whatever good that would do. Their hands were tied. The president would make his pick, and the Republicans would take a few potshots. But all in all they'd be forced to just stand there and watch. Helplessly.

16

THERE WASN'T MUCH TIME, AND THEY HAD TO MAKE SOME quick decisions. Allan had phoned Lanna at the hospital. She'd come home and gone straight into panic mode. He sat her on the bed and got her to calm down. They had to get their bearings. He didn't like the idea of packing up to leave Lanna and the kids. But under the current circumstances, they would just have to deal with it.

A big problem was the late hour. Lanna would have caught a jet with him first thing in the morning, but on such short notice there just wasn't time to make arrangements for all the kids. Allan started making calls while she stuffed clothes into a suitcase for him.

Allan appeared in the bedroom doorway, holding the cordless phone against his hip.

She was folding a pair of his underwear into the suitcase when she glanced up and saw him standing there. "Anything?"

He nodded. "Got a hold of the Landers. They'll keep Cody and Claire, no problem. They said not to worry, they'll keep them as long as necessary. Evelyn said she'd get the spare bedroom ready tonight. You can drop them off tomorrow as early as you like."

Lanna let out a breath she hadn't realized she'd held in. "Evelyn is such a saint. What about Parker?"

"Yeah, I've been thinking about that. What's your feeling about Parker staying here with Dermott? They get along well enough. I'd lay down the law. Dermott would pick him up from school and they'd have to come straight home. It'd give him a chance to prove himself a bit. I think they'd be okay. It's up to you though."

She put her hands flat against her cheeks, closing her eyes. "I don't know. No. No, I'd prefer someone looking after Parker. An *adult*. Dermott can stay here and look after the house and feed the animals. But I want the children under adult supervision. Call the Lollers or the Brauns, they'll help."

Allan turned from the doorway.

Lanna ate half a slice of cooled garlic bread for dinner. The suitcase was packed and staged by the front door. Everything he'd need was in it except his toothbrush, which would go in after breakfast in the morning. She had the peace of mind of knowing Cody and Claire were set to be taken care of for at least the next few days. Arrangements for Parker were still up in the air. She'd have to deal with that in the morning. She prayed that Dermott wouldn't burn the house down.

All she could think about was Steven. He was sitting in a cold jail cell somewhere on the other side of the country. Was he okay? Were they treating him well? What could he possibly have done?

By the time they got into bed it was after two in the morning. Neither of them slept. They both stared at the ceiling until the alarm went off at 5:30 a.m.

Allan peeled himself out of bed. He wandered into the bathroom and stared at himself in the mirror. It wasn't a pretty sight.

Lanna made her rounds through the house, rousing the troops, getting them bathed and fed. She had to pack a travel bag for each of them. She slapped together some breakfast while she kept the phone pressed to her ear, still trying to make various arrangements. If she was going to take any time off from work, she'd have to beg someone to fill in for her. She poured a cup of coffee.

Lanna saw Allan to the front porch, embracing him, tears in her eyes.

"See you in a day or two," he said.

He kissed her, then turned for his truck, the suitcase in one hand and a cup of coffee in the other. He set the suitcase flat on its side in the back of the truck, then eased down the driveway, turning onto the highway.

The lawyer, Swanson, had been vague. Allan had gotten in touch with him shortly after hearing Steven's message. Swanson was in a meeting at the time and couldn't speak long. He said that Steven was in FBI custody in Boston. They were holding him for questioning. Charges were pending while evidence was gathered and organized. Swanson had been very brief. He gave the phone number and address of the building where Steven was being held, then quickly ended the conversation.

Allan drove his Dodge through a gate at the airport and grabbed a stub from an automated dispenser for long-term parking. He parked and lifted the suitcase from the back of the truck. At the moment there were no flights departing. It was too early. Allan needed the first available flight to Boston. He found a seat and sipped his coffee and stared at the buffed floor, contemplating the day ahead, hoping for the best and expecting the worst.

17

HAVING SPENT TWENTY-FOUR HOURS AND AN UNGODLY amount of money, they'd narrowed the list to three. Three names. Three potential nominees. Two of them were solid prospects, and one was a big if.

It was a tremendous amount of information to have gathered and cycled through in a single day. There was a thick dossier for each of the names. Dossiers packed with life histories. Glorious careers and towering achievement. The finest legal minds the country had to offer. There were pages and pages of glowing commendations. And that was all fine and good. But what they were interested in was the dirt. Was there any dirt?

Crystal Easterling flipped through one of the dossiers, reading quickly and silently. She tossed one on the table and grabbed up another. They had to pick the perfect nominee. Even a hint of scandal or controversy was too much.

It all boiled down to these:

(1) Sherman Reid. Seventy-one years of age. California supreme court justice. Graduate of Tulane Law School. Pro-choice. Marched with Martin Luther King Jr. Opposed Vietnam. Campaigned heavily for Mondale and Ferraro. Author of twelve books on liberal issues, including several currently used as academic texts at a number of universities. Opposed the death penalty and was renowned for his scathing dissents. Married with four children and a dozen grandkids.

(2) Tonya Compton. Forty-seven years of age. A former federal prosecutor. Law school at Georgetown, graduated in the top three in her class. Currently a professor of law at Columbia. A liberal with a tendency to go moderate on certain issues, especially concerning U.S. military involvement on foreign soil. Opposed the death penalty. Big advocate of gay rights. Married

once. Divorced once. The divorce was amicable, and the two remained close friends. They'd simply married too young. Currently single.

Crystal winced. She frowned and shook her head slightly. She was sitting at Jasper's desk at CI headquarters in Austin. Tonya Compton had looked promising. But the divorce put a damper on things. It probably wouldn't be a problem, but it couldn't be chanced. Pushing a woman through the confirmation process would be difficult enough. But a forty-seven-year-old single woman with a divorce was against the odds. They needed a sure thing.

Crystal tucked the photo inside the dossier folder and tossed it onto the table. She rubbed her eyes. They had to make a decision in less than six hours. Jasper had stayed out at his lake house. She'd slept in his office, doing what work she could online, always staying close to the phone. They'd hired an intelligence firm out of Bethesda to dig for skeletons. It was a firm that Anwar Claussen had used before, one that he trusted. The firm in Bethesda had balked at the twenty-four-hour time frame, but within eighteen hours the dossiers were flown, via Gulfstream V, to Austin.

She had the office door locked. The business day was sluggishly coming to life. Jasper was still south of town. Claussen was in D.C., awaiting word. Highfill and Strunyin were in the building, though she hadn't seen them in an hour. Jasper had phoned saying he'd be there shortly. They were to meet as a group by 10:00 a.m. to hash this thing out and make a decision. She was barefoot, in jeans and a Dave Matthews Band sweatshirt.

The wall farthest from Jasper's desk was made of glass, floor to ceiling, and looked out over the expanse of the production floor. She stood near the glass, paying no attention to the activity slowly gearing up below. She balled her toes in the carpeting, one hand squirreling through her hair, the other hand bearing the not inconsiderable weight of the third dossier. Her eyes ached but the clock was ticking. Then she continued reading.

(3) Getty Fairfield. Sixty-seven years of age. Born in Portland, Oregon. Undergraduate degree from Stanford. Law school at NYU. Was an appellate court judge. Was elected to a term in the House before being appointed to the Joint Chiefs of Staff in a civilian capacity, where he spent fifteen years at the Pentagon in Military Intelligence. According to the dossier, Fairfield had friends over every square inch of D.C. turf. They loved him on the Hill, as did the boys in the Pentagon. For his final go-round he'd eventually settled into a professorship at a law school, teaching one course a semester.

He'd been married to the same woman for forty years, with a half-dozen children and a flock of grandchildren. He was more vocally liberal than Reid or Compton but had the diplomatic skills to not alienate either side of the aisle. He was prochoice but a good Methodist. He was vehemently against the death penalty but had the hearts and minds of both the military and law enforcement squarely under his thumb. In his years in Congress he'd managed to endear the labor unions to him.

Crystal stopped reading and abruptly raised her head. Her heart soared. Getty Fairfield was their man. It was all there on the page. No enemies. No controversy. A fixture in all corners of Washington. He lived in deep left field but had the skills to finesse anybody and everybody. He was the one nobody could say no to. He'd be nominated by a Democratic White House and confirmed by a Republican Senate. It was perfect. Just perfect.

She couldn't help but smile. She wanted to start calling people immediately. Fairfield would hand them their verdict on a silver platter. They would take Amethyst to the mat.

Crystal threw her hands up, letting go of the dossier, hundreds of pages of copied documents fluttering to the floor around her feet. She held her hands over her head, making fists.

"Yesss! . . . *Yesssss!*" she screamed at the ceiling.

She could smell victory.

18

"IT'S FAIRFIELD, THEN. AGREED?" NEWTON HIGHFILL SAID, his back to the wall, facing out across the massive burled mahogany table.

Heads nodded all around the table.

"If he's the one, there's no turning back."

"We couldn't have built a better nominee in our lab," Sandy Strunyin said with a smirk. "Fairfield is the best of all possible worlds."

Newton Highfill and Crystal Easterling both nodded.

Highfill motioned toward the far end of the room, where Jasper Cone was standing with his back to the door. "Jasper, your thoughts?"

Jasper was dressed in a faded blue T-shirt, which was untucked. His chinos were slightly wrinkled. The cuffs of his pants bunched atop a pair of lightweight hiking shoes. His arms were crossed over his chest. At the moment that his name was called, his eyes were downcast. His expression was of deep displeasure.

For the longest time an awkward hush fell upon the room.

Sandy Strunyin was seated on one side of the table, his hands together on the surface in front of him. Crystal was seated catty-corner from him. He tried to make eye contact with her, to urge her to stir Jasper from his stupor, but her eyes remained fixed on her reflection in the polished surface of the tabletop.

Growing more agitated by the second, Highfill could barely contain his nervous energy. He combed at his hair, laboring to cover a balding spot with the surrounding brown scraps. Highfill was a doer. He preferred to be given his orders and get the job done. In that, Jasper drove him nuts. Highfill was born to be part of a hierarchical structure, whereas Jasper certainly was not. So therein lay the eternal conflict between the two. In the rockiest years at CI, post-Jasper, when the company slogged behind, when R & D offered little or nothing in the way of innovation, when profits tumbled and debts soared, when it was clear to everyone that they desperately needed Jasper back, Highfill had fought tirelessly against it. Just the thought of having him back in the building, tearing apart the corporate structure, had given Highfill cold shivers. Jasper was simply impossible to cage, in mind or body.

Highfill stood there watching him, waiting for some sign that he was even part of the conversation, because, frankly, so much of the time it was nearly impossible to tell.

Finally, unable to stand it any longer, Highfill cleared his throat and spoke. "Uh, Jasper?"

Jasper cupped an elbow in one hand, touching the index and middle fingers of his other hand to his lips and the tip of his nose. He inhaled a long breath.

Then he said, slowly, "How could it have come to this?"

"It's all about money," Highfill said. "We are sinking in debt. We are *smothered* by it."

Jasper finally let his eyes rise. He took a full stride from the door and sank his hands in the pockets of his pants. He shrugged his shoulders. "Do what you have to. I've nothing to add."

After he'd left, Crystal broke the silence, saying, "Forget all that. He's just out of his element. Give him time to cool off."

"Will he be a problem?" Strunyin said.

Crystal said emphatically, "Obviously he's uncomfortable. But I'm a realist."

Sandy Strunyin sighed. Jasper was correct. They had taken this to an extreme. But with so much at stake, who was he to make waves?

"Sandy?" Highfill said.

Strunyin made brief eye contact with Crystal, then faced Highfill. He seemed to be holding his breath.

Highfill watched him expectantly.

Strunyin turned from Highfill, gazing beyond Crystal to

nothing in particular. He let his breath out ever so slowly. "Count me in."

Crystal stared hard at Highfill.

A look of mixed relief and satisfaction buttered Highfill's face. He leaned away from the wall. He snatched up his copy of the Fairfield dossier and strode the length of the table, breezing past Crystal. When he reached the end of the table, he halted, rapped a knuckle against the mahogany surface, and spoke without facing them.

"Very well, then," he said. "It's decided. Fairfield's our man. I'll make the call."

19

FOR A SHORT TIME THE PLANE PASSED THROUGH A STRETCH of amazingly blue sky. Allan Adler, assigned to a window seat, looked out over the world below. He was keyed up but managed to nap for twenty minutes. When he woke, the clouds engulfing the plane were gray and threatening. Quite symbolic, he thought.

Neither Allan nor Lanna had ever made it out to Boston to see their son's school. It was just an expensive, time-consuming trip. That was part of the sacrifice of having the oldest child attend one of the finest universities in the world. They'd planned on indulging in round-trip tickets to his graduation at the end of the following year. Until then, they'd have to settle for his trips home at Christmas and at the end of the spring semester. Money was simply too tight.

The plane encountered a shelf of turbulence. Allan sat up. The pilot announced that they should be on the ground in another twenty minutes.

Boston gradually crawled into view.

At the Avis counter he produced a credit card and was soon presented the keys to a midsize sedan. Before heading out to the parking area to find the car, he stopped at a bank of pay phones and dialed Swanson's number.

The lawyer answered on the second ring. "Swanson," he said in a hurried tone.

He was at the courthouse, he said, working a separate case and unable to talk. He assured Allan that Steven was fine. He offered some crude directions on how to navigate from the airport to where Steven was being held, which Allan frantically scribbled on the back of his Avis rental agreement.

Swanson said he'd try to drop by early afternoon.

He found the car and made his way into the city. With every mile his stomach tightened. The unknown lay ahead. He just couldn't fathom what the boy had done. His son was guilty or innocent of a crime or crimes, and Allan wasn't altogether certain he was prepared to hear the story.

20

ATTORNEY ANWAR CLAUSSEN ENTERED THE THEATER alone. At the box office he paid for a ticket to an early matinee showing of a children's animated feature. He bought a tub of buttered popcorn at the concessions counter, then slipped into the darkness, finding his way between the rows of seats.

It was a nice theater, big and newly renovated, not one of those new ones divided into cubicles with a screen the size of a big-screen TV. He crept slowly down the aisle, letting his eyes adjust to the dark. There was a young woman with two small children seated a third of the way back from the massive screen.

Twelve or thirteen rows behind them, Claussen spotted his contact. He sidestepped down the long, curving row and took a seat next to Rowan Lipscomb.

Lipscomb kept his eyes on the screen and said, "You've got three minutes. Start talking."

Claussen wedged the tub of corn between his knees, ignoring it. "How close is the president to naming a nominee?"

"He's nervous, and understandably so. He's worried about his legacy." Lipscomb shrugged. "I do know he's narrowed the short list down to four or five."

"Got any names?"

"Me? No, I've heard nothing."

"And your boss?"

Lipscomb was working on a box of mint candies. He put one on his tongue and sucked on it for a few seconds before answering. "They're cousins, joined at the hip and all that. The president has included the senator in the talks thus far. If anybody has the inside scoop, it's Henbest. I hear bits and pieces but nothing of value. They're still batting things around."

"What about the name Getty Fairfield? Has he made the top five?"

"Fairfield?" Lipscomb held a candy to his lips, pausing to think. "Name means nothing to me."

"Well, Fairfield was on the original list from the Justice Department. He's our boy. It's in my client's best interest to make certain that Fairfield's name is whispered in the president's ear."

Lipscomb offered no reaction.

"What might that cost?"

Lipscomb sucked chocolate off his middle finger. "Hard to say. I'd have to consult my employer. Might help, though, if I could have a solid figure to run past him. Give him something concrete to mull over. Got anything in mind?"

From an inside pocket of his suit coat, Claussen withdrew a fold of cash. "First off," he said, edging his shoulder nearer to Lipscomb. "A little thank-you in advance from my client." He pressed the cash into Lipscomb's palm.

Glancing at the mound in his hand in the dark, Lipscomb leafed through it fleetingly. Thirty grand. Not bad for an afternoon errand.

The kids seated up front appeared to be getting restless. They stood in their seats, their mother fussing at them in a firm but hushed tone.

From the same pocket Claussen produced a business-size card, blank on one side, handwriting on the other. He placed it flat on the armrest between them.

Lipscomb slid the business card to the edge of the armrest, then palmed it, squinting at it, aided only by the dim flicker of the projector light. There was a dollar amount written on it.

The attorney spoke directly into Lipscomb's ear. "That amount is currently sitting in an offshore account, ready to be wired to a location of the senator's choosing. If this is satisfactory to him, he simply needs to furnish a destination account number, through you. And once the nomination of Getty Fairfield is finalized and made official, the money will be wired immediately."

"He'll want a guarantee before he sticks his neck out."

"My client is prepared to advance him one-third. Give me the routing number and the destination account and the money will be wired."

One of the children ran up the aisle headed for the restroom.

"One-third," Claussen repeated. "Five million. If that doesn't demonstrate my client's commitment, nothing will. And once the nomination is made public, the remaining ten million will magically appear in his account."

Lipscomb had what he needed. "If the senator is pleased, you'll hear from me shortly. Otherwise, no deal. Your three minutes are up."

Lipscomb was gone.

Claussen stared at the back of the seat in front of him for ninety seconds, then made a dash for the exit.

21

SENATOR FRANKLIN HENBEST GLANCED AT THE TEXT MESsage on his cell phone.

Outside, Urgent—LIP

His eyes lingered for a moment. It would be another ten minutes before he could get away. He was in a meeting for the Senate Committee on Banking, Housing, and Urban Affairs. He couldn't just stand up and walk out in the middle of business.

Suddenly fidgety, Henbest fooled with his wedding band. The meeting had gone on forever. The committee chairman, a right-winger from Iowa, was droning on in monotone.

What might Lipscomb want?

Henbest debated on making a break for the door, but that would draw attention. Time seemed to creep by.

Nobody wanted to talk business. The new obsession was the vacancy on the Court. Who was on the president's short list? Who were his top contenders? Would he swing wide to the left or stick to the middle of the road where it was safe? Everyone had an opinion. Everyone was an expert. And it was an excruciating act of discipline for everyone in the room not to stare at Senator Henbest, because if anyone was privy to what the president was thinking, it was Franklin Henbest. They wanted to know. Wanted to pick his brain. To get in there and wallow around and get the inside scoop. So it was imperative that he keep his game face on, to make as if everything was simply business as usual. Inwardly, though, he was a wreck.

His cousin, the president, had indeed narrowed the potential nominees to two. Cole Baxter, a federal judge in the Northwest, and Ella McCaullin, Michigan's attorney general. Both quite moderate. Uncontroversial and essentially unremarkable. As had been the case with many issues, the president had sought Henbest's counsel. Washington, D.C., was full of jackals and yes-men, and a trustworthy adviser was treasured. It was a power-hungry town. Everyone looking for an angle.

The president trusted him.

They'd grown up in small farmhouses, two miles apart down a country road, surrounded on all sides by an ocean of wheat fields. They'd fished and fought, hunted squirrel, chased after the same girls. Their relationship was widely publicized and scruti-nized. Certainly he'd used his cousin's influence to his best ad-vantage whenever necessary. His critics were many.

One set of wary eyes discreetly watched him from nearby in the room. Republican Senator Les Faulkenberry had seen him steal a glance at his cell phone. Faulkenberry didn't know what to make of Henbest. He was suspicious of the man, but more than that, he feared his influence and feared his power. Having the ear of the president was no small privilege and of no small concern. It gave the Democrats on the Hill an added strategic advantage.

Unlike so many of his peers, Henbest wasn't one to instantly gravitate toward the spotlight. He could smile at the cameras and press the flesh with the best of them, but his most danger-ous skills were as a behind-the-scenes manipulator. And that ter-rified the Republican senator, because that's where the real damage was done. Something was up. He couldn't put a finger on it, but he'd kept a close eye on his adversary, and his suspicion was that things certainly were not as they appeared on the sur-face. The goon from Amethyst had put the fear of God in him, and the shadowy actions of the Democratic senator did nothing to ease his rattled nerves. All he could do for now, though, was to watch from a distance and wait for Henbest to make a mistake.

He watched and waited. Yes, something was definitely cook-ing behind those cool blue eyes.

The meeting adjourned.

The Republican senator stood, stowing his papers inside his

attaché case. His eyes were on Henbest. Henbest appeared strangely disconnected from the energy of the room. He made a move past a thicket of debating senators, heading quickly around the massive conference table and along the wall toward an exit. Faulkenberry, approached by a highly conversational golfing pal, politely excused himself and hurried out the door, keeping Henbest in view but maintaining a discreet distance.

He rounded a corner and momentarily lost sight of his fellow senator. A storm of civil servants and staff filled the corridor. He heard his name and turned to shake hands with several of them. Then, looking past the shoulder of one of his brethren, he spotted Henbest standing near a large window in the corridor overlooking the lawn, cell phone to his ear.

Faulkenberry tensed. Distracted by another friendly voice, he shook a hand and managed a bit of banter before escaping, crossing to the opposite wall of the corridor, careful to maintain a candid perspective.

Franklin Henbest stepped away from the brightly lit windows and passed through a security checkpoint and out a door into the fresh air and sunshine.

Faulkenberry held his ground. His paranoia and suspicions had suddenly elevated to a new level. Should he follow? He crossed to the windows where Henbest had stood moments before.

A second man, his back to Faulkenberry, was standing conspicuously close to the Democratic senator. Henbest appeared to be listening intently, occasionally nodding. Something was exchanged hand to hand.

Henbest was gazing off contemplatively. After what seemed an eternity, he gave a curt nod, placing a hand on the man's shoulder. The exchange of words was brief.

The mystery man nodded vigorously, then stepped around the senator and strode briskly away, walking into sunshine.

The senator remained facing the Senate Office Building but was clearly lost in his thoughts. Suddenly his eyes snapped up toward the glass.

Faulkenberry froze.

It appeared they were staring eye to eye. But Faulkenberry knew that with the intense glare on the outer surface of the windows, Henbest was seeing nothing more than a reflection of the outside world. Perhaps he was even staring at his own reflection.

Whatever the case, Faulkenberry felt unhinged and took a single step back away from the glass. A passing staffer clapped him on the back, and he turned to say hello. When he turned back, Senator Henbest was gone.

22

THE PARK HAD PLENTY OF TREES AND A KIDNEY-SHAPED pond with a tiny island in the middle. There were several decent walking trails, one of which followed the perimeter of the water. It was spring, and the grass and leaves were thick and green. A few squirrels darted from trunk to trunk, always on the lookout for a quick snack. Various waterfowl dropped from a blotchy sky with wings cupped, gliding to the surface of the pond, happily bathing and feeding.

Few joggers were attracted to the park for whatever reason, perhaps its distance from the more upmarket neighborhoods. The dome of the Capitol Building was visible. A narrow two-lane road bisected the park's west side, at one point passing beneath a stone bridge that formed a perfect arch over the pavement.

Two cars had pulled alongside one another, facing opposite directions, concealed beneath the bulk of the bridge. Trails of exhaust fumes sputtered out each open end of the stone arch.

Anwar Claussen, buckled inside his Mercedes S-class, lowered his power window. The cars were barely nine inches apart.

Lipscomb's window was already down.

"Must be your lucky day," Lipscomb said. "My boss has agreed to play ball."

"The senator is a wise man," Claussen said, eyes on his rear-view mirror, wearing his paranoia on his sleeve.

Lipscomb marked something on the palm of his hand with ink. He said, "The deal is five million up front." He extended his left arm out the window, facing his open palm so that Claussen could easily see what he'd written. "Dial this number. You will be given the destination account, and you are to wire the money immediately. Hold on the line and you will be alerted the instant the money transfer is confirmed."

"When will he talk to the president?" Claussen asked.

"Be patient. You'll have your nominee."

"My clients are nervous. They want a guarantee."

"Sounds like your clients are in the wrong business."

Claussen stiffened, unaccustomed to being verbally back-handed.

Lipscomb ended, stating, "You'll hear from me soon enough. Until then, advise your clients not to wander too far from camp." He raised his window and disappeared out one end of the park.

In a flash Claussen was on the phone, moving a great deal of U.S. currency from one home to another.

23

WES SWANSON WASN'T HALF WHAT ALLAN HAD EXPECTED. The attorney looked barely twenty-five. He in fact looked just old enough to have gotten *into* law school, let alone to have graduated and found employment with the state as a public defender. His voice over the phone had sounded bold and worldly, likely a guise he'd acquired to cover for his boyish exterior. He was short and rail thin.

Swanson talked for forty-five minutes. He'd requested that Allan meet him at a local restaurant. They sat in a booth. Swanson ordered a burger and talked while he devoured his meal.

The authorities had allowed Allan to see his son, but only briefly. Steven was scared. The FBI was pushing him around. Steven had guided him through his version of events: the weekend in Manhattan, the drive from New York, the encounter with Calther on I-90, Nick killing Calther and hiding the body, the missing wallet, all the way through to his arrest.

Swanson now filled in more of the blanks.

"What about the kid in the car with him?" Allan said.

Swanson nodded. "Name's Nick Calevetti. Born and raised in Manhattan. His father is a Wall Street type. Big money family."

"Yeah, Steven has mentioned him a few times."

Allan took this in.

"Well, the Calevettis are hiding behind their team of lawyers. They are denying everything. Their boy is of course an angel. Steven says Nick's license is revoked, funny thing for an angel, right? Anyway, the story goes that they clip this pedestrian out on I-90, west of here." Swanson glanced at his notes. "The body has been identified as one Ronald Calther, midthirties, worked third shift at a local cannery, guts fish or something. Married, with a baby girl. A sheriff's deputy came across his abandoned car the other day, parked along the side of the interstate just a couple of miles from where his body was discovered. Steven claims Calther was alive when they found the body. He says Calevetti panicked because he was driving with a revoked license and while intoxicated, and proceeded to finish Calther off with a tire iron."

"Same story Steven told me," Allan said.

"Right. Anyway, the problem we face at the moment is the issue of evidence. The car belongs to Steven, and there were no witnesses to the fact that Calevetti was driving. We can't necessarily prove that Calevetti was even in the car at the time, though we can make a very fair assumption, and friends and classmates will be interviewed. That will tell us if anyone knew for a fact that Steven and Nick had made their travel plans public knowledge. The FBI isn't saying whether or not they've recovered the tire tool. But even if they have, Steven claims that Calevetti held it with a rag, so no fingerprints. Whatever prints they lift will likely be Steven's."

Allan could feel himself turning pale. Listening to what Swanson had to say was like trying to outrun a wall of water. "What about Steven's wallet?" Allan asked. "How did they find it?"

Swanson shrugged. "Dumb luck. Some lackey from the sheriff's department happened to drop his cigarette lighter, bent down to pick it up, and bingo, there's a wallet in the grass between his feet."

Allan winced. He looked away and shook his head. "If only Nick had been the one to lose his wallet."

"That's assuming that Steven is telling the truth. So far it's Steven's word against Calevetti's." Swanson got the attention of the waitress and requested a refill of his drink. He continued, "And the first question a jury will ask is why, if things unfolded as Steven alleges, why didn't he march straight to the authorities and lay it all out?"

"He was scared, wasn't thinking straight," Allan offered.

"Fine, whatever. If that's the case, he didn't do himself any favors. What he did was rush the car to a body shop in an attempt to get rid of the evidence. Bad idea. The FBI found the Mustang sitting in the weeds beside the shop, still waiting in line to be worked on. He says Calevetti told him to. Maybe I believe that, and maybe I don't. Regardless, that was probably the worst thing Steven could have done for himself. I'd be willing to bet that Calevetti's fingerprints were all over the vehicle at some point, and I'd also bet that he took the time soon after to wipe it down.

That probably never occurred to Steven. I've got a suspicion that Calevetti is quite an operator." Swanson stopped chewing for a moment, swallowed. He tapped a finger on the tabletop. "So, picture this. The two of them are on the side of the road with Calther's body. Calevetti does his thing with the tire iron, and Steven freaks. Calevetti ditches the body. Steven is prepared to do the right thing. So, instinctively, Calevetti plays the money card. Why make a big a deal of a dead guy? He buys Steven's silence. Everything is fine now, right? Only thing is, Steven's wallet is found not far from Calther's body. FBI puts two-and-two together, and here we are."

"Will they bring Nick in?"

"They'll want to talk to him. But the lawyers won't make it easy. The Calevettis have very deep pockets, and no expense will be spared to ensure that their boy comes out of this without so much as a scratch."

"What about Steven?"

"He's in serious trouble. Somebody beat Ronald Calther to death, and we know for a fact that your son was in the area at the time of the crime."

Allan stared out at the parking lot.

They discussed bail.

"The arraignment is this afternoon. It will be quick and quiet and over in about three minutes. The judge will decide whether or not to set bail, and if so, how much."

That would prove to be a stumbling block. Money was a huge issue. There was simply not enough. Swanson suggested that they contact friends and relatives, even consider taking out a second mortgage on their house if need be.

"Even if he's released on bail," Swanson continued. "To mount the kind of defense needed here, I'm not gonna be a whole lot of good to you. A defense against these charges—a *good* defense—will get expensive in a hurry. You'll need to hire a big gun. That kind of lawyer could break the bank. Between you and me, Mr. Adler, that's the one real shot you've got. I'll work whatever magic

I can up front, but after the preliminary maneuvers, you are going to have to spend some money. Lots of it."

Standing in an empty space between their respective vehicles, Allan was more discouraged than at any other point in the past eighteen hours.

Swanson seemed to read his thoughts.

"Mr. Adler, it's not hopeless. We're far from that. Bleak, yes. Steven has certainly stepped into some serious trouble." Swanson had his hands stuck in the pockets of his suit coat, and he flapped them at his sides. "Don't let the FBI get to you. Most of those agents are just thugs in government threads. They want under your skin. Don't let them bully you. I told Steven the same thing."

"I'm in a daze," Allan confided.

"Understood." Swanson glanced at his watch. "Listen, gotta run. I'm stretched pretty thin lately. But I tell you what, let me make a few calls. I've got a few contacts in the city. I'll do what I can on my end, if you'll see what kind of dough you can scrape together." He yanked open his car door, nodded back to Allan, and sped off.

Allan Adler was left alone. He felt positively at a loss.

An oblong cloud blocked out the sun, casting him in shadow.

He unlocked the door to the rental car, realizing as he stood there that he had no idea where he should go now.

24

WEDNESDAY EVENING THERE WAS NOT A CLOUD IN THE SKY. It was warm out, the night air caressed by a cool, mild breeze. A good night for a party. And as luck would have it, the president's youngest daughter was celebrating her fourteenth birthday.

A healthy crowd of invited guests had begun gathering on the front lawn of the White House. Catering vans were parked nearby so that cakes could be carefully hoisted across the newly mowed grass to folding tables. The Secret Service kept watch.

The president was in the Oval Office handling a last bit of unavoidable business before he'd wander out to join the guests. The conversation behind closed doors was actually growing rather heated. A tone of confrontation had descended, sparked by a suggestion made, seemingly from out of the blue, by Senator Franklin Henbest, blood relative to the executive in chief himself.

Senator Henbest was in the room, along with White House counsel Bob Chapman and Chief of Staff Rusty Schwartzman.

The president was seated at his desk moderating what had become essentially a shouting match between his staff members and the senator.

"Settle down, Bob," the president said, frowning. "Just cool your jets."

Chapman was on his feet at the back of the room, pacing, and snorting every time he laid eyes on Senator Henbest.

Schwartzman was seated in a wing chair, arms crossed over his tailored suit, lips pursed.

"What's your objection, Bob?" the president said.

"My objection is that we had already narrowed the list to Reid and Compton. I thought we were agreed on this."

"Compton won't get past the Judiciary Committee," Henbest countered, seated alone on a sofa. He didn't make eye contact with anyone when he spoke. "It will be a waste of our time and energy, and we'll be right back to the drawing board."

"And Reid?" Schwartzman said.

Henbest rejoined, "In my opinion Sherman Reid is a lame duck. He has opposed every military conflict since 1812. The Republicans will shred him. Am I the only one here who sees that?"

"Getty Fairfield does have a solid record, gentlemen," the

president chimed in. "He's still remembered with fondness in the House, and his years at the Pentagon endeared him to the armed forces as well as the intelligence community."

"I say he's too far left." Schwartzman pressed a wrinkle out of his pant leg with the flat of his hand.

"Agreed," the White House counsel seconded with an overly enthusiastic nod. "Which, I mean, is fine and dandy and good with *me*, but the right-wingers will have his head!"

Taking in a long breath, then releasing it as a sigh, the president looked hard at his cousin, indicating that this was his battle.

Senator Henbest had arrived at the White House without an appointment. He had, of course, planned to attend the birthday celebration, but decided to make a preemptive strike in the nomination debate by cornering his cousin while they were alone and announcing that he'd had an epiphany. He'd done just that. The assault had been sudden and surprisingly decisive. The case Henbest made for Getty Fairfield sounded solid and, more or less, beyond reproach.

The president, after all, was in the enviable position of having the opportunity to reshape the Court, but also in the decidedly *un*enviable position of having to put his precious nominee up against those Republican savages in the Senate Judiciary Committee. Clearly, if he was to nominate a true pansy, a spineless moderate, the left would surely be hardly better off than before. But a card-carrying out-and-out liberal wouldn't stand a chance.

In the course of their private conversation, the president had gone so far as to candidly confess that he himself hadn't yet managed to generate much enthusiasm for either Reid or Compton. But still, Henbest's eager suggestion of Getty Fairfield seemed to have come from out of the blue.

"Trust me on this one," was the best the senator had offered at the time, in a suspiciously conspiratorial tone.

Now, on the president's cue, all eyes fell upon Senator Henbest.

Twenty-four hours earlier he'd been fully onboard with the

majority opinion. Reid and Compton had looked like a rather rosy pair to pick from. Up to this evening, the name of Getty Fairfield hadn't so much as passed his lips, and he'd voiced no fault with Sherman Reid or Tonya Compton. The change of tune sounded conspicuous even to him. He could only hope the others would fail to read too much into his radical reversal of direction. Fortunately, the argument in support of Fairfield was sound and well grounded.

Butting heads with the likes of Chapman and Schwartzman was certainly not a great pleasure. Neither man had climbed to these great heights by being easily dissuaded. They were bulldogs, aggressive and tenacious. But at the moment they seemed to be on the ropes. The president had warmed to the notion of Fairfield as chief justice with astonishing ease. After all, Henbest hadn't plucked the name out of thin air—Fairfield had been on the original list sent over from the Justice Department. Thank God, Cone Intermedia had someone on their staff who knew about something other than computer chips. If they had selected some suspiciously obscure candidate, this task would have been impossible to pull off. From the outside, Henbest was confident that he simply looked like he had done his homework.

The thought of five million dollars sitting in an account overseas, awaiting him, made a drop of sweat run down his back. He was adrenalized by a giddy nervousness. It was a truly beautiful scenario he'd been selected to deploy. He was as familiar with Cone Intermedia's plight as anyone in the Senate. In reality, Henbest had had little more than a passing interest in the whole affair, observing its progress through the judiciary system, as it evolved from a curiosity at the state level to a massive entanglement as an antitrust case argued before the highest court in the land.

In the few short days since Bourgeous's passing, all attention in Washington had zeroed in on the White House and who would be tapped to fill the vacancy on the bench—including Henbest. Only in the past half a day had it occurred to him just how immediate an effect a new chief justice would have on the Court. Literally billions of dollars were ultimately at stake in *Cone Intermedia v. Amethyst Technologies*, and that was just one out of hundreds of cases the current Supreme Court was debating. It boggled the mind, Henbest mused, to consider how one individual could wield so much power.

A sting of guilt nipped at the back of his neck. He reached a hand around and massaged the flesh just above his shirt collar. The guilt receded, though its shadow lingered. The knowledge of the five million helped to stave off the discomfort, and if the president fully took the bait and proceeded in favor of Fairfield, the account in Zurich would triple overnight. This, indeed, was his moment to shine. It was his job to mend fences with Chapman and Schwartzman, to alleviate their concerns, to anesthetize their lingering anxieties and aid them in coming to see the light.

The president certainly needed no one's approval to make his decision, but these men were his most trusted advisers—trust not easily tossed aside, and he would ever so thoughtfully take into consideration any nagging doubt they felt obliged to voice. Franklin Henbest was perhaps his oldest, dearest friend, but in the political arena it would be asinine to invest full faith in one specific individual without regard to opposing views.

But under no circumstance was Henbest going to let the fifteen million slip through his fingers without a fight. Not while it was there for the taking. Sure, he was manipulating the system for immense personal gain, but that was par for the course in this city. And he eased his mind with the logical justification that Getty Fairfield would actually make a fine chief justice. Another fat drop of perspiration traveled down the contours of his spine.

Of course none of these men were saints. Henbest had known the president too many decades to have any illusions about that. And neither Chapman nor Schwartzman was above indulging in shady dealings in order to get the job done. It had thus occurred to him to broach the subject of the money to the president, to offer an agreeable division of funds in exchange for

Fairfield's nomination. The money could remain overseas, accessible yet safely tucked away. If either of the other two men refused to budge on the potential nominees, the president was then free to include them in dividing up the nest egg.

And there had come a moment during his private tête-à-tête with the president when the words had been right there on the tip of his tongue. But ultimately he'd resisted, for two reasons: first, and perhaps foremost, his cousin was in many ways far less predictable than either the White House counsel or the chief of staff. He might flip out at just the suggestion of impropriety. In that way, the president was very much a Boy Scout. The scenario was too fragile. Henbest couldn't risk being excluded from the decision-making process. Secondly, he fell victim to his own greed. Why share the wealth? Why divide the fifteen million four ways? Already, wild fantasies blossomed and danced in his imagination; how the money could be spent, how he could indulge himself in a life of leisure and luxury. There was but a single year left in his term as senator. He could decline seeking reelection to a fifth term. Retire to Switzerland. Forget America and its taxes. Learn a language, maybe three. He could adapt to Europe easily enough, he figured. Working in the federal government had exposed him to the underbelly of the nation of his birth. It was nothing to be admired. The country was held together by Scotch tape, spackle, and the gravitational pull of material consumption. The pollution-free air of the Alps was just what the doctor ordered. He would invest the money and live off the interest. It was his shot at a pot of gold.

Senator Henbest said, "I'm not here to step on anyone's toes. Just to offer my opinion. In my view Fairfield is the right man to reverse the downward slide of the Court." He stood and approached one end of the president's desk. Shoving his hands in the pockets of his slacks, he made deliberate eye contact, one at a time, with both Chapman and Schwartzman, an effort to appear nonconfrontational. "I don't think you would argue that there's no room on the Court for mediocrity. This is our chance

to shake up the Court, to get the judicial branch back on track."
Henbest continued, "Getty Fairfield represents everything the
Democratic Party stands for. I'm not going to filibuster, gentlemen, but I wouldn't have slept well for a while had I not voiced
my concerns. Ultimately it's the president's call, though—it's his
vote that counts, not mine. And I hope he'll look past our petty
differences and do what's in the best interest of our country."

For better or worse, he'd done his part. The rest was out of
his hands.

No one spoke immediately following, and the dead air was
filled with awkward, unsure visual exchanges. The ball had been
served into the opposite court, and no one was too eager to take
a whack at it. The deflated expression on Chapman's face spoke
volumes.

Schwartzman kept a subtle eye on the president, hoping for
a telltale giveaway. But the president was apparently captivated
by something of insignificance atop his desk. Schwartzman, con-
trary to his typical aggressiveness, offered no rebuttal.

The president, the leather of his plush captain's chair creak-
ing as he rocked in it oh so gently, cocked his gaze toward Senator Henbest, and proffered an almost unnoticeable wink.

Henbest had hit his mark.

He nodded cordially at the two men facing him. "Well, I've
said enough. I leave here secure in the knowledge that the future
of the nation is in the best of hands. Now, if you'll excuse me,
rumor has it that someone special is turning fourteen this
evening, and I believe there might be a piece of cake with my
name on it." He clapped his cousin on the back and gave his
hand a firm shake.

On his way out the door, he glanced briefly back over his
shoulder. The president was rising from behind his desk, his
chest puffed out like a bull elk in rut. Bob Chapman sank into
the sofa. The last image he caught before the door snapped shut
was of Rusty Schwartzman looking totally stunned, as if to say,
What just happened here?

25

D.C. ALWAYS LOVED A GOOD FUNERAL. THURSDAY MORNING
the dignitaries and the cameras gathered among the gravestones
to watch Kenneth Bourgeous be interred in his final resting
place. It was a fine morning—a clear sky and birds in the trees.
The forecast had called for scattered showers, but there was not
a gray cloud in sight. A perfect spring day.

A few former members of the Court were there—one foot
in the grave themselves. Most of the Senate showed, as well as
a hearty turnout of congressmen. The remaining eight justices
had good seats up front. The entire mob had started the morning at the National Cathedral, where Bourgeous and his wife
had attended services for the past twenty-five years, and gradually migrated to the grave site for the burial service. The
widow was front and center, just out of arm's reach of the fabulous casket.

The president was the first at the podium, offering stirring
words of respect, playing as much to the cameras as to the audi-
ence on the grass before him. A Republican senator shared a
handful of anecdotes about the late chief justice, a few of them
humorous, a few of them profound, and then he relinquished
the podium to the minister, who closed with a final thought and
a prayer.

The buzz was passing through the gathering like a wave before they'd reached the cars. A rumor was circulating among the
Democrats that a nominee had been chosen, and the right-
wingers were salivating for a name. The gossip scorched through
the crowd like a fire across the prairie.

Amid the whispers and hushed conspiratorial musings, a few
overheard the name Getty Fairfield.

Who? someone said.

Impossible, said another.

Speculation soared at a frenzied rate.

Fairfield *who?*

Impossible.

Several more potential nominees were mentioned. But the buzz surrounding this Fairfield character seemed to have some bounce to it, some substance. There were still plenty of skeptics, though. Still, by the time the funeral procession had made it out beyond the cemetery wall, the name Getty Fairfield was on everyone's lips.

Could a nomination be soon in coming? There was no short-age of uninformed opinions. The rumor, of course, had been strategically leaked. And the rumor was true.

The jet carrying the president's nominee to the White House was in the sky even as the procession of mourners headed back to work inside the Beltway.

26

GETTY FAIRFIELD HAD BEEN IN THE MIDDLE OF TEACHING his one class of the day when his lecture was interrupted by the phone call. The call was transferred to his closet-size office up-stairs, and he took a quick moment to compose himself before picking up the phone.

The conversation with the president of the United States was short and surreal. And when he'd hung up the phone and settled back in his plush chair to take a few seconds to decompress, he realized he could hardly remember a single word that had been spoken. Soon enough, though, the circuits of his brain made the proper connections and relays of data, and he understood that, yes, he had in fact accepted the president's nomination as chief justice of the U.S. Supreme Court.

The call had actually come about an hour before the funeral for Kenneth Bourgeous. He watched the church service on a television set at LAX but was in the air, resting comfortably with his wife in first-class, somewhere over the Rocky Mountains, as the graveside proceedings were carried out.

A limo greeted them at the airport and whisked them away through the streets of the nation's capital.

Even at sixty-seven, Getty Fairfield was disarmingly handsome. Thick, wavy blond hair and a tan face with chiseled features. He stood six three. His solid stature, rugged good looks, and towering intellect had made him a magnet to the young coeds and coworkers through the years. Mrs. Fairfield was a former Miss Oregon.

Anyone who'd ever passed through law school and logged any amount of time as a cog in the machinery of the judicial system had entertained far-off dreams of sitting on the Court. Fairfield had not been immune to such fantasies. And to find himself in D.C. now, preparing to stand before the lights and the cameras and the microphones to accept a nomination, was simply too much to fathom.

But there he was.

Their escort explained that their presence in the city was to be kept strictly under wraps until the announcement, by order of the president. Her wording of the decree gave him goose bumps.

The limo followed a circuitous route—national landmarks spread out before them. He was no stranger to D.C., but it was as if he were seeing it for the first time. Then something fell into place, waking his ego, and as he gazed out the window at the center of the political universe, he understood that this was where he'd always deserved to be, and that the power afforded the chief justice of the United States Supreme Court was his birthright.

27

ALLAN AND STEVEN HAD A FEW MINUTES TO THEMSELVES before the lawyer showed up. Swanson was late, but Allan didn't mind because it gave him some quiet time alone with his boy, just to get a feel for how he was holding up.

"You been getting any sleep?"

"Some. Not a lot," Steven said, his cuffed hands under the table, his upper body slouching forward in a weary posture. "You wouldn't believe how many creepy sounds fill this place at night."

"What happened to your head?"

Steven touched the bandage on his forehead. "Just banged it up a little in the accident. It's fine."

"Are they feeding you?"

Steven nodded.

Allan assessed his son. He was starting to look very much like a kid getting his first up-close viewing of the downside of the law. It was also probably his first true encounter with adulthood. A sobering encounter.

"I didn't kill that man, Dad. I tried to stop Nick, but he wouldn't listen. I swear that I'm telling the truth," said Steven in a measured tone. Allan could tell it was all his son could do to not succumb to complete panic.

"I know that, Steven. I know. Mom's flying in," Allan said, easing the tension. "I'll pick her up a little later."

Steven didn't look up. Just nodded his head slightly.

The sound of the door opening was a welcome distraction. Wes Swanson barreled in, looking harried, his briefcase in one hand, a paper cup of coffee in the other.

"Morning," Swanson said, careful not to spill coffee as he swung the briefcase onto the table with a clatter.

Steven improved his posture for his attorney, sitting up straight in his chair.

"How are we doing this morning, gentlemen? Okay, first off, the prosecutor faxed the results from your urine test to my office." He popped the snaps on the briefcase and went about sloshing paperwork. He found what he'd been after, and grew still for a moment, his attention going from a printout in his hands to Steven. "Clean as a whistle."

Steven nodded.

"Nick Calevetti's lawyers are certainly earning their money," Swanson said. "I've demanded a urine sample from him, but they've managed to delay long enough that his system would have likely flushed most of it out by now. That's the reason they make five hundred dollars an hour. Also, the judge denied our request for bail, but I expected that."

"Why the problem with bail?" Allan asked.

The lawyer gave a half shrug, sat back in the stiff, wood chair, and crossed his arms over his chest. "Steven is a flight risk. He is accused of killing a man and fleeing the scene, Mr. Adler. The court will want to ensure that he doesn't wind up in Canada or Mexico before he can be brought to trial."

Allan shook his head slowly, releasing a long, deep breath. "Do we have any options?"

Swanson nodded, diving a hand back inside his briefcase. He produced a business card. "You're going to see about getting some legal-eagle wizardry on your side. Her name is Rochelle Giovannucci. Her office is downtown. She's a criminal defense attorney, and her paychecks have a few more zeroes at the end than mine, to say the least. If you can afford her, she'll come as close as anyone on earth to getting Steven off the hook. She can twist a prosecutor's argument into balloon animals. She's nasty and rich and one of the best at what she does."

Eyebrows arched, Allan asked, "When do I contact her?"

"I've already made an appointment. She and I share mutual friends. I begged and pleaded and managed to squeeze you in to see her this afternoon. Do *not* be late. One thing Giovannucci is in short supply of is patience. I've faxed her everything I've got on Steven. She'll offer an assessment, quote you a fee, and—if you decide to go forward with her as Steven's legal counsel—require a sizable retainer, paid up front."

Allan fingered the card Swanson had passed him.

Steven was sitting pensively, rubbing his hands together.

"What if we can't afford her?" Allan asked.

"I'd advise you to beg, borrow, and steal—whatever it takes." Swanson stood, snapping the gold-plated latches on the briefcase. "If your son is really innocent, Mr. Adler, you're going to need all the help you can get because Nick Calevetti has all the legal muscle in the world behind him. So my advice is, find the money. Be creative. The funds are out there. Where there's a will there's a way."

28

BY LUNCH THE RUMORS HAD ESCALATED, FLYING FAST AND furious. The White House had alerted the media of an impending press conference to be held at 4:00 p.m. but refused to add specifics. When they couldn't coax another drop from sources at the Capitol Building, they lit up the phone lines on Capitol Hill, which set off a maelstrom of chatter and renewed speculation. But most of the mystery had evaporated: Getty Fairfield was the president's nominee.

When he simply couldn't take it any longer, Senator Les Faulkenberry locked himself in the privacy of his office and dialed the phone. Shortly he was speaking with attorney Ben Clement, head counsel to Amethyst Technology.

"The name is Getty Fairfield. He teaches law somewhere in Southern California, I think," Faulkenberry said, buzzing with nervous energy. "The announcement will be made late this afternoon. The White House is keeping it all cloak-and-dagger until then."

Clement was idling in Seattle traffic in his Jaguar, rain misting his windshield. He'd been heading home for lunch after a series of meetings at the sprawling Amethyst complex when the cell phone rang.

"Fairfield?" he said, signaling for a left turn at a red light.

"Yeah. I've only heard bits and pieces, but word has it he swings wide left. They say he was in the intelligence racket for a long time—in what capacity, I have no idea yet. I'm working on that, though."

"Fairfield," Clement repeated to himself, nearly under his breath. "Keep digging. Give me a call if there's anything of value."

Faulkenberry had opened his mouth to reply, but Clement was gone.

Clement folded shut the tiny cell phone, changing lanes without even checking his mirrors. He passed the turnoff in the highway that led to his house. He wasn't going home.

Costas Goodchapel's estate overlooking Puget Sound encompassed some sixty acres. Much of its perimeter was enclosed by a ten-foot, camera-monitored fence, designed to blend unobtrusively into the surrounding environment. Clement waved at the guard as the gate opened for him, and the Jaguar accelerated, zipping around the lazy curves of the long, paved driveway.

In his years employed by Amethyst, Clement had seen only a fraction of the Goodchapel estate. It was the ultimate state-of-the-art property. Legend contended that construction costs had run north of five hundred million dollars. Considering that the owner ranked among the twelve wealthiest individuals in the world, Clement didn't doubt it for a second.

He parked the sedan beneath an expansive portico and made his way up a spectacular stone path to the massive double front doors. Goodchapel had imported the giant matching slabs of wood from Japan. Scenes depicting warring samurai were carved down the length of each door. A laser eye embedded in the wood scanned his facial features as he approached, and a soothing feminine voice greeted him by name.

"Good afternoon, Mr. Clement. Please wait in the foyer. Dr. Goodchapel will be with you shortly." It was such a sexy voice. He often wondered how those computer geeks had managed to suffuse such sultriness into synthetic diction. The automated program released the titanium bolt in the door, and he was able to enter without complication.

The entire mansion was hard-wired from floor to ceiling with cutting-edge technology, and the architecture was spare, heavily influenced by Asian culture and design. The layout was the very definition of simplicity. Clean lines. Sweeping, open spaces. But the walls concealed hundreds of miles of wiring and cable, enough to rival the schematics of a battleship.

The foyer was expansive and awe-inspiring unto itself, with richly swirled marble and a sky-high vaulted ceiling braced up by rough-hewn beams. The floor was a quarter-mile of richly swirled marble. A wonderful scent he couldn't readily identify had been added to the filtered air. And the climate controller maintained a perfect, soothing environment twelve months out of the year. It was always a pleasure to visit the Goodchapel mansion.

Clement knew the drill. He strode to the far end of the foyer, where a plasma screen was mounted on a wall to his right. It was displaying a screen saver featuring multiple, shifting scenes of a lush Amazonian rain forest. As he approached, the screen saver faded to pearly white, and suddenly the face of Costas Goodchapel appeared on-screen.

"Ben, I didn't expect to see you today."

Clement said, "I would have called ahead but thought this would be better if discussed face-to-face."

"I'm in the third-floor dining room," Goodchapel replied.

Clement could see that Goodchapel was eating. He'd interrupted lunch.

"Check the diagram on any plasma screen if you lose your way." Goodchapel was referring to a three-dimensional grid of the home located in the bottom-left corner of each of the dozens of identical plasma screens located throughout the enormous mansion.

Third-floor dining room, Clement mused. Exactly how many does one *need*?

"Of course," Clement said, and headed for an elevator.

The elevator door had barely closed before it opened onto the third floor. Various members of the house staff acknowledged him in passing. Like Clement, they worked exceedingly hard to please their employer.

The third-floor dining room was the smallest of the four in the home. It was near his main office and allowed quick, easy access for meals or snacks. There were no kitchen facilities on the third level, though. The kitchen staff had to cater the rest of the mansion from the massive kitchen area located on the basement level.

When Clement found his employer, a member of the kitchen staff was standing next to Goodchapel's table, transferring emptied dishes onto a stainless steel cart to be wheeled away.

Goodchapel was hovering over a steaming bowl, spooning soup into his mouth. "Have you eaten, Ben?"

"No, actually I haven't."

Goodchapel nodded. "Marcel, Mr. Clement will have the duck. And . . . yes, the egg-drop soup as well," he said. Then he said to Clement, "Marcel makes the most fabulous egg-drop."

It was always a special treat to take a meal at the Goodchapel mansion, though the man was rarely as hospitable as he appeared on this day. Costas Goodchapel wasn't tall. But he was stout—thick through the chest, with powerful arms, and solid legs beneath him. Short, curly dark hair and an intensely handsome face completed the picture. His dark, beaming eyes could scold or seduce with equal ease and success. And money was the lifeblood that coursed through his body. He preached profits, and fools were not tolerated.

"Down to business, then," Goodchapel said, sipping water from a stemmed glass.

A plate of roasted duck was placed before the lawyer. The aroma emanating from the cooked fowl was divine. His mouth was watering. But he hesitated before grabbing up his utensils to carve the bird.

"A source in Washington says the president will announce his nominee this afternoon."

Goodchapel flashed his eyes at his lead counsel.

"A liberal named Fairfield," Clement added.

"Who is he?"

"That's still coming."

"Any background at all?"

"My source—the senator—mentioned a possible background in intelligence. Once the announcement is made, the media will have his résumé condensed to a twenty-second sound bite—that we can count on."

"Bury him. I don't care where he came from or what he's done. Find something on him. Cut him off at the knees. Nobody in D.C. is a Boy Scout."

True to form, Clement thought to himself. Goodchapel was a take-no-prisoners capitalist. All he could see with his tunnel vision was the potential threat to his empire. Cone Intermedia was a thorn in his side. Any nominee for chief justice who'd likely back CI was a threat, and therefore the enemy. Plain and simple.

In Goodchapel's world, the rules were written and rewritten as needed. And his mission was to make bloody well sure that the rules always favored Amethyst. He'd started from scratch. He was the embodiment of the American Dream. Building a global company from out of the dust. Buying out or destroying competitors. Annexing companies whose products or resources complemented Amethyst's strategy for growth and expansion and dominance in the high-tech sector.

In the few short years since CI had filed suit, Clement and his team of legal masterminds had steamrolled through the various levels of judiciary, claiming victory every step along the way. No way was Goodchapel about to let a liberal chief justice be allowed a seat on the Court.

"We'll get him," Clement said confidently.

"Bring me his head."

You did not become one of the richest people on earth by being meek or by staying within the lines—Clement had no illusions about that. Fortunes were built and sustained upon the corpses of weaker opponents. Goodchapel fed on weakness.

If Getty Fairfield had any weak spot at all, they would tear him apart, limb by limb.

29

THE AFTERNOON TURNED HOT. RATHER THAN TURN ON THE AC in the rented sedan, Allan cranked down his window, preferring the fresh air. He drove with both eyes focused on the road, ignoring the densely layered traffic all around him. He was too preoccupied with the crisis impacting his family to concern himself with the maddening rush of everyday life in the city. Eventually he stumbled upon the correct exit and followed the road signs to Logan International Airport.

Allan glanced up at an arrivals display to check the status of Lanna's flight. It was right on time.

She came out of the plane looking like she could use a vacation. She dropped her carry-on and hugged him tightly. Allan grabbed her bag, and they headed off to fetch the rest of her luggage as he told her about their afternoon appointment with the high-priced lawyer.

"I want to see Steven!" she protested.

"We'll see him soon," Allan promised. "This lawyer is a big deal. She might be able to help us. Steven's fine. A little tired and scared but still in one piece."

They made the long hike to the car in short-term parking and put her luggage in the trunk. During the drive downtown, Lanna caught him up on business at home. The kids were all where they should be, and Dermott was keeping everything under check at the house.

Allan tried to prepare her for the financial toll Steven's situation was going to place on them.

She said, "I filled out a loan application at the bank. We have some equity in the farm. Now we have to decide if we are willing to risk it for this."

They parked in an underground lot and took an elevator up thirty-five floors. Allan held the door for his wife as they entered a lushly furnished reception area. The plaque outside the door declared it the offices of Birnbaum, Cass, and Giovannucci, Attorneys-at-Law. A panel of receptionists sat behind a massive crescent-shaped reception counter. The women wore sleek headsets allowing them hands-free communication by phone or intercom.

A very prim-looking young woman with pink lipstick tapped their names into her computer and had them take a seat. They sat for all of three minutes before a secretary appeared and escorted them down a series of hallways to an open door.

"Please go right on in. Ms. Giovannucci will see you now," the secretary said.

Rochelle Giovannucci looked barely three or four years older than Wes Swanson, Allan noted. The legal profession, it seemed, had been overrun by teenagers. But he could see why she had risen so high up the ranks. She was clearly possessed of all the class and poise that Swanson lacked. She was dressed all in red— a power suit. She was just hanging up the phone when the couple eased into her office.

"Mr. and Mrs. Adler," she said, greeting each with a firm but feminine handshake. She closed the door behind them.

"As you're probably aware," she began after offering them a seat, "I had to wedge you in today. My schedule is packed as it is, so, without wanting to sound rude, this *is* a bit of an inconvenience, and we'll have to be as brief as possible."

Awkward nods from the Adlers.

"Wes gave me a quick but thorough briefing of the case, and faxed all available and pertinent information and documentation." She paused a beat, choosing her words. "Let me be blunt. A man is dead, Mr. and Mrs. Adler. There appears to be strong evidence to suggest that it was a homicide. Steven left the scene of the crime, and he also tampered with evidence by attempting to have the damage to his car repaired. I can list all the charges the prosecutor has brought against your son, but we are short on time here, so I'll let Wes fill in those blanks for you if he hasn't already. An additional factor is that the victim has a widow. She could sue. She could take everything you own and it would not be pretty. Steven has an uphill battle ahead of him, and without someone of my caliber fighting for him, he will almost certainly go away for a long, long time."

"What about Nick Calevetti?" Allan asked.

"Your son is now locked in a game of he said/he said with the son of one of the wealthiest families in New York. This is no small matter. Quite honestly, your son could become the next *Court TV* celebrity."

Lanna ingested a deep breath, both hands clutching her purse.

Allan ran a hand through his hair and puffed out his cheeks.

"Well," he began, emotionally off-balance. "How much would a defense like that cost?"

Rochelle Giovannucci didn't so much as bat an eyelash. She spoke as if she'd been waiting with her finger on the trigger. "My fee is six hundred dollars an hour. You are looking at a very expensive defense here. I have no intention of sugarcoating that fact. And I can promise you this case will not come to a conclusion overnight. Our court system moves forward at a glacial pace. I do not come cheap, but you have to decide what the next few decades of Steven's life are worth."

A stunned silence followed. They would have come unglued at half the price.

"Now if you'll excuse me, I have a busy schedule to keep. You have my card. You have a lot to think about, and time is not on your side." And in a flash she was at the door, showing them out.

They rode the elevator to the garage in silence.

They would not—*could not*—hire Rochelle Giovannucci. Such an endeavor would leave them in financial ruin. The money they would receive by taking out a second mortgage was a mere drop in the bucket compared to her potential legal fees. There was no reason to even waste energy discussing it.

Swanson was useless. Giovannucci was out of their league. What else was there?

Standing at the rental car, Allan reached into a pocket and fumbled with the key.

Lanna put her face in her hands and openly wept. "I thought this Calevetti boy was Steven's friend! What kind of friend does this? What kind of *human being* does this?"

He didn't even attempt to say anything to console her. He was barely holding it together himself. He was one stitch away from coming apart at the seams. Steven was going to prison, and there wasn't a thing they could do about it.

30

IT WAS OFFICIAL.

Getty Fairfield was the president's nominee. The announcement was timed so that it would make the evening news. The photo op on the steps of the White House was perfectly choreographed.

As instructed, the call was made shortly after the president's announcement. Anwar Claussen dialed the number, and the now-familiar voice spoke briefly, then fell silent while the money transfer took place. Claussen was in the hotel room provided to him by Cone Intermedia but made the call using his cell phone.

When at last the sum in the account was confirmed, Claussen snapped his phone shut and casually spun it across the glass surface of the table he was using as a desk. The American justice system was an amazing machine, he thought. A few bucks could buy you just about anything.

The next call Claussen made was to Newton Highfill. Whatever it was worth, they agreed, the investment had been made.

Highfill was scheduled to depart for Malaysia bright and early in the morning, and having the knowledge that the nomination was in their pocket would make the drudgery of business travel that much easier to bear. It would give him a lot to mull over at thirty thousand feet.

Crystal had spent the late afternoon in Sandy Strunyin's office, watching the president's presentation of Getty Fairfield. At the end of the announcement, Strunyin had muted the TV and looked over at her. They were both standing, their backsides supported by his massive desk.

"Well?" he had said.

Without turning to him, she'd replied, "It's a start, anyway."

And then she had climbed into her Porsche and sped across town to the home in Austin she shared with Jasper.

Jasper was waiting.

She had opened the front door and found him in the foyer, leaning against a wall, shirtless and barefoot, wearing only his trademark wrinkled chinos. A bottle of wine in one hand, two stemmed glasses in the other.

"Having a change of heart, are you?" she said in her elegant accent.

Jasper shrugged and smiled, and then he poured her a glass of wine.

They got drunk and made love for hours.

31

DARKNESS FELL QUICKLY ON SEATTLE. WITH A DRAMATIC flourish the sky blackened with amassed clouds, and the rains came. Thunder boomed and lightning slashed overhead. The winds blew unrestrained, driving the rain horizontally.

Sitting alone with the lights off, Costas Goodchapel reclined on an exquisite leather sofa he'd had shipped to his home from South Africa. The whites of his eyes glowed intensely as he stared at an immense plasma screen TV mounted to the wall.

In his hand was a very compact remote control. He thumbed a button for the umpteenth time in the past few hours, once again cueing up the footage he'd recorded on the DVR unit inset into the wall below the plasma screen.

The image froze as it was cued; then the hard drive proceeded to replay the downloaded footage. The sequence began the moment the president took a step back, amid light applause from those gathered, ushering the nominee to the podium.

Getty Fairfield entered the frame and faced the cameras.

Goodchapel froze the picture. He stared for a long moment, studying. Then he thumbed the remote, watching with rapt interest as Fairfield made a brief statement.

Outside his office window a cannon shot of thunder exploded. He could feel a slight vibration from it even through the plush leather sofa. The windows above him were glazed with trickling rivulets of rain, casting creeping, disjointed shadows on the carpet.

When Fairfield finished his few words, he made a move to turn toward the president. But Goodchapel didn't give him a chance. He thumbed the remote, and once again Fairfield was frozen in time.

Goodchapel spoke toward the face on the plasma screen, his voice rich and commanding, filling the room.

"Don't get too comfortable," he said, staring up at eyes that could not see him. He turned off the TV. Then he repeated the threat, "Don't get too comfortable."

32

THE VISIT WITH STEVEN WAS ABSURDLY BRIEF.

He looked better, actually. He was sitting up straight, with his hair combed, and he even managed a smile.

They were given only a couple of minutes. Just time enough for a hug and to say good-bye. They'd be back tomorrow, they promised. Not much was said about the visit with the lawyer. Then they watched as he was led away.

Lanna stared out the window as they meandered through

traffic looking for a good place to eat. Allan let her have her space. She kept her face from him, fiercely holding back her tears. If he'd done anything even as benign as touch her leg or say her name, she'd have lost it.

They rode in silence.

Dinner was the buffet at a Chinese restaurant.

They ate mostly in silence. Allan asked about home. She warmed to conversation gradually. He held her hand from across the table. She couldn't keep her eyes from misting. They held hands on the way out to the car.

At the hotel, Allan fetched her luggage from the trunk. Lanna set about tidying the room.

Finally, when there was no longer any way to avoid the inevitable, they sat in chairs at the small round table near the window to hammer out an approach to the coming days, weeks, and months.

There were no easy answers. They had no money to spare. What little savings they had would be of no benefit to Steven, and by the end of this trip would be all but depleted anyway. And of course there was the house. That was a sticky proposition. If they lost the house to pay for Steven's defense, they'd have nowhere to turn. Allan put his foot down. They simply couldn't risk losing their home.

"This can't be happening," Lanna said through tears.

Allan peeked through the blinds and out the window at the street below. Directly across the street was a bus stop—just a park bench bathed in light from a street lamp. A few cars zipped past. The sidewalks were all but clear of pedestrians.

"We will do what we can," he said. "But I don't see any way out of this."

She stared past him toward the wall at his back, her eyes eerily vacant. "He's our own child, and there's not one thing in this world we can do to protect him. That's always been my greatest fear in life."

"Please don't," Allan said, but wanted to say more.

The only reasonable course of action was to forge ahead. A feasible solution had to be out there somewhere.

The hours passed.

His spiral notebook lay on the table, crisscrossed with financial calculations, tackling the issue from every imaginable angle. They'd listed every friend, family member, and acquaintance who'd ever crossed their path, building the most comprehensive potential donor list possible. There was Mitchell Lundberg, of course. He had some money tucked away somewhere, but that was just too much to ask of a friendship. Asking—*begging*—for money, would be humiliating. In the end it would be a matter of how much they were willing to endure. But parents weren't in the business of drawing lines denoting where their devotion to their children began and ended.

Sometime just after midnight, Allan glanced at the cheap digital alarm clock on the nightstand and pushed his chair away from the table.

"Geez . . . that's enough for one night."

Lanna's eyes were streaked red, both from tears and exhaustion.

"You need a snack?" he asked.

"No. Maybe a water, though."

He nodded. "There's a machine down the hall. I'll fill the ice bucket and grab a bottle of water for you. Then I've got to have a shower."

He brought back a granola bar with the water. Lanna peeled back the wrapper and took a small bite. It tasted surprisingly good. She hadn't realized how little she'd eaten at dinner. It didn't take long to finish her snack.

Allan retreated to the bathroom and shut the door. Soon enough, Lanna heard the shower running. She turned on the TV and changed into a cotton nightgown. She lay across the bed, propped up on an elbow, flipping channels. Her eyes grew heavy. She was fading fast.

Fox News was repeating the day's headlines. The volume was

down. She bumped it up enough to hear what the talking heads were saying. Her eyelids fluttered but she managed to keep them open. There was something familiar about a name at the bottom of the screen, though she couldn't place it. She flipped channels, hesitated a second or two, then flipped back to Fox News. *Curious*, she thought to herself. The name was listed below a topic-of-the-day caption.

Amid a cloud of steam, Allan yanked the shower curtain to one side and reached for the towel he'd left on the toilet seat. He slid into his boxers and had the towel draped over his head when he came out of the bathroom door.

Lanna heard him and turned his way.

"This is driving me crazy," she said.

"What?" he said, only half-listening.

"Honey, that fellow you used to chauffeur around—what was his name?"

Allan was preoccupied with the suitcase.

"Honey?"

"Huh?"

"In the army—that bigwig you carted around, who was that?"

"What, at the Pentagon?"

"Yeah."

"Geez, babe . . . that had to have been—what, close to seventeen, eighteen years ago."

"Yeah, so what was that guy's name?"

"Fairfield, if I'm not mistaken."

"Well," she said, "he's on TV."

He stood at the corner of the bed, careful not to block her view. "Turn it up."

The face on the screen had certainly aged, but Allan immediately recognized it as the man he'd spent a portion of every day with, back so many years ago.

"Well, sure enough," he said. "That's a face I didn't expect to see again in this lifetime."

"I *knew* that name was familiar," she said, passing him the remote. "No big deal, it was just driving me crazy. One of those things that sticks in your brain funny, and you can't shake it loose till you've pieced it together."

Watching Getty Fairfield on TV took him back a lot of years, to a simpler time—at least it seemed simple *now*. Every stage of life was equally chaotic, he found. Only time and distance had a way of creating nostalgia for the past. Seventeen years! He'd have been—what, twenty-five at the time? He'd had a young family by then. In reality, now that he thought back on it, those few years spent chauffeuring Fairfield from his home in Virginia to work at the Pentagon, or anywhere else the man had the inclination to go, were every bit as hectic and stress-filled as any other time in his life.

Easing down on the edge of the bed, he bumped the volume another notch. Lanna had squirreled around into her spot, her head on her pillow, eyes closed.

Allan listened.

Memories of his time in the company of Getty Fairfield gradually came cascading back. Allan had been a staff sergeant, simply assigned at random as a driver. Not the greatest gig in the world, but there were a few perks. Fairfield, as he remembered, kept to himself in the car—not one for a lot of small talk. But then again, the man worked on the second floor of B-wing at the Pentagon—Military Intelligence. He was an SES, the highest-level civilian. He was friendly enough, but not prone to chatter. That surely came with the territory. Given his position, with access to highly sensitive intelligence, Fairfield had been the keeper of many secrets.

Allan served as his driver until the end of his enlistment. Getty Fairfield hadn't crossed his mind since that day. And now he was nominated for chief justice.

Who'd have imagined?

Allan watched until the topic switched to some international matter. He clicked the remote and the TV screen blinked to gray. He sat still for a few moments, smiling. It was a small world. A small world, indeed. He folded back the bedspread on his side of the bed and, careful not to wake Lanna, switched off the light over the table. He lay there between the sheets, still wide-awake, staring up at the ceiling, the past slowly coming back to life.

33

LANNA WOKE AND ROLLED ONTO HER BACK, THE PERFECT stillness in the room filling her with uneasiness. Their bedroom at home had a ceiling fan, and she'd grown accustomed to its rhythmic sounds. This room was too quiet. She reached out her left hand to touch Allan, for reassurance that everything was okay. Her hand found nothing but sheets and the bedspread.

She sat up. Surely he'd just gone to the bathroom, she thought. But the bathroom door was open, and there was no sign of light. It took only an instant for her to find a light switch and put on her robe. Allan wasn't in the room. The vending machines were right down the hall. Had he gotten hungry? She peeked her head out the door. The hallway was empty.

Startled, she ducked back inside the room, locking the door. She paused, gathering her thoughts, puzzled. She approached the window, brushing the blinds aside. The other hand she clutched to her chest and breathed a big sigh of relief.

Allan was seated on the bench across the street, beneath the street lamp. He was alone, faintly aglow in a pool of white light.

Lanna released the blinds and turned to look at the alarm clock on the bedside table. It was a few minutes past 3:00 a.m. She dressed quickly, pulling on a pair of jeans and a V-neck sweater, and threw on some sandals. She grabbed her key card on her way out the door and stuffed it in a pants pocket.

The night was still and cool. Lanna came down the stairwell and emerged into the open air. She rounded the corner of the brick building and could just make out the figure sitting on the bench across the street.

At that hour there was minimal traffic. She crossed the street and stood before him.

"Couldn't sleep, huh?" she said, hands in her pockets.

He looked up into her eyes and offered a weary smile.

There was something going on behind those eyes, she thought. She knew that look.

"I woke up and you weren't there," she said. "You had me worried for a minute."

"Needed some fresh air, is all."

"It's pleasant out. A little cool, though." She tucked her arms in against her body, shivering.

"Have a seat." He patted the empty length of bench beside him.

Lanna snuggled up next to him.

"You been out here long?" she asked.

He kind of shrugged. "A little while."

"Thinking about Steven?"

"Thinking about a lot of things. The way things work out in life, the way the pieces of the puzzle fit together."

She tucked a hand between his legs for warmth.

"I slept for maybe half an hour, then woke up and stared at the ceiling forever. Then the craziest notion got stuck in my brain," he said, a far-off look in his eyes. "It was like a lightbulb flashing on in my head. It was the craziest idea, and I couldn't shake it."

Lanna put her head on his shoulder, closing her eyes, wishing they were warm in bed rather than out in the chill of the early morning.

"What are you talking about?" she said, almost as a yawn.

Allan sat for a moment, his arm around her. Then he said, "Let me tell you a story. Something that happened years ago, something I never told you. When I was stationed at the Pentagon as a driver for Getty Fairfield—"

"The guy on the TV?"

He nodded. "I drove him all over D.C. Took him to work every morning, then home at the end of the day. He'd have meetings at the White House on very rare occasions. He was a big dog at the Pentagon—a member of the Joint Chiefs of Staff, in fact. He was a civilian in Military Intelligence. Anywhere he wanted or needed to be, I was the man behind the wheel. I was assigned to him for over two years. And tonight, seeing him on TV, brought back memories that hadn't crossed my mind in years. They came flooding back. I stared at the ceiling until I fell asleep. Then I woke and stared at the ceiling some more. And out of nowhere came a memory that I'd pushed way down."

Lanna kind of tilted her chin up toward the sound of his voice. "What?" she asked.

"A woman," Allan said, his eyes closed, remembering.

Lanna blinked, suddenly very interested.

He continued, "I can remember I picked Fairfield up from the Pentagon one evening after a day of work. We headed across town and, quite out of character for him, he had me make a detour. He gave me an address, told me to go there. It was an apartment building. I knew the place—or at least knew *of* it. But what was strange was what he said to me then, en route. Something about how much trust he put in me as his personal driver, that I was a soldier and that it wasn't my job to question but to simply follow orders and keep my mouth shut. I was to speak of his business only if authorized by him. He asked if I understood. I remember looking at him in the mirror and saying yes sir. He told me to drop him outside the apartment and circle around for an hour, then pick him up. That's exactly what I did. The first night."

Lanna sat up. She watched his face as he told the story.

"The stop-offs at the apartment were once or twice a week at first. Then every other day. I first saw her on . . . on a Thursday, I believe. They came out of the apartment entrance together, and he ushered her into the backseat of the car. I kept my eyes on the road. At first, anyway. He could barely keep his hands off her. And let me tell you—she was stunning. Like a model. Tall and blond, with a figure you couldn't ignore. I knew nothing about her and didn't care. If Fairfield wanted to run around on his wife, that was his business. I was a soldier sticking to orders. But I didn't like it. Shuttling him and his mistress around D.C. was not the reason I'd joined the service.

"It got to the point they were seeing each other nearly every day, for longer periods at a time. Fairfield would tip me a couple times a week—which, you know, he didn't have to. I was assigned to him. Thirty, forty . . . sometimes fifty bucks a pop. Which I wasn't about to turn down because money was tight. I didn't know how long this would persist, but it was getting tiresome because their affair was cutting into my off-duty hours. But what could I say?"

Lanna, now truly caught up in his tale, rested her back against the bench, folding her arms across her chest. She was slightly flabbergasted by his narrative, to a great extent because they'd been married for two or three years by then, with two kids already, and he'd never once mentioned his boss's illicit behavior. She had no idea where this might be going, or why the memory of it had driven him from bed to sit out in the dark in the wee hours of the morning.

"One afternoon," he said. "The Joint Chiefs of Staff were in an unscheduled meeting. I parked the car and went inside the Pentagon and took an elevator up to the second floor, to B-wing, to see what time they thought he'd be out and ready to leave. In the elevator I saw a buddy of mine from my days in PLDC. We got to talking, and I followed him out to the offices where he worked. That's when I saw her."

"The woman?"

Allan nodded. "She didn't see me, and I didn't stick around to give her a chance to spot me. I excused myself and headed for the offices at Satellite Imagery, to inquire on the status of the Joint Chiefs. Turns out she was a secretary at the Pentagon. Then one day, not long after that . . . about as suddenly as it all began . . . it ended. No more detours to her apartment. No more dinners out. No more anything. And that was that. Shortly thereafter, my enlistment ended, and I came home to you."

He then looked at her, and she looked at him, and she could tell that the story wasn't complete.

"What is it? What are you leaving out?"

He held his tongue, staring into her eyes.

"What . . . what was her name, Allan? Didn't you at least ever learn her name?"

Allan nodded. "Yes, I did. But not until months later, when her face was splashed all over the news, all over every magazine in existence."

"Who was she, Allan? Tell me."

"Rosemary Hitchins."

The name didn't register at first. She turned from him, her gaze drifting, her eyes lingering on the darkened street. He could tell she was scanning her memory for some sort of recollection. He gave her time, wanting her to find it on her own.

Her eyes narrowed, frustration building. Then, suddenly, those same eyes opened wide, her mouth agape, and her head turned slowly to face him.

She croaked the words: "The spy?"

Allan gave a single nod.

"*The* Rosemary Hitchins?"

"Yes."

"Oh my . . ." Lanna gasped.

"Understand now?" he asked flatly.

She appeared stunned. For a long moment she stared into the distance, trying to process it all. At last she looked at him and said, "I remember she had a nickname. What was she called?"

He nodded. "The media christened her the Red Fox because she was a beautiful Russian spy."

"The Red Fox," Lanna repeated. "I remember now. That is incredible."

"Exactly."

"Didn't . . . didn't she, like, go to prison?"

He nodded. "As far as I know, she'll spend the rest of her life behind bars. Consecutive life sentences. No chance for parole, if I remember correctly. That name hadn't crossed my mind in so many years . . ."

Clearly dumbfounded, Lanna simply sat there wide-eyed. "How'd she get caught?"

"She was sleeping with some other intelligence official, and in the course of their affair, she got caught passing documents to the Russians. Both of them were convicted of treason. She got life, and last I heard, he's still sitting on death row."

"And you never told me . . ."

"Lanna, it was something I wrestled with. We are talking about treason against the government of the United States of America. It could just as easily have been Getty Fairfield taking the fall, and almost certainly I would have gotten dragged in and grilled for weeks regarding my involvement. Those were dangerous times. It felt somehow sleazy, being so close to it all. I was scared and chose to protect you by keeping it to myself. I was paranoid for a long time. At some point I realized it was safe to go on with life, and I did my best to put the whole thing out of my head."

She looked at him. "Why now?"

"That's what I've been sitting here pondering. There might actually be something useful about what I witnessed back then."

"Fairfield and Hitchins?"

"Yes, I think so."

"To help Steven?"

"Yes. Maybe. I don't know just yet."

Lanna stood and took his hand. "I'm interested in hearing it," she said. "But let's go inside where it's warm."

34

IN THE HOURS LEADING UP TO SUNRISE, THEY TALKED strategy. Allan struggled but was able to recall in some detail the case history of the Red Fox and her entanglement with the U.S. government. Rosemary Hitchins had been thirty-one at the time of her arrest, having served in various secretarial capacities over a period of about six years at the Pentagon. She'd been caught in the act of physically passing classified documents to a Russian agent. Based on the recovery of those specific documents, it was speculated that she'd significantly compromised the United States' intelligence community. But there was no definitive way of tallying the actual damage.

The Rosemary Hitchins affair had been among the most scandalous incidents in the past quarter-century of U.S. history. She was an instant cover girl, both because of her infamous acts and her striking physical beauty; thus the nickname. She was born and raised in Madison, Wisconsin, where she had lived with her single mother. She did well in school and put herself through the University of Wisconsin. Desperate for a more glamorous, exciting life, she rode the coattails of her much older boyfriend to New York City in her early twenties. Her looks and her sharp mind opened many doors. Through a network of friends and contacts, she was offered a job in Washington, D.C. Her roundabout journey to the Pentagon was fueled by her lust for adventure.

It was that same lust for adventure that ultimately led her into the arms of a handsome and roguish Russian agent and allowed her to be seduced and manipulated by him. Her treasonous acts had nothing to do with money—none changed hands. It was about love.

Her lover, though, was never identified. The Russian agent

arrested at the fateful exchange was a comrade of his. She was also sleeping with a high-level Pentagon official named Ellis Crabtree, her source for the sensitive data. At the time of her arrest, Crabtree was waiting in the car for her, nervous and fretful. As the FBI descended on the car, Crabtree pulled a snub-nosed pistol from his boot and pressed it to his right temple. Unfortunately for him, a federal agent intervened at the last possible instant, causing the bullet to enter Crabtree's skull but miss his brain by a matter of millimeters. A surgeon saved his life, so that he could spend the next two decades awaiting the chair.

There were books written about her, and a movie of the week. She was a footnote in history books, and any time old spy stories were traded on TV or in college lecture halls or in smoky pubs, inevitably the name of Rosemary Hitchins surfaced.

What fascinated Allan Adler was why Hitchins had never ratted out Getty Fairfield. It had perplexed him seventeen years ago, and sitting there now, the question had lost none of its intrigue. The revelation of their affair would have destroyed Fairfield, as it had Crabtree.

The effect would certainly be equally destructive today.

Whatever the reason, their relationship had remained a secret known only to Fairfield, Hitchins, and, of course, Allan Adler.

And that secret, Allan thought, might just provide enough leverage to save Steven.

PART 2

PART 2

35

QUIETLY AND METHODICALLY A SMALL ARMY OF SNOOPS had been dispatched across the country with strict orders to leave no stone unturned. These were specialists, highly trained in the art of information gathering.

Costas Goodchapel was now a man possessed. The reality of Getty Fairfield's nomination for chief justice had slowly sunk in, and there was a quiet rage building inside him. In the years since Cone Intermedia had first filed suit against Amethyst, Goodchapel had felt very little threat to his empire. Especially since the Supreme Court had been stacked in favor of the right. Another week or two and it would have all been history. Bourgeous would have led the charge, and the conservatives would have handed Amethyst a license to crush the competition.

Fairfield could change all that.

Goodchapel couldn't let that happen. So he'd authorized Ben Clement to take whatever measures necessary to strike down the president's nominee.

Brenner Walsh had retired from Interpol, and now ran his own consulting firm, Pike & Associates. There were offices in L.A., London, Paris, and Hong Kong. Amethyst had a long-standing contract with P & A. Clement got hold of Walsh through the Los Angeles office. They took what was known of Getty Fairfield's career history, dismantled it on paper, broke it down piece by piece, organized it in spreadsheet format, and developed a plan of attack.

Within twenty-four hours, Walsh had his troops on the ground in a half-dozen U.S. cities.

Money was no object. All that mattered was that a legitimate flaw be found in Getty Fairfield, anything of even limited severity. Enough to either cause him to withdraw his name from consideration out of embarrassment or cause the White House to quietly drop him before a scandal had time to erupt. They were to dig deep and dig fast. Time was the enemy.

36

GETTY FAIRFIELD—THE MAN OF THE MOMENT.

He'd gone from lecturing a class full of law school students one moment to literally being the center of a media whirlwind the next. Had he truly understood the immediate shake-up that would hit him, maybe he would've taken at least a few minutes to mull over the president's offer before jumping in with both feet. But now here he was, and there was no turning back the clock, so he was trying his best to enjoy the ride.

They had paraded him all over Washington, with cameras in his face every step of the way. The Supreme Court wasn't as sexy an entity as, say, the White House or the FBI or CIA, but then, never had a potential justice been as camera-ready as Fairfield. Editors from coast to coast were licking their chops to get him on the covers of their magazines. Every senator from the Democratic boat wanted a photo op with him.

By day two he'd already been exhausted. By that first weekend he was running on fumes. It was a far cry from lazy campus life. He'd thought his golden years would be mellow and uneventful.

The hearings before the Senate Judiciary Committee were coming up shortly. Whenever that thought crossed his mind, a second thought was always close on its heels: the current investigation of his past by the FBI and the Justice Department. He just couldn't shake the bad vibes. Why worry, though? He'd already slipped through the cracks back when the heat was *really* on. And there was nothing new now that hadn't been available back then.

Surely there was nothing to worry about. After all, the Red Fox was locked away. Locked away where no one could hear her.

37

THEY STARTED AT THE TOP AND WORKED THEIR WAY DOWN. Fairfield's career was easy to track, given his many years as a public servant. Brenner Walsh had teams in D.C. sniffing around Capitol Hill, the Capitol Building, and the Pentagon. Teams also descended upon the Stanford University campus where Fairfield spent his undergraduate years, NYU Law School, and the districts where he served as appellate court judge.

Fairfield was a Methodist. Any church he'd ever attended on even a semiregular basis was probed in the hopes of discovering something untoward in his past.

Pike & Associates employed some of the finest hackers in the world. Walsh had them plug into the mainframes at the Pentagon. There was little they couldn't find or do with a keyboard and a mouse.

They spent days on it, snooping and sniffing, always on high alert for any morsel of gossip or hearsay, any whisper that they could take and elaborate on until it blossomed into something more substantial.

And eventually they indeed did unearth what they needed to find out about Getty Fairfield.

It was the middle of the afternoon on Tuesday. Ben Clement
had battled a migraine all day, but quickly forgot about it when
the phone rang and he heard the news. He turned on a dime,
leaving a meeting without wasting time on an explanation. He
phoned Goodchapel from his car and said he was on his way to
San Diego.

38

SOMEHOW THEY HAD STUMBLED UPON GWEN PAPPAGEOR-
gio. She lived in an apartment in San Diego, California. She was
once divorced and now had a husband of three years—a UPS
driver named Dimitri.

Clement didn't want her pressed too hard until he got there.
Just contain her, he'd said. *Just don't let her slip away.*

Walsh said he'd wait. Walsh had flown in from L.A. earlier in
the day when his people alerted him to their lead.

Pappageorgio's apartment was located above a small market
that sold only organically grown produce. When the Buick carrying Clement pulled alongside the curb and he hurried out, a
clerk in a green apron was standing outside with a spray bottle,
misting a crate of leafy greens.

Two men in black suits got out of the car and strode alongside Clement. He instructed them to stay near the door and
keep an eye out. Nobody of questionable intent was to enter
the building without authorization from either Clement or
Walsh.

Somebody from Pike & Associates had made the mistake of
getting Gwen Pappageorgio a little spooked, and she'd called her
husband. That one error had complicated matters. Gwen was

seated on a divan, with Dimitri standing near her, his beefy arms folded over his chest. He'd been at work when she had finally reached him and convinced him to hurry home. He was still wearing his UPS uniform—brown shirt and shorts.

Walsh met Clement at the front door, took him by the arm, and led him to a hall bathroom. He closed the door, and leaned in close to speak.

"What a mess," he said.

"What does she know?"

"She's a paralegal for a megafirm here in the city. But she worked for a while in D.C. at the Pentagon, in the secretarial pool. We found her among the payroll records. We were only interested in the time period during which Fairfield was there. Now understand, she did not work with Fairfield, not even in the same office." Walsh paused, and patted a shirt pocket with one hand. He withdrew a pack of skinny cigarettes and lit one.

"Okay, and . . ." Clement prompted.

"And . . . secretaries talk, they gossip. She had a girlfriend she ate lunch with, and smoked with, and drank—"

"Yeah, yeah, okay . . . got it. Go on."

A bit miffed, Walsh plucked the cigarette from his lips and blew smoke at the textured ceiling. "Very well. This girlfriend of hers bragged that she was screwing one of the joint chiefs. She wouldn't name names, but she couldn't keep all the juicy details to herself, either. Pappageorgio didn't believe her at first, of course. But her friend was insistent. Every other day she had a new tale. Her powerful boyfriend was apparently insatiable."

"The boyfriend . . . was Fairfield?"

Walsh tapped ash into the sink basin and shrugged. "For a long time she says she didn't know *who* it might be, if there was any truth to it at all. Then, purely by chance, she happens upon her friend one night in the city, and the friend is with a man—an older man. An isolated incident. They were alone, in Washington, locked in an embrace. She did not approach them. And she never mentioned the sighting to her friend. Now, she claims the man the president has nominated for chief justice is that same man."

"You believe her?" Clement asked, keeping his voice down.

Walsh shrugged again and made a sort of flippant gesture with the hand holding the cigarette, brushing his thumb across his upper lip. "Who's to say?" he said. "She saw him, she didn't see him."

"And what would it mean?"

"Yes, of course—what would it mean? It would mean that Getty Fairfield was an adulterer. Maybe. At that time, yes, he was married, with children, and yet apparently keeping company with a young woman. If their relationship was indeed physical, then we're in luck. No?"

Clement was staring hard at him.

"Is she sure he's the same guy she saw back then?" Clement asked.

"She claims it to be so, yes."

"Okay, so who's the girl?"

Walsh frowned and tapped another quarter-inch of ash into the basin. "That is where it's gotten complicated."

"Complicated how?"

"She got nervous and called her husband—the Greek in the brown shorts in there."

"Yeah, so?"

"He came storming in, threatening my people, threatening to phone the police."

"Why? What had they done?"

Walsh shrugged, looking away from the lawyer for a moment, taking a lingering drag on the cigarette. "Nothing, really. You know, maybe they got a little *pushy*, is all. But she got excited."

"How much had you gotten out of her before her husband got home?"

"Dimitri."

"Whatever."

"Most of it. He shut her up. They slipped away to the back room, and she apparently filled him in. They were back there a while. My men kept the apartment sealed off—no way in, no way out. Anyway, the husband is apparently brighter than he looks."

"How do you mean?"

"He sized us up quickly, realizing we were not federal agents. That complicated things. He could have called the police, of course. But obviously he didn't. He saw an opportunity."

"Money?"

"Yes, of course, money."

"So he shuts her up before she gives up the whole golden goose, and now he wants money for the rest of it?"

Walsh nodded slightly, squinting as a trail of cigarette smoke found its way to his eyes.

"Great . . ." Clement said.

"So you see . . . it's *complicated.*"

"How much does he want?"

Walsh rested his hip against the edge of the bathroom counter. "Actually, he won't say."

"Why?"

"He's waiting for you, actually—someone with authority to make an offer."

"So he can counter it."

"That would be my guess, yes."

"He gave you nothing to work with?"

Walsh shook his head.

"Tell me this," Clement said. "How did you *not* get the girl's name?"

"It happens." Walsh offered a sheepish grin.

"Do you think the husband's a sap?"

"See for yourself."

Walsh followed Clement out the door and down the short hallway to the living room where the Pappageorgios were waiting nervously.

Clement took one look at the two of them and wished that all his opponents in a court of law were so pathetic-looking. He'd be able to rattle their cages in a heartbeat.

Dimitri Pappageorgio was all neck and forearms. He could not have stood five five, Clement guessed with only a cursory assessment. The man stood like a tree stump at the edge of the divan.

"We need to know what your wife knows, sir," Clement said directly and without hesitation, as if he were prepared to break out the handcuffs and take her downtown for questioning.

"What if she don't know nothing?" Pappageorgio said.

"Then we're all out of luck."

"Well, she knows plenty," Pappageorgio said in a sudden shift of tact. "She knows plenty, but it will cost you."

"Okay. What do you want? How much?"

"Cash."

"Okay. How much?"

"No, no. You make an offer to *me.*"

Clement understood that the poor chump didn't want to lowball himself out of a big score. This should be fun, he thought. Just like batting a mouse around a little bit before having it for lunch.

"You've got me in sort of a pickle, sir. I'm just a lawyer, but I could maybe go as high as five hundred dollars."

Dimitri Pappageorgio looked as if he'd been gut shot. Five hundred bucks was certainly not what he'd had in mind. For a moment he looked deflated, then regrouped. He suddenly realized he had nothing to lose by throwing out a number, which played directly into Clement's hands.

"Ten grand, I want ten thousand—*cash!*" Pappageorgio said firmly.

Clement, having expected this, just shrugged.

"Looks like we won't be doing business today, after all," Clement said. "Too rich for my blood." He motioned for his people and all of Walsh's people toward the door. "I apologize for the inconvenience, Mr. and Mrs. Pappageorgio. Sorry to have bothered you. Have a nice afternoon." His back was already turned to them as he marched with his small gang of staff toward the opened door.

Shock set in quickly. Dimitri Pappageorgio's master plan had crumbled at his feet. Easy cash was walking out the door, and no way could he let that happen. Whatever it was that Gwen knew, that these cats wanted, was trivial to him, but he'd gladly give it up for five hundred.

"Hey, hey! Whoa, whoa!" Pappageorgio was waving his arms, desperate to salvage the situation.

Clement ignored him, following his men out the door.

"Hey, hey, hey! Wait! Come on . . ."

Clement paused, then looked back over his shoulder.

"I didn't mean it like *that*," Pappageorgio said, his poker face long gone. "Let's talk this over."

Walsh was already out the door. Clement motioned to him, took him by the elbow, and whispered in his ear for him to wait with his people downstairs. Then Clement shut the front door, leaving himself alone with the husband and wife.

"Okay," Clement said. "I'm listening. But I've got one minute . . . so time's wasting."

"There's no reason to get all excited," Dimitri said, relieved to have calmed the lawyer down. They might just make a few bucks out of this after all! "I was just throwing you a number, you know?"

Clement took a seat on an ottoman. He flashed an impatient smile at them, and said, "Listen, Mr. Pappageorgio, I've got an envelope here with two thousand dollars in it. I'm in no mood to negotiate." He produced a business-size white envelope from a coat pocket and held it out between his pinky and ring fingers. "So let's cut the crap, okay? If your wife tells me what I want to know, the money's yours. Otherwise, I find what I'm after somewhere else. But I've got no time to screw with you today."

Dimitri Pappageorgio fixed his eyes on the white envelope.

This was easy money. He wasn't about to make an idiot of himself and piss it away. He wet his lips with his tongue, then nodded at his wife.

"Tell him," he said.

Gwen looked torn.

Clement fixed her with an expectant look.

She looked at her hands in her lap, nervously shifting on the divan.

"The man on TV," Clement said. "The same man you saw all those years ago, he was with your friend from work, right?"

She nodded hesitantly.

"You understood who he was back then, and you understand who he is now, don't you?"

"Yes."

"They were having an affair, weren't they?"

"I . . . believe so. Yes."

"Who was your friend, Gwen? What was her name?" It was all Clement could do not to pounce forward and shake it out of her.

She had her hands balled in her lap. She cut her eyes toward her husband, and he made a gesture with his eyes, urging her on, giving a slight nod.

"I . . . I never wanted to get in trouble," she said, again looking down at her hands. They were trembling. "I mean, that's why I never said anything, never told a soul. It was just better to keep to myself, to keep my mouth shut. I knew they'd come to me, asking questions, accusing me of being in on it with her, of being a part of it. I was scared, that's all."

"Help me understand, Gwen," Clement said, inching forward on the edge of the ottoman. "Tell me, so that I can understand. Who was your friend?"

Gwen Pappageorgio was growing more and more uncomfortable by the second. She asked Dimitri if he'd go to the kitchen and bring her a glass of water.

Dimitri reluctantly agreed and left the room.

"Everyone was so suspicious," she said, glancing up at Clement. "After they arrested her, you could barely trust anyone. Everybody was nervous. I got so scared. That's why I quit my job and moved to San Diego. I got to where I couldn't watch the news. For a long time after that, I had stomach problems—from the stress, I mean."

Clement, nearing the end of his patience, pressed his palms together as if to pray, and pointed his fingers at her.

In a level, nonthreatening voice, he asked once again, "Gwen, who was she? Who was your friend?"

"I've never told anyone, not my first husband, not even Dimitri. I was afraid it would get out, and I'd be in trouble."

"You'll be fine," he said. "I just need you to tell me her name."

She took a breath, held it, and closed her eyes.

"My friend," she began. "Her name was Rosemary Hitchins."

Five or ten seconds passed in complete dead silence.

Dimitri returned from the kitchen with a glass half-full of water, a single cube of ice bobbing at the surface.

It had taken a few seconds for all the connections in Clement's brain to fall into place, and when they did, he nearly gasped. Chills ran up and down his spine. He met Gwen's eyes.

"Gwen, are you absolutely certain? Are you *positive*?"

She nodded.

"You have to be sure. There can be no doubts here, understand?"

She nodded.

Clement stood and dropped the white envelope on top of the ottoman.

Dimitri snatched it up and leafed through the cash.

"Thank you, Gwen," Clement said. "You've done a good thing."

Gwen put her face in her hands, beginning to sob.

Dimitri ignored his wife's distress, transfixed by the two grand they'd just earned for nothing.

Clement shut the door behind him as he left. Then he stood outside, with his hand still on the doorknob, truly astounded by what he'd just discovered. His luck was unbelievable. This was perhaps the greatest news he'd ever heard.

He could hardly wait to tell Goodchapel.

Fairfield had slept with a Russian spy. And not just any spy.

The tables had turned. Suddenly, they were back in the game.

39

THE PRIVATE JET TAXIED ONTO A RUNWAY, AND WAS QUICKLY airborne. Ben Clement threw his coat over a leather seat and loosened his tie in his shirt collar. He was ecstatic. In his mind he was already thinking three or four steps ahead. If Gwen Pappageorgio was on the level, the news would rock Washington. Fairfield would be plunged into ruin, and the White House would look like fools.

What a beautiful day to be a lawyer, Clement mused.

If what she'd described was in fact the real deal, it would be up to himself and Goodchapel to compose a strategy for how best to leak the news. But first, the claim had to be verified.

They had to find Rosemary Hitchins and get her to talk.

He dialed the number for Goodchapel's home office. Voice mail picked up. So he tried Goodchapel's cell phone, and Costas picked up on the second ring.

"Good news?" Goodchapel asked.

Clement could tell that his employer was outside, probably on one of the half-dozen decks that extended from the back of the mansion, overlooking Puget Sound.

"You wouldn't believe it if you read it in a book. Stranger than fiction," Clement said with glee.

"What'd you find?"

"Fairfield had a mistress."

"When?"

"At the Pentagon."

"Perfect!"

"Oh, believe me, Costas, you don't know the half of it."

"I'm listening."

"Costas, he was screwing a Russian spy." Clement couldn't keep the smile off his face.

"You cannot be serious."

"God's honest truth. Just get ready to celebrate. The White House is sitting on a time bomb, and they don't even know it."

40

MARCEL ULON WAS SCANDINAVIAN. HE WAS SIX ONE AND lean, with a strong jawline, and long, straight blond hair he kept fixed in a ponytail. He had trained at one of the finest culinary schools in Denmark and had used that education to gain employment as head chef at the home of Costas Goodchapel, one of the wealthiest men in the world.

It was easy work with outstanding pay. The only real drawback was that the position was so low profile; there was little or no recognition for the exquisite work he did on a daily basis. He felt his soul dying a little more every day. But it was just so hard to walk away from the money.

For the past six years he'd wasted his immense skills toiling in obscurity, cooking mainly for Goodchapel and the rest of the staff at the mansion. He could have worked in New York or London or Paris for half the pay and a thousand times the glory.

But glory alone bought few of the luxuries he'd come to enjoy.

For a time, early on in his employment with Goodchapel, he'd resided in staff quarters on the basement level of the mansion. But soon he desired his own space and rented a town house a short drive from work. He was a fitness fanatic who spent much of his off-hours toning his body and tending a small herb garden he'd cultivated on the terrace of his town house. There was a superb outdoor market within walking distance of his front door, and one of his greatest joys in life was to spend hours sorting through the moist bushels in search of the most splendid produce for his personal kitchen.

It was at this outdoor market that representatives of Cone Intermedia had first approached him, eighteen months ago, with an offer he couldn't refuse.

They needed his help, they said. And they were willing to pay generously for it.

How much, exactly? Marcel had asked straightaway.

The number they mentioned had left him speechless. He would finally have the opportunity to leave Goodchapel forever and live the life he'd dreamed of since culinary school.

But not just yet. It would take time and patience.

They needed him to be their eyes and ears. He would be paid a regular fee; then, when and if he delivered the ultimate scoop, the big payday would arrive.

The temptation was too great. He would take the money, do what he must, and end his wasted years.

Once he was on board, they furnished him with the necessary hardware and taught him how to use it. It was basic surveillance. He spent weeks choosing the spots in the mansion to plant bugs, and did so stealthily. In the kitchen, he mounted a device beneath a refrigeration unit that relayed audio transmissions to a personal computer located in his town house.

For the past year and a half, his evenings had mainly consisted of sitting at home at the PC, a set of headphones over his ears, scanning through telephone conversations using special software.

Occasionally there'd be something worth passing on to his contacts at Cone Intermedia. But rarely.

Today, that all changed.

After lunch he made a stop at the outdoor market, purchased some fish fillets, and returned home for an hour or two to work on a menu for dinner at the mansion. As he often did while scribbling in his daily planner at the kitchen counter, he popped on the headphones for a quick listen.

He was using his favorite gold-nib fountain pen, marking down the ingredients he'd need for an elaborate cream sauce. As he wrote and listened, his eyes drifted from the page, his pen trailing off at an angle. His mouth hung open for a moment. He could hardly believe what he was hearing. Today was the day.

He did not hesitate. Leaving things at the table as they were, he headed for the front door, taking his bicycle with him on his way out. He pedaled as hard and fast as he could, rounding the block, shooting across traffic, ignoring traffic lights.

Up ahead was a row of pay phones. He dropped his bicycle to the ground with a clatter and hurried over, quickly dialing the number he'd memorized months ago. They had warned him of the dangers of calling from home or even using his own cell phone.

He breathlessly summarized the recorded conversation between Costas Goodchapel and attorney Ben Clement regarding a woman named Rosemary Hitchins. He then hung up the phone, hands shaking.

He'd done it! He was so happy he wanted to cry. For so long it had seemed this day would never come.

Yes, he was a traitor, but that was something he could live with.

He picked his bicycle off the ground and walked it back the way he'd come, his hands still shaking.

41

NOTHING EVER TOTALLY SHOCKED ANWAR CLAUSSEN ANY-more. *Nothing.* In his career he'd seen everything. He'd seen the best possible situation go south in the blink of an eye, and vice versa.

In a court of law both sides were bloodthirsty, and rarely was one or the other unwilling to step over the line if they could get away with it. Personally, he'd learned long ago to park his ethics at the door.

So he certainly wasn't shocked at the news from Cone Intermedia's intelligence outfit. In fact, Claussen had to tip his hat to Goodchapel. It was dirty pool but well played. Claussen strongly doubted the validity of the allegation but what an astounding premise. Fairfield had had an affair with an infamous Russian spy? The Red Fox?

But if there was even an ounce of truth to it, and if it could be proved, it would be the deathblow to Fairfield's nomination. And truth or fiction, it would have to be squashed before it even got out of the gate. CI and the White House had to take decisive action. Drastic steps were needed. There wasn't time to sit around and scheme.

He was immediately on the horn, putting corrective measures in motion. He had to plug the leaks. Amethyst had to be stopped.

42

THE JAGUAR PULLED BENEATH THE PORTICO, AND BEN CLEMent hurried up the walkway toward the door of the mansion. He was startled to find Costas Goodchapel outside waiting for him.

Clement offered a sly grin.

"We found the needle in the haystack," Clement said.

"Do you believe the woman?"

"Honestly, I do," Clement said.

The day was cool but pleasant, sunny with a mottling of clouds against the pale blue sky. Clement heard the distant hum of mowers trimming the lawn, and the light, fresh smell of cut grass was in the air.

Goodchapel felt reinvigorated. It was not in his nature to leave a challenge unmet. And he never underestimated a threat. CI had taken swings at him for years now, but this was the first time they'd come so dangerously close to actually landing a blow. He wouldn't sit still and take it.

"What do you recommend now?" Goodchapel asked. "Talk from your gut."

They were standing on the stone walkway, surrounded by immaculate landscaping and lush foliage. Small birds flitted among the thistles and branches. It was a perfect place to sit alone and ponder, and Clement had to assume that Goodchapel did that quite often. The man was brilliant and innovative, and was serenely and singularly self-confident. Nothing in Costas Goodchapel's world happened by accident. He was a man of calculation and purpose, and when he asked for an opinion, he was by no means asking to be patronized. He was interested only in results.

"We must be cautious," Clement said, looking away contemplatively. "This could certainly prove to be the straw that breaks the camel's back. But the situation must be navigated with the utmost delicacy. We must act with speed and precision."

"Why not leak the Rosemary Hitchins angle now, and let them deal with it in Washington?"

Clement shook his head. "Not a good idea."

"But all we need is to cast a shadow over Fairfield."

"Wrong. If it proves to be untrue, the Democrats will cry slander. And that would hurt us more than help. Besides, what could be better than having Rosemary Hitchins in the flesh, claiming to have had an affair with Fairfield?"

Clement folded his arms over his chest, focusing on Goodchapel. "Let's keep a lid on this. Time is the big enemy. We've already found her, and I'm on a plane in ten minutes."

"What if she won't talk?"

"Let's deal with that when the time comes."

"What if she denies an affair?"

"Every inmate has a price," Clement said at last. Then he added: "Everybody has something they want or need, and they're willing to say or do just about anything to get it. Trust me, whether or not Rosemary Hitchins has ever laid eyes on Getty Fairfield, she has nothing to lose by making a fuss. Remember, the truth is basically irrelevant. What matters is which side puts on the best show."

43

HE WAS KNOWN ON THE STREET AS FABIAN. HE WAS STRICTLY a low-tech operator. He'd been paid cash and told to do the job quietly and get out. Fabian was given only the apartment address and a brief description of the targets. Late that afternoon he found the produce market and waited across the street with a slice of pizza and a beer. Then he made his move.

The stairs led to a landing, with doors on either side. He knocked at the door. After a minute, the door opened against its chain.

"Rudy here?" he asked, peering in at the partially obscured face.

Gwen Pappageorgio gave him a suspicious look.

"Wrong apartment, now leave me alone," she said, and bolted the door.

He'd been told a husband and wife lived there. He went back down the stairs and waited across the street in the door of a record shop.

Dimitri had returned to work after the incident with the lawyer. Gwen apparently couldn't sit still. She left with her purse, perhaps going out for a drink to unwind.

Fabian watched her pass in front of the market and disappear among the foot traffic on the sidewalk. He slipped up the stairs and sidled up next to the door.

From a pocket of his jeans he produced a modified flat-head screwdriver. He punched it into the keyhole, squirreled it around, then gave the screwdriver handle a practiced twist. In seconds he was standing inside the apartment with the door closed behind him.

A lamp was on in the living room, but besides that all lights were off. He moved through the shadows, eventually ducking into the hall bathroom, taking cover behind the door, where he could watch through the gap between the hinges.

He didn't have to wait long.

In less than an hour, Gwen Pappageorgio returned home. She turned on a light and got something from the fridge.

Fabian could hear the TV. He waited.

Gwen fell asleep on the divan with the TV on. She had only dozed, really, and soon awoke, hungry. The day had exhausted her.

She was squatting in the open door of the refrigerator, taking inventory of the lower shelves, when a hand from behind her covered her mouth, followed by a sharp pain at the back of her neck. The pain was blindingly intense. Then she thought she heard a grotesque crackling sound, then a quick pop. Then she felt nothing at all. Her life was over.

The knife blade had severed her spine. When her body stopped twitching, Fabian jerked the blade free from the base of her neck and wiped it clean on the fabric of her blouse.

He took her under the arms and dragged her body to a closet in the bedroom, covering her with a blanket from a shelf above the clothes.

In the front room he turned off the TV, killed the lights, and made sure the front door was locked.

Dimitri Pappageorgio returned home late that afternoon. He worked long hours delivering parcels, and customarily stopped off for a beer or two before calling it a day. He wasn't drunk when he got home, but the liquor slowed his reflexes. It would be just enough to cost him his life.

He fumbled with his key, got inside, and fumbled for the light switch.

Fabian pounced. He slashed the blade across Dimitri's throat. Dimitri struggled briefly, then went down on both knees. Lying on his back, bleeding to death, suffocating, he gazed up at the thin white man standing over him. The man was holding a pillow from the divan, which he proceeded to press over Dimitri's face.

Dimitri's body was heaped on that of his wife in the bedroom closet.

Fabian tidied up, made sure the lights were out, and used Dimitri's key to lock the door behind him. He paused on the street corner to light a cigarette. He dropped the apartment key into a trash receptacle along the sidewalk and casually made his way into the anonymity of the bustling city.

44

EVERYBODY, IT SEEMED, HAD SOMETHING TO LOSE.

The president. The Democrats on Capitol Hill. Cone Intermedia. Amethyst. Getty Fairfield.

Everybody, with the possible exception of Franklin Henbest. His fifteen million was safely tucked away halfway around the world, and win, lose, or draw, nobody could touch it. But there was a white-hot spotlight on him right now, and he was sweating, desperate to find a way out of the situation.

He had brought Fairfield to the president's attention, so it was up to him to bail out the president by making sure nothing ever developed from this Hitchins rumor.

News of the Red Fox had hit him like a brick to the head. Lipscomb had phoned him in a panic, relaying a message from Anwar Claussen. Claussen was in D.C., scrambling to patch leaks. His sources had picked up on the Gwen Pappageorgio situation, and they'd arranged for her and her husband to be disposed of. Any and every link to Rosemary Hitchins had to be eliminated.

Every hour that passed put them a step behind Costas Goodchapel and his forces. Goodchapel had the resources to move mountains.

They knew that Rosemary Hitchins was locked away, but for the moment he couldn't be sure that Pappageorgio's tale was anything but fiction. After all, she'd been offered cash for her story. All the excitement might prove premature. But until there was a definitive confirmation of an affair between Fairfield and the Red Fox, Henbest had to move forward as if the world were coming to an end.

The only logical move was to confront Fairfield himself.

If there was any substance to the allegations, Fairfield needed to come clean about it to those closest to him.

An emergency meeting had been called at the White House. Henbest had personally phoned the president. The president came unglued. Not only would he lose his shot at nominating a left-wing chief justice, the odds of his seeing reelection in a year would simply evaporate. It had the makings of a scandal that would haunt him beyond the grave.

Henbest went into damage-control mode. He suggested they get Fairfield alone, put him in the hot seat, and pry the truth out of him.

The president simmered down and agreed to the meeting. And now Senator Henbest was on his way to the White House, unsure what to expect but wise enough to expect the worst.

His driver slowed the car on Pennsylvania Avenue and turned into the drive, stopping at a security post. Secret Service personnel did their job, then quickly sent the car on its way, waving it through.

There was naturally a degree of guilt involved in what Henbest had done. But only because he'd abused his relationship with his cousin. The president had trusted him, and the senator had taken that trust and soiled it for personal gain. By doing so he'd placed the president's head on the block.

It was now his full intention, though, to salvage what he could. After all, the facts were still largely unknown. There might very well be nothing to the rumor. Fairfield might waltz in, blatantly deny it, and it could all blow away like a bad dream. But something in his gut told him he was in for a rude awakening.

The president was in his private study, and Henbest was immediately sent in. The president had had ample time for his anger to build, but also to size up the situation.

"Franklin, you've put me in a tight spot," the president said, a little coldly. "You marched in here last week singing Fairfield's praises like he was the Second Coming, and I took a leap of faith based on that."

"Don't count him out just yet," Henbest said. "You know

how these games are played. The Republicans are desperate. This is an act of desperation."

The president turned away, pushing his hands through his graying hair. He shook his head. "It was a mistake listening to you, Franklin."

"They're provoking you. That's their job. Your job is to make the big decisions, to look ahead and do what's right for the country. Nominating Fairfield was a brilliant strategic move—I still firmly believe that."

There was a call for the president.

"Fine. Show him in," the president said, then looked at Henbest and motioned toward the door.

Getty Fairfield was standing in the Oval Office, waiting nervously.

The door opened quietly, and Henbest followed the president into the Oval Office.

"Getty . . ." the president said, cordially. "I appreciate your promptness." He offered his hand, and with the other, clapped Fairfield on the shoulder.

Fairfield next shook hands with Senator Henbest. Then Henbest backed away, taking up position behind a wing chair, placing his hands on the back of it.

The president sat on the front edge of his desk and folded his arms over his chest. He nodded at a couch. "Have a seat."

Fairfield quickly gauged the atmosphere in the room. The two men facing him—his biggest allies and supporters over the past week—now wore expressions of concern and apprehension. He took a seat on the couch, bracing himself for whatever was coming.

Outside, a mild breeze was stirring the branches of trees. The rosebushes looked dazzling in the late afternoon sunshine. Soon enough, the sun would fade and long shadows would fall across the lawn.

The president's sudden frostiness toward him was unsettling, and he could think of only one reason for it. But surely they

couldn't know. After seventeen years, why now? Fairfield stead-
ied himself, determined to stay levelheaded. He was being paranoid. Whichever the case, he would know soon enough.

"Getty," the president said. "Let me get straight to the point."

"Of course."

"Something rather disturbing has come to my attention. It's
rather off-the-wall, and my first inclination is to dismiss it right
out of hand. But because of its severity, and because of the potential ramifications, I have no choice but to pursue it until I
know the truth. For the time being, I'm treating this report as
rumor. I've called you here this afternoon because I believe you
can clear up the confusion."

"I will certainly help in any way I can," Fairfield said.

The president cleared his throat, then continued, "What can
you tell us about a woman named Rosemary Hitchins?"

It was a moment of both complete release and unbridled ter-
ror. There was no more hiding, no more pretending. He wondered
how they'd found out. How much did they know, actually? His
head was swimming. A thousand separate emotions clashed in a
storm inside him. For so long now he'd thought he had outrun it.

Still, perhaps they were merely fishing. The worst thing he
could do right out of the gate was reveal the full hand he was
holding. He had no way of knowing if they'd seen his cards, so he
had to proceed as if they were only speculating.

At last, Fairfield pursed his lips and asked, "Why?"

"You can do better than that," the president growled.

"Okay," he responded evenly. "The spy. Of course I remember. But I don't see how—"

"Did you have a relationship with her?" Henbest snapped,
cutting him off.

"And what would make you think—"

"Just answer the question."

"Am I being accused of something?"

Both the president and Henbest were watching closely, losing
patience.

Fairfield considered their line of questioning for a moment. "Where is this coming from?" he asked.

"Did you sleep with her?" Henbest again. Fairfield was stalling, dodging the question.

Fairfield flinched, not a lot, but noticeably. He looked to the president for a little moral support against the senator but didn't find any.

"It's best if we know the facts, Getty. Whether something happened or didn't happen, you need to let us in on it," the president said. "Because that allows us to act accordingly. Understand?"

Fairfield nodded.

"Good." The president eased around the end of his desk so that he was facing out the window of the Oval Office. His face was backlit by waning afternoon sunshine and dappled with shadows. "Allegations are beginning to circulate that you had a physical relationship with her. Getty, if there is even an *ounce* of substance to this, I want to know."

Fairfield was seated with his back against the couch, one leg elegantly crossed over the other, his hands at his sides. Every instinct told him to continue evasive maneuvers, to duck and hide. His instincts pleaded with him to hold the words inside his mouth, to swallow them back before his tongue had a chance to let them out into the world.

What infuriated him was that he'd done nothing illegal. Yes, he'd been an adulterer, but not a traitor. He'd actually not suspected anything of her until late in their relationship, at which time he broke it off. But none of that mattered. They would crucify him. His only hope was to ally himself with someone with the power and influence to at least attempt a cover-up. With the president in his corner, he could keep up the facade. He knew this was now in the best interest of the White House. After all, the notion that the sitting chief executive had nominated an individual to the Court who'd had an illicit affair with a traitor to national security would almost certainly crush the current administration.

He was cornered. All of them were cornered.

Fairfield sighed. "Very well. Yes, I had a brief relationship with that woman."

The president closed his eyes and shook his head.

Henbest clenched his jaw, banging his fist against his leg.

"Do you have any idea the position you've placed me in?" the president hissed.

"You've jeopardized this entire administration!" Henbest interjected.

"It was just such a long—"

"*Enough!*" The president turned from the windows, fuming.

"What did you tell her?" Henbest asked. "How much did you give away?"

"Absolutely nothing."

"How long did it last?"

"Not . . . not long. Perhaps five or six months."

Henbest mumbled to himself, "Might as well have been a decade."

"How and when were you able to see her?" the president asked.

Fairfield shrugged. "Usually we'd stay in at her apartment."

"How do you know no one ever saw you?"

"I was careful. Besides, it's a big city."

"And the two of you were always alone?"

"Of course."

"How do you know she didn't confide in her friends or family?"

"I guess I trusted her."

"We already know of at least one person she told," Henbest said bluntly.

Fairfield flinched.

"Why didn't she rat you out when they caught her?" the president asked.

"Honestly, I don't know. Other than the fact that it wouldn't have helped her. They had caught her red-handed with Crabtree, and maybe she just didn't see the need to drag me down with them. I've never really understood it myself."

"It never occurred to you what she might be after?"

"I was head-over-heels. You wouldn't believe the things she was willing to do in the bedroom. At those moments, gentlemen, the furthest thing from my mind was national security."

"Could there be anyone else with knowledge of the relationship? One mouth has already been silenced. So that leaves yourself and Hitchins," the president said.

Fairfield shook his head. "We were rarely in public together. I was married, remember."

Suddenly his stomach dropped. A face from the past flashed onto the screen in his mind's eye. For the moment he couldn't recall a name, but the face was fairly clear.

His driver at the Pentagon.

That was the only conceivable remaining tie to the affair. Would it do him any good to broach the subject? Would it do any further harm to keep it to himself? For the time being, he held his tongue. It happened so long ago, and his driver had been just some lowly staff sergeant.

Both the other men in the room noted the slight contemplative shift in Fairfield's expression.

"Don't even *think* of holding back on us," Henbest prompted. "If you know something, now is the time to lay it all out on the table. Now is when we can help you—not later."

"No. I swear, I've told you everything I remember." His tone was unconvincing.

Henbest and the president exchanged skeptical glances.

The president settled in behind his desk. He glared hard at Fairfield for a long moment, then said, "Avoid the press for the next few days." The president busied himself with paperwork on his desk, signing his name like mad. He didn't look up as he finished with Fairfield. "By then things will have been dealt with, and the storm should have blown over. Senator Henbest will see to that."

So be it, Henbest decided, my money is sitting pretty, safe and sound across the Atlantic.

The president shoved documents out of his way. "We're done here, Getty," he said with a dismissive wave of his hand.

Shaken and reeling, Fairfield rose to his feet and strode to the door.

With the door shut, Henbest approached the president's desk.

Without looking up, the president growled, "This is your mess, Senator—clean it up."

"I'm on it," Henbest said.

45

THE LINCOLN TURNED ONTO PENNSYLVANIA AVENUE AND fell into the sluggish ebb and flow of traffic. Senator Henbest was tired from the day but had hours of work still ahead of him. In the backseat of the car he closed his eyes for a few short moments, hoping to recharge his batteries.

He had to get hold of Lipscomb. Lipscomb took care of the dirty work that the senator couldn't get near. As the car sputtered from light to light, he pulled his cell phone from a coat pocket and dialed Lipscomb's number.

Two car lengths behind the Lincoln sat Senator Les Faulkenberry in a green Saturn hatchback. The car belonged to a member of his staff—it was discreet camouflage for a senator. He had stalked Senator Henbest halfway across Capitol Hill earlier in the afternoon and followed him to the White House, where he parked and waited a half a block away, within view of the drive turning in to the gate. He had sat hunched over the wheel, glassing the driveway with a pair of collapsible binoculars. When the Lincoln pulled into traffic, Faulkenberry resumed his pursuit.

He was doing his best to stay close to Henbest, to catalog his every movement, because something significant was afoot. He was itching to know what was going on. Faulkenberry didn't like being kept out of the loop. But if something worthwhile fell into his lap, maybe Clement would start treating him like a U.S. senator instead of some low-tier errand boy.

He changed lanes, maneuvering the small car until he had a visual of Henbest in the backseat of the Lincoln. Henbest was on the phone.

There was nothing he could do now but stick tight to him and hope something came of his effort. He desperately wanted to phone Clement, but Clement wanted results, and Faulkenberry had nothing to offer. So he sat in traffic, scooting along a few feet at a time, with his window down, smelling exhaust fumes.

46

ROWAN LIPSCOMB ENJOYED HIS WORK. IT AFFORDED HIM tremendous freedom. He had a reputation in the city's underground, and those with the need to hire him for whatever the reason (lawyers, PIs, thugs, etc.) knew how to reach him. He was on call day and night, but for the most part he could come and go as he pleased. Senator Henbest was his primary source of income and could be a demanding boss and expected results, but Lipscomb had worked for worse for a lot less money.

His paycheck came from a variety of sources—nothing out of

the senator's own pocket, though. And that was the beauty of the arrangement. Lipscomb could pretty well ask for what he wanted, and the senator rarely put up much of a fuss. Some of that came from campaign funds, and some from backdoor lobbyists and PACs. And a lot came in the form of contributions from private donors. It was soft money that found its way in and magically remained unaccounted for. He was not an official member of the senator's staff, and if he were ever taken down for whatever reason, he was essentially on his own. But the benefits outweighed any drawbacks. Most of the time Lipscomb actually did very little at all. The flexibility of his employment arrangement allowed him to pursue other interests.

But now Henbest was asking for a lot. He wanted a woman out of the picture. And not just any woman, but one who was incarcerated in a federal prison. This was a job he'd have to contract out. So now he was on the road, on his way to meet with a couple of characters he hadn't encountered in quite some time.

Baltimore wasn't his favorite place in the world, but that was where he'd have to go find the Brothers. Patton and Metcalf were as capable as anyone of finding a way to Rosemary Hitchins. But they didn't come cheap.

They were popular with the Russian Mafia. That's how Lipscomb first ran into them, in a deal bringing over opium on a freightliner from Afghanistan.

By his second pack of Camels, he could vaguely make out the Baltimore skyline on the distant horizon. He reached over and dropped open the glove compartment. His Ruger automatic was inside beneath his vehicle registration. These guys made him nervous.

He picked an exit, and the car roared up the ramp to a red light.

Because they weren't available by phone, he had to track them down one step at a time. You had to have a history with them; otherwise they were like ghosts. They weren't easy to find, but they were certainly worth the effort.

An old pal name R.J. owned an S & M shop not far from a railway depot. Lipscomb hadn't been around there in two or three years at best, but the area hadn't changed much. He parked by a telephone pole and crossed a weedy lot to a street that ran through a decaying business district. A few kids in hooded sweatshirts watched him stalk down the sidewalk. His Ruger was tucked down the back of his pants, and periodically he'd reach a hand back just to feel that it was there.

R.J.'s shop was aptly named The Whipping Post. It was in the basement, accessed through a low door in a narrow alleyway pinched between two brick buildings. Narrow stairs descended between gritty walls, a musty stench growing stronger the farther you sank into the depths. At a landing at the base of the steps was a second door, this one to your left. Immediately beyond this door Lipscomb found himself bathed in a pungent smell—a hefty mixture of sweat and rubbing oils.

On his way in, a young woman and a male companion brushed past him on their way out the door. She had a thick bolt through her lower lip, and her boyfriend wore more eye makeup than a hooker. He'd once dated a girl who was into S & M, and he hadn't been too impressed.

On the walls were racks loaded with merchandise—all breeds of buckles and straps and whips and other paraphernalia, most of it laced with wicked-looking metal points or brass studs. Display mannequins had been arranged in all manner of out-landish sexual poses, each of them fully outfitted in grotesque leather gear. They were visible throughout the shop, and just the sight of them gave him mental flashbacks of his short time with Ella, the girl with the fetish.

The woman behind the counter had a red-colored contact lens in one eye.

Freak, he thought.

"Looking for somethin'?" The red eye was glaring at him.

"R.J. Is he around?"

"He's on the phone, man," she said, apparently bored to tears.

"Would you tell him Rowan Lipscomb is here to talk to him?"

"Whatever." She disappeared through a side door, leaving him to stare at the gadgets under the glass.

"Rowan . . ."

Lipscomb turned to see R.J. standing in the side door.

"Come on back."

He followed R.J. through a dark hall to a small office. R.J. wore a silk shirt unbuttoned to his navel. His hair was too long and gelled to a sheen.

"Long time no see," R.J. said, picking a smoldering cigarette butt from a cheap ashtray.

"Yeah. How's business?"

"No shortage of kinky inbreeds out there, know what I'm sayin'?"

Lipscomb nodded.

"What brings you to Baltimore?"

"Business."

"Yeah?"

Lipscomb shrugged. "Yeah."

"What's the play?"

"Nothing you'd be interested in."

"Never know."

"I'm looking for Mick Costaldi."

"Yeah?"

"Yeah."

R.J. squinted as he pulled on the cigarette. "Mick comes through now and then."

"I figured as much. That's why I came to see you first. Mick's not so easy to find."

"What's Mick got that you want?"

"Like I said, it's business."

"Right, sure. Business."

Lipscomb could only imagine the viruses coursing through that man's veins. Lipscomb was no puritan, but R.J. was a vile creature who dwelt in a vile underworld.

"So can you help me or not?"

"We're old friends, right? I'd never turn away a friend in need."

Lipscomb produced a fifty, folded it in half, and stood it on the desk like a little tent.

R.J. pulled open a desk drawer and slapped a matchbook onto the desktop. Then scribbled something on the backside.

"You can usually find him there," he said, flicking the matchbook across the desk.

A phone number was handwritten in a sloppy scrawl.

"You didn't get that number from me," R.J. said, crushing out the remains of the cigarette.

"Sure." Lipscomb stood and turned for the door.

"Gone so soon?"

Lipscomb nodded.

"You should hang around awhile," R.J. said, sliding around his desk. "I'd introduce you to Paige out there."

"The girl at the counter?"

"Hell yeah!"

"I'll pass."

47

LIPSCOMB CROSSED THE WEEDY LOT BACK TO HIS CAR. HE whipped out his cell phone, dialed the number, and waited.

The phone rang twelve times without answer. And no machine picked up. It occurred to him that R.J. had just been screwing with him. But R.J. was generally on the level.

He dialed again, letting it ring forever.

Still no answer.

He leaned against the hood of the car. He had neither the energy nor the desire to march back over to R.J.'s shop. The sky was quickly darkening; shades of deep orange and purple bruised the horizon over the cityscape. He was losing daylight in a hurry, and that wasn't good. It meant he was getting nowhere fast. Senator Henbest wanted results, and the senator was not a patient man. A lot was riding on finding Patton and Metcalf as soon as humanly possible.

He unlocked the car door and slid in behind the wheel. Without Mick Costaldi, the trail ended here. It was too late to change direction and follow some other plan. He dialed the number again, and again let it ring for an eternity.

Someone answered, snapping at the phone, "What?"

Lipscomb sat up, startled. He nearly fumbled the phone. It was a woman's voice, and she sounded husky and more than a little scary.

"Who's this?" he asked finally.

"Who's askin'?"

"I'm looking for Mick."

"Mick's not around."

"I'm an old friend."

"You got a name or what?"

"Lipscomb. My name's Lipscomb. I need to find Mick."

He heard a muffled sound, like she'd put her hand over the phone, and then what sounded like shuffling or moving about in the room, and the distant clash of voices.

Then suddenly she was back. "What do you want with Mick?"

"It's business."

"Yeah, well, he's gonna want to know."

"Tell him I'm looking for the Brothers. He'll understand. And tell him it's urgent. Tell him I need to find them tonight." A major downside of associating with this sort of underworld was that everybody was steeped in acute paranoia. They assumed everybody was a fed. That was the only reliable policy. It often took years to build a reputation, and even then trust was a very fragile commodity.

He suspected Costaldi was there next to her, listening in and debating whether Lipscomb was clean. There was additional muffled conversation; then she was back on the line.

"How'd you get this number?" she asked accusingly.

"A friend of a friend."

"Give me your number."

He told her.

The line went dead.

So here he was, sitting in his car in a nearly forgotten section of Baltimore, having to wait for a call. He'd be pissed beyond words if Costaldi left him hanging out to dry. But what choice did he have? Mick Costaldi was his link to the Brothers.

He started his car. He began cruising the neighborhood, just to keep moving. Nearly fourteen minutes had passed when his cell phone chirped from the passenger seat. He pressed Talk and put it to his face.

"Mick?"

"You tell R.J. I'm gonna nail his balls to the wall. He knows better than to spread my number around."

"Yeah, next time I'm over that way, I'll be sure he knows. But it was just a favor to me."

"Whatever. You familiar with the shipyards?"

"Sure."

Costaldi rattled off an address and told him to be there in forty-five minutes. Lipscomb did a U-turn and sped back in the opposite direction.

He knew the road. Much of the trafficking he'd been involved with over the years had passed through these same shipyards.

Ships stood in the water, their rusting hulls high in the air, glinting in his passing headlights. The warehouses were motley-looking at night. He parked a few hundred feet away from the one he was looking for and approached on foot. He checked that his Ruger was loaded.

A late-model Chevy Nova was parked on a gravel strip beneath a floodlight. A gangway led to a door in the side of the sheet metal building. He tested the doorknob. It was unlocked. He opened the door, and beyond it was complete darkness save for a faint moon glow coming through a series of small high windows near the ceiling. His footsteps echoed on the slab floor. He felt along the wall for a light switch.

He heard a footstep that wasn't his, then felt the distinct sensation of a gun barrel pressed to the back of his head.

"Welcome to Baltimore." Mick Costaldi sounded different in person than he had on the phone. He sounded congested, like he had a severe head cold.

"Step back toward the door where I can see you better, Rowan. And open it."

Outside in better light, Costaldi held the gun to Lipscomb's head and patted him down, running a hand up and down the inside of his legs. Lipscomb winced when the Ruger was removed from his waistband.

"I *like*, I *like*," Costaldi said, turning the Ruger over in his hand. "You came packing, eh? Can't say that I blame you, but I gotta keep it for now. The Brothers wouldn't appreciate you carrying a piece like this to meet them. Might give the wrong impression."

Lipscomb swallowed hard.

With the pat down complete, Costaldi lowered his own gun and clapped him on the back. "Just procedure, you know."

"Sure. So, the Brothers in town? I've got a rush job for them. I need them ready to roll tonight."

"Cash? Up front?"

Lipscomb nodded. "Big payday."

"You bring it?"

Lipscomb hooked a thumb in the direction of his car.

"Let's have a look, then," Costaldi said.

The money was in the trunk of Lipscomb's car. Nice tight bundles of thousand-dollar bills stacked in a waterproof metal case.

"Sweet," Costaldi said.

It was astounding how large sums of cash could materialize in Washington, D.C., Lipscomb thought. If Capitol Hill ever got serious about clamping down on soft money, so little of the dirty work of politics would ever get done.

Costaldi fastened the snaps on the metal case and jerked it out of Lipscomb's car. "I'll be keeping an eye on that from now on," he said, quickly stashing the cache of pirated currency into the trunk of his Nova. "Follow me out with your car, and try to keep up. I've already called the Brothers. They're waiting on us."

48

EVERYBODY CALLED THEM THE BROTHERS AS SORT OF A JOKE. It started in prison. That's where they met. And that's where Mick Costaldi met them.

Legend had it that Costaldi had foiled an attempt by another group of inmates to ambush the Brothers and had thus gained their trust. So now he was one of the few able to make contact with them. He assessed offers for work, winnowed out the less promising, and in return took a cut from every job. He made enough to live the way he wanted, hadn't pulled down an honest paycheck in over a decade, and had never in his life had a bank account of any sort. He didn't have many needs aside from booze, drugs, and women. His one advantage in an otherwise inept life was his link to the Brothers.

Lipscomb kept his eyes on the Nova's taillights. The road followed the water's edge. The sea was surprisingly still. Moonlight swam across the glassy ripples.

The Nova followed a gentle curve to the left. He saw a pier. It jutted out from shore, standing in the Atlantic. The road sloped rather generously.

The Nova parked and Lipscomb pulled up alongside. They were facing the water. The sky had darkened so that there was no discernible horizon. The Nova's headlights flashed off and on three times quickly. Then the driver-side door opened, and Costaldi motioned to him.

They moved along wordlessly. Lipscomb could feel the tiny hairs on the back of his neck standing on end. They reached the planked causeway that extended out for the entire length of the pier.

"Stay here," Costaldi said.

Lipscomb nodded.

Costaldi went on ahead. When he'd neared the far end of the wood pier, a point of light blinked on and off just once in the distance amid the black water. Costaldi waved an arm back and forth, signaling out, then stood and waited.

Soon he could see movement in the water just beyond where Costaldi was standing. Then a sleek watercraft appeared. Lipscomb strained to see more. Costaldi was pointing and gesturing. The tide was lapping against the hulls of the boats, rocking them gently.

Finally, Costaldi turned and gestured at him.

He came up next to Costaldi.

There in a yellow and white fiberglass speedboat were Patton and Metcalf, the Brothers.

"The money is acceptable," Costaldi said. "But they want to hear details."

"Okay . . . right . . . sure."

"I told them you needed them to be ready to travel tonight."

Lipscomb nodded.

"Is the job hot or cold?" Patton spoke up from the stern of the boat.

"Hot," Lipscomb said, meaning it was a kill job.

Then Patton said, "Leave your car. Get in the boat."

He felt a swell of relief.

Metcalf gunned the throttle and the front of the boat rose out of the water as they sliced across the incoming tide. Lipscomb turned to look back and saw Costaldi still standing at the edge of the pier, growing smaller and smaller.

Lipscomb realized he'd crossed the point of no return. Money had changed hands. The job had been sanctioned. The Red Fox would be dead inside of twenty-four hours.

49

FOR THE PAST THREE DAYS, THERE HAD HARDLY BEEN ENOUGH time to eat, sleep, or breathe. Allan and Lanna had flown home together from Boston the day after Allan's late-night epiphany. There was nothing to be done for Steven sitting in a hotel room in Massachusetts, fretting. It was best to go on home and regroup. Things had changed, and they knew what had to be done. Walking away from Steven, leaving him alone in that cell, had been painfully difficult. As hard as it was to leave, there was solace in the knowledge that there was now a plan. The two of them were cautiously optimistic. The plan was still in its developmental stage, but the more they hammered it out, scheming and theorizing, the more they truly began to believe that, yes . . . *it just might work*.

Saturday morning they had met with their loan officer at the bank and had gotten a check for fifteen thousand dollars—a loan against the equity in the house. Allan didn't plan on needing it all, but it felt better having some breathing room, just knowing the funds were at arm's length. It also helped knowing the cash wasn't going to pad some attorney's wallet. Instead, it would go to real use.

He phoned Rob Kiernan, the longtime owner of the lumberyard, at home on Sunday, and they met at the office for a long
closed-door meeting. Allan asked to cash in additional unused vacation time. Kiernan was a bit nosy, but Allan was successfully evasive. Allan agreed to come in for most of the day on Monday to get
things around the office semiorganized and to make sure that
business in general would be kept on track during his absence.

Monday morning he skipped breakfast and left a little early,
wanting to get to the office while it was still relatively quiet.
Things weren't quiet for long. People were in and out of his door
for the next eight hours straight. First chance he got, late in the
afternoon, he bolted for the door, not even pausing long enough
to announce his exit.

He settled into a chair at a computer terminal in the public
library and was quickly on the Internet, going straight to a search
engine. In the blank he typed: Rosemary Hitchins, Spy, Russia,
Treason, Prison, Red Fox. He hit Enter and waited.

The search results filled the monitor's screen. He went down
the page, clicking and reading. His spiral notebook was close at
hand. At last he found what he was after: Rosemary Hitchins
was incarcerated at Fort James Federal Penitentiary in Fort
James, Ohio. An hour later he entered a Radio Shack and purchased a tiny cassette recorder and a package of blank cassette
tapes. He sat in his truck in the parking lot testing the cassette
recorder, deeply concerned with how well it would pick up the
conversation between himself and Rosemary. He wasn't pleased
with the results. He began to have serious doubts.

·◆··◆·

The sky was still dark when Lanna followed him out onto the
porch very early Tuesday morning. She had kissed him good-bye,
holding him close, not wanting to let him go but understanding
what had to be done. "Be careful," she had said, still clutching

him in her arms. She stood watching until his truck was gone from view.

The route took him through the northeast corner of his home state, then through Missouri, Illinois, and Indiana, before he crossed the Ohio state line. It was dark by the time he found a hotel. The bored woman behind the counter took seventy-five bucks cash and gave him a card key.

From a rack of brochures he grabbed a map of the area and then went to find his room. The shower had just enough hot water to get his hair wet. He came out of the bathroom, crawling straight into bed, ignoring the TV. He unfolded the map on the bed. He was about forty-five miles from Fort James.

He slept in fits and starts. He tossed and turned in his sleep, dreaming of Rosemary Hitchins. The photos he'd found of her on the Internet were the first he'd seen of her in the greater part of two decades, and now he could not get that face out of his head.

She'd been so beautiful. Was she still?

It wasn't her appearance that disturbed his sleep but the prospect of approaching her from out of the blue after so many years. Her secret was more valuable than all of Nick Calevetti's money. It could mean Steven's freedom. No matter what it took, Allan could not blow this opportunity.

50

CLEMENT ARGUED WITH THE PILOT, BUT TO NO AVAIL. THEY had to make an emergency landing and it had to be done right away. Clement threatened and screamed, losing his cool. The pilot stood firm. Either they land the Gulfstream V immediately or delay even further and suffer the deadly consequences.

They dropped from the sky in a hurry, desperate to find a safe place to set the bird down. The pilot sent out a distress call and was quickly directed to a rural airfield somewhere in South Dakota. He brought the jet down smoothly onto the narrow runway and taxied it over to the one and only aircraft hangar.

A mechanical problem had arisen in flight. Up to that moment things had cruised along so smoothly and on schedule that Clement had found himself beginning to relax, at least a little. They had pinpointed the location of Rosemary Hitchins and they were only hours away when misfortune struck.

The jet landed outside the small community of Olivet, South Dakota, at an airfield the size of a pocket calculator. The aircraft hangar was empty. A small metal building at one end of one of the hangars served as the office. A man in a blue windbreaker greeted the pilot and they shook hands. There was no mechanic on duty.

The pilot opened a panel door along the belly of the jet to begin his diagnostic investigation. He rolled up his sleeves and went to work.

Clement had taken along Karla Gormaine, Philip Hopfner, and Brent Sneed, his core team that had stoically faced down the Cone Intermedia assault for the past few years. They were out for blood. Clement stood out on the asphalt apron that bordered the tiny office and anxiously glanced at his watch every thirty seconds. Time was eating them alive. The longer it took them to get to Fort James, Ohio, the greater the margin for error. He wouldn't be able to rest until he'd personally laid eyes on Rosemary Hitchins. Who'd have ever imagined that the linchpin in the lawsuit brought against them by CI would come in the form of a female Russian spy? This was a lawyer's dream. No story could do a better job of grabbing headlines. It would be beautiful. They'd set up a video camera and have her say the words that would destroy Getty Fairfield, and ultimately Jasper Cone. Clement was buzzing with anticipation.

He dialed Goodchapel at home. The exchange was brief and vicious. Goodchapel was not pleased.

Forty-five minutes later the pilot presented the bad news. The Gulfstream couldn't leave the ground without replacing a part. The pilot had tracked one down in Omaha, and they'd have to have it delivered by chartered plane. But of course it would take hours.

The pilot had streaks of grease on his chin and both forearms. He waited for instructions from Clement.

"How long will it take to install the part?"

"If all goes well, maybe half an hour. Ironically, this part we need is about the size of my thumb and costs next to nothing."

Clement grimaced and glanced at his watch, imagining how Goodchapel would respond to this latest bit of news. What other choice did they have?

He was terrified of not getting to Rosemary Hitchins soon enough, that they'd blow this one tiny window of opportunity. But perhaps all the fussing and fretting was unwarranted. She had been locked away for nearly two decades. She wasn't going anywhere. No one had given a rip about her in years and years, so why should that change within the next twelve hours? The anxiety was wasting too much mental energy. Better to just patiently ride out the delay. They'd be back in the air soon enough. Then they'd have Rosemary Hitchins, and that would put them back in the driver's seat. CI would never see it coming.

"Do it," Clement said.

The pilot rushed off.

They were stranded in the middle of a prairie, a twenty-million-dollar aircraft handicapped by a throwaway part the size of a thumb. Casually, Clement glanced down at his hand, sticking his thumb up. How many billions of dollars were at stake because of something so trivial? He couldn't resist shaking his head and grinning. *For want of a nail the kingdom was lost.*

51

IN THE PREDAWN HOURS OF WEDNESDAY MORNING, LONG before the light of the new day would begin to show itself on the crest of the horizon, the air was crisp, with fog hanging along the contours of the ground. It was a soybean field, soft from a recent rain. The wet earth made the long hike across it something more of a chore than it should have been.

The sky was overcast, so there was little or no moonlight peeking through the cloud cover to aid Patton in his traverse across the gummy farmland. He wasn't far from the road—barely a couple hundred yards—but the crisp air burned his lungs and the mud swallowed him up to his ankles. When at last he spotted the glow of the prison lights up ahead, he slowed his pace and crouched low to the ground.

He came to a slight rise that fell quickly away, sloping down to level ground, which led directly to the acreage on which Fort James Federal Penitentiary stood. Patton had endured enough years of his life in just such a facility to not relish the sight of this one. A sort of reflexive spasm shot through his nervous system as he took up position looking ahead at the complex of buildings and fencing and razor wire.

Patton raised his field glasses to his face. His was lying on his stomach, with his arms braced up on his elbows. He crawled forward using his elbows to work himself nearer to the peak of the rise. As he panned the layout before him through the field glasses, the world seeped into focus, and he saw mainly darkness. The exterior facade of the prison was nothing impressive. There was razor wire and a guard tower with spotlights, but it was no Alcatraz.

He unclipped a walkie-talkie from the waist of his pants. "I have visual," he said.

"Acknowledged," Metcalf responded from the SUV they'd stolen from the airport.

Everything appeared quiet. At least for the moment, no one seemed to be coming or going. Patton glassed the guard tower and spotted a man in uniform leaning against a railing, working on a cigarette. Most of the exterior of the prison complex lay in darkness. The road curled in through an outermost gate, passing beneath the guard tower. Entrance through an interior gate required first stopping at a guard post.

A half hour later, headlights approached the outer gate. Patton stirred. He was dressed all in black.

The car was a yellow Hyundai. It swung through the outer gate without slowing. The car followed a slight elbow in the road, which angled to the right, then continued toward the gate that would grant it access to the parking lot and the rest of the prison complex.

Patton had his fingers around his field glasses, pressing them to his face. The car was far enough away that he couldn't hear it. When the Hyundai was fifty or sixty feet from the lighted guard post, the car's headlights flashed off and on a single time and barely slowed at all as it continued on. Before the Hyundai even reached the guard post, the motorized gate began to pull open.

Patton figured the guards would be accustomed to a small number of familiar vehicles that they saw on a daily or nightly basis. These they would pay little attention to. These were their friends, their pals.

The car found an empty slot in the parking lot, the headlights died, and the driver's door opened. The driver made his way across the dimly lit asphalt to an outer door in the prison wall, punched a string of digits into a touchpad on the door, and entered.

Almost immediately that same door opened, and a man in a guard's uniform sauntered to his own car and backed out of the lot. It was a Ford Escort station wagon. The gate opened, and the car meandered out the way it had come in eight hours before.

Without a moment's hesitation, Patton was on his feet.

"Blue Ford wagon headed your way," Patton said. "Be ready." He darted back across the edge of the field, his boots tearing through the wet slop.

Metcalf was sitting in the quiet, the SUV idling in the chill of the early morning. Headlights appeared in the distance.

He put the SUV in gear and turned into the road. He quickly pulled to a stop, popped the hood, and hopped out. The oncoming headlights approached in a hurry. Metcalf turned to face the lights, and took a long stride into the other lane. The light was blinding.

The car slowed significantly. Metcalf stepped around the front of the car, approaching the driver's side window. He tapped on the glass. The window slowly came down.

"Sorry, man. You know anything about motors and stuff?" Metcalf said, hooking a thumb in the direction of his SUV.

The man inside looked out suspiciously.

"What are you doing out here, anyway?"

Metcalf shrugged. "I could really use some help."

The man's face was deeply skeptical. Something was not right, and the man could feel it.

There was an awkward moment of silence.

"I'll stop at the gas station a few miles down the road and have them send some help," he said, nodding at the road ahead.

Just then he turned back, and the barrel of Metcalf's gun poked him between the eyes.

"Easy now," Metcalf said. He opened the door and gestured with the gun for the man to slide across the seat to the passenger side. The man obeyed. Metcalf climbed in behind the wheel, keeping the gun trained on his captive. He shut the door and turned the car around in the road, taking them in the direction of the prison.

Not far down the road, Metcalf saw a small point of light flash from the fencerow to his left. He slowed the car, coming to a stop near where the light had appeared. A figure hurried to the road from the darkness of the field.

Patton slid into the back, poking his head over the front seat. He took Metcalf's gun and pressed it to the guard's neck. "Let's take a drive to your house," Patton said. "That'll be a good place for us to have a little talk."

52

LIGHTS APPEARED ON THE DISTANT HORIZON. PHILIP HOPFNER was the first to spot them. He was outside standing on a patch of gravel smoking a cigar. Clement and Karla Gormaine were inside the Gulfstream, Karla with her head down and eyes shut, sneaking a nap, Clement on his cell, moving whatever mountains he could from the middle of nowhere.

Hopfner watched as the lights of a small Learjet grew gradually larger in the night sky. He launched up the steps and poked his head into the passenger cabin.

"Heads up," he said, gesturing skyward.

Karla woke with a start, her eyes heavy with sleep.

Clement shot out of his seat, snapping his cell phone shut.

Brent Sneed was outside having a cigarette.

The Learjet floated in and touched down with ease. It taxied up alongside the Gulfstream V. The delivery was completed with a bare minimum of discussion, and the Learjet lifted off without delay and quickly disappeared into the slate-black night.

The pilot ground his cigarette into the asphalt and went to work without a word to anyone.

The clock was ticking.

53

JACK BROWNE HAD LITTLE DESIRE TO DIE JUST YET. SO HE kept his hands to himself and spoke only when spoken to. At this point he wasn't altogether certain what these two thugs were after, but he had no plans of getting a bullet in the head for trying to be a hero.

One of the men was driving him in his Ford, while the second man followed in the SUV. He still couldn't believe he'd fallen for their little trap. But what in the world could they want from him? He had no money. Browne was a goat farmer, so he took third shift at the prison in order to work the farm during daylight hours. He lived in a clapboard house with his wife, Jenna, and their unwed, unemployed thirty-year-old daughter, Ria, and her son. His stomach tightened as his blue wagon turned into the gravel drive to his home.

"Get out." Patton held the gun on him.

The lights from the SUV washed over the two men and the Ford.

Patton kept the barrel of the gun drilled into Browne's back as they moved up the porch to the front door.

Jenna Browne stirred from sleep. She just shrugged the blanket higher up on her shoulders and mashed her face in the pillow. She'd barely shut her eyes when the front door clapped shut and there was the sound of footfalls in the next room. With one sleepy eye she glanced at the clock and saw the time. She knew it was just Jack getting home from work, and so she did her best to disregard him and tried to get back to sleep.

The only light in the front room was a small lamp on a reading table next to a tattered recliner. The lampshade was stained and dusty. Browne kept his hands up where Patton could see them. The sensation of the gun barrel jabbing him between his shoulder blades was making him weak in the knees. He eased forward as directed, every movement slow and deliberate.

Patton entered with caution. The house was small and dirty. A goat farmer's house. The furniture was old, and a good portion of it was in a state of disrepair. The front living area was small, no more than twelve feet by fifteen feet, with a kitchen area along one wall. There were dirty dishes scattered along the short counter space. On the floor at one end of the kitchen counter sat a litter box. The place stank.

Metcalf rounded the side of the house in the dark, and eased onto the porch. He was quickly inside the house and pushed the door shut with one elbow.

Patton put a hand to Browne's shoulder, halting him. Patton's eyes were highly active, probing every corner of the room. He leaned up near Browne's ear.

"Who's home?" Patton said.

"My wife and daughter, and my daughter's boy." Browne licked nervously at his lower lip. "They's all asleep," he added.

"Yeah, well, not for long." Patton motioned to Metcalf.

Metcalf nodded, pulling a gun from the waistband of his pants. A short hallway led to the bedrooms. There was a door on the right and a door on the left. Both doors were shut, and no light was apparent beneath either. Metcalf approached the one on the right. He put his ear to the door and listened for a moment. Then he gently turned the knob. He threw on the light switch and saw two small beds in a tiny room. The beds formed a right angle. A young woman sat up in the larger of the two beds. He held his gun on her.

Her mouth opened.

Before she could make a peep, Metcalf said, "Take it easy."

The small boy in the second bed twisted around to face the door. He squinted against the light.

"Mommy?" he said sleepily.

"Get in the front room!" Metcalf said, waving the gun.

Mother and child hurried into the hall and huddled next to Browne.

Metcalf opened the door on the left, swatting blindly for the light switch. Jenna was standing in the center of the room, facing the door, having gotten up to investigate all the sudden commotion. She froze midstep, her nightgown brushing her ankles. Metcalf held the barrel of the gun an inch from her nose.

The family was assembled in a corner of the front room near the kitchen. While Patton held them at gunpoint, Metcalf went through the kitchen drawers and bedroom closets, hunting twine or rope or packing tape—anything that would sufficiently bind them.

The nearest neighbor was a quarter-mile down the road. There was little chance of being surprised. Metcalf used some heavy cord he'd found in the bottom of a junk drawer to bind their ankles and wrists. Then he wrapped their upper bodies with layer upon layer of duct tape. When at last he was satisfied that not one of them could budge so much as an inch, he fell in alongside Patton.

Patton dragged a kitchen chair from the dining area and sat in it facing Browne.

"Here's the way it's going to be, Jack," Patton began, straddling the chair. "You've got one shot to do this right, so don't get stupid."

"I don't understand," Browne said. "We got nothing to give you. What do you want?"

"What time does your shift start tomorrow?"

"Huh?"

"What time do you clock in for work, Jack?"

"Eight o'clock in the evening."

Patton glanced up at Metcalf. 8:00 p.m. That was awfully late. They needed to take care of Rosemary Hitchins as early in the day as possible. Lipscomb had been very clear about that.

"That won't work, Jack."

Browne was dumbfounded, bewildered, thinking fast.

Patton, wearing a blank expression, raised his handgun and pressed the end of the barrel to the center of Jenna Browne's forehead.

"Pay attention, Jack," Patton said. "Otherwise I start killing."

"Please . . ." Browne said, his voice unsteady. "I'll give you whatever you want. Just don't hurt them."

"I need you to think, Jack. How early can you get to work at the penitentiary? That's a simple question."

Browne thought a moment.

"It's payday," he said. "I usually just pick up my check during my scheduled shift. But our checks are available all day. Occasionally I'll swing by and pick mine up early."

Patton stood, withdrawing the point of the barrel from the woman's head. It left a pink ring indention in her flesh. He conferred with Metcalf next to the refrigerator. Browne had given them an important detail. As simple as it sounded, it made a great impact on their planning. They would have him go for his paycheck late in the morning, or early in the afternoon. They'd gotten lucky. It would almost certainly draw unwanted attention if Browne were to show up early on any other day for some concocted reason. But this just might work.

It was a quarter of five in the morning. For the Brothers, the length of their day was catching up to them, and a few hours of sleep would do a world of good. Patton took out his cell phone and dialed Lipscomb. The conversation was brief. Lipscomb sounded slightly nervous.

Metcalf put an empty pillowcase over the head of each of the four family members after placing duct tape over their mouths. The curtains were drawn, and the small lamp remained the only source of light in the house.

The plan was straightforward but tricky. A lot could go wrong. They were forced to put a lot of faith in Jack Browne and his love for his family.

Patton sat on the floor in a corner of the kitchen, his gun on the floor between his legs. He crossed his arms over his knees and put his head down, closing his eyes. Metcalf checked the windows one last time. The property surrounding the house was quiet and still. The road out front was dark and silent. There was nearly two hours till sunup.

Metcalf sank to the floor beside the door. The secret to napping was to never get comfortable. His eyelids fluttered and his breathing slowed. Very soon he was asleep, his head braced against the wall.

The house was perfectly still. The only sounds were those of the Browne family, bunched together in the center of the kitchen floor, crying.

54

THEY WERE AIRBORNE.

Clement held his breath until they reached cruising altitude. The copilot stepped into the passenger cabin and delivered the good news that everything was again in tip-top shape. He announced their new ETA, ignored the scowl from Clement, then returned to his post in the cockpit.

They were hours away and still had to land, find ground transportation, and make the long drive to the prison.

Clement swallowed an antacid. His staff busied themselves in an effort to avoid him.

They sped eastward at nearly five hundred knots.

55

BROWNE HAD PROVED TO BE JUST WHAT THEY WERE HOPING for. His family wasn't exactly a Norman Rockwell painting, but he appeared to be a faithful provider and protector. Patton learned that Browne was a deacon in his tiny church and served on the board of the local coop. He'd been married for thirty years, and anyone who allowed his grown daughter and her kid to move back in indefinitely was surely willing to go to some rather extreme lengths to ensure that no harm came to them. They had nabbed a simpleminded farmer who wasn't likely to try anything brave or stupid.

Morning light found its way into the small farmhouse despite their attempt at covering the windows. Metcalf was the first to rise, peeking out the windows and even cracking open the front door so that he could better see the road in either direction.

Soon Patton was up and alert, and the two of them set about their work. Patton hooked Browne under one arm and lifted him to his feet. He hauled the farmer to the rear of the house, shoving him to the floor and slamming shut the door. Metcalf made sure the rest of the family was properly bound, then headed back to join his partner.

Browne was on his back on the floor, his legs bent at the knees. He was shaking with fear. Patton circled him, stomping the floor inches from his head. Metcalf entered and took a seat on the bed.

Patton squatted, and pressed his gun to the prison employee's forehead. They needed Browne to talk. They wanted him scared out of his mind. People were most cooperative when they were unmistakably certain you meant business.

"Are you listening?" Patton growled.

Browne nodded vigorously, whimpering, tears running down the sides of his head, past his ears.

"The first lie you tell, somebody dies. Understand?"

Browne was blubbering.

Patton snapped a finger at Metcalf, gesturing for something. Metcalf fished an item from a pocket of his jacket and leaned forward to pass it. It was a lined three-by-five index card. On it was information provided to them by Lipscomb. The information had cost Lipscomb's employer a rather princely sum, especially for the speed at which it had been obtained. Chick Mancini had invested no more than forty-five minutes at his computer keyboard cracking into secure government databases before handing over what Lipscomb had desired. Information specific to Rosemary Hitchins and her incarceration at Fort James Penitentiary. All the guesswork had been taken out of finding her. They simply needed someone who could get inside and get within arm's reach.

"Today it's up to you whether you and your family die," Patton said. "Is that clear enough?"

Browne nodded, his mouth still covered with a strip of duct tape. Patton reached down and tore the tape from the man's lips. Browne flinched, his lips stinging.

Patton then proceeded to describe exactly what they required of him. He was to enter the grounds of the prison, somehow find his way to the inmate named Rosemary Hitchins, and ultimately put a bullet in her head. Patton read aloud the information on the index card. He read the details slowly and carefully, making certain Browne understood every word spoken.

Browne was beside himself. He immediately knew where Hitchins was being held. "Her cell is nowhere near the payroll office," he said, jerking his head side to side, wildly. "If I'm simply there to pick up my check, I'd have no reason to be anywhere near that section of the prison."

"So you'll get lost for a few minutes," Metcalf instructed, hunched forward on the edge of the bed.

"And even if I get near her, I can't be waving a gun. They'd be all over me."

Patton put the barrel of his gun to the prison guard's right ear, grinding it into the meat of his inner ear. "You know what your problem is, Jack? You think about yourself too much. Maybe I should bring that little grandson of yours in here and let you listen to him scream when I explode one of his kneecaps. Hmmm? How about it? That seem easier than finding your way through the prison with a firearm?"

Browne grew still, his hands bound behind him. For the first time he fully understood that there was no way he would be able to talk his way out of this situation. These guys, whoever they were, were sick and twisted, and they meant business. They had his family, and he had no doubt they would follow through on their threats. They were specific about what they wanted him to do, and their knowledge of the inside of the prison was astoundingly accurate. He was too scared to think straight. There had to be a way out of this. Though perhaps the only way to come out the other end alive was to just follow orders and get it over with. Then maybe they'd leave his family alone.

What Browne didn't understand was that Patton and Metcalf had no intention of leaving them alive. That was not their style. There would be a bullet in each of the four heads. That was simply a given. But it was hard to motivate a person unless he believed he had a shot at survival. When the time was right, Patton would leave with the prison guard, and Metcalf would stay behind with the family. Before the little blue Ford Escort wagon was even out of sight, the wife and kids would be finished off, and Metcalf would head out. That was the plan.

They went through a dry run of sorts. They agreed that he would go in for his paycheck just after 10:30 a.m. He'd have to swing by payroll and sign for his check; then, of course, he'd have to waste a few minutes chatting with the first-shift guards as he passed them in the corridors. The more relaxed everyone was with him there, the less they'd care if he wandered off on his own. All of these things taken into consideration, Rosemary Hitchins should be dead by 11:00 a.m. at the latest.

A few minutes before 10:00 a.m., Metcalf led Browne to the bathroom. Metcalf sat on the toilet seat while Browne lathered himself behind the cheap plastic shower curtain. Browne rinsed off and asked for a towel. He put on fresh jeans and a button-down shirt and parted his wet hair neatly to one side.

At a quarter after, Patton eased out the door and into the Escort wagon. It started, and a thin cloud of exhaust fumes floated past the opened car door. The morning was quiet and cool, though warming quickly. The sky was clear except for a few wispy clouds, and the sun was reflected in the car's hatchback.

The atmosphere in the house was apprehensive. The boy was crying. Jenna Browne pleaded for them not to take her husband. Browne, though, had resolved to complete the task before him and assured his wife that everything would be fine.

Patton and Metcalf conferred one last time, finalizing any loose ends. They would meet in an hour and would be on their way back to Baltimore by noon.

Metcalf held the front door open, and Patton led Browne down the porch steps to the idling Ford. Patton rode in the backseat with his gun held beneath the driver's headrest, barely a half inch from Browne's spine. The car bucked slightly as the transmission was shifted into gear. As he drove past the fencerow bordering his farm, Browne resisted the impulse to glance back at his home.

Soon the car was little more than a vague shape a mile down the dirt road, obscured by a dark cloud of dust. From that distance Browne couldn't hear the three pops of gunfire that left him alone in the world.

56

THERE WAS NOTHING AROUND THE PRISON FOR MILES. THE road leading in was arrow straight, with only open pasture on either side. The penitentiary itself was a series of unremarkable low cement buildings bordered on all sides by twenty-foot-high fencing, topped with coils of razor wire.

A loud buzzer sounded somewhere above Allan Adler's head. The guard standing next to him spoke to someone on the other side of a thick metal barrier, and the lock released with a clang. Allan had never been so nervous in his life. He immediately had a greater appreciation for the law and civilized society. This was no place to waste your life. His resolve to keep Steven out of a place like this was cemented at that moment.

The concrete slab floor was mopped to a perfect shine. The guard's heavy boots echoed loudly off the floor, walls, and ceiling as they progressed down a long, colorless corridor. The guard was tall and lean and offered no conversation at all. Allan was glad for that.

He was shown to a small office where he sat in a stiff plastic chair next to a fern. A form on a clipboard was shoved in front of his face.

He made quick work of filling in the blanks on the form, then slid it through a small window to the unsmiling clerk. He was told to have a seat and wait. A small transistor radio on a shelf inside the office was playing country and western. Allan sat in his chair by the fern and tried to shut the music out of his head.

For thirty minutes he stared at a crack in the wall and listened to the heavy woman behind the window typing at her computer keyboard . . . *peck* . . . *peck* . . . *peck* . . . one finger at a time.

Allan had presented himself as a freelance journalist. He suspected that once upon a time reporters had swarmed to her like
flies, just as he also suspected that that kind of interest had
ended years ago. Mostly what the Internet had had to offer were
only fragments, bits and pieces, brief mentions of Rosemary
Hitchins. In the early years after her conviction and imprisonment she'd shunned journalists. On rare occasions a high-profile
media personality would make it in to her for a few questions,
but the years passed and interest faded, and now Rosemary was
left alone to rot away the remainder of her natural life.

After all these years, Allan hoped, she might very well be re-
ceptive to an unexpected visitor just to diffuse the unending
monotony. His name would mean nothing to her, just as he'd
never known hers until the arrest on spy charges. Only a face-to-
face encounter would have any chance of sparking her memory
of him.

Everything hinged on getting Rosemary Hitchins on tape. He
needed her voice, speaking clearly, acknowledging events known
only to herself, Getty Fairfield, and Allan Adler. She needed to
clearly and unmistakably confess to an affair with Fairfield.
Nothing less would suffice. If he could gently coax her into acknowledging that relationship, and get it recorded on tape, he'd
have something to use for leverage.

Fairfield was in a precarious position. He'd be going up
against a ravenous Republican majority in the Senate, and a
taped confession from his former mistress would obliterate any
chance at a confirmation to the Supreme Court. So Allan had to
put himself in a position to play one side of Capitol Hill against
the other.

Allan knew enough about politicians in D.C. to understand
what a wily and devious bunch they were. A taped confession of
the most infamous female spy in United States history revealing
a sexual relationship with the man now nominated by the president to be chief justice would leave one side salivating and devastate the other.

Allan planned to go to Washington armed with the confession and a few demands. No jail time; no reduced charges; no probation; no plea bargains; and no six-hundred-dollar-an-hour lawyers—Steven had to be allowed to walk away unscathed. He wasn't about to let his son pay for another man's crime. But by embarking on this mission, Allan realized that he was walking head-on into the meat grinder. He had to be careful and watch his back. Because things could very easily blow up in his face.

But first he had to get inside the prison to see her.

Finally, a door to one side of the small window opened, and a short man with a wide tie asked him to step inside.

Allan found himself in yet another office, this one featuring a gray government-issue metal desk that faced two chairs.

"I'm Mr. Wollard. Have a seat, please," the man said.

The conversation didn't last long. Wollard basically expounded on the same questions presented on the form Allan had just filled out. He looked at the world through thick glasses with cheap, heavy frames.

"Has the article you're writing been commissioned by a publication?"

Allan kind of shifted in his chair. "No . . . not exactly. I'm hoping if the interview is fruitful, I'll be able to generate a feature article which might drum up some interest among the more distinguished periodicals."

Wollard had a pen in hand, which he used to make notes along the margins of the completed form.

"And you have a recording device you'd like to take inside with you?"

"Yes, that's correct," Allan said, reaching a hand inside his jacket pocket and holding up the microcassette player for inspection.

Wollard stared at it a moment with absolute disinterest. Then he added something to his notes.

"Have you had any previous or outside contact with the specified inmate?"

"No." A nervous shiver up the back of his neck.

He set down his pen and looked up at Allan.

"I'm a busy man, Mr. Adler. This sort of matter takes me away from other responsibilities. The inmates here prefer not to be bothered with this sort of request. Rarely will an inmate cooperate. Mostly they are interested in legal help or visits with spouses or loved ones, not members of the media."

"I'd appreciate any effort you could make on my behalf," Allan said.

Wollard glared at Allan, then at the request form. Then he glared once again at Allan. He pushed his heavy glasses up on the bridge of his nose with the knuckle of his middle finger and grabbed up his telephone. He punched in a three-digit extension, barked at whoever answered, and hung up.

Allan held his breath.

They stared at one another across the desk for what seemed like hours. The administrator seemed content to not say a word. Allan could feel the sweat beading in his armpits.

Finally the phone rang. The administrator let it ring a second time before answering. Allan watched the man's eyes.

Wollard frowned slightly, thanked the caller, then hung up the phone. He cleared his throat.

"Well, Mr. Adler, today must be your lucky day. The inmate has agreed to speak with you, under the conditions that the interview will not exceed ten minutes and that the conversation not be recorded."

Allan felt equally euphoric and devastated. The relief was beyond description, yet he desperately needed her voice on tape. He was barely aware of himself standing and moving toward the door. He'd been so terrified of not being granted an opportunity to speak with Rosemary, and of how devastating that rejection would be, that he'd been totally blindsided by her stipulations. Somehow he'd have to cope with this shocking development.

Within moments a guard arrived to escort him.

The guard walked a full stride ahead of him. It was slightly cooler this deep inside the prison walls, and Allan felt the skin on his arms prickle. They stopped at a lockout, and a second guard stepped forward and ran a wand across and down Allan's upper body, then swept it from top to bottom of each leg.

The wand made a chirping, whirring sound as it passed over one pocket of his jacket.

"Empty the pocket, please," the guard said.

He produced the microcassette recorder and its extra tapes.

"Just a tape recorder," Allan said, offering it for examination.

The guard gave it only a cursory glance. "All right. Good enough."

The door slammed shut behind them.

"She's kinda famous, you know," the guard said without glancing back.

Allan said, "That's what I hear."

"I've worked here nineteen years. Back in the day, reporters were eight deep on any given morning. Not anymore."

"Has she changed much?"

They had arrived at another security lockout. The guard drew up beside him and made fleeting eye contact.

"She's still a knockout," the guard said, as if only to himself.

It was difficult not to suspect that a great percentage of the immense media attention that had been aimed at Rosemary those many years ago hadn't had to do with her spectacular beauty. Sure, she'd conspired for the Russians and was one of only a tiny number of female spies to ever be caught on U.S. soil, but nothing sells like a pretty face. The picture in his mind's eye had long ago faded, though the images he'd downloaded off the Internet at the library had brought a rush of memories. It didn't require a great deal of imagination to comprehend how or why Getty Fairfield could have become fixated on her. Any man with a pulse would have been hard-pressed to not be tempted by her advances.

A short flight of stairs ended at a blue-painted door with a rectangular window inset at eye level. The guard turned the knob and held the door open for Allan.

Beyond the door was a long, narrow room divided by brick and wire-reinforced glass. A metal counter ran the length of the room on either side of the glass partition.

"Have a seat," the guard said, gesturing to a string of metal folding chairs spaced at intervals along the counter. "She'll be brought in momentarily. I'll be right outside this door if you need anything."

When at last the door behind him shut and the guard was gone, Allan was alone. It was early enough in the day that he had the visiting room to himself, at least for the moment. The room was all flat, cold surfaces. He pulled out a folding chair and took a seat. He could feel his heart hammering in his chest. He took a deep breath and held it, focusing to calm himself.

So many years had passed since he'd been in the presence of Rosemary Hitchins. His palms were clammy. He wiped them on the insides of his pant legs. The room was slightly cool, but he could feel the perspiration forming along his brow. He stared straight ahead, past the glass partition, to the door on the other side. Soon enough, he saw movement in the rectangular window inset in that door. Then a flash of color, and the door opened.

Allan's heart caught in his throat.

A woman dressed in prison denim and handcuffs stepped through the open door and looked his way. She frowned slightly at the sight of him, and paused. A mixture of curiosity and confusion registered in her eyes. She had to be wondering who in the world this person was who'd requested a visit with her.

Allan watched with rapt attention as she shuffled toward the chair directly across from him on the other side of the glass. The first thing that struck him was that she'd aged. It had been seventeen years since he'd last laid eyes upon her, after all. She wore no makeup at all. And her hair was now cut fairly short. The uniform was none too flattering, though he could tell there was still a fabulous body hidden underneath. At any rate, the picture before him certainly didn't match the image filed away in his mind's eye.

Rosemary hesitantly approached the chair, eyeing him with great suspicion. The guard exited the room, pulling the door shut behind her. Rosemary sat down, her hands in her lap.

Allan went blank. He was suddenly rattled. Forget the past two weeks—he'd have never dreamed he'd again find himself face-to-face with this woman. The word *surreal* flashed through his mind. All the manic energy that had carried him this far suddenly short-circuited, leaving him at a complete loss for words.

She was still beautiful. Rosemary was actually taller than he'd remembered. Her skin was pale, but the quality of her features more than made up for it.

A telephone receiver was mounted on each side of the glass. She reached for hers first, holding it to her face, waiting. Allan followed suit.

She sat looking him squarely in the eyes. A lot was going on behind them, he could tell. She was assessing him. After a minute or two had passed between them in silence, her expression turned first to annoyance, and then to puzzlement.

Allan realized he'd been staring. He shook his head slightly, then opened his mouth to apologize.

"I . . ." he stammered, scrambling to collect his thoughts.

"Oh my . . ." she said softly, interrupting. "It's you."

Allan's eyes widened. "You *remember*?"

"Of course I remember."

"It's been so many years. I didn't expect you to know me from Adam."

"What's your name?"

"Allan. Allan Adler."

"I didn't recognize the face at first, though I think you've aged well. But I remember those eyes."

"We never even spoke to one another," he said.

She shrugged. "I was always good with faces."

"Ms. Hitchins, I want to thank—"

"Rosemary . . ." she interrupted.

"Sure, okay. Rosemary, I want to thank you for meeting with me."

She said, "I can't imagine why you're here. As you said, we never spoke. It's been nearly twenty years. I'm here because I betrayed the country of my birth. I will spend the rest of my life behind these bars. You mean nothing to me, and I can't imagine that I would mean anything to you. For a brief time we had Getty Fairfield in common. Beyond that . . ."

Allan nodded, then edged forward in the folding chair, his elbows on the metal counter.

"This must be perplexing, I know. I apologize for this. It's not my intention to cause you any discomfort by bringing the past rushing back."

"They told me you were with the media."

He shifted in his chair. "Yeah. About that, again, I'm sorry. But I wasn't sure how else to get in to speak with you."

Abruptly, Rosemary sat up straight in her chair, her expression turning serious as stone. The handcuffs on her wrists rattled as she shook them lightly, shrugging. She spoke up, the tone of her voice rising noticeably.

"Tell me, Allan, why are you here? You've obviously gone through considerable effort to speak to me. And you're clearly no reporter. So why? What do you want from me?"

The fine hairs on the back of his neck were standing on end. This was the moment. It all boiled down to this. His stomach tightened like a fist. His breathing became more labored. It was time to plead his case. Steven's future was at stake.

"Actually, Rosemary . . . I'm here to ask for your help." It sounded absurd, and he knew it.

Her expression of puzzlement deepened. But she didn't respond just yet; instead, she waited and listened, knowing there was more on the way.

"After your arrest, you never betrayed Fairfield. Why?"

She looked sad. She pondered the question for a moment. Finally, she said, "There was simply no point. I was going to prison for the rest of my life, and nothing I could say or do could have changed that. If I had mentioned Getty, it would have served only to destroy him. I wouldn't have benefited. And he'd treated me well. I didn't love him, I simply used him." She shrugged, and her shoulders dropped slightly.

"As painful as this is for you, your secret is the only chance I have of saving my son."

It took a moment for his words to settle over her. The conversation had already taken a toll on her. For him it was simply a matter of history. For her, though, the topic represented the end of life in the outside world. But now he'd said something outside her loop of understanding, and it took a few beats for her to comprehend that the tone of the conversation had shifted.

Slowly she raised her head. "What?"

"Rosemary, my son is in serious trouble. He's a good kid, with a bright future ahead of him. But he is accused of a crime he did not commit. A man was murdered, and my son has been blamed. He is completely innocent."

She shook her head, and shrugged, clearly taken off guard. "Allan, I'm confused. What does your son's problem have to do with me? I'm in here, locked away from the world."

"Have you watched the news lately?"

"The news? No."

"Getty Fairfield has been nominated for one of the most powerful positions in the nation. And I believe he would be willing to do most anything to keep your secret buried in the past."

"You intend to *blackmail* Getty Fairfield?"

"Yes. That is exactly what I intend to do. But without your help my hands are tied. I don't have a lot of money and the cost for the defense attorney my son will need is astronomical—more than I could ever hope to afford."

She stared at him.

He added, "I simply can't let my son pay for a crime that someone else committed—someone who was supposed to be his friend. As his father, I must do everything I can to help him. You're our only hope."

Rosemary held the phone in both hands, and lowered it to her chin. Her gaze seemed to look right through him to some unknown point. Again, he got a glimpse of just how much damage life behind these walls had done to her.

The silence that filled the moments that followed seemed to linger forever. Allan dared not move a muscle. He dared not breathe. The subjects of Getty Fairfield and blackmail and Steven's fate had been broached. He had asked for her help. Now all he could do was to wait in breathless anticipation.

Through the small rectangular window inset in the door behind Rosemary, he caught a fleeting glimpse of the female guard checking in on them. Then she was gone. He was stunned by a sudden sense of panic that the guard might barge inside and whisk Rosemary away before he'd had time to get what he'd come for. His heart was bursting with urgency.

He stared hard at the door behind Rosemary.

Her voice startled him. She had said something that he hadn't caught.

He politely asked her to repeat it.

Her eyes had softened just a touch, and it was evident that they were probing him. "Tell me about your son," she said.

Allan blinked. She had blindsided him with the request. He held the phone to his ear, and stared at her through the glass. She seemed genuinely curious.

"Well, his name is Steven, and he's twenty-one. He was just a small boy when I worked for Getty Fairfield. He's a student at Harvard University."

"Harvard? That's impressive." Her elbows were on the metal counter. Allan didn't reckon she got much in the way of real conversation. Perhaps talking about his son made her reflect on the fact that having lived the bulk of her adult life behind prison walls had prevented her from having a family of her own.

"Yeah. His mother and I are proud."

"I bet he's a good student."

Allan nodded. "He's worked hard to get where he is. That's why I'm terrified to see it all be thrown away."

"Does he take after your looks?"

Stunned by the intimate tone of her queries, Allan couldn't help but grin. "Actually, yeah, I guess he pretty much does. Though he's got more of his mother in personality and temperament."

She was quiet for a moment, then she said, "Allan, I will help any way I can."

His heart leaped. Despite his deepest hopes, he was overwhelmed by her willingness to help him. He took a deep breath, and leaned forward, his face now mere inches from the glass, tears forming at the corners of his eyes.

She continued, "On some level we share something, a moment in time, a moment of history. You, me, Getty. I stare at the walls month in and month out. My future is sealed, I cannot change it. So perhaps the one power I have left is to help you, to help your son. Tell me what you need."

He paused a moment, having to redirect his train of thought. Then it all came back to him, everything that needed to be done.

He then spoke slowly and deliberately. "Your relationship with Getty Fairfield would devastate him at this moment in time. His supporters have the power to move mountains, and there is nothing they wouldn't do to protect him. They have power, money, influence. Only you, me, and Getty, have any knowledge of your relationship. If I confront his supporters and threaten them, I just might be able get enough leverage to buy Steven's freedom. It's a long shot, I know, but it's all I've got."

"So why come here? Why not just go straight to them and cut a deal?"

"Yeah, I thought about that," Allan said, nodding, scratching at the back of his neck. "But in order to make it convincing, I decided my threat needed to pack a little more muscle. Otherwise they might see me as just some nut making loony accusations."

"And so . . . ?"

Allan unzipped his jacket pocket. He removed the cassette recorder and set it on the counter. Her eyes were immediately drawn to it.

She gave him a confused look. "What?"

"I need it on tape," he said.

"You need what on tape?"

"Your voice," he said, tapping a finger against the cassette recorder. "I need you to tell your story, in your own words, with your own voice. I need it on tape so that I have something to take before them. Understand?"

"Right here? Right now?" She gestured with her bound hands, indicating their surroundings, her face registering bemused shock. "You want me to just blurt it out? The whole sordid tale?"

He looked her straight in the eyes, unblinking.

"It's the only thing that will do." He stood the cassette recorder on end atop the metal counter. "Your words, Rosemary. Nothing else will scare those people enough to do my boy any good."

"I specifically stipulated that no part of this conversation be recorded."

"Rosemary, I have no other alternative. Please . . ."

The slender, rectangular recording device stood on the counter between them like a monument to secrets and lies. They both stared at it a moment. In the distance, beyond the door behind Allan, were sounds of prison life. Iron doors slamming shut, foot-falls on the vast cement floor, someone calling to someone else. Allan ignored the sounds, his heart tightening in his chest.

The guard's face appeared in the window again, staring. Then she was gone.

Rosemary appeared momentarily transfixed by the presence of the tiny cassette recorder. Allan glanced at her as she stared at it. He tried not to imagine what she was thinking. It terrified him to think he'd pushed his luck one step too far. But what other choice did he have?

Rosemary took a deep breath. Her eyes continued to linger on the object on the metal counter.

He opened his mouth to apologize. But she spoke first.

"Allan, I'm sorry," she said quietly. She was looking down at her hands on the edge of the metal counter. "As I told you, I'd like to help you any way I can. But this, this I can't do. I've had many years to come to terms with the fact that I deserve to be here. Getty did nothing wrong. His only sin was against his wife. That's between them. He didn't know what I was after. So he shouldn't be punished for my crime. If I let you record my secret and make it public, it . . . it just wouldn't be right."

The blood rushed from Allan's head. He felt the intense need to gasp for air. He'd been so close! So *close*! And now the door was slamming shut right before his eyes. It was astonishing.

"Rosemary, please . . ." Allan was dumbfounded. He'd been caught off guard by her abrupt change of heart.

She held up a hand to silence him.

He hushed, his eyes beseeching her.

"Allan, it's complicated."

"You're my one hope."

"I'm sorry."

"I just . . ." His words trailed off. He grabbed the cassette recorder and stashed it in a jacket pocket. "I shouldn't have come." It was now difficult for him to allow himself to make eye contact with her. He could tell that she wasn't going to come around. This was now officially a waste of time. He felt utterly humiliated. He couldn't get out fast enough.

Rosemary leaned forward, her elbows on the metal ledge. She pressed the bridge of her nose against the balls of her hands.

He turned away from her, saying, "I'll just let the guard know that I'm ready to—"

"Allan, wait . . ."

He ignored her, rising from his chair, taking a step toward the door.

"*Allan!*" This time her tone was sharp and insistent, calling out to him through the Plexiglas partition.

Allan paused, pivoting to face her.

She looked at him and said, "Please, sit down."

He remained standing, hesitant.

She sighed, "I . . . there's something you need to know . . . just so you'll understand where I'm coming from."

He returned to the chair and put the phone to his ear.

"It's about Getty Fairfield," she said.

"Okay. So tell me."

"Like I said, it's complicated."

"For a guy you haven't seen or heard from in seventeen years, he's sure got you wrapped around his little finger."

She didn't speak, but something shifted in her eyes. It was a subtle change that told him he'd hit closer to the truth than he realized.

"What?" he said. "What am I missing? What are you not telling me?"

She interlaced her fingers, butting her knuckles against the underside of her chin. It was then that he noticed that tears had formed at the corners of her eyes. There was great turmoil inside this woman.

"Tell me, Rosemary."

Slowly her mouth opened, and she spoke. "Getty is the father of my child," she said in a fragile tone. "I had his baby."

57

A HALF MILE FROM THE PRISON, THE BLUE ESCORT WAGON pulled to the side of the road, and Patton got out. He walked around the front of the car, looking in both directions down the road to make sure no other traffic was coming. He continued pointing the gun at Jack Browne. He motioned for Browne to lower his window.

"I'll be right here, waiting on you," Patton said. "You try to be a hero, your family dies. You leave without killing the woman, they die. It's real simple."

Browne's knuckles were white as he gripped the steering wheel.

"You got that?" Patton said.

"Yes," Browne said through gritted teeth.

Patton unzipped a jacket pocket and withdrew two small Motorola walkie-talkie radios. He held one out to Browne.

"These are two-way radios. I've taped down the transmission button on yours so I can hear everything going on around you. Clip it on your belt and leave it turned on. I've got the other one here with me. I'll be listening to every word you say, every move you make. If I hear any funny business, I'll make a call to my partner, and he'll be more than happy to take care of the dirty work back at your place. Understand?"

Browne grabbed the radio out of Patton's hand and put it in his lap. "Just let me get on with it, you *monster*!"

Patton knew full well he'd never be seeing Browne again. If he made it to Hitchins and managed to pull the trigger, either his fellow guards would immediately put a bullet in him, or they'd wrestle him to the ground and he'd be looking at his own time behind bars. The Motorola put out a fairly strong signal. Metcalf would be along any minute, and they'd sit a safe distance away and listen.

"Go," Patton said, gesturing with the barrel of the gun.

The Escort motored away, heading toward the prison.

Patton trotted off toward a line of trees not far from the road. He kept an eye out for Metcalf, and kept the Motorola radio to his ear.

58

Jack Browne offered a wave to the man in uniform stationed inside the guard post. Then he steered the Escort through the gate and into the parking lot. He turned off the engine and remained seated behind the wheel. A sharp pain was thumping inside his head. He stared straight ahead at the thin strip of grass in front of the car. He was numb from head to toe.

He was desperately seeking a way out of this mess. He'd been in the wrong place at the wrong time last night. And now he was in a no-win situation. He grabbed the steering wheel with both hands and squeezed with all his might, his fingers and knuckles turning from white to blue. It sickened him to know that he was being monitored. He glanced down at the walkie-talkie in his lap. They had really thought of everything. He had briefly entertained the notion of calling the police from inside the prison to have them quietly encircle his house and smoke the second guy out. Maybe he could have pulled it off, but not now. The second he dialed the phone and opened his mouth, the man up the road would send word, and Jenna and the kids would quickly be dead.

He opened the door and climbed out of the car. He hooked the Motorola radio on the waistband of his jeans and let his shirt sag over it slightly to disguise its presence. The gun they'd given him was under the front seat. It was a .22-caliber pistol. It was slim and compact and fitted with a suppressor tube on the end of the barrel. He lifted the tail of his shirt and tucked the gun in his jeans. His hands were shaking.

The short trek from his parking spot to the entrance of the penitentiary felt like miles. His heart was thrumming away inside his chest, and he genuinely feared that he might have a heart attack. He was, after all, the perfect age for the old ticker to finally give out.

He paused, took a breath, then opened the door.

First he would head to payroll. That was a normal thing to do. It wouldn't raise so much as an iota of suspicion. He'd then slide over to a restroom, just to get his bearings. By then nobody would pay him much mind, and he'd have a few minutes in which to wander freely. It wasn't uncommon, when you worked a strange shift, to want to kick around a little on payday and shoot the breeze with some of the personnel you didn't get to chat with on a regular basis.

Rosemary Hitchins was housed in security level C-4. He knew that much. He rarely ventured that way, but he was friendly with a couple of the guards in that area of the prison complex. He'd just have to march through like he owned the place.

The payroll office was on the second floor of Building One. He took the stairs as casually as possible. His back was sweating. He prayed that the gun wouldn't come loose and drop into the baggy seat of his drawers.

There was a small cluster of people bunched around the front desk in payroll. It was payday, after all—the most festive day of the month. Browne generally waited until his shift to pick up his check, so there were a few surprised looks when he came through the door. He shook hands and smiled and did his very best not to think about the pistol in the back of his pants or the guy in his house ready to kill his family. His shirt was soaking up perspiration.

A secretary produced his check from a drawer in a tall filing cabinet. He reflexively glanced at the sum printed on the face of the check, for the first time in his life not giving a rip about taxes or insurance holdouts. His mouth was dry as he folded the check into a shirt pocket and said his good-byes. A couple of the fellows hanging out there offered to join him for a cigarette outside.

He declined, saying he wanted to say "hey" to a few folks before heading off to the farm.

By the time he found a restroom, he thought he might vomit. He locked himself in a stall and sat on the toilet seat, clenching his fists, trying desperately to get a grip on his nerves.

It was now or never. Wasting time wouldn't do him a lick of good.

Knowing that Patton would be listening, he lowered his mouth near the radio and said softly, "Okay, I'm on my way to find her now."

He peeked out the door to make sure no one was nearby, then turned the corner and headed in the direction of security level C-4.

59

"HOW CAN THAT BE POSSIBLE?" NOTHING COULD HAVE PREpared Allan for what Rosemary Hitchins had just told him.

"It just happened," Rosemary said, looking away from him for a moment. "It shouldn't come as a great mystery. What do you think Getty and I did all those nights?"

"But . . ." Allan shook his head slowly back and forth. "Did he know?"

"No. He ended our relationship before I discovered I was pregnant. When I found out, I originally was convinced it belonged to the Russian agent I was in love with."

"How'd you find out otherwise?"

Rosemary blinked. "I did the math. I hadn't been with Alexie in nearly two months. It was only a few weeks after Getty called it off that I started feeling ill in the mornings, and that month I was late."

"Alexie? Your lover, the Russian?"

She nodded, "Yes."

"You could have aborted the child."

"I didn't have the heart. I desperately wanted to have Alexie's child. More than anything in the world. And I would have gladly lied to him and told him the baby was his, but I ran out of time."

"That's when they caught you?"

"Yes. I was in the process of giving Alexie exactly what he was after, and I had every intention of leaving the country and joining him in Russia, when the FBI came crashing in on me. I was terrified. There I was, alone, pregnant, unmarried, and under arrest, charged with treason. They kept me hidden away until my trial date came around. That alone took over a year. They kept me in seclusion. I gave birth to the child, and she was immediately whisked away, taken from me before I even had a chance to hold her in my arms." Tears rolled from her eyes, and she made no attempt to wipe them away or shroud her face from him. The pain of having given up her baby was clearly greater than any sorrow imprisonment caused her.

Allan was stunned. All these years, he'd known only half the truth. No wonder she'd not been anxious to drag Getty Fairfield through the mud.

An awkward silence stood between them.

Allan was shocked at the intimate secret she'd revealed to him. He asked softly, "It was a girl?"

She nodded.

"What . . . do you know what happened to her?"

Rosemary shrugged. "They either found her a foster home or put her up for adoption." She paused. Then she continued, "The nurse who delivered her, Nurse Spagnazio, promised me she'd personally make sure Lucy was cared for."

"Lucy?"

Rosemary forced a smile through the rain of tears. She nodded, then shrugged. "That's what I called the baby. I wanted to call her something, something to at least remember her by, and that's all I could think of in the few seconds I got to see her. Nurse Spagnazio held her at my side in the delivery room, and I said, "Good-bye, Lucy. Know that I love you forever . . ." Her words trailed off as her lips began to quiver.

"That's incredible," Allan said, and he meant it.

"I'm powerless in here. They've taken my freedom, and they've taken Lucy. The only way I could protect her was to keep her a secret. If I had made the affair public knowledge, I would have put her in jeopardy. I had to make a choice, and I did what I thought best. I wish the best for you and your son, Allan, but I have to save something for myself."

And with that, Rosemary rose from her chair.

Frantic, Allan called out to her. "Rosemary . . . *please* . . ."

She already had her back to him. She knocked at the door, waiting for the guard to come for her.

"I'm begging you!"

The guard unlocked the door and opened it for her. Before she left, she turned and said, "I'm sorry, Allan. Really, I am."

And then she was gone.

Allan was standing, leaning over the metal counter, his hands pressed against the glass.

His plan had failed.

60

THE FEMALE GUARD WITH ROSEMARY WAS NAMED SHURELLE. She had Rosemary by the arm, casually leading her along the corridor the way they'd come barely twenty minutes ago.

Rosemary used the sleeve of her prison-issue shirt to wipe tears from her face. It had taken her a decade and a half to heal the wounds of giving up Lucy, and out of nowhere they had been suddenly reopened. It hurt so bad she could barely stand it.

The guard was used to emotional outbreaks from inmates, and she marched the prisoner ahead without a word.

Rosemary suddenly deeply regretted having agreed to speak with Allan Adler. It had served no purpose, and she felt that her heart had been broken all over again. All she wanted to do now was to get back to her cell as quickly as possible and crumble into bed, to press her face into her pillow and cry.

Her child, Lucy, was seventeen years old by now—a young lady. Lucy crossed her mind frequently, but never had Rosemary desired so badly to hold her daughter as she did at this moment. That was a joy of motherhood she would never experience.

She closed her eyes, a fresh spring of tears coursing down her cheeks. She could only hope that Nurse Spagnazio had kept her word and had found Lucy a caring home where she had been loved and nurtured.

Overcome with grief, her knees went weak and she stumbled. Shurelle reacted in a flash, trying to hold her up by her arm, but she lost her grip and Rosemary went down hard on both knees. Shurelle attempted to haul her back to her feet.

"I'm sorry," Rosemary said, looking up. "I tripped over my own feet."

"You all right?" Shurelle asked.

Rosemary nodded, but then winced. "I . . . I might have twisted my ankle."

"Can you stand?"

Rosemary probed a hand down the back of her leg. "It's tender. I don't know if I can put any weight on it."

The guard frowned, glancing up and down the corridor, hoping some help might wander by.

Rosemary twisted around into a sitting position, with her back to the wall, nursing her lame ankle. It really didn't hurt very much; she just wanted a few seconds to sit there and collect herself. She put her face in her hands, trying to keep from shaking, wishing all her pain, both physical and emotional, could somehow be washed away.

61

BROWNE HAD WORKED AT THE PRISON LONG ENOUGH TO BE pretty familiar with the faces of the inmate population. Rosemary Hitchins was no exception. The prison housed every breed of criminal under the sun, but none were more infamous than the woman who had spied for the Russians. Hers wasn't a face he saw on a weekly or monthly basis, necessarily, but it was a face he knew very well nevertheless, and so, at that moment as he moved through the prison's corridors en route to security level C-4, he knew precisely whom he was looking for.

But he hadn't expected to find her so easily.

First he heard a woman's voice beckoning him by name. He looked ahead. It was Shurelle, a guard from E-wing. She was waving him to her. Someone was seated on the floor, back against the wall.

Browne approached, not wanting to get stalled by having to help out.

Shurelle said, "Help me get her up. She might need to get to the infirmary. Says she twisted her ankle."

He was about to protest, when the woman on the floor raised her face from her hands and glanced up at him. He couldn't believe his luck.

Their eyes met.

"Give me a hand with her, Jack," Shurelle said.

He knew this was his moment of opportunity. It was now or never.

Shurelle started forward to reach down for Rosemary. But Browne stiff-armed her, catching the large woman at the base of her throat with the flat of his hand. She was rocked back on her heels and lost her balance.

Rosemary saw Shurelle hit the floor with a heavy thump, then looked in astonishment at Browne. She didn't understand. She didn't know what to think.

Browne lifted the tail of his shirt and pulled the .22-caliber pistol from the waistband of his pants. He held the gun inches from Rosemary's face.

The reality of what was unfolding before her clicked in her brain. But it was simply too late to react.

His finger tensed around the trigger, hesitating for just a second.

Shurelle, having sprawled out on the floor in the middle of the corridor, lifted her head and saw Browne and Rosemary and the gun, and she began screaming.

Browne ignored the screaming guard. He took aim.

"I'm sorry, but I have to," he said to Rosemary. Then he pulled the trigger repeatedly, firing round after round into her head.

The force of the shots knocked her over, and she slumped onto her side. He fired several more bullets into her upper body until he was certain she was dead.

Shurelle was backed up against the wall and screaming for help.

Browne looked down at Rosemary's lifeless body. Then he put his back against the wall. He'd done a terrible thing, but he had done it to protect his family, though he was now certain in his heart of hearts that those two monsters would not leave witnesses behind. They would kill his wife, child, and grandchild, if they hadn't already. Life as he'd known it was over. Now he was a criminal himself. But he couldn't face life behind bars without his family. Better to join them now in a better place. He put the gun to his head and pulled the trigger. His head jerked with the shot; then he folded to his knees and slumped forward lifelessly.

Blood was pooling around Rosemary Hitchins.

Shurelle was still screaming for assistance. She scrambled over to Rosemary's body, feeling for a pulse. But there was no need. It was too late. The Red Fox was dead.

62

THE CALL RANG THROUGH TO THE PHONE IN ROOM 1911. The shades were drawn and the lights were on. The hotel was in downtown Cincinnati. Lipscomb was dressed in chinos and a tank-top undershirt. He answered the phone with a lit cigarette between his lips.

The voice on the line was Patton. He had good news.

"You're positive she's dead?" Lipscomb said.

Patton assured him.

Lipscomb was all smiles.

The Brothers had taken care of Rosemary Hitchins in less than twenty-four hours. It was hard not to be impressed.

The three of them had arrived in the city on the same flight, but they'd be leaving separately. The Brothers were heading straight for the airport.

Lipscomb grabbed his button-up shirt off the back of a chair and was pulling it on a sleeve at a time as he dialed a number.

Claussen answered on the second ring.

"She's toast," Lipscomb said. "Pass it on."

Claussen didn't need to say a word.

Lipscomb found his shoes, snatched his wallet from the desk, and bolted for the door.

63

SENATOR HENBEST WAS AT A LUNCHEON LISTENING TO A rich white man expound on the plight of the nation's inner cities when his cell phone rang. He stepped outside for no more than a minute and was quickly back in his seat staring at his plate of cold pasta.

Lipscomb's report had been brief but clear.

It seemed that everything was back under control. The thorn in Fairfield's side had been removed. The remedy hadn't come cheap, but the problem was solved. They could once again take a breath of relief.

But this was Washington, D.C.

Henbest knew better than to be optimistic.

⁘

Word trickled down to Austin via D.C.

Claussen tracked Sandy Strunyin down on his car phone, and Strunyin had to pull to the side to keep from rear-ending the vehicle in front of him. He was suddenly short of breath.

Claussen chose his words carefully.

Strunyin put down the phone and pressed the flat of his hand over his heart. There was a bottle of prescription pills in the console between the seats. He popped the cap and tapped three into his sweaty palm. He sucked them down without the benefit of water. This business, he decided, was getting way out of hand. In fact, it seemed that it was no longer about business at all. The reality was that he was a part of something that had clearly spiraled out of control.

As much as it sickened him, he had to phone Newton Highfill and Jasper Cone. The pills kicked in, and he mellowed considerably. He made the two calls, then found the nearest bar and went inside for a stiff drink.

.◆...◆.

Jasper asked to be left alone for a while. Crystal didn't argue with him. A line had been crossed today, and they each had their own way of coming to terms with it.

Jasper strolled out to the garden and sat among the vines and blooms. She watched him from the kitchen windows, but lost sight of him when he crossed the lawn and passed the fountain. She poured a glass of wine and decided she needed to get very drunk.

It had been a mistake to get involved, she now realized. It had been arrogant for them to think that they could use political power in this way. That they could manipulate the president, for God's sake. Now their compulsion to crush Amethyst had led to murder. They were responsible for the murders of the Pappageorgios, and now they were linked to Rosemary's death. They had taken it too far. No amount of money was worth what they'd become.

64

THE MASSIVE CADILLAC SEDAN PARKED BETWEEN A HANDIcap spot and a blue Ford Escort station wagon. Ben Clement climbed out of the Cadillac's passenger side and gave the Ohio air a quick sniff. He wasn't a big fan of the Midwest.

The car's rear doors opened, Karla Gormaine and Philip Hopfner quickly popping out of the plush leather seats.

Brent Sneed thumbed a button on the keyless remote and the trunk lid released. Hopfner was immediately at the rear of the car, raising the trunk and digging for his gear.

Clement came around the car, hands on hips, and snapped a finger at Hopfner. "Hold up," he said.

Hopfner paused, turning his way.

"I don't want to be trudging in with all that equipment until we've been cleared," Clement said, gesturing at the video and sound equipment stowed in metal cases inside the trunk. "These administrative types get pretty fussy about that kind of thing."

Hopfner released the rubber-coated handle of one of the cases and shrugged.

"And I don't want the four of us piling in there like special ops dropping into Panama. Brent, you and Philip keep an eye on the car. Karla and I will go and do the meet-and-greet. Wait for my call." He gave Karla a wink and motioned toward the side-walk that led to the prison entrance.

"These boys won't know what hit them," Clement said, holding the front door for her.

It was immediately apparent that there had been a distur-bance of some sort. Prison employees were standing outside the administration offices, buzzing with chatter. Men and women in business suits, pointing and whispering, wide-eyed and talking animatedly. No one seemed too dazzled by the presence of a big-time lawyer and his lovely staffer.

They found the office without much effort, and Clement spoke to a secretary through the small window in the wall. They didn't have to wait long.

The administrator was out his door in a flash. He looked clearly frazzled.

"I'm Mr. Wollard," the administrator said, nudging his glasses up the bridge of his nose.

"Benjamin R. Clement, attorney at law," Clement said in his most magisterial tone.

Wollard didn't so much as blink. "Well, you're gonna have to excuse me, Mr. Clement, but you've chosen a decidedly bad moment to visit. I'll have to ask you to come back at a better time."

Being a lawyer, Clement was first and foremost a salesman. "I'm afraid my business can't wait, Mr. Wollard. I'm here on behalf of one of your inmates."

"With all due respect, Mr. Clement, please feel free to reschedule with Miss Anderson over there."

Clement glanced briefly at the enormous woman seated behind the window.

"You're misunderstanding me, sir," Clement said, stiffening, ready for a fight. "We have—"

"Who, then?" Wollard interrupted, about the time Miss Anderson bellowed at him and stuck her phone out through her window. He held up a finger to Clement and took a mighty stride toward the phone.

"Rosemary Hitchins, actually," Clement asserted, with a little more volume than was probably needed.

Wollard had no more than curled his fingers around the receiver before he froze in his tracks and wheeled his head back around to face the lawyer.

"Pardon me?" Wollard said, turning on his heels.

"Rosemary Hitchins. She's been incarcerated here since—"

"I *know* who she *is*!" Wollard said with a look of bewilderment. "She's *dead*!" He whacked the telephone receiver against the narrow ledge outside Miss Anderson's window and released it.

"Dead?"

Karla, who'd been listening over Clement's shoulder, took a step closer. She and Clement exchanged a shocked look. Before either could mouth a word, Wollard continued.

"Nobody shows interest in her in nearly a decade, then yesterday and today she's more popular than Elvis, and one of my own guards pulls a gun *right inside these very walls* and blows her head off!" Wollard shook his head and turned away from them. "You'll forgive me for being rude, but this is going to be one hell of a day."

Clement had to ask, "What *about* yesterday and today?"

Wollard paused, standing with the office door open. "That reporter, he shows up twice, and now the two of you."

Clement shot a quick look at Karla even as he fired off the next question at the administrator. "Reporter?"

But Wollard had already slammed his office door shut, cutting the exchange to an abrupt end.

They were left hanging. For a long moment they stared wordlessly at the closed office door. He felt like he'd just taken a blow to the head by a stout, blunt object. Karla looked as though Wollard had exposed himself to her.

"I didn't hear that," she said flatly. "I *couldn't* have heard that."

But Clement's mind was already zipping ahead. Someone had beat them to Rosemary Hitchins. They had to find out who exactly this reporter was, and what he'd been doing here. And why—*why*—would a prison guard murder an inmate? This situation reeked of Cone Intermedia. Clearly, somehow word had leaked.

Their big shot at slam-dunking CI had been derailed. He'd gotten so close to Hitchins he could almost taste it. And what a bitter taste it was. If he'd been only an hour earlier, maybe it would have made a difference.

Goodchapel would not be pleased. Clement switched into full battle mode. No more games. There still had to be a way to get to Getty Fairfield.

What had the reporter uncovered? They had to find him. Find him and bribe him . . . then kill him.

65

THE FACE OF THE HACKER WAS REFLECTED IN THE THIRTY-inch flat-screen computer terminal. Her name was Snow and she had a tattoo on the back of her neck that said WORLD PEACE? NO THANKS. She wasn't old enough to legally drink, but there wasn't a security system in the world she couldn't penetrate.

This one was absurdly simple. Snow had been seated at her keyboard in L.A. for less than ten minutes when she turned in her chair and smiled triumphantly at Brenner Walsh.

"You're fabulous," Walsh said.

"I hate to brag," Snow said, "but I *am* the queen bee!"

Walsh was seated on the front edge of a desk in the Pike & Associates L.A. office. He leaned around and grabbed a phone, dialing from memory.

Ben Clement was riding in the plush passenger seat of the Cadillac when his cell phone chirped. He checked his watch, then put the tiny phone to his ear.

"Tell me something good," Clement said without preamble.

"Inmate number WP99762 had one visitor today. We got a name off the Fort James visitor log. That translated into a home address and home phone number, Social Security number, credit history, work number, and, if you like, the balance of his 401(k)." Walsh gave a wink at Snow as he glanced at the printout she'd handed him from the laser printer.

"Ready when you are," Clement said, snapping his fingers at the passengers in the backseat, gesturing for a pen and paper.

"We're looking for a guy named Adler, Joseph Allan, a resident of Oklahoma City, Oklahoma."

"Okla-*who?* Is that even a state? What's he doing in Fort James, Ohio?"

"Apparently visiting inmate number WP99762," Walsh said flatly.

Clement ignored him. "Okay, so who's he work for?"

"According to this, he sells construction supplies."

Clement lowered the phone, holding it out away from his head. He gave a sideways glance at Sneed, who was driving. He ran this data through his brain, then put the phone back to his ear. "Something's off, and I don't like it. I want you down there in Oklahoma. I can't be running around chasing dead ends. Get down there, sniff around. Find out who this Adler character really is. I'm not buying this. Either he's not who you say he is, or he's nobody."

"Whether he's somebody or nobody," Walsh said, "he was at Fort James Penitentiary this morning with Rosemary Hitchins."

"Call me when you get to Oklahoma," Clement said. "We're running out of time."

66

OF COURSE NO ONE WAS HOME. ALLAN HAD DIALED THE number and stood there letting it ring until finally the machine picked up and he listened to Lanna's voice telling him what he already knew. He had hoped he might catch her having lunch at home, though she rarely did that. It was too much of a hassle to battle traffic twenty minutes each way just to grab a sandwich and a diet cola.

He was standing at a pay phone outside a coin laundry within sight of the interstate. There was traffic sitting at a light not thirty feet from the phone. He had to plug one ear with a finger just to hear himself think. When the message ended, he waited for the tone, then left a brief message that he'd try back later.

He was emotionally drained. Allan decided he'd had enough of Fort James Federal Penitentiary. He wanted to put as much distance between himself and Rosemary Hitchins as possible in the shortest time possible. Outside the prison gate he had stopped along the side of the road and sat behind the wheel for a moment, silent and still, just hoping to clear his head a little. His head was spinning. His worst nightmare had been realized. Rosemary Hitchins had denied him the one thing he most needed. An unsubstantiated story would get him only so far in D.C. To get results he'd have to have hard physical evidence. His cassette recorder was now useless. He had fished it from his jacket pocket and, in a surge of frustration, slung it across the cab of the truck. It slammed into the passenger-side door a few inches below the window and clattered to the floorboard.

A pickup lacking any sort of muffler was idling at the light, its engine rumbling like it was ready for a fight. Allan had to wait till it passed to make his call.

He next tried the hospital. Someone at the nurses' station picked up. She said Lanna was busy helping strip bandages from a burn victim. No message, he insisted. "I'll try later."

He had wanted to update her on how the morning had gone. He wanted to tell her that he was coming home to think things over and to regroup.

He hoped she was holding up okay. More than anything he wished she were still with him. Having her close was comforting.

Lanna's face was still on his mind as he crossed the pavement to his truck. His front left tire was seriously low. He knelt beside the truck to inspect it. Most likely he'd picked up a nail or something on the drive out from the prison. He stood and glanced around. There was a tire and lube garage beyond the next intersection. He decided the tire could make it if he hurried. Idling in the turn lane, signaling to turn in at the tire and lube, he heard sirens blaring nearby. He turned in and watched as an ambulance screamed past, not so much as slowing for the red light. Then, within seconds, a pair of police cruisers sped by as well.

Two fiftysomething men in stained work coveralls ignored him as he entered the open bay of the garage. A police scanner in the window had their attention. They listened to the radio chatter, one of the men frowning, straining to hear, the other half-grinning.

"Wow," Allan said. "What's all the excitement?"

"That ambulance that flew by," the grinning one said, still focused on the police scanner.

"There was a shooting out at the prison," the other one added. "One of the inmates took a bullet in the head."

Allan's blood ran cold. "What?"

"Yeah, a closed-custody inmate got popped on the way back to her cell. We've been listening. It's all over the police band."

It couldn't be. That was impossible.

But something on a gut level told him that yes, it was Rosemary. Someone had killed Rosemary.

His mind raced forward. His thoughts were a jumbled mess, strewn with mental images of Rosemary and Fairfield and the face of the president on TV. Fairfield was the president's nominee for chief justice, and Rosemary had represented a threat to his confirmation. Her sudden death couldn't possibly be a coincidence. *Could it?*

No. No way.

Allan had never considered himself any sort of conspiracy theorist, but he would have had to be blind not to see the connection between these players. Something big was going down. Which told him he'd been on the right track coming to see Rosemary. Someone had been scared of what she had to say. And they had made sure she was taken out of the picture. She'd been silenced. Something in his gut was telling him that he was in way over his head. He could be in serious danger and . . .

Then it hit him. There was one more link. Even better than Rosemary's words on tape. Her child, the girl. Lucy.

Lucy was the blood link between Rosemary and Fairfield. And Fairfield didn't know she existed. It was no longer a matter of he said/she said. DNA didn't lie. Lucy's DNA was a thousand times more valuable and dangerous than Rosemary's secret preserved on tape.

Allan knew exactly what he had to do now: he had to find Lucy.

67

THERE WAS A SMALL LIBERAL ARTS COLLEGE IN THE CENTER of Fort James. The town was basically built around it. It was barely large enough to accommodate two or three thousand students, and the word *sprawling* didn't exactly come to mind when describing the campus.

The library was two stories of brick and glass. Allan took the steps leading up to the front doors two at a time. He held the door for a pair of coeds who were much too caught up in their own conversation to even notice him. He stepped into the air-conditioning and wandered across the open atrium, goosenecking his way past vast rows of texts and resource materials.

A work-study staffer directed him to the computer room, and he settled in behind a monitor and keyboard and began pushing the mouse around. He'd brought with him the pages he'd printed at the library in Oklahoma City. They were badly creased down the middle, and he had to make a concerted effort to flatten them with his forearm. Working the mouse, he deftly found his way onto the Internet.

He uncapped a ballpoint pen and quickly scanned his printed pages looking for pertinent information, circling and underscoring anything that caught his eye. Most of what he'd previously found offered a brief history of the Rosemary Hitchins affair. Basically what he had was a crude timeline of events—a curt summary of her early life, through her arrest, trial, conviction, and finally, imprisonment.

He flipped a page over to use its blank side for scratching down notes. He directed the web browser to a popular search engine and typed a string of key words into the space provided. The hard drive hummed and droned for a few seconds, and he watched as literally thousands of matches registered in the hit count at the top of the screen.

Between the dates of her arrest and trial, she was denied bail and was held in a jail in Maryland. Many of the records he scanned stated this as fact. She was jailed in an unspecified county.

That was a start, but he'd have to go deeper.

He was after the nurse who delivered Lucy. It would take more than a few vague details found in random Internet records to pinpoint her. Very shortly it became clear that he could sit there day and night, having to scan through hundreds, or even thousands of files to find just one mention of the jailhouse in question. Even then, he considered, if he happened upon the location where she'd been held for the better part of that year, it might not draw him any closer to this Spagnazio woman.

Would Spagnazio have any direct connection to the jail itself? Allan leaned back in his chair and rolled his eyes toward the ceiling. He puffed his cheeks out, sighing. His conclusion? Perhaps not. In fact, it was a very, very slim possibility.

So, what else?

He rattled off more keystrokes, toying with any and every notion that came to mind.

In the search engine blank he typed items at random: Spagnazio. Nurse. Lucy. Russia. Spy. Adoption. Foster homes. Rosemary Hitchins. Washington, D.C. Government. Federal government. Federal employee. Pentagon . . .

It was maddening having to be so ambiguous and receiving such vague, unrelated results in return. The truth was he was looking for a needle in a haystack.

He pushed back in his chair and rubbed his eyes. He sighed and glanced at his watch. Time was wasting. But he was fully aware that he couldn't make the answers magically appear. He could stare at the computer screen for days on end, but if nothing hit him, then that's just the way it had to be.

He rolled his head around on his shoulders, then called up a map website and keyed in Washington, D.C. A map of the D.C. area sprang onto the screen. A mouse click asked it to list area hospitals. The website displayed a thorough list. There were over a hundred and fifty hospitals cataloged down a column that went on for nearly twenty pages. Calling every hospital, hunting just one solitary nurse who'd worked there seventeen years ago, was just not an efficient distribution of time or effort.

Next, he looked up an Internet telephone directory site. He entered the name Spagnazio and specified the search to the state of Maryland. It produced zero results. He repeated the process for Virginia, then for the District of Columbia. Nothing.

This was pointless!

He began slowly tapping the delete key, erasing the name he'd typed. As the blinking cursor backed over the O, I, and Z, Allan hesitated, narrowing his eyes and leaning closer to the monitor.

He had spelled her name with a Z.

Why?

He turned the question over in his brain. He thought he remembered Rosemary pronouncing it that way. And perhaps she had, but that didn't necessarily mean the name was spelled as such. The name had an Italian ring to it. Maybe it was spelled with a C or an S.

Following that tack, he typed the name as Spagnasio, searching the records from the same states he had under the previous spelling. He waited anxiously.

Again, nothing.

He frowned.

Allan typed over the second, replacing it with Spagnacio. He performed a search for Maryland and the District of Columbia, coming up empty on both counts. Virginia, though, produced one hit.

David & Mia Spagnacio—Richmond, Virginia.

Suddenly recharged, Allan jotted down the Spagnacios' home phone number.

Outside the computer room he stopped a passing student and asked if there were any pay phones nearby.

"Dude, you passed them on your way in," the kid said with a smirk.

And sure enough, he had breezed right past a bank of four phones bolted to the brick facade just inside the tall, glass entrance at the front of the library.

He dialed the number.

A woman's voice answered.

"Mrs. Spagna-*zio?*" He put great emphasis on the Z.

There was a moment of slight hesitation.

"Yes?"

"Uh, my name is Allan Adler, and I'm trying to get hold of a Mrs. Spagna-*zio* who either is, or used to be, a nurse in the D.C. area." Allan held his breath and hoped for the best.

This time the pause was a few beats longer in its duration.

Allan thought her voice sounded awfully young to have already been working as a nurse some seventeen years ago.

Finally, she spoke up. *"Unbelievable,"* she said, a certain amount of irritation edging into her tone. "We haven't gotten one of *these* calls in years!"

"Excuse me?"

"Our name is pronounced *see-oh*, not *zee-oh*. For about the first ten years after my husband and I moved to Richmond we were constantly getting calls for that nurse at that Presbyterian hospital. But it's been quiet for so long, I'd just about forgotten.

Wait until I tell David. What a hoot! People were always calling information, and the operators always tangled up the pronunciations. I'm sure that nurse got plenty of calls for us, too."

On the back of his hand Allan scribbled *Presbyterian*.

"You wouldn't happen to remember the name of that hospital, would you?"

She sighed. "Maybe . . ."

He could hear her fumbling through a drawer.

"Actually," she said. "I believe we had it marked down somewhere, so we could give people the right number. We got so many calls, you know, we just got used to it . . . ah, yeah, here it is."

Allan's heart soared. He made a fist and pumped it in the air, doing a little dance right there with the phone in his hand. A student with a book pack slung over one shoulder walked past and gave him a bemused look.

"Ready?"

Allan poised his pen. "Go ahead."

"Madison Heights Presbyterian Hospital. It's in Alexandria, if I remember."

He wrote as fast as he could.

"I have her old number, you want it?"

"That'd be great!"

She dictated it to him, he thanked her, and she hung up.

It was like getting a new lease on life. But until he had Spagnazio on the line, there was still no room for letting down. He dialed the number, reading it off the back of his hand. A recording informed him that the number was no longer in service. He cursed under his breath and hung up the phone.

All was not lost, though. He had the name of the hospital where she had apparently worked. He dialed information for Alexandria, Virginia, and requested the number for Madison Heights Presbyterian Hospital. The operator automatically put the call through for him.

Eventually he was directed to the personnel office. A man

with a very effeminate voice fielded his call and put the name Spagnazio through the hospital's computer system.

"I'm sorry, sir, nothing comes up under that name. That doesn't mean she didn't work here. Every couple of years we clean out old records. Our system simply isn't capable of warehousing such a vast amount. When everything was done on paper and stored in boxes across town, you could find just about anything you wanted going back for decades. Especially employment records. We keep that information for as long as the government requires for tax purposes, and then it's simply jettisoned."

Allan, staring at the wall of brick above the phone, chewed on his lower lip. "So there's no way of knowing whether she worked there?"

"All I have to work with is what's in this computer in front of me, sir. Outside of that . . . hey, wait a second," the man said. There was a pause, and Allan heard him shuffle through stuff on his desk. Then he came back on the line. "Tell you what, the best I can do is transfer you to the nurses' station on the fifth floor. That's pediatrics. You say your nurse worked with babies?"

"I believe so, yes."

"Okay, well, there's a nurse up there who's been with the hospital practically since Pearl Harbor. Her name is Ruth Levine. If she doesn't know, then God himself probably can't help you. Best of luck."

Allan waited through series of clicks and tones and then sat through two minutes of really bad Musak. Finally, a nurse answered.

"Pediatrics."

He asked for Ruth Levine.

"She's . . . let me see. Here she comes," the nurse said. "Can you hold for just a second?"

"Sure."

More Musak.

Then the line was picked up.

"This is Ruth," a fairly elderly but chipper voice said.

"Mrs. Levine?"

"Ah, Ruth will do, hon."

"My name is Allan Adler, and I'd like to know if you remember a nurse who might've worked there with the last name Spagnazio?"

She barely missed a beat. "Nell Spagnazio, sure."

"Nell? And she was a nurse there?" His excitement level was quickly rising.

"That's right, sugar. She's been retired the better part of a decade, though, that lucky devil. Me, I'll probably work till I just keel over in the break room."

"You wouldn't know if she was still living in that area?"

"Last I heard, her and that man of hers had sold out and headed for the wilderness. They built a cabin in Colorado, and they only trek down out of the mountains for groceries once a month or so. That help you, hon?"

"Absolutely," he said. "More than you know."

He hung up the phone and pressed his hands against the brick on either side of the phone, letting out a long sigh of relief. Then he made a mad dash back to the computer room.

He called up the Internet telephone directly and plugged in the name Nell Spagnazio, and clicked on Colorado.

Bingo!

Berg and Nell Spagnazio, Gunnison, Colorado.

Without a moment's hesitation, he printed off the page, gathered his few things, and bolted for the door. He'd done all he could out here. It was time to head west.

PART 3

PART 3

68

THE HOUSE WAS EASY TO FIND. IT WAS JUST OFF THE HIGH-way at the end of a dirt lane that wound through the trees and over a rise. Brenner Walsh guided the Mercury Marquis carefully down the crude driveway. He'd brought a freelance man with him, a guy named Sheridan, whom he paid in cash because in Sheridan's line of work paper trails were dangerous.

They had seen the Adlers' mailbox at the head of the drive-way. The name Adler was spelled out in uneven, peeling letter-ing. Walsh found himself agreeing with Clement's logic. It didn't make a lot of sense that a reporter doing a piece on someone like Rosemary Hitchins would live in a place like this. There had to be more to this Adler character than what they saw on paper.

Walsh planned to case the property on a quick drive-by, then return later for a closer look. Walsh was driving. Sheridan rode in silence in the passenger seat, his eyes hidden behind dark sun-glasses. Sheridan possessed some truly gruesome skills, though Walsh hoped they wouldn't be needed in dealing with Allan Adler. But Clement had made it clear that the stakes were now too high to take any chances. If blood had to be shed, so be it.

The driveway spit them out on a gravel strip that bordered a barbed-wire fence. The home was a two-story and sheathed in vinyl siding.

The Mercury eased up alongside the gravel strip and slowed to a complete stop. Walsh removed a sleek digital camera from a zippered bag and proceeded to photograph the Adler home.

Suddenly there was movement at the front of the house. The front door opened and a teenage boy emerged, at first staying right at the door, then gradually moving farther out on the porch.

Walsh put away the camera, turned the car around, and followed the driveway out the way they'd come.

Dermott Adler watched until the car was gone. He had happened to catch a glimpse of it as he passed a window. He honestly didn't think anything of it. Periodically someone would wander up the driveway to the house, figure out there was nothing there worth seeing, and quickly leave. He stood for a few moments with the door open, shrugged, and went back inside.

69

IT WAS A CURIOUS BIT OF NEWS, MENTIONED BRIEFLY BY each of the three major networks on their evening telecasts, though only in passing. The American woman convicted of passing secret documents to the Russians had been murdered in prison. Not much was said. The news anchors proclaimed that the alleged perpetrator was a prison employee, but few details had been released to the public. The story was wedged between other, more timely and relevant pieces.

Allan Adler didn't hear the news. At the moment it aired, he was at cruising altitude, trying to catch a nap before his flight landed in Denver.

Lanna Adler was fixing dinner, distracted by kids and the ringing phone.

Getty Fairfield had learned the news early in the afternoon, and he now watched the *CBS Evening News* with a glass of gin and tonic. The finality of the report filled him with both immense relief, as well as a number of secondary emotions that he chose not to acknowledge.

Crystal Easterling listened to it as she lay on a sofa with her eyes closed.

Jasper Cone hadn't watched television in years.

On the West Coast, Costas Goodchapel was swimming laps in his Olympic-size pool at the moment the report aired. He couldn't resurrect a dead woman, so why dwell on it? Instead, he focused only on things he could affect. He reached the end of the pool, flipped and turned, pushed off, and exploded through the water toward the far end. At this point, his mind was not so much on Rosemary Hitchins as it was on Brenner Walsh and his visit to Oklahoma.

70

BY THE TIME THE PLANE HAD LANDED IN DENVER AND ALLAN had filled out the paperwork for a rental car and managed to navigate his way out of the airport, he was starving. They had fed him a cold sandwich and a glass of tea on the plane, but he would need a real meal in his stomach if he planned to be on the road for most of the night.

To save money he'd requested the cheapest car the rental agency offered. In this case it was a Ford Fiesta. Allan opened the tiny hatchback and checked for a spare tire. In the country he was going to be driving through he didn't want to find himself stranded. The spare was a doughnut that looked better designed for use on a tricycle.

On the western outskirts of Denver he pulled into a steakhouse and ordered a Kansas City strip off a laminated menu. The waitresses wore kerchiefs around their necks, rodeo style. The slab of beef was still sizzling on the metal platter when dinner was served. The baked potato was slathered with butter and sour cream.

After dinner he pointed the tiny car toward the mountains and drove at full throttle into the sunset. He'd been up since early morning and could feel his body and mind beginning to drag. But he knew he had to keep trucking. If those who were protecting Fairfield discovered the existence of the child Rosemary claimed to have had, then she was in danger too, and his plan could once again be in jeopardy. At his point, Allan realized, it wouldn't just be Steven's future he was out to save, it would also be his own life and that of Rosemary's child.

The sun dropped behind the mighty peaks of the Rocky Mountains. The headlights of the little Fiesta swung around the curves in the steep mountain passes. Its puny engine groaned and whined like it was in the throes of death. He wasn't sure how much of this kind of driving it could take, but he couldn't afford to slow down or give it a break.

The farther away he drove from the lights of Denver, the fewer cars he saw on the road. In the higher elevations he would go fifteen or twenty minutes without seeing another pair of headlights. He kept the pedal pressed nearly to the floor, but the car did well to top seventy on the speedometer.

In Ohio he had called information for Colorado, requesting the number for the Spagnazios, but there was no listing. In Denver he tried again, and again came up empty-handed. The hope had been that maybe he could get hold of her by phone and ask if she remembered what arrangement she'd made for Rosemary's child. In the end he'd seen little alternative but to find them at their mountain hideaway and speak to her face-to-face, and just hope—*hope*—that she'd be open to helping him find Lucy.

And what if she didn't remember? What if she'd simply handed the baby over to someone else who'd then passed her on to the next set of hands, who may or may not have placed the child with an adoption agency or foster care? Then he'd be off chasing another rabbit. It could very likely turn out to be a time-wasting, fruitless endeavor.

The road unspooled before him like a ribbon of asphalt. He tuned into an FM station on the radio and hummed along with a song he'd never heard before.

Several hours into the trip he could no longer hold his eyes open. He pulled the car onto the side of the road and walked around in the chill for ten minutes, doing jumping jacks and running in place, anything to wake up his mind and body enough to get him a few hours closer to Gunnison. Then he fell in behind the wheel, cracked his window three or four inches, and punched the accelerator. Ninety minutes later, he pulled over at a scenic overlook along the highway and crawled into the backseat to submit to three hours of sleep.

71

LANNA CLEANED THE KITCHEN, AND DERMOTT TOOK CARE of the outside chores and helped his mother put the younger kids to bed. Dermott had then watched TV in the front room for a couple hours before finally wandering down the hall and disappearing behind his bedroom door. Lanna sat at the kitchen table, alone, absorbing the silence of the house.

The first message on the answering machine had been from Wes Swanson. He was just checking in and wanted to tell her Steven was doing fine. Allan had called also, saying only that he loved her and that he would try back later. The house didn't feel right without him. Nothing felt right without him.

She rested her chin on the flat of one hand, her elbow on the table. Her gut told her that maybe they'd allowed this whole mess to spin out of control. Now they'd taken out money on the house, spent savings they'd surely need someday, and Allan was out gallivanting across the country wasting more time and money. But she understood his motivation. They had to do everything possible for Steven.

It was well after midnight. She began shutting the house down. She made sure the doors were all locked and the lights were off. She peeked out the front window to make sure the gate was closed. Dermott had taken care of that hours ago. Then she peeked in on the little ones on her way to bed.

Because of the dark outside and the heavy cover of trees, she hadn't noticed the big Mercury sedan parked at the bend in the driveway with its headlights off.

72

WHEN THE LAST LIGHT IN THE HOUSE WENT OUT, BOTH Walsh and Sheridan got out of the car. They had parked behind a utility shed, out of sight of both the house and the driveway. The night was intensely deep and dark, and the Adler home stood featureless against a moonless, starless backdrop, but Walsh had set to memory the exterior of the house, and knew how and where to make their approach.

Rather than entering through the front gate, Walsh moved along the perimeter of the tree line, advancing on the house from the left side. Within minutes they had crossed the lawn to one corner of the house. Walsh breathed a sigh of relief—there was no sign of the dogs they'd seen that afternoon. No matter, Sheridan was armed with a pneumatic pistol with tranquilizer darts in case the animals showed up.

Snow had been on the phone with Walsh throughout the afternoon and evening, updating him the instant she uncovered anything of value regarding the Adler clan. She had begun with what she'd hacked from the prison's computer, and since then had been camped out online, focusing her immense skills on trying to peel back the veil to look into Allan Adler's past. She was slowly building a life history, stick by stick. They needed to know who he was and where he'd come from.

The family was inside, they knew. There was an older boy, three younger children, and the mother, Lanna. Snow had provided Walsh with names and ages. But so far there was no sign of Adler. They each wore tiny earpieces so that they could communicate at a whisper. This little errand would be brief. There wasn't much they could hope to accomplish, but Clement had been emphatic that they make an effort. Rosemary Hitchins was dead, and Adler might be their one link to Fairfield. Goodchapel wanted answers.

Walsh wanted to be on the way back to the car inside of five minutes. Sheridan was to poke around in the building out back while Walsh made his way inside the house.

Walsh was quickly at the door at the rear of the house. Careful to remain in the cover of shadow, he reached up and gently eased open the storm door. From his pocket he withdrew a slender tool that he inserted into the keyhole of the door lock. A simple twist was all that was required, and within seconds he was standing in a short hallway. He pushed the door closed, careful not to make a sound. Right away he found himself in the kitchen. He produced a slim penlight and went straight to the telephone located on the kitchen counter. This was easy work. He'd done it a thousand times. With a small tool he removed two screws from the handset of the phone and placed a listening device the size of a grain of rice therein.

As he was replacing the second screw, he heard a sound. He froze. A door had opened.

Seized with panic, Walsh spun his head, desperate for a place to hide. Footsteps were approaching. He shoved the penlight into his pants pocket and took two long, silent strides across the kitchen, putting his back to a wall.

The footsteps approached the kitchen, and he saw movement. He felt very naked and exposed. Sheridan was the only one with a gun. In all his career, Walsh had never carried one.

Suddenly the kitchen light flickered on. Walsh did his best to melt into the wall.

It was the four-year-old, Claire. Her eyes looked sleepy. She was wearing a cotton nightdress that swished across her ankles. She padded over to a broom closet and picked up a plastic stool with steps molded into one side. She staggered with her load to the kitchen counter, sitting it on the floor directly beneath the sink. Then she climbed up and filled a glass with water.

Walsh hadn't breathed since the girl had entered the room. A bead of perspiration popped out on his forehead and made a path between his eyes, finally catching on the tip of his nose and hanging there for what seemed like a lifetime. All the girl had to do was turn his way for a half second and he'd be busted.

Instead, when her thirst was satisfied, she set her glass on the counter and labored to get the stool back inside the broom closet where it belonged. Then, reaching up on tiptoes, she cut the light and felt her way along the wall to her bedroom.

Walsh reached up with one hand and pinched off the droplet of sweat from the tip of his nose. He felt the muscles of his back slowly relax. He finished with the phone.

There wasn't much to say about the house, at least what he could see of it. Even if they came back tomorrow and turned the place inside out while the family was away, he failed to believe they'd find anything newsworthy. Which made the entire scenario that much more puzzling.

The question was where was Allan Adler *now*? If he hadn't returned home after visiting Rosemary Hitchins at the prison, where had he gone instead?

73

SNOW WAS GETTING VERY CLOSE TO FINDING AN ANSWER. Though she was only nineteen, her personal view of the world was bleak at best. She ranked among the ten most paranoid individuals on earth. It never ceased to amaze her how in this day and age people continued to put so much trust in government and industry. Her major goal in life was complete anonymity, to put her faith in no one. She'd never applied for a driver's license. Had no credit cards. Had no checking or savings accounts. She had never used her Social Security number, and she had a thousand different ways of avoiding taxes.

She had good reason for the paranoia. She could take even the tiniest scrap of information, go online, and instantly look into a person's soul, completely uninvited.

Her hair was cropped short and was the color of fire. Her IQ was off the charts, and Walsh paid her off the books. She was currently on her fifth Diet Coke of the night. Her fingers blazed across the keyboard of her computer in the L.A. office of P & A. She wore a headset so that she could use the phone without having to miss a beat as she worked.

Keeping a keen eye on the fields of data rushing down the screen of her monitor, she began to get that giddy feeling in her stomach she always got when she was hot on the trail of something juicy. All she had used was Allan Adler's Social Security number, and she'd simply sat back and let it unlock all the doors to his past.

She kept a small pad of pink sticky notes at her elbow, and periodically she'd grab her pen and scribble something best not forgotten.

She grinned, making a quick note to herself on a sticky note. She circled what she'd written. "Ah," she said, "our boy was a soldier." Then, without taking her eyes from the screen, she reached over and dialed Walsh's cell phone number.

The Mercury was blowing down the highway. Walsh answered immediately.

"Adler was in the army," Snow stated straight out of the gate.

"Okay. When?"

"Let's see . . . let's see . . . let's . . . yeah, there . . . it's been awhile. He's on file with the VA," Snow said as if she were speaking to herself, which she usually was. "It's coming up . . . right . . . now. According to the VA's database, he's been out for like, sixteen, seventeen years. He was last stationed at . . . let's see . . . *huh?* . . . oh, yeah, yeah, that's what I thought it said . . ."

"Spit it out."

"The Pentagon."

"Say again."

"His last few years of service he was assigned to the Pentagon."

"What rank?"

"Mmmm . . . staff sergeant, 92 Yankee. Whatever that means."

"Could mean a lot of things. You're sure he was at the Pentagon?"

"That's what it says. Want me to email it to you?"

"Good idea."

Her hands thundered over the keys. "It's on its way."

"Keep digging," he said and ended the call.

He quickly dialed Clement.

"It's late, make it good."

Walsh said, "Adler was assigned to the Pentagon in the army while Fairfield was there."

Clement shot straight up in bed. Chill bumps stood up on the back of his neck. His wife was in the bed next to him. He slid out from the covers and crept to the bathroom, flipping on the light and taking a seat on the toilet. His mind was churning madly. It didn't take him long to connect the dots.

"Adler knew about Fairfield and Hitchins!"

"I'm not saying one thing or another," Walsh said flatly. "I'm just passing you the facts as we uncover them."

"So why would he have been with Hitchins just before her murder?"

"I have to guess that was just bad timing. This guy's life is *Little House on the Prairie*. My professional instincts tell me that whatever he's up to, he's not necessarily in competition with us."

"All I care about is what he knows. He heard or saw something or someone at the Pentagon, I'm betting money on it."

"We'll know for sure very shortly," Walsh said.

74

DESPITE HAVING FOLDED HIMSELF INTO THE BACKSEAT OF the compact car, causing his neck to cramp and making his knees feel like they belonged to an eighty-year-old arthritic man, Allan Adler had managed to wake fairly rested. Morning light angled into the car through the hatchback window. He twisted around on his bottom, fighting with his legs to get himself arranged in a proper upright sitting position.

He rose up—light blinding him for a moment—and yawned. He rubbed his eyes, then his neck, which ached fearsomely from his awkward sleeping posture. He managed to squeeze himself through the gap between the front seats and kicked open the driver's side door with his foot.

It was barely forty degrees out, and a stiff wind cut him to the bone. But the brisk cold was exactly what he needed first thing this morning. The wind was a cold slap in the face, and he loved it.

He vaguely remembered pulling the car over at a scenic overlook, but in the middle of the night every turnoff along the highway looked no different from the next. This morning, however, he realized that the term *scenic overlook* was a vast understate-ment. The view before him was awe-inspiring. The gravel turnoff where he'd brought the car to a halt faced out at a grand am-phitheater of towering mountains, the highest peaks of which appeared to be capped with snow.

He had to get moving.

The little Ford was stubborn when he first turned the key in the ignition. It had sat in the cold for too long and the battery had taken a beating. He cranked the ignition three times, unsuc-cessfully. He let it sit for two or three minutes, blowing into his hands to warm them, then gave the key another twist. The en-gine rattled to life.

There was no time for breakfast. He needed to get plenty of highway behind him as early as possible. Passing through a small ski town, he stopped to fill the tank with gas, and grabbed a tall cup of coffee and a banana-nut muffin wrapped in plastic. He paid with a credit card and held the coffee between his thighs as he drove.

He'd made better time the night before than he'd realized. Not far outside the ski town he passed a sign that said Gunnison 45. He'd be there within the hour.

The map he'd printed at the university library gave the Spag-nazios' address as not being within the city limits of Gunnison itself but rather off a county road a good half-hour's drive south of town. The map was quite lacking in details, and he offered a silent prayer that he wouldn't get lost or stuck or fall off the side of the mountain.

Gunnison came and went.

He watched the road signs with great care. He arrived at a T in the highway, where he could continue straight and hit Mont-rose, or take a left. He turned left.

The highway seemed to wind on forever. The scenery was splendid, but it felt like he was getting nowhere fast. He suspected the turnoff for the county road would either be dirt or gravel and wouldn't be well marked. He was correct on both counts.

If he had blinked he'd have missed it. The county road branched off where the highway made a dramatic curve around the mountain it was cut into. Allan had to throw the Fiesta into reverse and back up about thirty feet in order to hit the dirt road. He pulled to a stop just a stone's throw from the highway and peered up ahead, observing the path he was about to follow into the wilderness. And that's precisely what he was looking at: wilderness. The road ahead of him was fairly primitive. His guess was that it was maintained by a county grater that came by no more often than once a month. The drive was sure to be rough going.

The road followed a stream for about a half mile, then crossed a small bridge that spanned the water, and began to work its way up a serpentine route through the mountains. The little four-cylinder whined as he urged it onward. It wasn't designed to function in such high altitudes.

Soon the highway was no longer visible. The road climbed through endless acreage thick with aspens. The sun was out and the sky was clear, and the morning was quickly warming. The dirt road was barely wider than the car itself, and Allan figured that in a hard rain it could wash out pretty easily. About the time he was wondering what he'd do if he encountered a vehicle coming from the opposite direction, he looked up ahead and saw a glare of sunlight reflecting off the windshield of an approaching SUV. He groaned.

As the distance between them shrank, Allan did his best to make room. The oncoming vehicle was a silver Toyota. It barely slowed as it passed. The driver, an older gentleman, offered a cordial wave. There appeared to be passengers in every seat. The SUV left him in a cloud of dust. He watched it grow small in his rearview mirror, then continued on.

He'd driven nearly forty-five minutes before he started to really worry. The last thing he wanted to do was spend the entire day wandering aimlessly through the mountains. Periodically he'd pass a cabin or a nice log home situated at the edge of the

forest. It was his best guess that most folks around those parts remained strangers to one another. But eventually he decided he'd
better stop.

He turned at a fork in the road and followed a split-rail fence
for a quarter-mile. A handsome log home was visible in a break
in the aspens. He made his way up the driveway and parked the
car not far from the front door. A short conversation produced
good news.

Another mile and a half down the bone-jarring county road
deposited him in a long valley where two mountainsides con-
verged. A narrow, gurgling stream divided it in half. The road
passed right through the stream, the skinny little tires splashing
through maybe five or six inches of snow-fed water. This was the
valley he was after. He'd been told what to look for, and that
he'd better have the eyes of a hawk.

Just past the stream he got out of the car and walked a few
yards ahead. He stopped and scanned the opposite mountainside, using his hand as a visor against the sun. If he hadn't been
told what to look for he'd have never spotted it. From that distance it was nothing more than a brown shape among the trees,
but it gave him a point of reference.

The road didn't follow the crease down the center of the valley, instead dipping now and again into the blanket of aspen and
pine, passing from dappled shadows into stark sunlight. He
cursed whoever had spent a lifetime forging such an erratic trail.
Finally he was able to glance to his left and spot the Spagnazios'
cabin directly uphill from him. The road, though, continued on,
eventually curving back around through the forest.

A crude dirt track branched off the road and stopped at a
closed gate less than a hundred yards farther down. It was held
shut by a short length of chain but was unlocked. He swung the
gate open, drove through, then closed the gate before continu-
ing.

The dirt track ended at a circle drive made of gravel. The
cabin was an A-frame structure made mostly of redwood. It was

of modest size, with a redwood deck protruding out the front. It faced the valley and the opposing mountainside, and Allan mused to himself that he wouldn't at all mind waking up there every morning for the next thirty years. The only sounds were of the wind in the trees and an occasional bird squawking from somewhere in a high perch.

There was a parking area to the right of the cabin with space enough for three vehicles, though only a minivan and a small four-door car were present. A metal pole stood in the ground on the far side of the deck, on top of which was mounted a solar panel. Well, he thought, they've got power at least. There were two other small structures staggered several yards behind the main cabin.

He knocked several times on the aluminum frame of the storm door, and put his face to the window, hoping someone was home. No one answered. He frowned and knocked again, this time putting a little force behind it. Still nothing.

Surely he hadn't come all this way just to miss them. He cupped his hands around his eyes and peered through the window. The first floor of the cabin was mainly one big room. There were a few pieces of furniture, but it was rather sparsely adorned.

He wandered down the steps on the other side of the deck. Most of the yard surrounding the cabin was scrub grass. A fence had been erected around the perimeter of the property to keep cattle from grazing right up against the house.

They turned and saw each other at the same moment.

"Oh my, you startled me!" the woman said.

Allan was equally jolted. He'd never had nerves of steel and had nearly jumped out of his socks as he caught a flash of her out of the corner of his eye.

She was fairly advanced in years, likely in her midseventies, maybe late sixties, with white hair sprouting out from beneath a floppy denim hat. She wore white pants, rolled at the cuffs, and an oversize khaki shirt unbuttoned over a red T-shirt. Both hands sported cotton gardening gloves, and in them she grasped a gardening spade.

A narrow gravel path led from the rear of the cabin off at an angle to one of the secondary structures. The woman had been returning down the path when they spotted each other.

"Oh Lordy," she said, placing a hand over her chest. "My heart. I believe you scared the next twenty years out of me!" Her expression was startled but cheery. "I didn't know anyone was here. Never heard you drive up."

Allan offered a smile. "It's so quiet up here I'd figure you could hear everything for half a mile."

She set the spade on a large gray rock and plucked off her work gloves. "When I'm working, you could set off a grenade and I'd not notice." She looked at him. "Are you lost, sir?"

He smiled. "I hope not, ma'am."

"For starters, I'm Nell, not ma'am, and we are the Spagnazios, Italian by blood but mountain goats at heart!"

"I'm Allan Adler."

"You've certainly wandered off the beaten path to get here."

"True."

She looked at him curiously. "Is there something I can help you with?"

"Possibly. I'm looking for someone. Maybe you can point me in the right direction."

"Well, Allan, it's cooler inside. We can talk more in there. How about some tea?"

"That's certainly a generous offer to make to a perfect stranger who shows up on your doorstep."

She smiled and touched his wrist. "Allan, when you live out in a place like this, trouble is not likely to come looking for you. Our best friends started out as strangers. Besides, you have kind eyes. So, come on in."

He followed her up the steps to the deck and they went inside.

Nell took two plastic cups from a cabinet and filled them

with ice from a small refrigerator. She found the pitcher of tea and filled both cups. "Berg and I—he's my husband—we're from out east. Not originally, but we spent over thirty years in the Washington, D.C., area. We built this place when we retired."

She handed him a drink.

"I'm sorry you missed Berg and the kids. They're off on some adventure this morning."

"I passed a Toyota on the way up."

"That would be them," she said.

A propane heater stood on the floor near one wall. A long shelf was mounted to the wall above the heater. She motioned him to join her. He saw that the shelf was lined with framed photographs.

"Family?" he asked.

She nodded, and waved a hand past the display of portraits with the grace of a game-show presenter. "Our kids and grand-kids. Berg and I had three, two boys and a girl. They're spread from here to there, all over the country."

The whole drive up he'd debated with himself the best way to approach Nell Spagnazio. She had apparently briefly encoun-tered Rosemary Hitchins and made what in all likelihood had been just an off-handed promise as a means of keeping the in-mate from getting distressed. But hers was the one and only name Rosemary had mentioned, and now Rosemary was gone. Nell Spagnazio was all he had. She was the only remaining link to the baby that Rosemary claimed Fairfield had fathered.

He had to think of some way to bring up the subject. He sipped his tea, listening but not listening, his eyes glancing over each photo as she pointed to it, but only half paying attention.

"That's Glen, our eldest. He's a chemist in Tupelo," she was saying excitedly. "Those are his kids. And that's Laney, our daugh-ter. That's her husband, Stan. They have a twelve-year-old, that's Ricky there, and a seventeen-year-old, Lucy, and that's her there. They live in Florida now. Stan imports wicker furniture . . ."

Her words echoed over and over in his ears. Had he really

heard what he thought he heard? Lucy. Had she said *Lucy*? He took a step closer to the framed photos, suddenly intently engrossed in her cataloging of the family. He zeroed in on a photo of a blond teenage girl. Chills ran up and down his spine.

Nell had continued on to the next batch of kin.

Despite the iced tea, Allan's mouth had suddenly gone dry. Surely it couldn't be. There had to be an explanation for the coincidence. Why couldn't Nell Spagnazio have a seventeen-year-old grandchild named Lucy? But deep down he knew better. Deep down he knew the truth. And the truth was that the search was over. He'd found Lucy.

". . . Tricia has worked there since—"

Allan politely interrupted. "Uh, Nell . . ."

She looked at him with bright eyes.

"I, uh . . . I think there's something . . . something you should know."

"Oh?"

He nodded, wanting to play this as delicately as possible. He glanced around and spotted a reading table beside a recliner. He set his cup of tea on a coaster on the table.

"Mrs. Spagnazio . . . Nell, I have to come clean with you. I didn't wander up here to your cabin by accident. Actually, it's you specifically that I've come to see. I've come to talk to you about a woman named Rosemary Hitchins, a prison inmate whose baby you helped deliver nearly two decades ago." He paused a few beats, letting his words find their mark. "Do you understand what I'm saying? Do you remember?"

The light went from Nell Spagnazio's face.

Outside, the sun had hidden behind cloud cover, and long shadows fell over the cabin.

She was looking at him differently now. She turned and walked quickly to the cramped kitchen area, dumping out her tea into the sink, setting the empty cup on the short kitchen counter. Allan could hear the sound of ice cubes sliding into the sink drain.

"Mr. Adler, I think you should leave now," she said sharply, refusing to make eye contact. "You're no longer welcome here."

"Nell, please . . . don't misunderstand . . . I—"

"Just go, please . . . *NOW!*" Her tone, like her countenance, had darkened considerably. She jerked open the front door, gesturing for him to leave.

"All I want to do is talk—"

Both of them at once heard the sound, and their heads turned in unison, looking past the deck and the gravel parking area toward the top of the driveway.

The Toyota was ambling down the drive, coming toward the cabin.

Her expression sank. She glanced up at him, her jaw tightening.

The SUV barreled around his rental car and slipped neatly into its parking space. Kids piled out of the backseat as well as the rear storage area. A man Nell's age appeared as the driver's side door swung open. A younger couple came around the rear end of the vehicle, the man snapping at the kids to behave.

"Company, huh?" the older man said, smiling. "We hadn't reached the highway yet and I realized I'd forgotten my heart medicine, so we had to turn around." He reached out to shake hands with Allan. "Berg Spagnazio," he said, pumping Allan's arm.

"Allan Adler."

"He was just leaving," Nell said anxiously.

"Nonsense!" Berg declared. "Nell, pour some tea and bring on the chips!"

"But . . . but . . ." Nell had her hands clutched at her bosom, her eyes wide and frantic.

The younger couple introduced themselves as Stan and Laney Pendleton. Stan had a toothy, boyish face but severely thinning blond hair. Laney was rather short, with dead-of-the-night black hair that fell to the middle of her back, and she had her mother's eyes. They were both congenial and very talkative.

Their boy, Ricky, had his father's face, which was covered with freckles. Their teenage daughter, whom they introduced as Lucy, had thick, gorgeous blond hair fixed in a long braid, but bore no notable resemblance to either parent.

Nell Spagnazio dispatched herself to the kitchen, where she fumbled flatware and dishes and seemed uncharacteristically agitated. She was the sole member of the family not currently enthralled by the concept of a surprise visitor.

The boy was full of energy. He said a quick hello to Allan at his parents' insistence, then quickly withdrew to more interesting matters. Lucy had a bright gleam to her eyes. She'd obviously been hauled off to the mountains away from her friends the moment school had let out for the summer. Here she was, seventeen years old, a lovely girl, stuck on a mountaintop with her parents, grandparents, and her twelve-year-old brother. He could only wonder how much she knew about where she'd come from.

Berg Spagnazio came down the short flight of stairs that led to the bedroom. He had a bottle of medication in one hand. He popped a couple of pills into his mouth, washing them down with a quick slurp of water from the sink faucet. He approached the rest of the gathering, patting his chest and smiling at Allan. "Got to the keep the old ticker ticking."

"Living out here should do wonders for your heart," Allan said.

"Right you are. What brings you out this way, Allan?" he said as he grabbed a folding chair from a small closet.

Nell still hadn't joined them. She was suddenly obsessed with kitchen utensils and mixing bowls, and was jerking open drawers and cabinet doors.

Allan wondered how much Berg and the kids knew, how much Nell had told them. He'd prepared for them to get defensive, and he knew that they might very well kick him out the door and chase him down the mountain. But Nell Spagnazio's reaction to even a mention of Rosemary Hitchins's name, and her present behavior in the kitchen, led him to believe that what

she'd done all those years ago she'd done on her own and had
lived with it on her own.

Perhaps that was how it should remain, Allan decided. He
had come so far and gotten so close. But this had to be Nell's decision. He wasn't going to bully her. Finally, Allan simply
shrugged. "Actually, Berg, I got turned around a few miles back
and ended up here." He glanced in Nell's direction, but she had
turned away from them. "I should be getting back on the road, I
guess."

"Don't be silly," Berg said. "Sit. Sit."

Allan was already at the door.

Berg put a hand on his shoulder. "What's the rush, Allan?
Stay for lunch, I insist."

Allan had the door open, one foot outside, a cool mountain
breeze in his hair.

"Sit for half an hour. Where's the harm in that?" Berg followed on his heels.

"I'm intruding—"

There was a loud crash and the sound of breaking glass, and
everyone jumped.

"*Stop it!*" Nell shouted. She was facing the kitchen window,
her hands clutching the edge of the counter. "*JUST STOP IT!*"

Berg spun to face her. Both Laney and Stan were quickly on
their feet. Laney was clearly alarmed at her mother's sudden
outburst.

Nell put her face in her hands, and she began weeping, backing away from the kitchen counter, catching the heel of her shoe
on a long rug on the floor and nearly tumbling over backward.
Berg rushed to her. He took her in his arms, guiding her to the
couch. He sat next to her, his arms around her shoulders.

She was sobbing.

Laney and Stan exchanged looks of mystification. Berg
glanced up at them, his eyes wide in confusion.

"Mother, what in the world?" Laney said, kneeling on the
floor in front of her parents. "Mother, what's *wrong*?"

The kids had been out on the deck away from the boring adult conversation. But now Lucy wandered in on her own, a look of deep concern in her eyes.

"Mom, is Grandma okay?"

"I don't know, honey."

"What's going on with you?" Berg said to his wife.

Finally, Nell looked up at them all. "Mr. Adler is here because of me."

All eyes shifted to Allan, and never in his life had he felt so uncomfortable.

She took a breath. "Allan, please stay. You might as well hear this, too." She didn't want to tell them, in fact that was the last thing on earth she wanted all of them to know. But if after all these years they were going to find out, she wanted it to come from her and not some stranger.

"Hear what?" Berg asked.

"Lucy," Nell said, her eyes red with tears. "Come over here by your mother."

Lucy circled around the couch and knelt on the floor beside Laney. Nell took their hands in her own, making eye contact first with her granddaughter, and then with her daughter.

"I never wanted it to come to this," she began, attempting to compose herself. "But the time has arrived, and I want you to hear it from me."

Laney nodded at her mother, waiting.

"When Lucy was born," Nell said, "it didn't come about in quite the way I led you to believe. Her adoption wasn't arranged by the hospital. There was always such a huge demand for newborn babies that they were always snapped up by people with money or influence. When you and Stan got married and you couldn't get pregnant, you were so devastated, remember?"

Tears welling in her eyes, Laney nodded her head.

"You tried and tried for years. Finally the doctors told you that you couldn't conceive, that you'd never have a child of your own. And the two of you had no money then. You couldn't afford the costs of a proper adoption. There was always so much paperwork to wade through, so much legal red tape. I knew it would take years if you followed the proper channels. And I simply couldn't bear watching you be miserable. I was a pediatric nurse, so I saw hundreds of babies a month, and so many of them were born into miserable families or no family at all."

Laney shook her head. "Mother . . . I don't understand. What are you saying?"

Nell continued, "An opportunity arose. An unwed woman was brought into the hospital on very short notice. She had already gone into labor and was about to give birth at any moment. We rushed her into the delivery room. It was a bizarre situation. She had been in jail, so there were armed guards everywhere. It was all very secretive and hush-hush. No paperwork was ever filled out. They simply wanted the baby delivered as quickly as possible so that they could return the woman to jail . . ." Her words trailed off as tears ran down her face.

Laney was overcome, her face shifting slowly from confusion to shock. She looked from her mother to Lucy. Lucy was already piecing together the meaning behind her grandmother's words, and her face was growing pale.

"What . . . what are you saying, Mother? That . . ."

"That woman was my biological mother, wasn't she?" Lucy said, blinking away tears.

"I knew she was born to an unwed mother," Laney said. "But a . . . a *criminal*?"

Nell raised her head, forcing a pained smile. "I wanted you to be happy. I did it for *you*. It was a chance for you to have a child, no questions asked. The doctor handed this beautiful baby girl to me in the delivery room, and I cleaned her up. It was late at night. There was only myself and one other nurse in the nursery. She left for a few minutes to check on some of the other expectant mothers, and while she was gone I scooped up Lucy and hid her until the end of my shift. There was no paperwork. No one missed her. It was a miracle."

"Who was she, Grandma? What had she done? Why was she in jail?" Lucy's eyes had cleared, and now there was a strength to them that was amazing to behold.

"Honestly," Nell said, "I didn't know at first. Not until later on did I learn. I saw her on TV."

"TV?" Laney said.

"Who was my mother?" Lucy asked again. "I deserve to know."

Nell again put her face in her hands, sobbing. She shook her head. She couldn't continue. She was too ashamed.

Stan Pendleton had backed away a few steps and dropped into one of the recliners, stunned. He sat with his hands on his knees, staring straight ahead. Berg Spagnazio was still seated next to his wife on the couch, his arm around her. Everyone was trying to cope with this revelation.

"I need to know," Lucy said. "Eventually I was going to try to find out anyway. This is no big deal, Grandma. I am who I am, and I have been raised by the most loving people in the world. But I need to know where I came from, my roots. Good or bad, it doesn't change who I am."

Nell simply shook her head from side to side. "I just can't do it. Please . . . please let Mr. Adler tell you."

Lucy released her grandmother's hand and stood. She turned and approached Allan. She looked directly at him with sober eyes. "Mr. Adler," she said. "Can you tell me who my biological mother is?"

Allan was more than impressed by the teenage girl before him. She was mature beyond her years. She was fully prepared for whatever he might say. He simply hated being the one to tell her. But he wasn't going to back down at this point.

"I can do you one better," he said. "I can tell you about your mother, and I can tell you about your father, as well. But before

I do, I'd like to ask for your help. My son is in trouble, and you are the one person with the power to help him."

She didn't bat an eyelash. She looked at him with an expression of absolute sincerity and said, "Mr. Adler, if you tell me about my biological parents, I'll help you any way I can. I promise."

75

THERE WERE MANY THINGS THAT NEEDED TO BE SAID. A LOT of water would have to pass under the bridge and many tears would have to fall before the air was cleared enough for their lives to ever get back to normal. But this day was the first step along that bumpy road to recovery.

Allan had explained things in much the same way as Rosemary had explained it to him. All four adults distinctly remembered the tale of Rosemary Hitchins. It was, after all, a part of American history. Berg and Nell were totally unfamiliar with the name Getty Fairfield. They spent more than half of every year sequestered far from television and listened to radio only for the weather report. So the activities in Washington over the past couple of weeks came as news to them.

The Pendletons, though, acknowledged an awareness of the death of Chief Justice Bourgeous and the president's nomination of Getty Fairfield to the Court. They grilled Allan with dozens of questions, some of which he answered, many of which he couldn't.

He pleaded his case.

How, exactly, did he think Lucy could help? they asked.

Allan didn't have a good answer for that. She was simply the physical result of a relationship between two high-profile people. And her DNA was the only remaining physical link between them. Allan insisted that he in no way wished for any harm to come to her. He promised that her identity would never be revealed, if that was her wish. He simply needed something he could take to D.C. to present to those with the power and resources to save Steven, something irrefutable. It would cost them nothing. He vowed to take care of all expenses.

Laney and Nell went for a walk down the dirt road. A lot had come out, and mother and daughter needed time alone. They walked slowly, holding hands as they gradually faded from view over the ridge.

Berg dutifully occupied Ricky, keeping him away from adult matters.

Lucy, having found herself the center of circumstances beyond her control, had asked if she could be alone for a while. She had crossed the fence and was presently strolling through the high sage, trying to make sense of the maelstrom spinning around her. She found a tree stump and had a seat, gazing up at the sky, studying the endless blue and wondering where she fit in all of this.

That left Stan Pendleton and Allan.

Stan leaned against his minivan, looking at the ground and shaking his head. Allan stood to one side of him, facing down the driveway toward the open gate. A silence lingered between them, a silence that Allan felt he himself was unmerited to fill.

After a few moments of contemplation, Stan said, "As a parent I can't see any wisdom or logic behind the idea of whisking my child off to D.C. to be used as a pawn in what amounts to political blackmail."

Allan nodded.

"I mean, really, I don't understand what you have in mind. But that city is a den of wolves, and I can't in any good conscience see myself allowing her to be cast into that. She'd be eaten alive."

Allan had his hands deep in his pants pockets. He stared at the taillights of the minivan, listening and agreeing. He was sickened by his own selfishness. He'd thought he was being a good father, but a good father was Stan Pendleton. So he stood at an impasse in his own heart and mind.

"I'm not going to argue with you, Mr. Pendleton. You're absolutely right. And if the roles were reversed, I'd choose likewise. But if the roles *were* reversed, where would you stand? Could you turn your back? That's not fair, I know. But that's the dilemma I face at this moment."

Stan started to respond but held back. This guy had appeared out of the blue with an absurd request. Allan had showed no aggression and appeared to be in no way a threat. He'd clearly pegged Nell correctly. But there had to be limits to what you exposed your child to. Stan might not have been nominated for any parent-of-the-year awards, but he wasn't a fool.

Allan could sense that he was losing. The simple truth was that Pendleton didn't have a single reason to go along with this thing. The man had nothing to gain except to put his adopted daughter in possible danger.

Finally, Stan spoke. "I'm sorry. I'm sorry you drove all this way, and I'm sorry for what your family is going through. But it's not our business. No parent in his or her right mind would even consider it. You clearly care a lot about the well-being of your boy, and I respect that. But I've got to draw a line somewhere." He made eye contact with Allan and motioned with his head toward Allan's rental car. "So I'm going to have to ask you to leave now."

Before Allan could respond, a voice came from nearby.

"No."

Both men turned in unison.

Lucy was standing between them and the fence. She had approached without their knowing. How long she'd been standing there or how much of their conversation she'd heard they could only guess.

"Lucy—" Stan began but was quickly cut off by his daughter.

"I want to help him," she said.

"Listen, sweetie—"

"No, you listen, Dad. This is something I've got to do. I'm glad Mr. Adler found me. I'm glad to know where I came from. And no matter what my biological mother may have done, she was still my mother."

"Sweetie, we don't know—"

"I believe him, Dad. I know you are just trying to protect me, but this happens to be a pretty extraordinary circumstance. And you can't protect me forever."

"I won't allow it," Stan chided in a fatherly, authoritative tone that Allan knew well.

Lucy took several steps closer. She was now only a few paces from them. Her face was set in a look of unwavering determination.

"Dad, please. This isn't your choice to make. I'll turn eighteen in a few months. I'll be an adult then, and there'll be nothing you can do to stop me. Mr. Adler's son would probably still be in jail paying the price for his friend's crime, and I'd go and help him. But I'd rather help him now."

Stan opened his mouth to rebuke her, but words failed him.

"I don't hate my biological father, but the time has come for him to know that I exist."

Allan could hardly believe his ears. There was still hope after all.

Flustered and desperate not to lose his tenuous hold on his daughter, Stan said, "But Lucy, what can you do? If they find out who you are, you will never again be able to live a normal life. You're too young to understand what a blessing anonymity is!"

"I understand, Dad. All he really needs is my blood. Just a blood sample, right, Mr. Adler? Just something to prove whose DNA I possess."

She's right, Allan thought. *That's all it would take.*

Allan offered a slow nod, wanting to acknowledge what she'd said but not wanting to show disrespect to her father.

For a long moment Stan Pendleton remained silent. He was clearly shaken. Finally, he slowly approached his daughter, placing his big hands on her shoulders.

"Baby, are you sure?" he asked, his eyes moist.

"Yes, Daddy."

"Then I can't stand in your way."

She grew teary, and they embraced.

"Thank you, Daddy."

They parted, and Stan composed himself. Then he turned to Allan. "Okay, then. What now?"

Stunned by the sudden turn of events, Allan had to take a moment to think. His head was spinning. There were three priorities that he could think of on the spot. In no particular order, they included: get a blood sample, take it to D.C., and guard Lucy's identity.

"Honestly," Allan said. "I'm kind of thinking on my feet here. But first I better make a phone call."

"Here," Stan said, offering the use of his cell phone.

"Thank you," Allan said, extending his hand to Stan Pendleton. "Thank you for everything."

76

THE KIDS WERE SCATTERED THROUGHOUT THE HOUSE, AND Lanna had the day off, though she usually worked harder at home than anywhere else. She was currently behind the house on a ladder, washing windows from the outside.

Cody pushed open the storm door and stuck his head out.

"Mom, Dad's on the phone!" he shouted; then the door clapped shut.

Lanna nearly fell off the ladder. She carefully backed down the aluminum rungs, setting her foamy sponge on the ground. With all that was going on with Steven, and Allan being away from home, busying herself with mindless chores was about the only thing keeping her sane.

She hurried into the kitchen and grabbed the phone. "Allan?"

"Hey, babe."

"Where are you? Are you okay?"

"I'm fine. Listen, I've only got a minute. Things are getting crazy. Have you by chance talked to Steven in the last couple of days?"

She pushed hair out of her face and said, "Uh, I talked to Wes Swanson the other night. He said Steven's holding up fine. He's exhausted and scared, but fine other than that. Nick Calevetti is still hiding behind his father's lawyers. The FBI is wanting to move forward with the charges against Steven as fast as they can. They believe it's an open-and-shut case. Swanson sounded tired and less than optimistic. What about Rosemary?"

The connection was poor, lots of static.

Allan said, "You're breaking up, I can barely hear you. So I've got to be quick."

"What happened at the prison?"

"Rosemary is dead."

"*What?*"

"Murdered. I don't have time to go into it."

"But—"

"Listen, Lanna. She had a baby in jail. She gave birth to a baby girl. It's Fairfield's kid."

The connection crackled, and she thought she'd lost him for a second. She could barely understand him and didn't for a second believe he'd actually said what she thought she'd heard.

"Lanna, you there?"

"Yes!"

"Bad connection."

"What did you say? A *baby*?"

"Take down . . . number . . ." But whatever number he was trying to communicate was lost in the static interference.

Lanna frantically searched for a notepad.

". . . got to go."

His voice was too distant to make out clearly.

". . . if you—me—call the . . ."

She could no longer hear him at all. The connection was gone.

.•─••─•─•.

In a small motel room five miles from the Adlers' house, Brenner Walsh removed his headphones and dived across the bed for his cell phone. He'd been sitting at the table with a briefcase fitted with electronic surveillance equipment designed to pick up the signal transmitted from the tiny bug he'd planted in the Adlers' telephone. He'd heard the entire conversation, as brief as it was.

He fumbled with the phone, finally managing to dial Clement's number. It seemed to ring for an eternity before Clement answered.

77

"WHO IS SHE?"

"We don't know," Clement said, holding his cell phone in one hand while steering with the other. The leased Mercedes was cutting through D.C. traffic, ignoring all laws of the road. He'd flown to Washington that morning to put out fires and keep tabs on developments there. The answer was nothing close to what Goodchapel wanted to hear, but it was the truth.

"Where are they?" Goodchapel was at his home office, pouring over research.

"Somewhere in Colorado. That's the only place Adler could be. He took a flight to Denver yesterday evening and rented a car from there."

Walsh had kept Clement updated minute to minute as details trickled in. In L.A., Snow had yet to budge from her workstation except for bathroom breaks. She'd crept as far into Allan Adler's life history as her skills would allow. Then she'd shifted her focus to his current movements, following the trail he left with his careless credit card transactions. She snickered every time another occurrence showed up on her screen. What a moron, she thought. If she ever chose to disappear, she'd vanish in a heartbeat, like a ghost. Of course this goofball probably had no idea anyone was after him.

From the moment Adler had rented the car in Denver, the great mystery had been where he could be headed. He'd left Ohio like a flash, taking them completely off guard. His actions had raised more questions than answers. But the phone call from Adler to his wife was the slipup they'd waited for. It filled in the missing piece to the puzzle. And the news was so much more than they could have ever hoped for.

Rosemary Hitchins had Fairfield's baby!

Truly, it was like hitting the lottery.

But Costas Goodchapel was quickly losing patience with Clement. The attorney had moved too slow getting to Rosemary Hitchins, and if they lost this girl—if indeed she was Fairfield's kid—they wouldn't get a third chance at shooting down Fairfield's nomination. They needed the kid. For the moment they had the jump on Cone and his friends. But Goodchapel knew all too well that that window of opportunity would be too brief. They had to move, and they had to act decisively.

Among the big questions in Goodchapel's mind now was why Adler had gone after the kid. What did he want? If they could answer that question, it might just pave the way to getting hold of the girl.

If the girl had both Hitchins's and Fairfield's blood, then finding her and keeping her alive was now the only thing that mattered.

"Why does Adler need the girl?" Goodchapel said.

"That's the billion-dollar question, isn't it?"

"So somehow he had a connection to Fairfield and Hitchins at the Pentagon, and out of nowhere he visits her minutes before she's killed, and then he goes straight for her kid. What am I missing?"

"Could he be working for Fairfield?"

It was a fair question. Goodchapel turned it over in his brain. He wanted so badly for it to fit. It wouldn't make life any easier, but at least it would be an answer. "So he knocks off Hitchins and then goes after the girl?"

"But he didn't touch Hitchins, we know that much. A guard killed her. It doesn't add up. Our big problem for the moment is that Adler knows where the girl is and we have no efficient way of tracking him. A credit card transaction every twelve hours won't help much."

"Stay put in Washington," Goodchapel said.

"What about you?" Clement asked, frustrated to have his hands tied like this.

"I'm going to deal with Adler." Goodchapel ended the call and tossed his cordless phone onto a chair as he rushed out the door.

78

IT WAS A HUGE MISTAKE. NEITHER GOODCHAPEL NOR CLEMENT could have ever guessed that their conversation would cost them so dearly. The firm hired long ago by Anwar Claussen on behalf of Cone Intermedia received a call from Marcel Ulon, and the communiqué between the head of Amethyst and his lead counsel was quickly streamed via email to Claussen's temporary office in Washington, D.C.

If it wasn't one thing it was another. And the curveballs were flying at his head harder and faster every step along the way. It was becoming increasingly difficult to react quickly enough to keep ahead of whatever might be flung at him next.

Claussen made two calls: one to Rowan Lipscomb, and the other to Austin, Texas.

79

THE COUNTRY CLUB WAS AMONG THE MOST EXCLUSIVE IN the nation. Rich white men of all ages fought like schoolchildren for a shot at membership or even an opportunity to walk the fairways of its golf course a single time. It was a paradise on earth, strewn with multimillion-dollar homes and available only to the chosen few. Getty Fairfield had certainly never set foot there before. But he had been summoned by the president himself within the hour.

The limousine delivering him glided through the immaculate

neighborhoods bordering the country club. He was deposited at the entrance to the clubhouse, where an escort was waiting with a golf cart. Fairfield went to retrieve his clubs but was told he wouldn't have need of them. He frowned and took a seat in the little motorized cart. The escort whisked him down a paved path at a brisk speed.

The president was on the fairway of the seventh hole. The usual group surrounded him: Secret Service agents and a few aides desperate to get some business done.

Fairfield approached, and the group hushed as the president lined up his shot and severely sliced it, driving the ball up into the edge of the trees. The president seemed not to care. He was a notoriously rotten golfer. His caddie stepped up, and the president dropped his seven-iron into the bag. He turned and spotted Fairfield.

"Ah, Getty!" he said. He motioned for Fairfield to hop into his cart. "Let's take a ride."

The cart hummed as they motored across the immaculately maintained grass in the general direction that his ball had traveled. Fairfield was puzzled.

Finally, the president spoke. "Getty, I thought we had everything out in the open."

The cart rattled to a stop a few yards from a handsome stand of trees. The president set the brake but remained seated.

The president's face was flushed with anger. A light breeze was playing with his hair. Fairfield wanted desperately to look away but dared not.

"Mr. President, I have to confess that I'm at a loss," Fairfield said.

"The games are coming to an end right here," the president snapped. "I have one question for you, and I'm only going to ask it once. If you lie to me and jeopardize my administration, that's not acceptable, and I will no longer offer you protection. Is that clear?"

The only thing he could do was nod. Fairfield felt completely in the dark.

The president said bluntly, "It has come to my attention, Getty, that Rosemary Hitchins had a daughter, fathered by *you*."

Fairfield stared at him blankly, a deer in the headlights.

"Do you deny this accusation?"

"That's . . . absurd!"

"I'll take that as your final word on the matter, then."

"Mr. President, I can assure—"

The president cut him off. "You've already admitted having a physical relationship with Hitchins, so how can you know with one hundred percent certainty that a pregnancy didn't result? Tell me that."

Fairfield's chest tightened. Never in a million years would such a hypothesis have ever occurred to him. The very suggestion was rubbish!

"Who is she?" Fairfield demanded, his voice wavering.

"If you cannot assure me that the allegation is without merit, I'll be forced to assume the child is yours and take the necessary actions to make sure that threat is extinguished."

The word *extinguished* rang eerily in Fairfield's ears. He had to interpret the president's words as meaning that unless Fairfield could without hesitation flush away all doubt, the girl would have to be killed. Rosemary Hitchins had never meant a thing to him, and this girl, whoever she was and wherever she was, was just an anonymous concept to him. But what if? That was the ominous question that he now had to consider. All these years, had he been the father of a child he didn't even know existed? *What if?* And now, here he was, with the president prepared to snuff out her life. But it had to be done.

"The only thing I'm certain of is that I've never had any knowledge of a child, Mr. President. And that, I swear, is the truth."

The president climbed out and stood beside the golf cart, only the lower portion of his face visible beneath the roof of the cart. Austerely he replied, "That's not good enough."

80

HALFWAY DOWN THE MOUNTAIN THE RAIN BEGAN. AFTER-noon showers were a nearly daily occurrence at that altitude. Lucy had requested to ride with Allan. It went against her parents' better judgment, but it was clear to them that under the current circumstances they could no longer treat her like a child. The remaining Pendletons followed in their minivan. The grand-parents had waved good-bye from the deck of the cabin. Nell was still quite upset, but Berg kept his arm around her as they watched the cars slowly creep down the mountain.

The rain made the trip rather slow going. The weather had lured a few deer out from the cover of the forest, and they stood on and beside the dirt road, cautious but curious. Allan honked the car horn a few times and the animals eventually strolled out of the way.

Lucy hadn't said much. She was buckled in, her hands in her lap. Allan wanted to ease her mind but found himself at a loss.

"What was my biological mother like?"

The question startled him. He'd been focused on the road ahead and lulled by the patter of rain on the roof of the car.

"Well, I didn't know her. For a brief period, a lot of years ago, I saw her a few times. But I'd never spoken to her until yester-day."

"Was she pretty?"

"Yes, actually. Truly one of the most beautiful women I've ever seen."

"Really?"

"Really."

"What'd she look like?"

"Well, blond hair, like yours. And she had your blue eyes, also. She would have been very proud of you."

"Do you believe she was a bad person for doing what she did?"

"I don't know. It's really not my place to make a judgment on that. She had her reasons, I guess. She said she was in love with someone at the time, and she did it for him."

Lucy turned and looked at him. "The Russian?"

Allan nodded. "Apparently."

She said, "Women will do strange things for love. That doesn't make her a bad person."

"True enough."

"Did you know my biological father well?"

"No. I drove him around for a few years when I was in the military. But he was a big deal, and I was just a soldier doing my job. Some days he'd be a little conversational—talk about sports or the weather, something benign like that."

"Do you think he's a bad person for letting Rosemary go to prison?"

"I don't think he could have helped her much, honestly. But the gesture sure would have been noble. I can't say that I would have done any differently."

She sat quietly for a long while, staring at the horizon. They reached the highway and turned north. Allan kept an eye on his rearview mirror for the minivan. The rain let up, and sunlight broke through the clouds. He lowered his visor, and Lucy did likewise. He accelerated to sixty-five, struggling to keep all four tires on the road as they flew around the mountain's treacherous curves.

"What do you think about this whole thing?" he asked, not wanting to press too hard or make her uncomfortable, but testing the waters a little, to try to gauge where she was emotionally.

"It's a little scary, I guess."

"I know."

"But I'm really not frightened."

He gave her a look. "No?"

She shook her head. "This is a good thing. I'm a little nervous, is all."

Allan offered her a smile. She smiled back.

"You're kind of a hero," he said.

"You *think?*"

"Absolutely. You're my family's hero, that's for sure."

By the time they reached the Gunnison city limits, the sun was out and steam was rising off the highway. They found the airport without incident. Allan parked and watched as the minivan pulled up beside him. He went in to arrange the charter flight while the Pendletons dealt with their luggage at the minivan.

Allan talked with the man at the front counter, a cheery fellow wearing a billed cap. The man said he could have the plane ready to fly in half an hour. Allan paid with a credit card, then stepped outside to wait with the Pendletons.

Allan, Stan, and Lucy would take the charter, which would save them the long drive to Denver. From there they'd catch an airliner to D.C. The small prop plane simply could not hold them all. Laney and Ricky were forced to make the trip to Denver by road, and they would remain there until summoned by Stan. They hugged Stan and Lucy and then hurried to the van and tore out of the gravel parking lot.

The prop plane was fueled and ready in no time at all. They lifted off from the small airstrip and circled around over Gunnison, casting a birdlike shadow over the mountains and buildings.

The flight to Denver was uneventful. Allan purchased three tickets to Washington, D.C., and after an hour's wait they boarded. None of the three seats were together. Again, he had paid with plastic.

◆—◆—◆

The credit transaction showed up almost immediately. Snow couldn't help but shake her head. Like taking candy from a baby, she thought, scanning through the info for the particulars. She felt kind of bad for the guy, though. He was either stupid or naive. He simply didn't know whom he was dealing with.

.•-•-•.

Another hacker had spotted the same thing. His name was Ryce and he lived in the basement of his parents' home in New Jersey. He was at least two years younger than Snow. He wore flannel pajama bottoms and a plain white T-shirt, and his face was blistered with acne. He was an independent contractor currently doing work for the firm Cone Intermedia had hired to do their snooping for them.

He smiled at his computer screen, a mouthful of braces smiling back at him in his reflection. He'd been given the name of Allan Adler barely a half hour ago and already he knew most of what there was to know about the guy. He picked up the phone and dialed. When the call was answered, he said simply, "He's headed to D.C."

81

THE BROTHERS WERE WILLING TO DO THE JOB, BUT THEIR price had gone up. Lipscomb haggled with them briefly, but without conviction. The money was available, and there frankly wasn't any time to waste. For the moment at least, Lipscomb didn't have much to tell them. Three people were on a flight to Reagan National Airport, he said. Two of them needed to die. He told them that the assumption was that one of the three was a girl in her late teens. She was the primary target. A forty-something-year-old male named Allan Adler was with her. Whether or not they nailed Adler, the girl was a must.

"And when they're dead," Lipscomb instructed, "be sure and burn the bodies."

The Brothers were ninety minutes from the Beltway when they got the call. Lipscomb told them that he would leave an envelope at the front desk of the Crowne Plaza Hotel near Reagan National. It would tell them everything they needed to know.

Metcalf pulled his 1970 Barracuda into the parking lot of a supermarket, and he and Patton opened the trunk to make sure they were properly armed for the job. They had enough firearms and ammo to take down a casino. Before storming onto the interstate in the Barracuda, they bought jumbo-size garbage bags, lighter fluid, and matches.

82

IT WAS NOT A DIRECT FLIGHT. TWO LAYOVERS WERE SCHEDuled before they touched down in D.C. Allan took advantage of the time in the air to rest. For the past two days he had been running on adrenaline, so as he allowed himself to relax he found it increasingly difficult to hold his eyes open. They would cross two time zones on their way east, and lost hours would likely place them on the ground just after dark. The coming days would be eventful, so Allan concluded that these few hours might be the most sleep he'd get for a while.

He turned in his seat, spotting Lucy. She smiled at him. From where he sat he could not see her father. He turned back around, put his head against the seat, and closed his eyes.

He slept hard, his dreams reflective of the upheaval in his life the past couple of weeks. In his dream unseen predators were stalking him through tall grass. He could hear Steven's voice, then Lanna's, calling to him in the darkness, though he could not find them. Steven's especially seemed to grow more distant with each cry for help. The sounds of the predators' footsteps were almost upon him. He crouched as low as he could, trying to hide. But it was too late, there was nowhere to turn, and he simply wasn't fast enough to run away.

83

LANNA HAD BEEN IN THE BATHROOM FOR THE BETTER PART of half an hour. She had shut the bedroom door, then locked herself in the bathroom. She wasn't feeling ill, just overwrought. She needed a few moments to herself, away from the kids. The call from Allan had unnerved her. He'd been so brief and vague. She ran cold water into the sink basin and splashed her face.

Allan had not said where he was going or why, or what was going on. That just wasn't fair. Here she was, holding things together at home on her own, worried day and night about Steven locked behind bars halfway across the country, and now Allan was telling her that someone had been murdered and that this was somehow linked to a baby or a girl or something.

Her hands were shaking. She badly needed to cry, to let go of some of it, to release some of the pressure, but she wouldn't allow herself. Breaking down would help no one. She had to forget about the money, forget about the financial hole they were digging for themselves, and understand that Steven didn't need his mother losing control of her emotions.

Where are you, Allan? she wanted to scream.

She needed fresh air. Groceries hadn't been dealt with since this debacle started. It would serve her well to wander the aisles of the supermarket. Maybe she would even treat herself to a cappuccino at the deli.

Dermott was in the kitchen when she rushed in. His shirt was off, and he had grease on his hands and forearms.

Lanna grabbed her purse off the kitchen counter. "Watch the little ones," she said. "I'm going for groceries."

Not surprising for a late afternoon, the supermarket was packed. She cruised the parking lot for a few minutes, willing to accept the first available parking space.

She grabbed a shopping cart and began the long, monotonous process of planning the meals for the coming weeks. Normally she'd have prepared a list, but the past couple of weeks had basically demolished her usual concepts of preparation and organization. She felt lucky just to have her clothes on right side out.

Nearly ninety minutes later she passed through the checkout line with two heaping carts. The teenager at the register and the teenager bagging her goods did their jobs without so much as acknowledging her presence. The receipt was nearly three feet long. About average.

"Need help out to your car with that, ma'am?" the bagger asked.

She responded with a smile of appreciation and a quick nod of her head. She led the way, pushing the lighter of the two carts herself.

She opened the trunk and the four doors of her car. The kid had the carts unloaded in a flash. He slapped the trunk shut and was gone.

Lanna fussed with the bags in the backseat. Then she shut the back door and fished her keys out of her purse. She turned to get in, and jumped back, startled.

A man was standing on the other side of her opened door, looking at her.

"Oh, you spooked me!" she said, her voice shaking slightly.

"I apologize," he said with a smile, his voice colored with a South American accent she couldn't readily place.

Lanna took a quick look around, surveying the parking lot. There was no one else in the immediate vicinity. She was alone with this stranger.

"Well, if you'd excuse me, I've got to get this food out of the sun," she said, doing her best to get out of there as quickly as possible.

"One moment, please, Mrs. Adler."

Her heart skipped a beat. She froze where she stood, her purse clutched with both hands. The man certainly didn't look like a mugger. He appeared well groomed, and he wore a very expensive-looking suit. He had dark skin, which fit well with his exotic accent. She tried to place him. Perhaps he worked at the bank. No, she was pretty familiar with most everyone there. Was he a doctor or a surgeon at the hospital? Many of them were foreigners. But again, she could name any one of them in a heartbeat. She was at a loss.

"I'm sorry," she said awkwardly. "Should I know you?"

"No, Mrs. Adler. But I know you and your husband, as well as your five children," Costas Goodchapel said, careful not to appear threatening in any way. "Who I am isn't really important, but what I can do for you *is*. For the benefit of conversation, though, you can call me Harper, if you like."

She had no idea where this might be going, but she was growing more uncomfortable by the second. "Mr. Harper, I've really—"

"Mrs. Adler, I know where your husband is at this moment, and I know who is with him. Your husband, Allan, doesn't know the extent of the danger he is in. There are people looking for him who want him dead. They want him dead because of the young girl who is with him. And I am here to help you ensure his safety. Am I being clear?"

She stared at him, frightened out of her mind but more

frightened to ignore what he was saying. He seemed to know a lot. And given the events of the past two weeks, anything was possible.

"I don't understand . . . who are you?"

"Please, Lanna . . ." he said, gesturing with his hand, smiling warmly at her. "Let's go someplace where we can talk."

"But my groceries!"

"They are the least of your concerns, believe me," Goodchapel said with just enough edge to his voice to convince her to forget the food for now.

"I . . . I don't know."

"I'm not here to harm you, Lanna. I'm here to help bring Allan back alive and in one piece. But I can't do that without your cooperation and assistance."

Against her better judgment, she shut her car door and nodded.

The Mercury Marquis pulled up alongside them, and Walsh hurried out to open the back door. Both Lanna and Goodchapel got in. They proceeded to cruise through a sleepy residential neighborhood.

"Lanna, your husband is on a flight bound for Washington, D.C., even as we speak. There are people there who want to kill him. But they are really after the girl he's with. She is approximately seventeen years old, and she is the child of some very important people."

"Rosemary's child . . ." Lanna said, replaying Allan's phone call in her mind. "She's the baby Allan mentioned, isn't she?"

Goodchapel nodded. "Yes."

"Why would anyone want to kill her?"

"For the same reason I need to protect her. I need her alive as badly as these other people need her dead and gone. These are my enemies, Lanna. They are trying to destroy me."

Just then she flashed on the rest of Allan's comments on the phone. "Rosemary Hitchins . . . she's *dead*. Did they . . ."

"Yes, Lanna, the same people are responsible for her murder.

They killed her and now they plan to kill her daughter, and your husband."

"Does this have to do with Getty Fairfield?"

"Ah, now you're seeing it," Goodchapel said. "I am trying to protect the very people they want to destroy."

"Who is the girl? What's her name?"

"There are two things I don't know, Lanna, and the girl's name is one of them . . . that's the major complication. The second thing I don't know is how Allan is connected to Rosemary Hitchins."

Lanna swallowed. It was amazing to her how complicated life had become based on a simple assignment Allan had had in his military days. She nodded and said, "He was just Fairfield's driver for a while at the Pentagon."

Goodchapel closed his eyes. It was all so simple and yet so stupid. Allan Adler was nothing. He'd been a chauffeur, nothing more. But clearly he'd known about the affair.

"Why did he go to visit Rosemary Hitchins?" he asked her.

"To blackmail Fairfield. Our oldest son is in jail in Boston, and we don't have the money to help."

More and more, the situation was playing beautifully into Goodchapel's hands. This was all about money. Their kid was in trouble. And Fairfield's dark secret was the one card they could play.

"I want to help," Goodchapel said, turning to her.

The Mercury was cruising along at precisely the posted speed limit. Walsh and Sheridan sat in the front in silence. The car made a left turn, passing modest brick homes on a tree-lined street.

"Lanna," he continued. "Allan will be landing in Washington within the next few hours. He will be in immediate danger. I need the girl alive. I am here to offer you a huge amount of money for the safe delivery of Rosemary's biological daughter."

"How much?"

"More money than you would see in twenty lifetimes.

Enough to wipe away all your debts, to pay for the best defense attorney money can buy for your son, with enough left over to never have to worry again for the rest of your life. This is the lottery, Lanna. And all you have to do to win is say yes, just tell Allan to keep the girl safe and sound until my people can get to her. She will not be harmed in any way. In fact she will be treated like royalty. There is no downside here, Lanna. We all win."

An ominous sensation floated over her. This man "Harper" seemed to know what he was talking about. He knew about Rosemary and her murder, about Getty Fairfield, and he knew about the girl Allan had mentioned to her just hours ago. And she had no reason to disbelieve that he had that kind of money. But could they trust that Harper wouldn't harm the girl? No amount of money was worth a child's life.

Every word out of Harper's mouth sounded reasonable and good, but his presence was intimidating, and she failed to believe that he could be blindly trusted.

"So, let me make sure I've got this straight, okay?"

Goodchapel nodded patiently.

"I tell Allan to keep the girl safe, and then once you have her in your custody, you hand over the money?"

"It's that simple."

"But *that* much money, how will you give it to us?"

"It will be wired to an account of your choosing. Just like transferring money to or from your personal bank account, though of course I would not recommend placing it there, Lanna, unless you want the IRS to know about it. The transfer will be untraceable; that way I don't have to worry about the money trail leading back to me."

She thought about it for a moment. "But why do we have to wait for Allan to call home? If you know where he's headed, your people can simply approach him when he lands."

"Our people will be there, but they won't be alone. That's likely to get messy. Besides, your husband isn't going to stop and chat. The offer will have to come through you. If you're comfortable with it, then he will be as well. But, Lanna, I need you to commit, because time is running out. When that plane touches the ground, things are going to happen fast. I need both you and Allan on my side, and you need me on yours. Trust me, Lanna."

"I want a number," she said, stiffening her tone with courage she didn't feel. "How much money?"

Goodchapel knew he had her, but he maintained his cool. He cut his eyes at her, and then looked straight ahead over the seat in front of him. For a long moment he maintained a look of intense deliberation.

"Three million dollars," he stated without looking at her.

Lanna remained silent, dumbfounded by the figure she'd just heard.

"Three million," he repeated. "Payable upon my taking possession of the girl."

She tried to steady her breathing. That amount of money would wash away every care in their world. They could save Steven and finally have their heads above water. No longer would debt have a choke hold on them. Three million dollars equaled freedom. She struggled to keep tears from filling her eyes.

The Mercury circled around and she could see the supermarket coming into view up ahead.

"What's it going to be, Lanna?"

They eased up behind her car and stopped.

She let out a breath, her heart going a thousand beats a minute.

"Okay," she said. "Okay, I'll tell Allan."

"You're doing the right thing, Mrs. Adler. Everyone comes out a winner . . . you, me, Allan, the girl . . . everyone. What could be better than that?"

Her hands were shaking. For the first time in as long as she could remember it felt like everything might work out for the best. And as welcome as that knowledge was, she'd never been so terrified in her life.

"What exactly do I tell him when he calls?" she asked.

"Tell him to call this number," he said, handing her a card. "This is my cell phone number. Give him the basics of the situation, and tell him about the money. But make sure he calls me. I'll work out the details with him at that time. Understand?"

Lanna took the card in her hand. It was blank except for the cell phone number. She nodded, afraid her heart might explode.

"Go straight home, Lanna, and stay by the phone. Every second from this moment forward is crucial. You're going to be rich in a few hours. And your son will win his freedom. Don't forget that. Just think about the money and everything else will fall into place."

She got out of the car and it quickly disappeared around the outskirts of the parking lot.

Could she be dreaming? she wondered.

No, she was still stuck in the same nightmare as before.

84

THE BARRACUDA PARKED ILLEGALLY IN A LOADING ZONE outside the Crowne Plaza Hotel, and Patton circled around the front end of the car and crossed the street. Metcalf waited behind the wheel, lighting a cigarette and keeping an eye on the mirror for cops.

They were three deep at the check-in desk. Patton didn't wear a watch. He glanced at a clock on the wall behind the counter. They didn't have much time to waste. A Hispanic girl with a slight mustache smiled at him as he stepped forward.

He asked if anyone had left an envelope with them for the

name Prescott. She ducked her head beneath the counter, then reappeared, a business-size envelope in one hand.

"Yes, Mr. Prescott, here it is."

He nodded his thanks and headed for the door.

There wasn't much inside. A folded printout with info on Adler, downloaded from the Oklahoma City DMV. There was a photo, along with his height, weight, eye color, and date of birth. As for the girl, there was only her estimated age of seventeen to eighteen years old. But two men and a teenager shouldn't be too tough to spot, Patton figured.

The car squealed its tires pulling out of the parking spot. The flight would be arriving shortly, and they'd need to take up a position in the terminal where they could see every face that got off that plane. Metcalf wheeled up to the entrance of Reagan National, and Patton bailed out. Metcalf was to leave the Barracuda in short-term parking and then hurry inside.

From his basement bedroom in New Jersey, Ryce had taken down the flight number, arrival time, and gate number of the plane Allan Adler & Co. would be sailing in on. Patton stopped to check an arrivals display to find out the status of the flight. He couldn't help but smile. Adler and his friends would simply walk into his arms. It couldn't get any easier.

Patton eased over to a row of machines and fed his cash into one of them. It dispensed the weakest cup of coffee he'd ever tasted. He spotted Metcalf.

"Any sign?" Metcalf asked.

Patton shook his head, blowing on the coffee. "Hasn't arrived yet."

They watched and waited. There was no way out of the airport without passing them. The plan was to assail them, separate the girl from the men, and quietly usher them outside to the Barracuda. A bullet for each of them; then they'd drive outside the city and have a little bonfire. No muss, no fuss.

Patton sipped his coffee. *Any minute now,* he thought, watching the door. *Any minute now.*

85

CLEMENT WAS OPPOSED TO DEALING WITH THIS HIMSELF, but Goodchapel had given him little choice. They couldn't afford to let this Adler business be handled by a third party. When and if Adler called his wife, and things began to roll, Goodchapel needed his right-hand man there to take care of the details.

Brenner Walsh's trusty hacker back in L.A. had provided the only available physical ID of Allan Adler, taken from the state's DMV computer system.

Hopfner and Sneed were with him in the car. Every extra set of eyes would help. Sneed was at the wheel of the Mercedes, with Clement in the passenger's seat and Hopfner in back. Rather than sitting around staring at the phone waiting for Adler to take the bait, Goodchapel wanted them to hurry to Reagan National ahead of the plane, so that maybe they'd get lucky and catch sight of Adler and the others. It probably wouldn't be productive to approach the three of them from out of the blue. They might freak out and bolt. Better to just keep them in sight.

Sneed parked the car while Clement and Hopfner dashed inside.

They had to hurry. The flight had arrived. There was a crush of travelers crowding the terminal exit, making it difficult to separate one face from another. Clement was on his toes, trying to see past the sea of heads. He glanced at the printout in his hand, hoping Adler hadn't changed much in the time since the photo was taken.

He didn't notice the man a few feet away glancing at a copy of the same photo, looking for the same face.

86

THEY WERE INSTRUCTED TO REMAIN SEATED UNTIL THE AIR-craft had come to a complete stop. As soon as they were allowed to unfasten their seat belts and stand, the aisle filled, and over-head compartments were flung open as passengers grabbed for carry-ons and shuffled toward the exit.

Allan stood at his seat, making eye contact first with Lucy, then, eventually, with her father. He had to give the girl credit—she was stepping into an adult world, facing the facts of who she was and where she'd come from. There was strength in her eyes, eyes she'd inherited from Rosemary. And he gave credit to Stan Pendleton as well. Stan clearly wasn't comfortable with the whole matter, but if his daughter was bound and determined to follow through with this, he was at least going to be by her side for security and support.

Lucy allowed the person seated next to her to squeeze past, and she waited at her seat for her father. When Stan finally made his way down the aisle to her, she stepped out in front of him and he put a hand on her shoulder. They shuffled forward, mak-ing their way slowly toward the exit. Lucy paused to let Allan in. The three of them entered the Jetway and followed the flow of travelers up the ramp to the gate.

On the plane Allan had done his best to formulate a rough game plan. Everything at this point was coming from the hip. The past couple of days had been a blur, and all he could do was take it a step at a time. But so far so good. He'd found Lucy and managed to get her safe and sound to D.C. The next stage required somehow getting to Fairfield, or someone near him, and making an offer. Threatening Fairfield with the exis-tence of a daughter he'd likely never known about would im-mediately put all of them in danger. They could grab a cab outside the airport and hide someplace in the city where they would be safe. From there he could call Lanna, just to check in and let her know that all was well. Then he'd sit back and gather his thoughts and debate how best to approach Fairfield.

They pushed through the crowded gate, moving quickly across the terminal toward an exit.

Allan felt a sharp jab in his back. Before he could turn to investigate there was a growling voice in his ear.

"Just keep moving," Patton said. He held the gun inside his jacket pocket.

Metcalf brushed up behind Stan, in the same motion scooping a hand around Lucy's waist, pulling her back to him. Stan made an effort to protect her, but thought better of his actions when he felt the distinctive jabbing in his back.

"*Daddy?*"

"Keep your mouth *shut*, darlin'!" Metcalf hissed.

"What . . . who are you?" Stan insisted.

"Shut up and walk!" Patton said. "Nobody makes a big show, understand?"

Allan's mind was working frantically, looking for pieces to the puzzle. These guys had to be somehow connected to Fairfield. But where had they come from and how had they known where to look?

The Brothers moved quickly to get their captives through the terminal and outside the airport as fast as possible. Everything would be simpler once they were out-of-doors. No one seemed to pay them any notice. Everyone was headed somewhere different and in a crazy rush to get there.

Of course it was instinctual to consider making a move on them. And the thought had occurred to both Allan and Stan. But neither was willing to risk what might happen to Lucy. Second by second, though, they were moving closer to the exit, and nothing good would come of that.

Clement and Hopfner exchanged a look. The look said: *What*

just happened here? They had spotted the trio straightaway, and, as planned, had begun to follow at a reasonable distance. And shortly thereafter, two men had appeared out of nowhere and commandeered Allan Adler, the girl, and the second adult male. This was bad. This was very, *very* bad. Something was going down right before their eyes.

The two strangers looked like they were capable of taking care of themselves—something neither Clement nor Hopfner was necessarily prepared to deal with. They were high-priced lawyers, after all, not men trained in hand-to-hand combat. But something had to be done.

The doors that opened onto the street were straight ahead.

Clement knew that if the thugs got outside it was over. He was sweating heavily under his suit. As they rushed to close the gap, Clement leaned in close to Hopfner and said, "Just break them up and get out of the way!"

Hopfner, wide-eyed, nodded.

Thirty feet from the exit they made their move.

Clement rushed Patton, bulldozing forward with his shoulder lowered. He caught Patton under the right arm, knocking him off-balance. Hopfner made a similar move on Metcalf, striking him in the back with a kidney punch. Metcalf grimaced, going down on both knees.

Suddenly and unexpectedly freed, Allan, Lucy, and Stan spun around, slightly disoriented.

"*Go!*" Clement bellowed at them. He then went for Patton's knees, throwing his body at the man's legs. Patton went over hard onto his back, his arms floundering out at his sides.

Allan wasted no time getting out the door.

Stan had his daughter by the arm.

They all said a collective prayer of thanks at the sight of a taxi idling at the curb and jumped into the backseat.

"Where to?" the driver asked.

"Just please *drive!*" Allan barked.

Lucy was seated in the middle.

Both Allan and Stan turned to look out the back window. They were safely away from the building by the time Patton and Metcalf emerged onto the street, pulled their guns, and began firing.

Allan ducked his head.

Stan put his arms around his daughter, holding on to her with all his might. His only thought was that this trip had been a huge mistake.

Allan had his own thoughts to consider. He was beginning to believe that the price to save his son was finally getting much too high. *Exactly how far*, he wondered, *am I willing to go?*

87

THE PHONE RANG AND NEARLY SCARED LANNA OUT OF HER skin.

She snapped a hand towel from the front of the stove with one hand, grabbing at the portable phone with the other.

She hit the Talk button and skipped any form of greeting.

"Allan?" she said, hoping beyond hope that it was indeed him.

"Hey, babe."

She wilted with relief, easing her bottom back onto the barstool.

"Allan, where *are* you?"

"I'm in D.C."

"Are you okay?"

"I'm fine, everything's fine."

"Allan, what's going on?"

Where to begin? he thought. The absurdity of where this endeavor had taken him was almost funny. Almost.

"Everything's crazy," he said.

"Is Rosemary's daughter with you?"

He nodded, staring at the wall. He was using Stan Pendleton's cellular phone. He was standing beneath an awning, around the corner from where Stan and Lucy waited in the cab.

"Yeah," he said, "she's with me, so is her father."

"Listen, Allan, there's something I've got to tell you. And you have to listen *carefully*, okay?"

"Yeah, okay, but make it quick, we've got to find a place to stay. What's wrong, babe? I can hear it in your voice."

The card Goodchapel had given her was on the counter, damp from the water. She shook it off.

"Allan, I was approached by a man today in town."

"And?"

"And he made us an offer. It has to do with this Getty Fairfield business."

"What are you talking about?"

"He said that you and this girl are in danger, that there are people who are going to try to kill both of you in order to protect Fairfield from word of his relationship with Rosemary leaking out."

Allan's stomach turned.

"So I was right about Lucy . . ."

"Lucy?"

"Rosemary's kid."

"Oh. Right. This guy, Harper, said that the people supporting Fairfield know they aren't safe until you and the girl are out of the picture."

"Do they know who she is?"

"No," she said. "They didn't know she existed until you found her, actually."

"Great . . ." Another sinking feeling.

"But Harper needs to protect her."

"Who is he?"

"I haven't a clue. He's obviously not on Fairfield's side, and he's loaded, Allan. And if you deliver her to him, he'll make us rich. We can finally get Steven a good lawyer."

That stopped him in his tracks. "How do you mean?"

"Allan, he's offered us three million dollars. That's tax free. Do you hear me? That kind of money would mean the end of our worries. We could pay for Steven's freedom."

Something *ping*ed in the back of his mind, something that didn't set well at all. It wasn't about the money. It was something else . . . something he couldn't quite put his finger on.

"Three million dollars, baby. I know it sounds too good to be true, but it's not. I swear this is the real thing!" She desperately wanted him to understand the reality the way she did. She wished he could have been in that car with them, to hear that Harper guy make his pitch.

If Allan was the one who'd found Lucy, and until then no one had known of her existence, then how had . . . ?

The phone . . .

Of course!

"Lanna, the phone is tapped! They can hear every word we say!"

"*What?*"

"That's how they know about the girl. We've got to get off," he said decisively. "Go out to the garage . . . are you listening?"

"Yes! Yes, I'm listening."

"In the shop out back, next to my workbench, is a metal filing cabinet—a short one. In the bottom drawer is one of our old rotary phones. Unplug the one you're using now. Plug in the old rotary. That way if I need to call you back, there won't be unwanted ears sharing our conversation. I've got to go."

"But Allan, wait!" she said with urgency. "I have to give you this number. It's how you get hold of the man with the money."

"I don't know about this, Lanna."

"Just *talk* to him, Allan! *Three million dollars!* We'd be fools not to at least talk to him. Right?" She was pleading now. Walking away from that sum of money seemed insane. Goodchapel had promised not to harm the girl, and Lanna so badly wanted to take him at his word.

"Talk to him, Allan. What would it hurt?"

"Stay by the phone. Take the old one and have Dermott smash it. I'll get back to you as soon as I can. I love you, babe."

"I love *you.* Please promise you'll call this number."

"Give it to me," he said after a moment of hesitation.

She read the number off the card.

88

IN THE PAST HALF HOUR ALLAN HAD BEEN SIDESWIPED twice. The first time was when the two men accosted them inside the airport. The second time was during his conversation with Lanna when he realized the phone was bugged. These incidences opened his eyes to a whole new reality. This business was no longer solely about helping Steven. No, he'd stepped into more than he'd bargained for. This had become much bigger and more dangerous than he could have ever anticipated. He'd been right on the money about Fairfield, though. But there was no doubt in his mind whatsoever that he'd bitten off far more than he could chew.

Paranoia set in.

They had tapped his home phone. And they'd known the destination of his flight. *How?*

Credit cards.

It took all of five seconds to put it together. He'd been paying with plastic for the past several days. And every time he charged a purchase, they knew about it.

Stupid . . . stupid . . . stupid . . .

Well, things had to change. He had to start thinking like a man with nasty folks on his tail.

And what about this guy with the money? Harper. What was that all about? The guy wanted Lucy. Well, *that* wasn't about to happen. Harper could keep the money and . . .

Then an idea occurred to him. It rattled in from somewhere in the back of his mind, and he sat up and took notice. It would take a little time to put together, but it just might work. He'd have to talk to Harper first, just to see what the man had to say.

It was a beautiful idea.

89

"Mr. Adler, I'm glad you called."

"Is this Harper?"

"Yes."

"Tell me about the money."

Goodchapel was aboard his private jet, flying east at a speed of 487 knots. He said, "Simply turn the girl over to us and the three million U.S. dollars will be wired to an account designated by you."

"How do I know that you are good for the money?" Allan asked.

"Mr. Adler, I have infinite resources at my disposal. I am like the genie in the bottle."

Listening to Harper's confident tone, Allan had little doubt that the man had deep pockets. He decided to push a little further. "For starters," Allan said, "make it five million."

Goodchapel was tiring of this. He was a man of industry. He built empires. His patience was running thin. "No."

"Then I take the girl elsewhere."

"You are putting your son in jeopardy."

Allan stiffened. "Let me worry about that."

"I am on your side, Mr. Adler. It is my desire to help you. All you have to do is help *me*."

"Prove it. Transfer the money. Five million."

A short pause. "Done. Where is the girl?"

"Slow down. I've got to make arrangements for the money. You'll hear from me shortly." And Allan hung up. His stomach was in knots. He just hoped he could pull this off.

90

THE FIRST LESSON LEARNED WAS TO FORGET THE CREDIT cards. From now on, cash only. The cab dropped them outside a Red Roof Inn. They hurried inside. It was dark by now, but they felt vulnerable being outside too long. Allan paid cash for two rooms, and the clerk behind the counter handed him the keys.

Lucy and her father took one room, Allan the other. He told them to stay put. If they needed anything, he'd get it for them.

From his room he dialed the number to his old friend's office phone. Mitchell Lundberg was still at his desk in Dallas when Allan called, and he answered on the second ring.

Lundberg sounded delighted to hear his voice. The conversation was brief. Allan told him what he needed. He gave his word that Lundberg would be well compensated for his efforts.

No problem, Lundberg insisted. It took a matter of minutes for him to set things in motion. He had Allan jot a few things down on paper.

Lundberg was a pro. He might not have had the best instincts when it came to automobiles, but he knew how to make money disappear in a hurry.

Allan knew he'd picked the right man for the job.

91

FRANKLIN HENBEST WAS SWEATING, SO HE KNEW THE PRESIdent had to be. The president, he figured, was probably hyperventilating. Lipscomb had called. The Brothers had lost them at the airport.

Henbest wanted to scream and kick holes in the wall. He wanted to shout and spit and hit somebody. When it rained it poured. It seemed that for every inch of progress they took three steps back. He'd thought Fairfield was a sure thing. Instead, he'd turned out to be a grenade with the pin pulled.

And now this Adler chump was on the loose somewhere in D.C., running around with the girl. Fairfield could deny he'd fathered the girl until they were all blue in the face, but he denied *everything*, and look where it had gotten them. How could it get any worse?

He popped the cap off a bottle of antacid and washed the tablets down with bourbon. There would be no sleep tonight.

92

BRENT SNEED HAD BEEN IN THE RIGHT PLACE AT THE RIGHT time. He had been in the Mercedes, attempting to find his way to short-term parking, when he ended up stuck behind a fender bender. A small Nissan pickup had rear-ended a Buick right at the entrance to the parking area, making it impossible to get around. A short man and a kid wearing a ball cap were near punches, trading insults as to who was to blame.

So Sneed had decided to circle around and come back to the loading zone. Cabs were lined up against the curb, waiting. A steady trickle of travelers appeared and disappeared under the wash of overhead lighting. He was hoping the accident had been cleared up, though it was doubtful much had been accomplished in the three or four minutes he'd managed to kill. But he couldn't just sit there and wait. There was traffic behind him. He had to keep moving. That's when it happened.

Doors at the entrance to the airport had flung open, two men and a girl rushing out into the night. They had jumped into a cab, four car lengths ahead of the Mercedes. Seconds later, two men burst out, guns drawn, running hard, chasing the cab on foot. It didn't take much imagination to fit the pieces together.

Sneed jerked the car into an open lane and punched the accelerator. He wasn't worried about Clement or Hopfner, the girl was all that mattered. A shot was fired up ahead. Sneed saw the flash. Then another shot, and another. The two men on foot were blasting away, flashes of gunfire visible as they ran. Sneed had only a second to react. He turned into them. Both Metcalf and Patton tumbled up and over the hood of the car, falling to the ground and out of view of the mirrors.

Flat on his back, Patton tried to move but couldn't. Something had snapped as he hit the ground. He couldn't feel anything from the neck down. Out of the corner of his eye he could see Metcalf struggling to his feet. But Metcalf collapsed, coming down hard on one shoulder, too weak and too busted up to stand. They heard footsteps running toward them and people shouting. Metcalf managed to glance up and saw airport security personnel rushing to the scene. A man in uniform held them at gunpoint as he radioed for backup.

Sneed lost sight of the cab several times as they sped down the highway. He hadn't gotten a clear view of any of the three. The cab reappeared, and Sneed did his best to tail them. He was cut off by a FedEx van, and by the time he got around it the cab was in the far right lane, signaling to take the next exit.

Tires screeched as he maneuvered across several lanes of traffic to make the exit. His heart was hammering away. He was a lawyer, not an action hero.

He watched and followed for quite some time. He was determined not to lose them. Visibility was poor in the swirl of shadows and light. Eventually, he glimpsed the cab turning in at a motel. Red Roof Inn, he noted. He pulled in, keeping a safe distance. One of the men paid the driver, and then the cab was gone. The three of them hurried inside. Sneed parked the car near an untrimmed hedge and, keeping to the shadows, loitered within eyeshot of the motel's office.

A few minutes later he dialed his cell phone.

•◆••◆•

Up to that moment, Clement had been in a state of flux. He and Hopfner and been nursing their wounds after the brief brawl with the thugs at the airport. There was no need for speculation—those men were sent by the enemy. That meant time was running out. There was no longer any room for error. The girl had been within minutes of death.

He and Hopfner had saved the day, but in the process had lost sight of them. Then Sneed called.

The lawyers caught a cab and rushed to the Red Roof Inn. For the moment, Sneed was a hero.

Adler and the girl were inside somewhere.

Clement had to regroup. He now had the upper hand. But he wasn't sure what to do with it.

93

ALLAN KNOCKED ON STAN AND LUCY'S DOOR. HE COULD feel an eye studying him through the peephole. The door opened. Stan waved him in. Lucy was sitting on the bed watching TV.

"How're you guys holding up?" Allan asked.

Stan got up in his face. "We were almost killed! *That's* how we're holding up!" He spoke through clenched teeth. He grabbed Allan by the arm and they stepped into the closet-size bathroom. Stan shut the door. "I don't like what you've gotten us involved in. I was a fool for giving you the benefit of the doubt. We are finished here. I won't put Lucy in harm's way any longer. I've got to get her home. She's in danger. You had no right dragging us here. Whatever your problems are, whatever your son's situation, it has nothing to do with us. This whole matter is insane. I want no part of it. I'm putting her on the next flight out. From this point on, you're on your own!" Stan spoke with such intensity and emotion he was nearly trembling. He backed off, catching his breath.

"I can't argue with anything you've said. I was wrong to bring you here. I apologize for that," Allan said. "If you want to walk out that door with her right now, I won't argue and I won't stand it your way, Stan. You've already gone above and beyond what any parent should ever be asked to do. For that, I thank you. But we are so close to the end. All I'm asking now is for you to sit tight with Lucy until morning; then we're gonna get the two of you out of here. Get you home. After tonight, it's over. Words can't adequately express my gratitude for what you've done by coming here. I promise to make it up. And if all goes well tonight, it might have been worth it after all."

Stan Pendleton glared hard at him. "Give me one good reason why we should stay."

"Stan, I'm asking one father to another. Please understand."

Stan was silent. He stood with his back to the wall. Then he opened the door and looked in to check that Lucy was all right. She smiled at him. He looked at Allan guardedly. "What is your plan?"

Allan bit his lower lip for a moment, looking for the right words. Then he said, "I need . . . something to offer them."

Stan raised an eyebrow.

"Proof," Allan added. "I need to offer them proof. A little blood would do, I'd think." Just saying the words made his stomach tighten. He was asking this man for his child's blood.

The bathroom door opened, and Lucy stood firmly, making eye contact with both men.

"No problem," she said, as if she'd just been asked to do the dishes or take out the garbage. Not the best of chores, but no big deal. "How much?"

"Shouldn't need much at all."

She shrugged, rolling up her shirtsleeve. "Then let's do it."

The process was impromptu. They made a tiny pinprick to her forearm, catching four or five drops of blood on a square of paper. Allan sealed it in a Ziploc Baggie.

"One other thing," Lucy said.

"What's that?"

"I've been thinking about something. I've talked it over with Dad, and he says that it's up to me."

For the next few minutes Lucy detailed her thoughts, then asked his opinion on the matter.

"If that's what you want, Lucy, I'll see what I can arrange."

"Thanks," she said.

"I don't know how long I'll be gone. A couple of hours, at least," Allan said. "Just keep this door shut."

Stan nodded. "Take my cell number just in case."

"Good idea." Allan scrawled the number on the back of a ticket stub in his wallet. "Okay, good enough. Stay safe." And then he was out the door.

94

THEY WATCHED FROM THE MERCEDES AS ADLER EXITED THE motel and hailed a cab. The immediate temptation was to take off and follow him, and if they'd had another car, that might have been a realistic option. But as it stood, the girl was the priority. She was the key. If they got their hands on her, they could put all other concerns to bed.

But who was the other man? Had to be the father.

For the moment, they needed to take advantage of Adler's absence. But that was tricky. Goodchapel had opened a dialogue with Adler, and negotiations had begun. An offer had been floated, but nothing was finalized. Clement didn't want to spook the girl. If she bolted, they might never find her. A thousand options buzzed through his mind. They needed her cooperation, so nabbing her and stuffing her in the trunk was simply not a reasonable proposition. But at least they had her cornered.

Clement decided to play this one conservatively. They'd wait it out. If the girl and her father made a move, Clement and his men would be right on top of it.

95

THE HOTEL WAS ONLY A FEW BLOCKS FROM THE WHITE House. The taxi stopped at a street corner and Allan got out. Allan glanced over both shoulders on his way inside, doubtful that he'd been followed but paranoid just the same. At the front desk he requested a room for one night. The desk clerk smiled and tapped away at his computer. He said the only rooms available started at four hundred per night, which ordinarily would have given Allan a coronary, but his financial future was looking up, so he shrugged and handed over his MasterCard. The clerk passed him his card key and pointed at the elevators across the lobby.

He had gone over his plan during the ride to the hotel. The major issue was how to get their attention. He needed to let the president and the president's people know that he was playing hardball. But Allan didn't see the likelihood of marching into the Oval Office making demands and threats. These people—the president included, most likely—would have very much liked to see Allan dead. So the objective became how to safely get his offer to the individuals with the power to make things happen. Clearly he couldn't go to them, so he'd simply make them come to him. His task over the next few hours would not be an easy one.

Room 3075 was on the third floor, ten or twelve doors down from the elevator. Allan's heart was racing. He ran the card key through the slot and pushed open the door.

He turned the bolt in the door and flipped on the light. The room was spectacular. For four hundred a night, he figured it better be.

He had to work fast.

96

WITHIN SECONDS THE MASTERCARD TRANSACTION AP-peared on his monitor screen like a bubble surfacing in a bath-tub. Ryce had been in the bathroom and didn't see it immediately. He sauntered back across the deep shag in his bare feet, scratching at the crotch of his flannel pajama bottoms, and flopped down in his swivel chair. There it was. He grinned, and shook his head. *These morons never learn,* he mused. Once again, he dialed the phone, earning another few thousand bucks.

·◆··◆·

Snow was really beginning to feel sorry for this Adler character. He was easier to track than a doped-up rhino. She sighed as she made the call to Brenner Walsh.

97

THE ALARM SOUNDED. THE ALERT WENT OUT ACROSS WASH-
ington. They finally had him pegged. Lipscomb made an illegal
U-turn and ran a red light in his desperation to not waste a second in getting to the hotel. Patton and Metcalf had blown one
golden opportunity, and he was determined not to blow this one.

As he sped through D.C. traffic, he reached over and
dropped open the glove compartment, retrieving his snub-nosed
handgun. At this point in the game, he could take no chances.
Even if he had to do the killing himself, the job had to get done
right this time. He had absolutely no reservations in popping
lead into both Adler and the girl.

The front end of the car dipped down a ramp as he entered a
parking garage. His headlights glanced past massive support
columns and gray cement walls as he hunted for an open parking
slot. He checked that his gun was loaded.

Lipscomb followed arrows painted on the cement walls that
led to an elevator. It deposited him on the third floor of the
hotel. He was pleased to observe no one else in the hallway at
the moment.

Room 3075 was to his left. He drew himself up alongside the
door, keeping to the wall. There was no light on beneath the
door. Perhaps they had already gone to bed. Perhaps they'd gone
out for dinner. Whichever the case, Lipscomb had no plans to
knock. He went to work on the lock with a couple of rather simple tools and was inside the room in less than a minute. The
lights were indeed off. He slipped inside and gently pressed the
door shut without making a sound.

He grinned, amused that less than twenty minutes had
passed from the moment Adler had paid for the room with his
credit card to now. Adler had made a stupid rookie mistake. And

both he and the girl would pay for that mistake with bullets in their brains. Lipscomb withdrew the handgun.

He moved his free hand along the wall, hunting for the light switch. Now he was standing in the light. He turned from the door and nearly stumbled over a chair placed directly in his path. A sheet of hotel stationery was placed in the seat. Once again, his stomach tightened.

There didn't appear to be anyone in the room.

Lipscomb snatched the sheet of stationery and read what had been scrawled on it in blue ink:

I know who you are and what you want. There is a pay phone at the coffee shop across the street. Be there to answer it at 9 p.m. Be ready to negotiate.

Not such a rookie after all, Lipscomb thought, wadding up the sheet of stationery and casting it aside. He put the gun away and left the room.

98

IT WAS NEARLY MIDNIGHT AND A LIGHT MIST WAS FALLING. The streets of D.C. weren't exactly quiet but traffic had thinned substantially. The clubs were hopping. Bars were full of revelers having a good time.

Senator Henbest had driven himself across town. Lipscomb had arranged a phone conversation with Adler just three hours ago. Adler claimed to have the girl, and claimed she was Getty Fairfield's biological daughter, via Rosemary Hitchins. Henbest still couldn't wrap his brain around that one. It sounded too out-landish to have even a shred of substance to it. But, unfortunately, they were in no position to take the risk that Adler's story was fiction.

Adler had lured Lipscomb to a phone outside a coffee shop a few blocks from the White House and demanded that he speak directly to the senator. Allan knew, as did the rest of the country, that Henbest was behind the president's every move. He knew whom he had to go to to save Steven and now Lucy. Then and there Adler had presented his case and made his demands. By the stroke of midnight tonight he wanted ten million dollars deposited in a numbered account in exchange for Fairfield's biological daughter to quietly fade away.

The president, of course, had initially balked at the notion. He would *not* cower to a threat. He was the leader of the Free World! Some snot-nosed teenage girl wasn't going to make him hide under his desk! Not for a second!

But Henbest played the voice of reason. After all, what would it really hurt to give the man what he was asking? The money was available. It would be a small price to pay. A very small price, indeed, if it enabled Fairfield to sail through the confirmation process untouched. The Republicans would be impotent. In Henbest's personal opinion, Adler could have asked for a lot more and gotten it.

On the passenger's seat next to him was a sealed envelope.

The meeting with the president and Fairfield had lasted the better part of two hours. A debate had raged. They had sought a strong alternative. They were being blackmailed. This Adler joker was some nobody and yet he had them by the balls. It seemed absurd. He'd come from nowhere, threatening the direction the Court would take by strong-arming the president of the United States.

Adler had warned against any form of aggression, stating that if anything happened to him, the girl and her father would immediately go public.

Fairfield was a wreck. As badly as he wanted to be chief justice, at that moment he longed for the serenity of the law school campus. If he survived this, he swore to himself, he'd live the rest of his life in absolute purity and righteousness.

In the end they reached the decision that it was worth the price. They would give Adler what he wanted in the hope that he would keep his word and simply go away. As for the girl, the best they could hope for was that she would forever remain a mystery. They agreed to meet Adler's demands, under one condition: that he give them a sample of the girl's DNA.

They were to meet at a sports bar in Georgetown. Henbest had been instructed to come alone. He parked his car along the curb a block and a half from the bar and carried the envelope in his right hand. He found a table inside near the rear of the bar, near the toilets. He stood a Zippo lighter on its end at the edge of the table. He ordered a beer and watched the door. Some college rowdies watched pro baseball on a television mounted behind the bar.

About ten minutes after midnight, a middle-aged man in a light jacket and jeans entered the bar and glanced around cautiously.

Allan saw the Zippo lighter and knew he'd found his man. He crossed to the table where Senator Henbest was seated.

"Senator?"

Henbest gestured toward one of the chairs around the table. Allan sat down.

"You're a lucky man, Mr. Adler. Lucky you aren't winding up in a landfill tonight with a knife in your back. You picked the wrong folks to screw with." Henbest downed his scotch, his eyes coolly assessing Allan.

Allan was fighting to keep his knees from knocking. He was fully aware that he'd jumped into the deep end of the river, and he had no idea how he'd managed to keep his head above water. For the moment, he planned to keep his mouth shut and listen to what the senator had to say.

"I don't know who you think you are, but this is not a wise

career move. Personally, I think you're full of crap. Where'd you find this girl, anyway?"

"Around."

"How did you know she even existed?"

"A birdie told me."

"You've got a smart mouth."

"Sorry, guess I've been under a lot of stress lately."

"You've got yourself to blame for that."

"You might be right."

Henbest slid the envelope across the table, but kept his hand flat on it. "Before you take this, we have one stipulation."

"What?"

"The girl's DNA. You owe us that much. You're getting what you wanted. We think you're a liar, so we want proof that she's got Fairfield's blood running through her veins."

Allan stared at the envelope for a long moment. Then he nodded slowly and shrugged. He took the Ziploc Baggie from his jacket pocket and dropped it on the table. "Her blood," he said.

Henbest held up the Baggie to his face, noticing the crimson-stained square of paper inside. His eyes cut from the Baggie to Allan.

Allan said softly, "There's enough DNA in that bag to create quite a shake-up in this town."

Henbest removed his hand from atop the envelope.

Allan broke the seal on the envelope and removed a folded sheet of paper. On it was an account number.

"The money is in Geneva, Switzerland."

"Thank you," Allan said, genuinely meaning it.

"Tell me," Henbest said. "Why should we believe that you'll keep your word, that you'll just go away and keep your mouth shut?"

Allan took a deep breath. He grinned nervously. "Have a little faith, Senator."

"What about the girl? How can we trust her?"

"She does want one thing."

"I'm listening."

"She'd like a few minutes alone with Fairfield. Somewhere safe, someplace where she won't be grabbed and hauled off."

"Why?"

"Just for . . . her own peace of mind. Just the two of them, you know. Four or five minutes, tops. She's a kid, going through a lot of emotions right now."

This was a new wrinkle that Henbest hadn't yet considered. But, really, what was the harm in it? He'd have to pass it by Fairfield, but what was there to debate?

"When?" Henbest asked, raising an eyebrow.

"First thing in the morning, 6:00 a.m. Tell him to be at the Vietnam Memorial . . . *alone*."

Henbest shrugged. "He'll be there."

"Good." Allan rose from his chair.

"I hope I've seen the last of you, Mr. Adler."

"That makes two of us."

99

SOMETHING FELT OUT OF PLACE. STAN PENDLETON JUST couldn't put his finger on it. For the past couple of hours he'd periodically peeked through curtains and the mist-streaked window at the parking lot. There was just something about the shifting shadows outside that didn't sit well with him. He was nervous, and growing more nervous by the minute. The cars outside were mere vague shapes, but he got the uncanny feeling that someone was out there watching and waiting.

He let go of the curtain and paced across the room.

"You okay, Daddy?"

Stan looked at his daughter. "I'm not sure, sweetie, I'm not sure."

Had they been followed? He wondered. It was a very real possibility. And Allan had been gone quite some time now. Might something have happened to him? Stan paced back to the window and peeked out one more time. He couldn't see anyone, but the feeling in his gut was stronger than ever.

"Honey," he said, "get your jacket on. We're gonna take a stroll."

Stan left the lights on, quietly shutting the door behind him as they eased into the hallway. If someone was outside watching for them, they had to make the run from the motel without being spotted. Approaching the front office, they ducked through a door that led to the service entrance. They nearly bumped into a woman wearing a Red Roof golf shirt and slacks. She gave them an odd look but seemed in too big a hurry to question what they were doing in a staff-only area. She turned a corner and disappeared from sight. To his right he saw the laundry room, bed sheets tumbling inside industrial-size dryers. He looked around quickly, thinking. A laundry cart was parked against a wall. The laundry room was momentarily unattended.

"Here," he said, and helped Lucy into the basket of the laundry cart. Someone's jacket hung from a peg on the wall. He put it on and turned up the collar. It wasn't much, but it would have to do. The service entrance door opened onto an alley. The alley was poorly lit. Parked just outside the door was a van with Red Roof Inn painted across the back doors. Stan glanced down both ends of the alley, then hauled the laundry cart out the door.

There was no one in the van. The lights were on and the engine was running. The woman they had passed outside the laundry room must have gone in for something and would return any moment. He opened the rear doors and stood guard while Lucy hustled into the van. They slipped away, apparently unnoticed. They abandoned the van several miles away, near an enormous shopping mall, then flagged down a cab and successfully vanished into the dark, wet streets of D.C.

100

IN THE SPAN OF ONLY A FEW MINUTES THE LIGHT MIST HAD turned to full-fledged rain. Allan stood in the shelter of a storefront, hands in his pockets, in no particular hurry to get soaked to the bone. The envelope was tucked safely away inside his zippered jacket.

A feeling of deep satisfaction and relief warmed him from the inside out. As much as he'd been through in the past couple of weeks, and despite the amount of wear and tear he'd endured both physically and mentally, he'd accomplished the unimaginable: he had found a way to save Steven. After consecutive days on the go, his body was beginning to let down. He felt his shoulders slumping, his knees going weak.

He put his back against a brick wall, the light of a street lamp glaring down on his face. He desperately wanted to find a bed— *any* bed—and curl up in a fetal position and sleep. But his work was not yet done. He had to hold out just a while longer.

He walked several blocks, keeping out of the weather as much as possible but unable to remain totally dry. He happened upon an outdoor mall. The shops were closed, but there were benches and vending machines and several banks of pay phones. The first call he made was to Stan's cell phone.

Stan told him that he and Lucy had abandoned the Red Roof Inn because of Stan's suspicion that the motel was under surveillance.

"Who do you think it was?"

"I've no idea," Stan answered.

Allan seriously doubted it was Senator Henbest's crew. Up until just moments ago, that team wanted Lucy dead. They wouldn't have waited patiently out in the rain. His best guess was that Harper was trying to get out of having to write that big check. Harper wasn't playing fair, and Allan planned to make him pay for getting greedy.

Stan and Lucy had taken a cab to a different hotel. Allan agreed to meet them there shortly.

His next call was to Wes Swanson. Swanson was asleep when the phone rang, and he sprang up as if he'd just taken a few thousand volts below the waist. He swatted at the nightstand, aiming for the phone but sweeping his lamp to the floor.

"Mr. *Adler?*" he said, no idea what planet he was on at the moment.

"Wes," Allan said, "sorry to wake you, but this couldn't wait till morning."

Swanson's young wife rolled over and planted her face in her feather pillow.

Allan broke into a monologue that fully caught the lawyer up to speed.

Swanson was left speechless by the words coming through the phone. "Could . . . could you . . . *repeat* that?"

"Just like I said, Wes. I've got the money. Get them to set bail, and then call Rochelle Giovannucci. Tell her she's got the job."

Swanson was certain he was dreaming the entire episode.

Allan explained that he'd be flying in to Boston at the first possible opportunity. He needed Swanson to make preparations.

Swanson, though, was still too foggy-headed to connect all the dots. Even after Allan had hung up the phone, Wes Swanson remained sitting upright in bed with the sleek handset of his phone resting against the side of his neck, his mouth open, his hair completely mashed on one side of his head. He sincerely wondered whether or not he'd remember or even *believe* this conversation in the morning.

Next, Allan dialed information for Washington, D.C. He requested the number for the *Washington Post*.

101

WASHINGTON, D.C., AT DAWN.

The rain had abated, leaving the ground wet and the air humid. Though it was still early, tourists could already be seen at the various memorials around the Mall. The Vietnam Memorial attracted a special breed of visitor and always had. It stood gleaming in the morning light. Getty Fairfield stood next to the Wall, his reflection staring back. He ignored the thousands of names. He wasn't there this morning to remember or commemorate or weep for those lost in battle. Though the past was very much on his mind.

He wore a long coat with the collar turned up. The morning was cool, and he would have rather still been in bed, or at least back at the hotel with a cup of hot coffee. But there was a part of him that was unable to turn down this opportunity. His wife didn't know he'd left this morning. He'd quietly stepped out, careful not to wake her.

Fairfield glanced at each passerby, then turned his face away. He tried to imagine what the girl looked like. Did she bear a greater resemblance to him or to Rosemary? he wondered. His eyes, or Rosemary's hands?

The tail of his coat flapped lightly against his legs at the urging of a breeze. He walked slowly down the length of one section of the Wall, his eyes on alert. He was looking for a teenage girl, but all he saw around him were middle-aged men and women, no one under the age of forty. Lipscomb was nearby, watching. He intended to pounce on the girl the moment she showed. Fairfield was the bait.

An adult male approached from the far end of the Wall. The man wore a cheap button-down jacket and jogging sneakers.

"You Fairfield?" the man asked.

A cautious nod. "Yes."

"Come with me."

They walked past a small gathering of elderly tourists speaking in hushed voices. The man walked at a brisk clip, forcing Fairfield to pick up his pace. They crossed a street, and the man led him to a cab. Then the man patted him down, checking for weapons and to see if Fairfield was wired.

"Get in," the man said.

Fairfield glanced around quickly but saw no one.

The cab peeled away from the curb and accelerated around a corner.

Lipscomb rushed to the street, out of breath. He was parked well away from there, and it would take several minutes to run to his car. He'd already lost sight of Fairfield.

The cabdriver had been paid handsomely for a simple job. He'd been instructed to take a circuitous route to his destination, winding through the streets of D.C.

"Where are we going?" Fairfield asked, attempting to sound authoritative but being betrayed by the slight tremor in his voice.

"You'll see soon enough," was all the driver would say.

They eventually entered a neighborhood of decaying homes and abandoned businesses. Weeds grew up through the sidewalks, and many of the vacant storefronts were decorated with bullet holes. Fairfield was now genuinely beginning to fear for his life.

"I demand to know where you're taking me!"

"Right here, friend," the driver said, bringing the cab to a halt alongside the curb.

Fairfield looked out his window and saw a paved expanse enclosed in chain-link fencing, a basketball hoop at each end.

"She's waiting for you out there," the driver said, glancing in his mirror.

Fairfield crossed the broken sidewalk, stepping out onto the neighborhood basketball court, now officially 110 percent out of his element. The painted line that demarked the half court was nearly completely worn away. He was truly frightened, prepared for a mugging.

Then he saw her.

She appeared at one corner of the fence, dressed in a coat and scarf. She slowly walked toward him.

Fairfield could only stare. She was the spitting image of Rosemary Hitchins. His knees wanted to buckle. His head felt spacey. She looked as lost for words as he was.

"*Mary and Joseph . . .*" he sputtered under his breath.

She stopped a few feet from him. The sky was gray with clouds, and a barely noticeable mist fell upon them.

"It's true, isn't it?" she said.

But all he could do was stare.

"You're my father."

He was speechless.

"My mother was sent to prison. Why didn't you at least try to help her?"

He longed to reach out and touch her, but resisted the temptation. "Because . . ." But the words wouldn't come.

Tears formed in Lucy's eyes and ran down her cheeks. Her lower lip trembled, but she managed to ask, "Did you love her?"

He hesitated for only a moment before answering, honestly, "No."

They stood nearly face-to-face. It was a beautiful shot. Zack Ronston, investigative reporter for the *Washington Post*, had them perfectly framed within the viewfinder of his Olympus E1 SLR digital camera. He had taken position behind the sycamore tree just outside the fence, concealed among the tall grass and sprawling weeds. He was within fifty feet of them. He adjusted the Zuiko 300mm digital zoom lens, magnifying them exponentially. Nice. This was the story that would make him a legend.

Crouching to one side of Ronston was Allan, and to the other, Stan Pendleton, both of them watching with rapt attention. Stan had been timid about letting Lucy go out there on her own. But they could be on top of Fairfield in a matter of seconds if anything went wrong.

Lucy wiped at her tears with her scarf, then shook her head and turned from Fairfield, finally just walking away from him. She understood in a purely academic way who he was and *what* he was, but she refused to let it go beyond that. There was no room in her heart for him. She had no use for Getty Fairfield.

Fairfield watched her walk back across the cement expanse for a beat or two before returning to the cab awaiting him curbside.

Lucy fell into her father's embrace, Stan enveloping her in his arms. She buried her face in his chest, her tears coming harder and faster now. The reporter was Lucy's idea. Both Allan and Stan had argued that it was vital to protect their identities, but she countered that they would be much safer with everything out in the open. With the media spotlight glaring, no one would dare lay a finger on them. Stan talked with her late into the night, but she wouldn't relent. She was going public.

Ronston was snapping on his lens cap.

Allan glanced at him and asked, "Was that good enough?"

Ronston couldn't conceal his toothy grin. "Perfect," he said. "Absolutely perfect."

102

FIFTEEN MILLION DOLLARS. THAT WAS THE AMOUNT HE would demand from Harper.

He'd take 25 percent off the top for Mitchell Lundberg for his efforts. Half of the remaining 75 percent, or $5,625,000, for the Pendletons. And the rest of the money would stay with the Adler family. It seemed to him a fair distribution of funds. The ten million from Henbest and his colleagues would remain safely tucked away, far away, untouched in some account in Europe. That brought the total to twenty-five million dollars.

Allan was certain that Harper was willing to go to some pretty staggering lengths to get his hands on the girl. Too bad it was going to cost the man a fortune for what would be public knowledge in a matter of days anyway. But his suspicion was that that kind of money was pocket change to a man like Harper.

Having returned to the hotel, Allan had sent Stan and Lucy down to one of the restaurants for coffee and breakfast. He remained in the room, staring out the window at the street, thinking, putting all the pieces into place. There was just one more call to make before he could jump on a plane and get out of D.C.

The phone rang only once.

"Adler?"

"Fifteen million," Allan said without the slightest hesitation, his tone a granite wall.

Goodchapel ignored the reference to money. "Where is she, Adler?"

"Fifteen million, Harper. Deposited inside the next half hour or she disappears forever."

Goodchapel had spent the night in D.C. himself. Throughout the past eight or ten hours he had remained in constant contact with Ben Clement. Clement had staked out the Red Roof Inn the entire night and was still there this morning. Allan Adler's attempt at a threat made Goodchapel smile. The chump had no idea they were sitting on top of the girl and her father. Clement and his team could make a move at any moment.

"The deal was five million."

"The price went up."

"You're getting greedy and stupid."

"I know what she's worth to you."

"You think you do?"

"Yes. Fifteen million is a bargain."

"And what if I stop playing generously? What if I change my mind and just grab the girl? What if I keep my money?" Goodchapel said in a slightly mocking tone. "What if I bump you out of the picture altogether? How would you like that?"

Allan stared out the window at traffic. The streets were visibly wet.

Finally, Allan said, "I doubt you'd do that."

"Oh? And why exactly is that?"

"Because you'll never find her."

Goodchapel relished the moment, taking his time with the words, because he knew that what he was about to say would drive an arrow through Adler's chest. "Interesting that you would say that, Mr. Adler, because the girl and her father are under my thumb even as we speak. We've been watching all night and all morning."

Allan shook his head, loving it. "Is that right?"

"It's too late for you, Mr. Adler. I believe I'll just take my money elsewhere."

"Why don't you do that. And I'll take the girl elsewhere. There are, after all, other interested parties."

"You've lost, Mr. Adler. Your threats are hollow now."

Allan grinned. "I'd suggest you make sure she is in the motel room before you turn your back on what I have to offer."

It took a few seconds for Goodchapel to understand what was being insinuated. Then his blood began to go cold.

Allan cut in before Goodchapel could respond. "You have two minutes to make up your mind. After that, you lose the girl for good."

The connection went dead.

103

WITHIN SECONDS CLEMENT AND SNEED AND HOPFNER WERE out of the Mercedes and rushing toward the motel. Clement knocked at the door to Room 91, but no one answered. He clenched his fists, and pounded again. No answer.

Sneed sprinted to the front office. No, the clerk on duty said, no one had checked out. Sneed declared an emergency and convinced the lady to bring a key to the room. She opened the door and they plowed inside, desperately hoping it was still occupied. No such luck.

The room was empty. They'd been duped.

Clement immediately gave Goodchapel the news.

104

ONE MINUTE AND FIFTY SECONDS HAD PASSED.

The phone rang.

"Where is she?" Goodchapel growled.

"Fifteen million," Allan said.

Goodchapel closed his eyes and pinched the bridge of his nose between two fingers.

"The girl first," Goodchapel insisted.

"Not a chance."

"That was the deal."

"No, that was the deal before you tried to pull the rug out

from under me. So the deal has changed. I want the money up front, then you'll get what you want."

"Fine. Fifteen million. Tell me where you want it."

And just like that, the world had turned on end. The impossible had just become possible. Millions of dollars were about to change hands. Allan repeated to Goodchapel the wiring instructions that Mitchell Lundberg had dictated to him, just as he had with Senator Henbest hours earlier, complete with the routing number and the account number. Goodchapel acknowledged that he understood the instructions, and then Allan told him to stand by.

From his home office in Dallas, Mitchell Lundberg went to work. He stared at his desktop computer, waiting, until finally the account he'd established the previous day suddenly registered a deposit of precisely fifteen million dollars. He lit a cigar and puffed on it, a thick cloud hanging over his head.

Now he would make the fifteen million disappear.

He proceeded to bounce the money all over the planet. It landed in the Cayman Islands, where it was broken up and rerouted, dozens of new accounts sprouting up instantaneously. Each of the new accounts received a different destination across the globe. Lundberg smiled to himself. Money hit in London, Zurich, Tokyo, South Africa, Sydney. New accounts were created, and old accounts evaporated as if they'd never existed.

At last, the money took its final form.

Lundberg notified Allan that all was well. The deed was done.

"You're now a rich man," Lundberg said.

It was too much to comprehend. Allan was exhausted. He didn't know what to think about the money, or whether or not to believe that it was even real. On some level, perhaps he understood that the money was his, but he'd have to deal with that later.

Goodchapel answered on the first ring.

"Okay," Allan said, "I've got the money."

"Where is she?"

"Don't worry about the girl, Harper . . . or whatever your name is. She's not important anymore. You're gonna get exactly what you want out of this."

Goodchapel was building into a slow rage. "You've got the money, Adler. Where's the girl?"

"Oh, you'll get your money's worth."

"Adler!"

"Relax."

"You promised me the girl! Who is she?"

"You'll find out soon enough."

"What's that mean?"

"It means," Allan said, "that you'll find out when the rest of the world does."

105

THERE WASN'T MUCH LEFT TO BE SAID.

Lucy understood she was about to find herself at the center of a media frenzy.

"You don't have to do this," Allan said. "Your anonymity is about to come to an end. There will be a big bright spotlight on you."

"If I don't go public," she responded, "I'll never be safe, and neither will you. I don't want the attention, but I want the truth to be told. This story will be with me forever, and it is now as much a part of my life as anything could ever be. Eventually, maybe, this will pass and life will get back to normal. I'm fine, either way. Really."

Lucy hugged Allan. She had tears in her eyes.

Stan shook his hand. "Good luck, Allan."

"I wish the best for your family," Allan said.

They parted ways at the hotel.

Lucy and Stan planned to wait at the hotel for the rest of their family to fly in from Denver. With the money that Allan had given them, they had hired a security team to thwart any unexpected threats. Zack Ronston from the *Washington Post* was anxious to interview Nell Spagnazio, offering both her and Berg first-class airfare from Colorado to D.C., as well as luxurious hotel accommodations during their stay in the nation's capital.

Outside the sun was peeking through the clouds, threatening to brighten the day. Allan flagged down a cab and headed for the airport.

106

LATE AFTERNOON.

Allan waited in Wes Swanson's car. Swanson had picked him up at Logan International in Boston and was absolutely beside himself. How in the world Allan had managed to pull this off, he'd never fully understand, but it was fascinating being a part of the process.

Swanson had spent most of the morning arguing, pulling strings, and doing the heavy lifting, eventually persuading a judge to set bail at one million dollars. Allan assured him that the money was on its way. Swanson was stunned. The Calevettis' lawyers went ballistic, ranting and raving, shocked and appalled that Steven was being released from custody. Swanson got the judge on the phone. The FBI agents working the case were dumbfounded. The prosecutor was livid. The plan was to move quickly and get Steven out of FBI custody as rapidly and quietly as possible, to get him on a plane and out of town before the feds could create complications and delay the process.

The day had turned hot and muggy. Allan had his window down, hoping a breeze might wander through. He held his breath and said a prayer. It seemed like months since he'd last seen Steven. He hoped the boy could grasp just how close he'd come to spending the next several decades of his life behind bars.

Allan borrowed Swanson's cell phone to call Lanna at home. It was almost over, he told her. He'd be home a little after dark, he figured. His news brought her to tears. He said he couldn't wait to see her. He couldn't wait to sleep in his own bed. He wanted to see his kids and to simply experience an average day in the life of Allan Adler.

Allan held his breath and waited anxiously.

In the car's side mirror he saw two figures appear. A tremendous wave of relief washed over him. He opened the car door and stood in the sunshine, waiting to greet them. Steven looked more than a little tired, but more or less in pretty decent shape, all things considered. It felt good to see him in the outside world again. The handcuffs were gone.

Steven grinned at his father. "What took you so long?"

Allan shrugged. "I didn't think you were in that big of a hurry."

"Yeah, I was just starting to make some friends in there."

"You okay?"

Steven nodded. "I'll live."

Allan glanced at Swanson. "Well, are you ready to roll?"

Swanson nodded and gestured at the car.

Allan let his son ride in the front seat.

They turned up the car stereo and roared toward the airport.

Steven turned in his seat to face his father, the wind howling through his hair, and said, "So who'd you have to sleep with to pull this off?"

Allan just sort of shook his head and grinned. "Oh, you wouldn't believe me if I told you."

PART 4

107

THE STORY BROKE EARLY IN THE WEEK, HAVING THE EFFECT of an atom bomb being detonated on the White House lawn. It started out as a piece in the *Washington Post* and quickly grew into a media spectacle. A previously undistinguished journalist named Zack Ronston became a familiar face to readers and television viewers. The idea that a nominee for chief justice of the United States Supreme Court had once upon a time had an affair with a Russian spy and fathered a child with her was too delicious to ignore. The media served it hot, and the general public seemingly couldn't get enough. The Red Fox was a bigger story than ever. For cable and network news, it was a ratings bonanza. There were more than enough juicy details to go around.

The president somehow managed to weather the storm. The administration's spin doctors worked their magic, masterfully siphoning the blame away from the commander in chief. The White House press secretary gallantly manhandled the media but resigned within weeks.

Getty Fairfield didn't survive the blitzkrieg. Overnight he was stripped of the nomination. He was crushed by the assault, and was swiftly and brutally driven from Washington, ruined and disgraced. His teaching position at the law school had been abruptly filled in his absence. Fairfield had once dreamed of becoming a famous historical figure, and now, much to his chagrin, that would indeed come to pass. He retired in seclusion to a modest lake house in the Sierra Nevada of California.

As expected, the Republicans pounced. After the Fairfield fiasco, the president had little choice but to nominate a conservative to the Court. The new chief justice was handpicked by

the right, restoring the Court to a status that would have made
the late great Kenneth Bourgeous proud, and she was arguably
more staunchly conservative than even the old man himself had
ever been.

108

Twenty-four hours before the new chief justice was
confirmed by the Senate, Jasper Cone drove his ancient Land
Cruiser to a self-storage unit on the outskirts of Austin, covered
it with a tarp, and exchanged it for a black Kia hatchback registered to a fictitious name. He drove to Houston and boarded a
flight to Stuttgart, Germany. He had not mentioned his travel
itinerary to a single soul, not even Crystal Easterling.

At Stuttgart, he leased a Peugeot using a second fictitious
identity, and drove to a bungalow in the forest outside Kurzen-
dorf. The bungalow was well furnished, complete with a satellite
dish bolted to the roof. He could be very comfortable there for
an indefinite stay. He intended to never return to North America. And for good reason. Word had leaked.

It was a rumor too big and unfathomable to be true. But by
the morning of the confirmation, the rumor had taken on a life
of its own, and at 11:00 a.m., the Justice Department announced that it was launching a massive investigation into allegations that Cone Intermedia had attempted to influence the
selection of the chief justice. They teased the cameras by hint-
ing that an insider had come forward with compelling evidence
that the company had conspired to manipulate the nomination
by a number of nefarious means, including murder.

No one from CI was immediately available for comment.

In the hours that followed, chaos ensued. The FBI arrived at the CI headquarters in Austin in full force. The siege began.

·━··━·

Canada

At a bus terminal in Ottawa, Ontario, Franklin Henbest had ducked inside a very unsanitary restroom and locked the stall door. He had walked casually out of his office on Capitol Hill nearly three days earlier without a word to anyone, and had then left the country as quickly and quietly as possible. His plan was to not stop moving until he had both feet planted safely in Europe. But he would never make it.

A custodian discovered the body several days later, Henbest strung up by the neck with piano wire, his feet a full six inches off the ground, his pants still bunched around his ankles. The killer, a very nondescript adult male, had followed him from D.C., waiting for the right moment in the right place. The killer had been instructed by his employer to remove all identifying documents from the body.

Henbest was placed in a drawer in a city morgue, with a toe tag labeled John Doe.

109

COSTAS GOODCHAPEL WAS FLOATING FACEDOWN IN THE Olympic-size swimming pool in his home. He had been dead at least half an hour when they found him. The paramedics went through the motions, but it was a futile effort.

In the days that followed, an autopsy revealed an aneurism in his brain. Death had come upon him without preamble, and the life of one of the most powerful and influential entrepreneurs of the age had come to an abrupt and unexpected end. The lawyers and the PR people kept a lid on the news as long as possible, knowing how the announcement would affect stock prices and such. The business world knew that without the driving force of its founder and CEO, Amethyst Technologies was now vulnerable, its future uncertain.

Eventually the iron giant was brought to its knees. The Court came down hard on Amethyst Technologies, condemning it for employing anticompetitive practices in its effort to dominate the marketplace. The new chief justice, it turned out, had very little tolerance for bullies, and in her majority opinion described Am-Tech as "perhaps the biggest bully in corporate America." The company would ultimately be broken up, ending its monopolistic stranglehold.

For Cone Intermedia, it was hardly a victorious moment at all. CI and all its hierarchy were going down in flames. They had scrambled, running for cover, desperate for escape. The lawyers tangled, filing suits and motions, producing mounds of indecipherable paperwork in an effort to delay whatever inevitably lay ahead for their very guilty clients.

The search was on for Jasper Cone. He had vanished.

Crystal Easterling wondered whether she'd ever see him again. She doubted it. He would never resurface, she was confident of that. It didn't matter. Things would never be the same. She only wished she'd had the foresight to make a run for it while there was still time. That was just one of many regrets.

110

MONEY WAS NO LONGER AN ISSUE. THE ADLERS COULD now afford any attorney at any price. Steven was guaranteed the best defense team that money could buy. Rochelle Giovannucci was hired without hesitation. She descended upon the scene with all the subtlety of a typhoon.

In the weeks and months that followed, evidence was gathered and cataloged and analyzed. Giovannucci left no stone unturned. Nick Calevetti's lawyers tried to play games with her. Giovannucci didn't play games. The momentum had shifted dramatically.

Soon it became clear that Nick could not hide behind his attorneys forever. The evidence against him was overwhelming. Nick was taken into custody and charged with the murder of Ronald Calther.

The day finally came. The case went to trial.

Giovannucci turned Nick's story inside out. There was simply too much evidence. She had the tire tool. She had the grease rag he had used. She put forensic experts on the stand. She mapped out the crime scene with photos and charts and diagrams. She presented a timeline of events for the jury and compared that with the testimony of friends and family members who had been aware of Steven and Nick's travel plans the night of the incident. She had photos of the damage to the Mustang, including close-up shots of the passenger-side windshield where Steven's head had shattered the glass. No way, she pointed out, could Steven have been driving that car.

Calevetti's legal team put on a good show, but ultimately it proved hollow. The writing was on the wall.

Steven took the witness stand and told his story. The jury listened to every word. Finally, the judge sent them off to reach a verdict. Three hours into the deliberations, Nick Calevetti made a plea agreement. He would do ten years, without the possibility of parole. He was led away in handcuffs to begin his sentence. The golden boy had been dethroned. His smug look of entitlement and privilege was gone, replaced by an expression of shock and disbelief. He made no attempt to make eye contact with Steven as he was taken from the courtroom. His world had come crashing down around him.

111

NINE MONTHS LATER, ON A QUIET TUESDAY AFTERNOON, AN attorney from a prominent West Coast law firm strolled into a local branch bank in Oklahoma City. He knew exactly which loan officer to speak with, and presented him with a check for the remaining amount due for the mortgage on the Adler property outside of town.

The paperwork was quickly completed, and the attorney left town as quietly as he had arrived.

The episode was whispered about of course. It had only served to deepen the mystery. After all, the Adler family had uprooted and left town in the middle of the night several months earlier, without so much as a word to anyone.

112

Somewhere in the Caribbean

THE PROPERTY WAS ON THE OPPOSITE SIDE OF THE ISLAND from all the gaudy condos and tourist resorts, the side ignored by everyone except a few of the locals. It was lush and beautiful, and as yet still relatively unspoiled by the desecration of overdevelopment.

The house was not visible from the main road. A dirt lane made its way patiently through immense vegetation, eventually emerging at a clearing where the jungle had been pushed back and a view of the sea had opened up. Bicycles lay in the front yard. Deck chairs stood in a staggered row along the porch.

The house sat on two acres of land, paid for in cash. The purchase price was a steal. Everyone wanted land on the far side of the island, not here. But the Adlers loved it.

There was a decent school located within half an hour's drive where the younger children had fit right in. Dermott was out of school now and had easily found work at one of the resorts. He was content for the moment.

Wishing to escape Boston and embrace his chance at a fresh start, Steven had transferred to Oxford University. He had always dreamed of seeing Europe. England was beautiful, and he was suddenly in no hurry. His desire for law school had vanished. He shifted his focus to international finance. The future looked bright.

Both Allan and Lanna were thrilled beyond words to be unemployed. Island life suited them. The locals were friendly and unintrusive. They slept late every day. There was enough money to live like this forever. They didn't desire anything, only to be left alone.

The house was beautiful. There was no debt. Allan bought himself a Jeep. They took long, exploratory walks, talking and laughing, kissing and hugging and making out like teenagers. At long last they were free.

Today, as most every day, Allan and Lanna had from late morning into early afternoon all to themselves. They casually strolled down the dirt lane to the beach.

Allan watched his wife wade into the water against the incoming tide. He smiled. There was much to smile about. It seemed too good to be true. And maybe it was. It would be a long while before he stopped looking over his shoulder at every turn and keeping one eye on the rearview mirror. He had certainly made enemies, government and otherwise. They had considered taking on new identities, completely erasing the past, but that seemed somehow far-fetched and a bit extreme. Instead, they had simply walked away, slipping into the night, with the hope that no one cared enough to make the effort to find them. Lundberg had helped with the money. He hid it where no government agency on earth could stumble upon it. The Adlers could use whatever they needed, but for the most part they planned to leave it alone. Allan wondered how many people actually knew about the twenty-five million dollars. It was dangerous to be associated with that kind of money—it could attract some very bad individuals. These thoughts kept Allan awake many a night, worrying.

He sat in the sand, his arms around his bare knees, and squinted up at the cloudless sky. Indeed, life had turned out all right. He heard Lanna laugh, running and splashing. She waved at him, and he waved back.

The sun was warm on his face. He was living the dream.

Just then, he thought he heard something not far behind him. A cold shiver stalked up his spine, and he made a quick glance over one shoulder, just to be on the safe side. He watched for anything that didn't belong. Nothing there but jungle and shadows.

Perhaps it was just his imagination, he decided, dismissing the unwarranted paranoia. *Perhaps.*

Allan tugged down the bill of his cap to block out the sun. He shook his head and grinned. He laughed at himself. Lanna dropped to the sand beside him and looked at him oddly.

"What's so funny?" she asked.

He kissed her and winked. "Never mind," he said.

Acknowledgments

The only thing more painful than writing a novel is the revision process. My attitude is that of the carpenter who said, "I've cut it twice and it's still too short." Well, if the job has got to be done, I am thankful to have Emily Bestler and Sarah Branham in my corner. They are brilliant at knowing what to leave in and what to take out.

Many thanks to my parents, Charles and Dana Moreton, for providing a key ingredient of this story, and for not charging me for it (yet).

But most of all, I thank Kari, for giving me a reason to get out of bed in the morning.